"Talking about faith is one thing; living it out is another. In Saving Grace, Denise Hunter's characters face unspeakable choices that can only be resolved by putting their faith on the line. An excellent book that will make you examine your own response to life's challenges."

Carol Cox—Author, *Sagebrush Brides*

"Pit gut-wrenching truth against biblical principles and Denise Hunter's characters never take the easy way out. Saving Grace grabs hold of the heart, forcing readers to think about God-challenges in their own lives. I loved it."

Lois Richer—Author, *Shadowed Secrets*

"Saving Grace kept me turning pages from the minute I opened the cover and kept me up way past bedtime. Denise Hunter has written a story of triumph over heartache, a book overflowing with hope and grace."

Deborah Raney—Author, *A Nest of Sparrows* and *Over the Waters*

"People who believe in a woman's "right to choose" often criticize those who believe in the sanctity of all human life. "They only care about the baby" is a common misconception. In Saving Grace, Denise illustrates that volunteers at the local Crisis Pregnancy Center are concerned deeply about the mother, as well as the baby. She also throws in a twist that makes this book almost impossible to put down!"

Becky Jones—Volunteer, A Hope Center

"With a cast of characters you will never forget, Hunter weaves a powerful story of God's grace and forgiveness in the midst of life's most challenging circumstances. You won't want to part with this one!"

Diann Hunt—Author, *Hearts under Construction*

"When faced with an impossible decision, how often do we have the courage to follow through with what we say we believe? Saving Grace by Denise Hunter is a gut-wrenching plunge into an emotional maelstrom that wouldn't let go until I finished the last page. This is a story that will challenge you and linger in your mind long after it's finished."

Colleen Coble—Author, the Aloha Reef series

DENISE HUNTER

A Novel

SAVING GRACE

HOWARD
Fiction

Our purpose at Howard Publishing is to:
- *Increase faith* in the hearts of growing Christians
- *Inspire holiness* in the lives of believers
- *Instill hope* in the hearts of struggling people everywhere

Because He's coming again!

Saving Grace © 2005 by Denise Hunter
All rights reserved. Printed in the United States of America
Published by Howard Publishing Co., Inc.
3117 North 7th Street, West Monroe, Louisiana 71291-2227
www.howardpublishing.com

05 06 07 08 09 10 11 12 13 14   10 9 8 7 6 5 4 3 2 1

Edited by Ramona Richards
Interior design by John Mark Luke Designs
Cover design by David Carlson

Library of Congress Cataloging-in-Publication Data
Hunter, Denise, 1968–
    Saving Grace : a novel / Denise Hunter
        p. cm. — (The new heights series ; bk. 2)
    ISBN 1-58229-433-X
        1. Single mothers—Fiction. 2. Teenage pregnancy—Fiction. 3. Teenage girls—
Fiction. I. Title.

PS3608.U5925S38 2005
813'.6—dc22
                                                                2005040267

ACKNOWLEDGMENTS

Many people helped shape this story into the book you hold in your hands.

I'd like to thank my mom, Sheri Huston, and Kristin Billerbeck for answering questions regarding the running of a pregnancy center and the volunteer's role there. Thanks especially to pregnancy center volunteer, Becky Jones, who read through the complete manuscript checking for accuracy. Thanks to Gayle Roper for answering my questions related to adoption. Any mistakes in the story are mine alone.

To the three best writer friends a girl could ask for: Kristin Billerbeck, Colleen Coble, and Diann Hunt. Thanks, girls, for countless hours of reading, brainstorming, and just hanging out.

Much gratitude goes to my agent, Pamela Harty, and my editors, Philis Boultinghouse and Ramona Richards. I wish to thank all the excellent people at Howard Publishing who get my stories into the hands of readers.

Finally, thanks to my husband, Kevin, without whom I would probably not be writing at all. Thanks, Honey, for being more wonderful than any hero I've ever written.

This book is dedicated to all the people who give of their time toward helping women in pregnancy centers all over the world. May God bless all your efforts!

CHAPTER ONE

"You won't tell my dad, will you?" she asked.

Natalie Coombs thought the girl across the desk looked eighteen or nineteen. She had a world-weary look in her eyes Natalie had seen before—deep pools of despair that reminded Natalie of someone else.

"No, everything is confidential." She extended her hand across the desk. "Most of my clients call me Miss C."

"I'm Linn." She shook Natalie's hand. Her dark hair hung down on both sides of her face like a curtain. "Can I take a test here?"

"Sure, you'll just need to fill out a form, then answer some questions first, all right?"

Linn nodded, and Natalie handed her a clipboard with the in-take form. "You can have a seat over there."

Linn settled into the farthest corner chair, and Natalie returned to the desk. Linn looked familiar, but then all the locals in Jackson Hole had seen each other at some point. Natalie was glad she'd sent this morning's volunteer, Amanda, upstairs to sort through the batch of baby clothing they'd just received. She had a feeling God had called her to help this girl. Her resemblance to Dana was uncanny, and Natalie prayed things would turn out differently for Linn than they had for her first client. Even though a year had passed, Dana's face still burned like a brand on Natalie's heart.

Natalie sneaked a glimpse at Linn. As the girl read the form, she toyed with the collar of her shirt. It looked as if she'd snagged it from the bottom of the pile in a cold dryer. At least she looked older than a lot of girls who walked through the doors. Old enough to get pregnant, young enough to be scared. And she was scared. Natalie could see it in her eyes. *Lord, help me to show her Your love.*

The phone rang, and Natalie reached for it. "Jackson Hole Hope Center."

"Hi, it's me."

His voice was a punch in the gut. He still took her breath away, just in a different way. She walked into the storage room and shut the door behind her. "I've asked you not to call me here."

"I can't help it. My plans have changed."

"What are you talking about?"

"Picking up the boys, going camping. I can't do it this weekend."

She closed her eyes. She could feel her shoulder and neck muscles drawing tight. "Don't do this to them again. You know they—"

"I can't help it, all right? I have to work. Half my crew deserted me today."

Well, you're an expert at desertion, aren't you? Natalie rubbed her temple. In her mind, she could see Taylor and Alex scrounging in their closet for their sleeping bags the night before. She could see them packing their clothes and filling baggies with Cheese Nips and pretzel sticks to take along.

"Will you quit it with the silent treatment? Tell them I'm sorry, all right? I'll take them next—"

"No way. You call them and tell them. I'm not doing it this time."

"Would you stop making it sound like I do this every week? I told you I've gotta work. Will you cut me some slack here?"

"Call them, Keith. I've got to go." She disconnected before he could argue. She could hear her pulse in her head, and her scalp felt two sizes too small. Maybe she could take the boys camping herself. She thought there was a tent in the basement somewhere.

But it wasn't the camping they'd so looked forward to; it was their dad's company. Besides, she wouldn't know a stake from a pole.

She stretched her neck, tilting her head to the side, feeling the pull of tightened muscles. She couldn't think about Keith right now. There was a girl in the lobby who needed her. She drew a breath and blew it out slowly, letting her facial muscles relax, then opened the door.

Linn was still in the corner chair. The clipboard rested on her lap, and she stared out the picture window where the words "Jackson Hole Hope Center" played in reverse. In the distance, Wyoming's Tetons rose majestically through the summer haze.

"All finished?" Natalie asked.

Linn nodded, then stood and walked toward her. The rubber sole of her shoe was loose at the toe and flipped with each step. Linn handed her the clipboard.

"Great. If you'll just step into that room there, I'll be right with you."

Normally, the volunteer would help the client, but Amanda lacked the experience to counsel with Linn. Anyway, Natalie felt drawn to help the girl.

Natalie called up the stairs. "Amanda . . . can you come watch the desk again?"

Moments later the volunteer bounded down the creaking steps. "Sure."

Natalie glanced at her watch. *Shoot.* "Could you do me a favor and call Paula?"

"No problem," Amanda said.

Natalie jotted down her sister's cell phone number. "Tell her something came up, and I have to cancel our lunch plans."

Amanda began punching the numbers.

"Thanks a bunch." Natalie grabbed a questionnaire clipboard from her desk and entered the counseling room.

"Now, then." She took a seat on the chair across from the girl. "I'll need to ask you some questions, and then I'll get you the pregnancy test. As I said before, all the information you give me is completely confidential, OK?"

3

"The test is free, right?" Linn blinked, and a stray hair caught in her lashes, bobbing down and back up.

"That's right. There's no charge." And that's why most of the girls came here. Most couldn't even afford a fifteen-dollar test from the drugstore.

Linn's gaze darted around the room from chart to chart, as if she were afraid the walls were going to collapse.

"I know you're anxious right now, but we're here to help, Linn, all right?"

She nodded, and Natalie perused her in-take form. "I know you've come because you think you're pregnant. Can you tell me why?"

She shrugged. "I'm late."

"When was your last period?"

"Seven, eight weeks ago, I think."

"Are you using any kind of birth control?"

She crossed her arms, cupping her elbows with her hands, the nails short and ragged. "Yes—well, usually."

"How long have you known the baby's father?"

She looked away. "Almost two years."

Natalie wrote it down. "Are you still seeing him?"

Linn's lashes fluttered down, and she shook her head.

"Have you ever been pregnant before?"

Her brows drew together. "No."

"I'm not making any assumptions about you, all right? I have to ask everyone these questions." When Linn nodded, Natalie continued. "What do you plan to do if you're pregnant?"

Her gaze fluttered to the floor. "I'll have to get rid of it. Have to . . . my dad would go postal if he found out."

Natalie carefully kept her expression bland, though her stomach clenched at the words. She zipped through countless other questions, from substance use to family relationships to dreams and goals. That's when Linn finally opened up.

"I'm going to college in the fall. I got a full scholarship to Loyola

University in Chicago, and I mean room and board and everything."
Her chin came up a bit.

"That's great, Linn. Congratulations. What will you be studying?"

"Psychology." She smiled for the first time and wiggled her brows
up and down. "I want to see what makes people tick."

"Well, when you find out, let me know, OK?"

Natalie tried to draw her out for a few more minutes, tried to put her
at ease. When Linn's shoulders curled forward and her hands lay loosely
on her lap, Natalie asked the last questions, the most important ones.

"Can you tell me what your religious background is like? Do you
belong to a church or synagogue?"

She shook her head. "No, I don't think so. My grandma was
Catholic . . . ," she offered feebly.

Natalie jotted it down. "How is your relationship with God?"

Linn's leg stopped bouncing. "Oh. It's fine, good." She nodded her
head vigorously.

Linn gave vague answers to the last questions concerning religion,
and Natalie knew the girl needed Christ. *Use me, Lord.*

"Well, you'll be happy to know we're finished playing Twenty
Questions." She pulled a release form from the desk and handed it to
Linn. "I'll need your signature on this form. Basically, it says you understand this is not a medical facility and that the pregnancy test may be
inconclusive."

As Linn read the form, Natalie retrieved the pregnancy test and slid
its contents onto the table. When Linn handed her the signed form,
Natalie gave her the instruction sheet and explained what to do. Linn
went to the adjoining bathroom with the plastic cup in hand.

Natalie watched the door shut and closed her eyes. *Lord, my heart is
burdened for this young woman. She doesn't know You, and she doesn't know
right from wrong. Father, if it's possible, let the test be negative. I don't want
to see another tiny life snuffed out, and I don't want to see another woman
scarred with the consequences. Yet, not as I will, Lord, but as You will.*

A few moments later, Linn returned with the urine sample and set it on the paper towel Natalie had laid out. Next, she opened the foil wrapper and pulled out the test cassette and dropper. She dipped the dropper into the urine, releasing the bulb to pull up the liquid. Pausing, with her hand over the test cassette, she looked at Natalie. "Four drops?" Her voice quivered.

"Yes." Natalie indicated the correct spot on the cassette. "Right in there." She pointed to the test window. "This other one is the window to watch. If there's a pink line there in five minutes, it means you're pregnant."

Linn's hand shook as she squeezed out the drops. When she was finished, she straightened and looked at Natalie.

"All righty." Natalie grabbed the egg timer and set it for five minutes. It began ticking off time. "I'll set the test over here where we can forget about it. Want a soda?" She smiled sympathetically. "This can be the longest five minutes of your life if you don't have something to do."

"No, thanks." The girl sat back down, and Natalie sat across from her.

Linn tilted her head back against the wall. "I can't be pregnant. I just can't."

"Well, we'll have the results of the test in just a few minutes, and if you are, there's a lot we can do to help you."

"You know somewhere I could get an abortion cheap? I don't have much money."

Cold fingers squeezed Natalie's gut until it was compacted into a hard knot. "If there is a pregnancy, this is a time of crisis. You're scared, confused. I know you just want this to be over with, but abortion doesn't solve that problem. It only creates new ones."

The girl's gaze fell on a picture on the wall. It was a photo of a newly formed baby. Just as quickly, Linn's gaze fell away.

"All the organs have formed; the heart is beating. It's not what you'd expect so early, is it?"

Linn's gaze swung to the test, though she couldn't see the windows from her seat. "There's just no way I'm ready to be a parent, and my dad's been telling me since I was twelve what would happen if I ever got knocked up."

Natalie offered what she hoped was a comforting smile. She wanted so badly to reach out to Linn, but she felt Linn closing up and changed the topic. "Did you graduate this past spring?"

"Yeah. With high honors. That's how I got the scholarship."

"That's wonderful, Linn. Your dad must be very proud."

She snorted. "He's just glad I'm cutting out in the fall." Linn tossed her dark hair as if that didn't bother her.

Natalie knew better. "Did you participate in any activities in high school?"

Linn shrugged. "Didn't have time. I worked part time and had to keep up with homework." Linn glanced toward the timer. "How much time left?"

"Three minutes." Natalie gave a sympathetic smile. "They creep by, don't they?"

Linn's leg bounced up and down as she looked around the room. Natalie didn't have to turn around to know what she was seeing. Charts of a baby's development from conception on, pamphlets on adoption, the bulletin board with pictures of clients and their babies. That was her favorite. Tangible evidence of the lives they'd helped touch and change.

"Do you have any brothers or sisters?" Natalie asked.

A faraway look entered her eye. "Nope. Just me."

Natalie smiled. "I always wanted to be an only child. Especially when my sisters were aggravating me."

"It's not all it's cracked up to be."

Natalie searched for a new topic. "What made you decide to be a psychology major?"

"I don't know. I like to guess what people are thinking, why they do things and stuff. I want a real job, you know? A career. I want to dress up when I go to work and have people respect me."

"Sure, that's understandable."

Linn's gaze flittered toward the timer.

"One minute left," Natalie said. "There'll be a pink line in the reference window, and if there's a pink line under it, the result is positive. Also, understand that sometimes if you're pregnant but there's not enough of the pregnancy hormone, the test can still read negative."

"How accurate is it?"

"The instruction pamphlet says ninety-nine percent."

Linn's brows ticked up, then down again, and she began twisting a ring on her finger.

"That's pretty. Can I see it?"

Linn held out her hand. A sapphire shimmered on the gold band. "It's beautiful. Is that your birthstone?"

Linn's eyes clouded. "No, I—"

The timer dinged, and Linn's startled gaze met Natalie's.

"Well, let's go see, shall we?"

They walked over to the table. The phone rang in the other room, and Natalie heard Amanda answer it. When they rounded the examination bed, Natalie could see the test cassette, could see clearly the test results. She stepped aside, allowing Linn to come near.

The girl's eyes fixed on the test. Natalie could see the moment she understood. Her eyes widened for just a moment before they closed. When she opened them, her gaze swung to Natalie's, her eyes lit with desperation.

"I'm pregnant."

CHAPTER TWO

Paula Landin-Cohen rinsed her hands under the automatic faucet, watching the sudsy water swirl down the drain. She almost wished she could go down with it. At least then it would all be over, and she wouldn't have to deal with this topsy-turvy cycle of hope and despair.

After drying her hands, she looked in the mirror one last time, making sure her makeup was still in place. Would David notice her puffy eyelids? She hadn't told him, had not gotten his hopes up, too. She never did. Maybe that's why she felt like she was alone on this mission. A mission she was failing. Her body felt like an empty temple, ornate on the outside, hollow on the inside. She had been so sure this time. How many times would she have to go through this?

Paula stepped back and checked her full-length image before exiting the restroom. The food must be on the table by now. As she made her way through the maze of tables, she was vaguely aware of heads turning. Sometimes people even approached her, as if seeing her on the news each night made them close friends. She avoided looking directly at anyone. She was not in the mood for PR.

When she reached the table, she saw the food had arrived. At her approach, David half-stood with the predictability of a geyser, then sank back onto his chair in unison with her.

"What took so long?"

Paula kept her gaze lowered, conscious of her tear-stricken eyes. Why did they have to get a window seat? "Nothing, just—someone stopped me in the restroom, wanted to chat, you know how it is." She scooted in her chair. "Mmm, this fruit looks delicious." She spread the white linen napkin in her lap, then speared a chunk of cantaloupe. She slid it into her mouth and chewed without tasting, then swallowed it around the lump in her throat. "Mmm, it is good."

"I thought you were meeting Natalie for lunch."

"She got hung up at the center. I'm glad you could meet me last-minute." She injected her last words with an enthusiasm she didn't feel, and fearing David might become suspicious of her downcast eyes, she dared a glance at him.

He was studying her, his forehead furrowed above his trendy glasses. Tiny creases lined his mouth and eyes. Why was it lines and wrinkles enhanced a man's appearance, yet worsened a woman's? She tried for a smile. "How did the closing go?"

He waited until he'd chewed the bite of glazed salmon before replying. "Fine. I have a showing at one, so I'll have to rush out when I'm done."

She nodded, and they continued to eat. When she'd called and asked him to meet her, her heart had been buoyed by hope. Now she wished she were alone. *Might as well be,* she thought as they finished their meals. Although the restaurant was filled with muted chatter, at their table, there was only silence. A strained, unsettling silence that felt like a rubber band stretching taut. She searched for something to say. Something that would release the band before it snapped.

"You started, didn't you?" he said.

She looked at him again. Shadows lurked in the depths of his eyes. The breath she didn't know she'd held rushed out. "I'm so tired of this."

He wiped his mouth with his napkin. "How long has it been, about a year?"

One year, two months, and seven days. "A little more." She looked away.

He laid the napkin on his empty plate. "Maybe you should see a doctor."

Her gaze snapped toward his. "It could be you, you know."

He looked away, his jaw hardening. Heaven forbid their problem should actually be his fault.

She didn't understand why they were having a hard time conceiving now when it had happened without effort before. Maybe David was thinking about that; maybe that's why he'd grown so quiet.

The server approached. "Everything all right?"

"Fine, thanks," David said.

The server set the bill tray on the table and removed the dirty plates. "You have a good day."

David withdrew his wallet, pulling out crisp bills and sliding them under the tray clip. "I've got to run." He rose from his seat and stepped toward her, bending to place an obligatory kiss on her cheek. "See you."

"Bye," she said, but he'd already started walking away. She watched him all the way to the door and wished the emptiness she felt inside would reach out and swallow her like a big black hole.

"I can't believe this." The dull throbbing in Linn's head turned to heavy jabs as she stared at the faint pink lines in the stick window. She couldn't be pregnant. This couldn't be happening to her. Her heart boomed against her rib cage, and her breaths came in shallow pants. A wave of dizziness passed over her, and she laid a hand on the table to steady herself. "The line's awful faint. Maybe I'm not really pregnant." She searched Miss C's eyes.

The woman's lips tipped up at the corners as she tilted her head to the side. "Even the faintest of lines indicate the presence of the pregnancy hormone. False positives are rare, but there's always a slight chance, so you should see a doctor to verify that you truly are pregnant."

Linn closed her eyes and covered them with a shaky hand. She wondered if she imagined the nausea that swelled in her stomach. She had felt sick several times over the past couple of weeks, but she'd thought it was a virus.

She felt a hand on her arm.

"Come back to my office where we can sit and talk."

Linn followed Miss C through the door and down a short hall. She had to get rid of it. She was going away to college. She was going to make something of herself.

Miss C ushered her through the door, and Linn sank onto the nearest chair by a desk. Miss C pulled another one close. "It's going to be all right, Linn."

This wasn't supposed to happen. Especially not now that he was gone. "No, it's not." Where would she get money for an abortion? They weren't cheap, she knew. Medical procedures never were. She couldn't even afford a pregnancy test; that's why she'd come here.

"We can help. We have resources. That's what we're here for."

Hope lit a fire in her belly. "You mean you can help me get an abortion?" Was it possible that the government helped low-income women with the cost of abortions? It was a medical procedure after all . . .

Miss C leaned forward and took something off her desk. "According to your calculations, you're seven or eight weeks along."

A stack of pamphlets on the desk drew Linn's gaze. She reached out and took one, opening it with trembling fingers. Her gaze fell to the page in her lap. The caption under the picture read "baby at eight weeks gestation." She looked closely at the picture she'd only glanced at earlier. Her breath sucked in. It was a photo of a tiny baby inside a bubble. The profile showed an enlarged head, but the limbs were developed with tiny fingers and toes. She could see an eye, an ear, and even the ridges where the ribcage was.

A painful knot tightened in her stomach. She tore her gaze away.

No. It didn't look like that. It was an embryo. A primitive collection of cells. The group that had come to her school had said so. Why would they lie about it?

She shut the pamphlet in her lap.

"Your baby's just as beautiful and precious as that one. You're holding the gift of life inside you . . . a marvelous, miraculous work of love."

Work of love. Yeah, right. If it was love, why'd he dump me? "You don't understand. I can't keep it." Her dad would flip if he found out about this. "I just have to get rid of it, then this'll all be over."

"Oh, Linn, it's not that way at all. I counsel girls all the time who've had an abortion. They deal with horrible guilt and remorse. One even committed suicide because the effects are just so staggering—"

"I don't want to hear about that." Linn flung the offensive pamphlet on the floor.

Miss C laid a hand on her arm. "It's going to be OK. What is it about having a baby that's upsetting you so? Is it your dad?"

"He'd kick me out of the house if he found out! I have no job, I'm supposed to be starting college soon, and the man who did this to me is long gone. Take your pick." Her head felt heavy and woozy.

"Let's take this one step at a time. Your dad would undoubtedly be upset, but many girls who come in here find that their parents are much more supportive than they thought. He'd adjust to the idea given time, just as you would."

Linn shook her head. *This lady doesn't get it.*

"If you choose not to keep the baby, there are many loving couples just waiting for the chance to adopt a baby. You could even have a say in who the parents are."

"No. I'm not having it. I can't." This was her choice, not Miss C's, and the thing inside of her wasn't even alive. The photo from the booklet flashed in her mind. She could still see the tiny human floating in the bubble. She had to get out of here. She stood. She brushed past the woman and reached for the handle.

"Wait, Linn, please."

Only the pleading in her tone stopped Linn. She turned and looked back.

Miss C grabbed a gray pamphlet off her desk and held it out. "Please, just promise you'll read this. I want the best for you, Linn. Truly, I do."

Linn just wanted out. Her stomach heaved, and she reached for the brochure. Without speaking, she turned and left. Her shaky legs carried her down the hall and through the lobby.

Everything she passed was a blur, her mind churning with a dozen different emotions. She felt a pebble bouncing in the flopping sole of her shoe, but she didn't stop to remove it. She felt the glossy pages of the brochure and held it up. "The Life Inside You."

A dark, ugly feeling swarmed over her. She didn't want to think about life. She only wanted to think of her plans to go to school, of her future career. A black trash barrel beside the sidewalk caught her attention. Without letting herself think any more about it, she lifted her hand and dropped the booklet in the gaping hole.

Natalie released a weary sigh as she heard the pregnancy center door swing shut. Her heart thundered in her chest like a stampede of cattle, and her legs ached to go after Linn. But what else could she do? Linn had made up her mind, and only God could change it.

She could see even now the flicker of fear in the girl's eyes. If anyone needed the Lord, Linn did. *Help me to show her Your love, Father. Give her guidance. Remind her that the little one she carries is a tiny human being. She needs You, God.*

Natalie wondered if Linn had anyone in her life she could trust. She'd seemed so alone and frantic at the news of her pregnancy. She said she was determined to have an abortion, but the shock on her face when she saw the photo was unmistakable. She believed the lies she was taught in school, just like thousands of others. But now she knew the truth about the little life within her, and she would be able to make an informed decision.

It had to be difficult to have an unplanned pregnancy and be so young. Natalie once had a rape victim who'd gotten pregnant, and that was even more heartbreaking. She'd never been in such a tough spot with such a difficult decision to make.

There were so many things that could happen in life to test a person's faith. If her faith were on the line, would she make the right choice? She'd always feared she wouldn't be up to the challenge. A part of her felt so alone now that it was just her and the boys. She had enough to handle without worrying about things that might never come to pass.

Natalie picked up the pamphlet that had wafted to the floor and placed it on her desk. She wished she could call Linn and talk to her more, but the center's privacy policy prevented that. Her legs wobbled beneath her, and she lowered herself into the chair. There was no more she could do for Linn unless the girl contacted her. *Please, God, let her see the truth before it's too late.*

The phone rang, and she picked up her office extension.

"Hi, honey," her mom's voice greeted her.

Natalie leaned back in the chair and released a cleansing breath. "Hi, Mom. Did Keith call the boys?"

She heard Alex whining in the background and listened while her mother settled him down. A few seconds later her mother whispered, "I hope that man knows how much he's hurt these boys. Alex has hardly said a word, and Taylor has been crying ever since he called."

Natalie laid her head back against the chair. It was amazing how one action by her ex-husband could hurt her and her boys in one fell swoop.

"Tell them we'll go rafting Friday, OK?" It would stretch her budget for the week, but she hated to see them disappointed again.

"Nat . . ." Amanda leaned through the door and mouthed that she was leaving. Natalie nodded and waved.

"Listen, Mom, I have to go. Just tell them we're going, OK?"

When she got off the phone, she dug an apple from her drawer and went to the front desk for her remaining hours at work. She processed Linn's forms and started on a mountain of paperwork. Even that could not distract her from the haunting image of Linn's hollow brown eyes.

CHAPTER THREE

Linn stepped off the bus and moved away from the tourist traffic. Once out of the way, she paused and took a breath. The diesel fumes caught in her throat and hung there. Her stomach churned, and she covered her nose with her hand. Lately, her stomach rebelled at smells. In the two weeks since the pregnancy test, it felt as if someone else controlled her body.

When her dad had cooked garlic chicken the night before, she thought she'd toss her cookies for sure. She'd only avoided it by going outside until dinner was over. She hated to puke. It reminded her of the time she'd stayed home from school sick in the third grade. Her dad had been home with her, and when she'd vomited all over her sheets, he'd made her clean it up. She could almost smell the sour stench now.

And if her stomach wasn't churning, her heart was racing, making her dizzy. Her emotions were a wreck, too. Two nights ago she'd cried when an old lady won a trip to Bermuda on *Wheel of Fortune*.

Linn uncovered her nose and started walking. Cars sped by, mostly tourists, probably off to see Old Faithful or go whitewater rafting. If only her plans for the afternoon were so insignificant.

Her thoughts swarmed like a dozen angry bees. She tried to push them away, but they kept returning. In desperation, she'd called her high-school guidance counselor at home. At first Miss Turley had seemed aggravated to be bothered, but when Linn explained her problem, she'd asked to meet her at the Shady Nook Café. Miss Turley's words replayed in her mind like a recording. *Of course, it's your choice, Linn, but why would you want to throw away the scholarship you've earned? Getting an abortion is really no big deal. They just scrape away the tissue, and it's over. Really harmless. Why would you want to ruin the rest of your life?*

Linn had left the café with her mind set. The counselor had been so convincing, Linn wondered if she'd had an abortion herself. Either way, she had to be right. She was a woman and a counselor. And when she'd seen her father tuck an envelope of cash into the coffee cupboard, Linn had thought it was a sign. She should just do it. By the time her dad missed the money, it would be over. She would pay it back eventually.

But now, all the counselor's points seemed as shaky as a rickety table. She couldn't forget that picture Miss C had shown her. It kept burrowing into her mind with the persistence of a termite. Everyone said it was only tissue this early on. Not a baby, just a lump of cells.

Could that picture be true?

No. Everyone else couldn't be wrong. They taught all about it at school. Smart people with degrees and everything. What did she know about this Miss C? Never mind the way the woman had looked into her heart. Never mind that it had been a long time since anyone had touched her so gently and listened to her so closely.

When she reached the end of the block, she made a right. One more block. A few yards away, a pregnant woman in a denim jumper approached on the other side of the sidewalk. The woman sipped on a water bottle as she passed. *If I don't do something, I'll look like that in a few months.* The thought rattled her and warmed her at the same time.

Her heart began racing, and she wondered if it was the pregnancy or her nerves. A wave of dizziness swept over her, and she stopped, wavering like a chairlift on a windy day. Her vision blackened down to two small focal points. She blinked and caught hold of a brick ledge on the building beside her, fearing she might faint. Slowly, the focal points widened until the black haze faded away.

Her stomach rumbled, and she realized she hadn't eaten lunch. Only some crackers for breakfast. Too late now.

She began walking again and saw ahead a green canopy with the words "Women's Health Clinic" written in neat, white script. Her heart tumbled in her chest. Her legs quivered like cooked noodles. She neared the entrance, her thoughts spinning, her vision clouding.

They just scrape away the tissue, then it's over.

Abortions don't solve problems; they just create new ones.

They just scrape away the tissue, then it's all over.

One even committed suicide.

It's just a blob of tissue.

All the organs have formed; the heart is beating.

Linn opened the heavy wooden door and entered the lobby. Soft tones of beige and clay surrounded her. Everything seemed surreal, as if someone else was looking out her eyes. She approached the window, where a kindly, middle-aged woman shuffled a stack of papers.

"May I help you?"

"My name is Lindsey Caldwell. I have an appointment."

CHAPTER
FOUR

Natalie opened the grill and checked the burgers. A blast of heat licked her arms, and she leaned back, letting the air escape. The edges of the burgers were crispy brown, so she began flipping.

Giggles erupted from the backyard, where Paula had pinned six-year-old Alex to the ground for a tickle-fest. "I warned you, Pal, and now you've had it!"

A smile touched Natalie's lips as she watched her three-year-old son Taylor enter the fray. "Get him, Aunt Paula!" His little fingers danced across his brother's chest.

"Stop!" Alex cried between laughs. "Stop, I gotta pee!"

Instantly Paula stopped, and Alex jumped up, dashed past Natalie, and slid through the sliding screen door.

Natalie and Paula chuckled at his abrupt departure.

"Do me!" Taylor said to Paula.

"Oh no you don't," Paula said. "I know what happens when I tickle you. Same thing that happens when I tickle Alex, only you don't make it to the bathroom." She tapped his nose.

Taylor put a hand to his mouth and giggled.

"Taylor," Natalie said. "Why don't you go swing for a while." Paula had been at their house for almost an hour, and Natalie had hardly gotten the chance to say a word to her.

As Taylor scooted off to the swing set, Paula collapsed in a lawn chair on the deck. "Your boys are a trip."

19

Natalie closed the grill lid and slid into the vinyl lawn chair beside her sister. "You're so good with them. You have a way with children."

Paula's only reply was silence. An awkward one that made Natalie wonder if she'd misspoken. Paula and David still had no children, and Natalie often wondered why. Wondered, but didn't ask. Paula had wanted to get her career on stable ground first. But she'd reached her short-term goal of becoming an evening news anchor and had never mentioned whether they were trying to get pregnant.

"David showing a house tonight?" Natalie asked.

"That's the rotten part of being a realtor. Evenings and weekends, down the tube. I was thinking of having you and Hanna and Micah over for dinner one night soon. Maybe Mom can watch the boys, and we'll have a grown-up night. Sound good?"

"I hate being a third wheel."

"You won't be. We're family."

A night of adult talk did sound tempting. "All right. Just let me know when, and I'll be there."

Again, it grew quiet. She wondered how Paula and David were doing but was afraid to ask.

In the silence, her own mind returned to the center. When she'd returned from an errand yesterday, a Post-it note had been stuck to her monitor. *Linn called. Seemed upset.* The details she'd gotten from her morning volunteer Valerie had been on her mind since yesterday. After two weeks of silence, Linn had finally called.

Oh, why had she run that errand? Linn had needed her, and she hadn't been there for her. Had she gone through with the abortion? *Please, Lord, let her call back.* Valerie said she'd been crying and that she'd taken the bus to the clinic alone. Natalie's heart ached for the girl. Linn had needed someone to be there for her, to listen to her, and Natalie had been the one she'd chosen. But Natalie had not been there. She'd prayed all day that Linn would call back.

Suddenly she realized she'd retreated into her own world. Her sister's leg ticked off time. Her type-A personality made sitting still difficult. "How's work going?"

Paula arched a finely groomed brow. "We have a new makeup artist, Dante—did I tell you about him?"

"Just that he's Italian and has a glorious mane of black hair." Natalie smiled.

"He sings when he's making you up, and I swear, it's like he's serenading you." Her copper-stained lips curved in a dreamy smile.

"You sound infatuated."

"Don't be silly." Paula rolled her eyes, but a flush blossomed in her cheeks.

Natalie knew better than to comment on the flush. Paula hated the fact that she blushed. Natalie suspected it was her inability to control something that Paula hated so much. "I'm just teasing."

The screen door slid open with a screech, and Alex burst through, forgetting to shut it.

"Alex . . ."

"Oops." He turned and slid the door so hard it slapped against the sill, then he ran off toward the swing set.

"Come push us, Aunt Paula," Taylor called from the swing.

Paula stood and followed Alex to the swing set.

"Just for a few minutes," Natalie called. "The burgers are almost done."

She walked to the grill and checked the meat again. Just a few more minutes. She closed the lid and leaned against the log exterior of the house, watching Paula push Taylor until he popped from his seat at the pinnacle of every swing.

"Higher!" he called.

Paula laughed. "If I push you any higher, you'll go all the way around."

"Sweet!" Alex said.

Natalie loved watching Paula with her boys. Not only did she have a wonderful way with them, but she looked so perfect while she was at it. So polished. Even today, on a Saturday, she wore a classic white blouse tucked into a pair of perfectly creased khaki pants. She wore her auburn hair in the latest short style that took years off her thirty-five-year-old face. Her makeup—even without the help of Dante—was flawless. And Natalie hadn't seen her without lipstick since junior high.

Natalie's gaze slid down to her own outfit. Levi shorts with a T-shirt, left untucked to disguise her not-quite-flat-anymore abdomen. She'd thrown her shoulder-length hair into a sloppy ponytail this morning and had gotten by with only tinted moisturizer and mascara. Not exactly a glamour girl. Her days of coifed hair and coordinated ensembles were at least temporarily on hold. Maybe when the boys were older . . . she needed to spend a lot of time with them now. Especially since the divorce. Still, she wouldn't trade her little guys for anything. And her job may not be as glamorous as Paula's, but it was rewarding.

A fire flared up beneath the burgers, and she quickly took them off the grill, then turned it off. "Come and get it!" she called.

After they scarfed down the meal, the boys started a game of soccer with the neighbor kids while she and Paula went inside to wash dishes.

When they were almost finished, Natalie nudged her sister. "There's some ice cream in the fridge." She wiggled her brows. "How 'bout we sneak a bowlful while the boys are occupied."

Paula shrugged as she dried her hands. "I've already blown it with the chips. What's a scoop of ice cream going to hurt?"

Paula opened the freezer door, and a puff of cold air smacked Natalie on her legs. "Mmm, Moose Tracks. You know how to spoil a girl."

Natalie pulled two glass bowls from the cupboard and set them down beside Paula.

"Natalie . . ." Paula tsked.

"What?" Natalie turned to see her sister holding the opened container. Inside, a frosty spoon leaned against the cardboard wall. Oh. That. One night this week, she'd had a terrible hankering for ice cream, and before she knew it, she'd plowed through half the container.

"Want to talk about it?" Paula put the chilled spoon in the dishwasher and began scooping the treat into bowls. "Must've been pretty bad if you ate out of the container."

Natalie wavered. Truthfully, the answer was yes. She did want to talk about it. She just wasn't sure Paula was the right one to hear it.

"Is it Keith? Hanna said he'd let the boys down this weekend."

It looked like the family grapevine was alive and well. Natalie mentally tracked the trail. Her mom had told her sister Hanna, and Hanna had told Paula. At least they meant well.

Natalie slid onto a barstool. "No, it's not Keith."

Paula slid a bowl her way, and Natalie slipped a bite of the creamy confection in her mouth.

"Work?"

Natalie savored the cool, sweet flavor and let it glide down her throat. She might as well tell Paula. She had to tell someone. "I had a client come in a couple weeks ago, and I just can't get her off my mind."

"Why not?"

Natalie paused. She would have to keep the conversation general because of the center's privacy policy. "Well, she's pregnant for starters."

"Young?"

Natalie shrugged. "Not terribly so. Just alone. And scared." She rested her spoon against the bowl. "She wanted to have an abortion. She called yesterday from the Women's Clinic. She had an appointment but was having second thoughts."

"Did she go through with it?"

Natalie wondered if she just imagined the coolness that seemed to emanate from Paula. "I don't know. That's what's killing me. She wouldn't talk to Val, and she didn't call back today."

Silence danced around them. Though Hanna and their parents were staunch pro-life supporters, Paula had always remained silent on the subject. Natalie and Hanna had once discussed Paula's silence, and both of them thought she might feel differently than the rest of the family.

Paula's spoon clinked against the side of the bowl. Outside, the boys' squeals carried across the yard. Why didn't her sister say something? Anything? The silence stretched awkwardly between them.

"Well, anyway, there's nothing I can do about it unless she calls again," Natalie said to break the silence. This time she let the subject die.

"Good night, girls," Natalie called as the parenting class participants filed past the desk on the way out the door.

"Night," they said.

McKenzie waddled past, her shirt swaying under her pregnant belly like a flag in the wind.

"When's that baby due, McKenzie?" Natalie asked.

The girl shot a look over her shoulder. "Not nearly soon enough."

Natalie hid a grin. How well she remembered the way the last weeks of pregnancy stretched out. She was so big with Taylor, she didn't want to be seen outside the house.

When all the girls had left, the volunteer and trainer packed up their things. "See you next week, Natalie," the volunteer called as she slid out the glass door. The room swelled with silence. Just a few more minutes to finish up these papers, and she could go pick up her boys. The night beyond the glass storefront was a black canvas, and in the glass she could see a reflection of herself sitting at her desk. Even in the distorted picture, she could see the dark circles under her eyes. It had been a long day with five new girls filing through the door. They all needed help, needed Christ, and sometimes it left her feeling so drained.

She looked at the Post-it note still stuck to her computer monitor. Linn had not called back today either. If she were still having second thoughts, wouldn't she have called back? Maybe she'd found someone else to talk to, someone who'd tell her an abortion was no big deal. Or maybe she'd gone through with the abortion. Maybe she was even now paralyzed with guilt and grief.

The fax machine kicked on, and Natalie started. When the paper started feeding through, she shook her head. Why was she so jumpy tonight? Earlier, as she'd walked back from Wendy's, she'd had the strangest feeling she was being watched. Which was silly, of course. This was Jackson Hole, not Los Angeles. Anyway, who'd want to stare at a middle-aged mom who hadn't had a haircut in six months?

Nonetheless, feeling suddenly vulnerable, she walked around the desk and flipped the metal lever. With a clank, the lock settled into place. Technically, they were closed, and there was no sense leaving the door unlocked while she finished up. With one last glance at the silent phone, she began wading through the stack of papers.

She worked quickly, eager to see the boys, wanting to tuck their covers snugly around their bodies and listen to their sweet prayers. After scrawling her signature on the last form, she grabbed her purse from the filing cabinet and dug her keys from its depths. She flipped out the lights, careful to leave on the exterior light. They really could use a security system, but it wasn't in the budget. Besides, they'd never had any problems before.

Natalie unlocked the door and slipped outside, fitting her key into the dead bolt and twisting. Warm air hugged her body, and the humidity seeped into her clothes and hair. Even at night, air conditioners hummed outside the nearby motel.

She set off for the back of the building, where her Suburban was parked. Habitually, her fingers found the little pepper spray canister attached to her key ring. She walked briskly, alert, trying to stay in the faint glow of the solitary streetlamp. The lot's crumbled concrete crunched under her loafers. As she rounded the corner to the lot, she felt it again. That strange feeling she'd had earlier. Her feet quickened.

She should have left with the others. Her finger easily found the lip of the pepper spray. There were no lights in the lot, but in the moonlight, she could see her lonely Suburban in the middle.

Almost there. Her lungs could hardly keep pace with her heart. All around the lot, the shadows danced as the wind moved the trees and shrubs. Her legs moved awkwardly, as if they were filled with helium.

At last, she reached the car door. Her fingers fumbled with the keys. Finally, they closed around the door key. She slid it in the lock and turned, her glance skating this way and that. She pulled open the door, jumped inside, then shut it behind her quickly. She depressed the automatic door lock, and the locks dropped with a satisfying clunk.

She took just a moment to catch her breath. How silly of her. Scared of her own shadow. She shook her head, inhaling deeply. A sour smell filled her nose and lungs. Probably an old cup of orange juice in one of the backseat cup holders. She would have to look later. She slipped the key in the ignition and turned it over.

Something grabbed the top of her head and slammed it against the headrest, holding it there. Her scalp tightened painfully on top. She grabbed at the source. A hand. The rearview mirror yielded only a view of her neck. Her gaze darted toward her pepper spray. She grabbed for it with desperate fingers. Closer, closer. She groaned. It dangled just out of reach.

She could hear her own breaths in the suffocating silence. Could feel puffs of hot air hitting her neck. Could smell the sour breath and knew that whatever it was, it was locked inside with her.

CHAPTER FIVE

A voice, soft and grating, filled the car.

"You been telling lies, haven't you?" His voice was low and calm. Eerily so. He yanked her hair.

Her scalp stung.

"That was a question."

Should she say yes? No? He decided for her, shaking her head up and down. She could feel strands of hair snapping.

"I thought so." His voice was in her ear. So close.

"It's not your business if girls get rid of their mistakes, is it?" He shook her head from side to side. Acid came up her throat.

"You're going to start telling the truth now, aren't you?" His other hand touched her head, and she flinched. He stroked the top of her head gently, as if he weren't hurting her with his other hand.

"Aren't you?"

She couldn't remember the question, but it didn't matter. He shook her head up and down.

"Good girl." His lips touched her ear in a kiss.

She flinched.

"I'd hate to see such a pretty girl get hurt. Bad things happen when you tell lies. You don't want to get hurt now, do you?"

He jerked her head back and forth. His breath reeked of cigarettes and cinnamon.

"Turn off the dome light."

It was off already. He must mean so it wouldn't come on when he opened the door. Opened the door . . . did that mean he was leaving? *Please, God.*

He loosened his grip on her hair enough that she could lean forward and flip the switch.

"Give me your hands."

Helpless, she lifted them up in the air. Her heart felt like it might burst from her chest like an airbag. Her hands trembled.

He took one hand and placed it on the headrest, then placed the other there, too. His hand twisted on her hair until she thought her scalp would rip loose from her head. She sucked in her breath.

"I'm going to let go in a minute. You're going to keep your hands here. You're going to close your eyes. Then you're going to sing a song. Let's see, what shall we make it . . . ?"

The pain combined with his putrid breath made her stomach twist with nausea. She arched her back, trying to relieve the pressure on her scalp.

"You know 'Pop Goes the Weasel,' don't you?"

She nodded her head, feeling the painful pull and wondering if she should've waited for him to do it for her.

"I'm going to leave this time, with just my friendly warning. Next time I won't be so nice, pretty girl."

She felt something warm and wet on her ear. His tongue. She squeezed her eyes shut.

"Good girl. You keep those eyes closed. I'll be watching you from outside for one minute. If you move or open your eyes, I'll have to come back in here and pick up where we left off. Got it?"

He yanked her head up and down. She kept her eyes closed. She heard him moving behind her, then the pressure on her head gave way. She had to force herself to keep her eyes shut.

The door clicked open behind her. "I can't hear you."

Singing. She was supposed to be singing. She scrambled for the words. "All around the cobbler's bench, the monkey chased the weasel. The monkey thought 'twas all in fun, Pop—goes the weasel."

"I'll be watching you."

She kept singing, her eyes closed. She struggled to hear something. Was he still standing there? She couldn't take the chance. "Johnny's got the whooping cough, and Mary's got the measles. That's the way the money goes, Pop—goes the weasel."

Natalie watched Sheriff Whitco walk out the center's door, followed by Hanna's husband, Micah.

Hanna was propped on the desk, eyeing Natalie carefully. "Are you sure you're all right?"

Natalie nodded and drew a shaky breath.

"I'll go call Mom again. She was a little frantic when I called before." Hanna went into Natalie's office, and she could hear Hanna punching in the phone number.

Natalie leaned back against her padded chair and closed her eyes, relaxing for the first time in what seemed like hours. She glanced at her watch. Had it really only been a little over an hour ago since she'd walked out into the night?

Those terrifying moments played out in her mind. When he'd grabbed her hair and jerked her head back, she'd thought he was going to kill her. She didn't know why, but she could feel death's cold fingers reaching out to grab her.

She wasn't sure how long she'd sat, elbows in the air, eyes shut, singing that stupid song. But when she opened her eyes, he was gone. She'd been too terrified to get out of the car. She'd pulled the back door closed, pressed the lock button, and dialed 9-1-1 on her cell phone. Then she'd called her sister.

"Mom's worried about you," Hanna said, drawing her back to the present.

Natalie hadn't even heard Hanna talking on the phone, hadn't heard her enter the room. "I'm OK," Natalie said.

"Sure you are. That's why you're white as a sheet."

"Are the boys all right?"

"All tucked in bed. They don't know anything. Mom just told them you stayed late at work."

Trying to recover some sense of normalcy, Natalie shuffled some papers on the desk and put the stapler in the drawer. When Sheriff Whitco had arrived on the scene, Natalie had still been locked in the car. He'd escorted her into the center, where he'd questioned her about the attacker. Hanna and Micah had arrived during the questioning.

"Who do you think it was?" Hanna asked.

Natalie shrugged. "You heard what I told Sheriff Whitco. I work with a lot of clients. It could be any number of angry boyfriends or fathers."

"Or it could be political. There are organizations that don't like what you're doing here one bit."

"Tough luck." Natalie drew the blinds beside her desk. She knew there were plenty of people who saw the Hope Center as anti-women. But, for heaven's sake, she was trying to help women, not hurt them.

"Ah, I see you've got your spunk back." Her sister's voice held amusement.

Spunk. She'd had no spunk in the car earlier. Her head had been trapped against the headrest while some psycho worked her like a marionette. The helplessness she'd felt hit her full force for the first time. She sank into her chair and buried her face in her hands. A sob tried to work its way out, but she forced it back. Instead, it lodged like a brick in her throat. She felt Hanna's hand on her shoulder.

"Want to talk about it?" Hanna asked.

If anyone would understand, it would be Hanna. She'd experienced the terror of being held against her will when she'd been raped years ago. But Natalie didn't want to talk about it. She just wanted to forget. She dragged her hands through her hair. Her scalp was tender. For the first time, she realized she had a throbbing headache.

"It must have been very scary," Hanna said.

It was. Too scary to think about right now. She felt a sudden longing to be home with her boys, watching them sleep in their beds. "I don't want to talk about it. I just want to go home."

"You'll need to talk about it soon. It's not good to brush over it as if it never happened."

Natalie stood abruptly and pushed the chair under the desk. "I just spent an hour talking about it, Hanna."

"I'm not talking about filing a complaint."

Her sister meant well, but Natalie could almost feel her nerves coming undone. She grabbed her purse off the filing cabinet and rooted for her ibuprofen. When she'd emptied two into her hand, she turned to see Hanna holding a paper cup filled with water. "Thanks." She gulped down the pills.

"I'm worried about you, Nat. Maybe you shouldn't work at night anymore." Hanna stood by the glass entryway. "Look at this piddly lock. It's just a thumb-turn, and with all this glass around it, someone would just have to break it."

"I'll be more careful."

"You should get a security system."

Natalie huffed. "The center can hardly afford that."

"Then stop working at night."

"And when are the parenting classes supposed to meet? Most of these girls work during the day." She threw her purse over her shoulder at the same time Hanna's husband walked through the door.

He stopped with the door still propped open, his gaze bouncing between the sisters. "Everything OK?"

"Fine." Natalie made her way toward the door, and they walked out into the summer night. She walked beside Micah, feeling reassured by his presence. "What did the sheriff say?"

"They don't have much to go on, really. But I'm sure they'll work on it. If you remember anything else, call them. Even if it seems insignificant."

"I will." They reached her Suburban, and Micah opened the door for her.

"We'll follow you home," he said.

She almost refused. She didn't want to be mollycoddled. She was a grown woman. But sinking into her seat behind the wheel, she could still smell him. Cigarettes and cinnamon. She choked back her refusal and nodded her head.

She made eye contact with Hanna. "Thanks for coming." She was starting to feel bad about being short with her sister.

Hanna nodded, and in a few minutes, they were driving down the deserted street. The headlights behind her offered a big measure of relief, but Natalie couldn't erase the memory of being attacked.

She suddenly remembered something she'd forgotten about before. Something she hadn't told Sheriff Whitco. *You're going to start telling the truth now, aren't you? Bad things happen when you tell lies.*

If he was talking about the things she told girls, about the viability of unborn babies, then she was still in danger. She couldn't stop telling girls the truth.

Bad things happen when you tell lies.

Natalie depressed the lock button as fear sucked the moisture from her mouth.

CHAPTER
SIX

Linn held the Hope Center card in her hands for the umpteenth time in the past three days since she'd fled the Women's Health Clinic. The woman behind the desk had called out to her, but she'd kept walking as fast as she could. She ended up by a gas station, where the pay phone seemed to be calling her name.

Miss C's name immediately flashed in her mind. *But you don't know the phone number.*

She walked toward the payphone anyway. Like magic, the phone book lay nestled in the cubby beneath the phone. With legs shaking and a mind gone numb from confusion, she found the number, picked up the phone, and dialed. But Miss C hadn't been there. The woman on the phone sounded nice enough, but she was a stranger. What could she do now?

Linn reached over to her bedside radio and turned down the volume. Should she call back? She flipped the card back and forth over her fingers. Why couldn't she make up her mind? On the one hand, it seemed so simple. She was alone and pregnant. She didn't want a baby. She had a scholarship in the fall that she would lose if she took the year off from school. She wanted to get on with her life. Having a baby right now would just be the worst.

But then she remembered everything Miss C had said. Remembered the charts on the wall that showed what was inside her right now. Could they be right? Why did the school counselor tell her it was just a blob of tissue? How come one group says one thing, and another group says something else?

Why did she get herself into this mess to begin with? She smacked her pillow and flung back against it. What had she ever seen in him anyway? He'd lied to her just like her dad did.

She laid a hand on her flat belly. Was it possible that what was growing in her had a heartbeat? Didn't that make it a living thing?

She held up the card again and ran a finger over the words. Miss C was practically a stranger, and yet, there had been something in her eyes. Like she really cared about what happened to her. Without giving herself any more time to think, Linn sat up, picked up the phone, and punched in the numbers.

A few minutes later a woman's voice came across the line. "Jackson Hole Hope Center, Janet speaking, may I help you?"

"Uh, yes, is Miss C there?"

"One moment please."

Linn drew a deep breath and let it out. Miss C must be there this time. She didn't know whether to be relieved or disappointed.

"Miss C speaking."

She finally had the woman on the phone, but suddenly her mind went blank. Her tongue stuck to the roof of her mouth like it was glued there. Maybe she should just hang up. Her hand moved.

"Hello? Can I help you?"

Linn brought the phone back to her ear. "It's me." *Dummy. Like she'd know your voice.* "Linn."

"Linn! Oh, I'm so glad you've called."

Linn could hear the smile in her voice.

"Are you all right? I'm so sorry I missed your call the other day."

"I'm OK. I guess."

"What can I do for you, Linn?"

Now, there was a question. She wished she could just turn time back a few months so she could make a better decision. She sighed. "I'm so confused. I don't know what to do."

"Tell me what you're confused about."

"This—this pregnancy! All my life I've been told a pregnancy is just a bunch of cells in the beginning. That's what that group that comes to my school said. That's what my high-school counselor said. And I came so close to getting rid of it." Her eyes stung, and she pressed her fingers against them. "And now I wish I'd just done it and got it over with."

"Oh, Linn. I'm so sorry you're having to deal with this. I know it's not easy. And it can be confusing when you don't know the facts."

"That's just it. Some people tell me one thing, and you've been telling me something else. What am I supposed to believe?"

"I see your point. And I know you're a smart young lady who wants to make an informed decision. I'll tell you what. Do you know what an ultrasound is?"

"Sure, it can see inside your body. My mom had one when she had gallstones."

"Right. Well, the center has an ultrasound machine that can look inside your uterus and give us a picture of your baby. It'll be kind of grainy, but it will show you that the heart is beating. Can I set up a time for you to come in?"

Just the thought of seeing the heart beating sent a shiver of fear up her spine. Maybe she didn't want to see it.

"Linn, is that all right?"

"Who would do it?"

"The ultrasound? That would be me. I used to be an obstetrics nurse at the hospital, and I've had special training on the machine. I'm the only one at the center who's allowed to use it."

"How much does it cost?"

"Nothing."

Miss C went on to describe the center's nonprofit status, but Linn's mind was spinning. She had to know the truth about what was inside of her. How could she make an intelligent decision without knowing? When Miss C stopped talking, Linn closed her eyes and did it.

"Count me in, I guess."

Natalie had no sooner knocked on the bevel-leaded front door than it swung open.

"Nat. Come on in." Paula moved aside.

Natalie brushed past her sister, noting her elegant pantsuit and glancing down at her own khakis and V-necked T-shirt. "I thought you said casual. Never mind. I guess that is casual for you."

Paula swooped past her, leading the way to the kitchen. "Mom have the boys?"

"Um-hmm." The house looked even more lovely than normal, its open space lighted dimly. When they passed through the dining room, Natalie noted the candles flickering on the table.

"What's for dinner? Can I help?" The huge kitchen featured a large island in the center with a black Corian countertop so smooth and shiny you could see your reflection in it.

"We're having a warm parsnip salad with carrots in an orange vinaigrette and roast duck with pecan stuffing. Can you toss the salad?"

"OK, what's up?"

"What do you mean?" Paula flipped on the oven light and peeked in.

"You only do gourmet when you're stressed."

"Can't a woman fix a fabulous meal for her family without questions?"

Natalie let it slide, but she was convinced something was nagging her sister. "Where's David?"

"He's around here somewhere. Probably picking out a CD."

Just then a jazz instrumental piece began flowing through the intercom speakers.

The sisters exchanged smiles. "What did I tell you?" Paula said.

The doorbell rang, and Paula, slipping the roasted duck platter from the oven, spared Natalie a glance. "Can you get that?"

"Sure." It would be Hanna and Micah, and Natalie was eager to tell Hanna that Linn had called the center. Though she couldn't share names with people outside the center, she did confide generalities to Hanna sometimes.

Her steps thudded across the marble foyer. She reached for the handle and pulled open the door, ready to greet her sister.

A man stood under the porch light. A man bearing a small bouquet of flowers. Natalie had seen him around town a time or two, but they'd never spoken.

"Can I help you?" She thought he must be at the wrong house.

"Is this Paula's house? Paula Landin-Cohen?" His eyebrows raised with the question, widening his grayish-green eyes.

"Yes." She still couldn't figure out what this man was doing standing on her sister's doorstep. Her married sister's doorstep, with flowers in his hand.

"She invited me."

His smile won him a few points, but she wasn't sure in what game.

It took a minute for her to break away from his enigmatic face. For his meaning to register. "For dinner? Oh. Oh, I'm so sorry, come in."

He stepped through the door and extended his hand. "I'm Kyle."

"Oh, sorry, I'm Natalie. Paula's sister." His hand was smooth and warm, just like his voice.

As she led him through the dining room, suspicious thoughts of another kind began to form. She remembered her comment to Paula about being a third wheel. *Oh no. She didn't.* And Paula had sent her to answer the door on purpose. *I'm going to smack that girl.*

"Kyle." Paula's lips widened in a disgustingly perfect smile. "I see you've met Natalie."

Kyle held the flowers out to Paula. "Thank you for inviting me. It's been a long time since I've had a home-cooked meal."

Paula took the flowers. "They're lovely. I have just the vase." She pulled a crystal vase from the cabinet and handed both to Natalie. "Will you arrange these for me?"

"Sure." Natalie was glad to turn her back to Kyle and Paula. She forced herself not to take it out on the flowers. They were lovely.

Just then, David entered the room. His dress slacks and tie made Natalie glad for the Dockers and polo Kyle was wearing. Not that she'd noticed.

David greeted Natalie and Kyle, then Paula explained that Kyle was an attorney who specialized in adoptions. "I interviewed him last week. Did you catch that one, Nat?"

She usually watched her sister's nightly news when she was home. "No, I'm afraid I missed it."

The vase was full of water, and the flowers were arranged, but she continued to move the stems around. The long night ahead stretched out in her mind like the Snake River. Maybe things would feel less awkward when Hanna and Micah arrived.

"All right, I think everything's ready. Kyle, you and David go ahead and have a seat at the table, and Nat and I will bring the food in."

The men filed into the other room, talking shop. Natalie turned to Paula and huffed. "Why did you do that?"

"Do what?" The sultry coyness in her voice only made Nat more angry.

"You know very well what," she whispered. "This is a blind date if I ever saw one, and one of us didn't even know about it."

Paula set a serving fork on the duck platter. "Relax. It's not a blind date."

Natalie narrowed her eyes, wondering if it was true.

"Look, he just seemed so nice at the station. Kind of like a lost puppy dog. Then I remembered what you said about being a third wheel and—"

"Where's Hanna and Micah?"

"Oh, they couldn't come. Some function at church for young marrieds."

Natalie's spirits sagged like a punctured tire. Now it would be really awkward. Kyle probably thought she was desperate. Too desperate to get her own date. Well, she wasn't desperate. And he wasn't her date.

"Grab the salad and bread, will you?" Without waiting for an answer, Paula slipped through the doorway.

Nat grabbed the salad bowl and breadbasket. The fresh aroma of yeast made her stomach growl. She took a deep breath and joined the others.

Natalie took the only empty seat, which was next to Kyle. Across from her, Paula took David's hand and asked him to say grace.

Natalie folded her own hands in her lap. She wished she could go back home and spend the night playing Trouble or Uno with her boys.

When the prayer ended, they passed the dishes around. To Paula's credit, the food was heavenly. It seemed like Natalie could barely manage grilled cheese and soup some nights. But, of course, her sister was not a single working mother. She had no children to rush through dinner in time to shuttle them to baseball or hockey. And she had a husband to help with things around the house.

Keith's face surfaced in her mind, but she shoved it away. She'd had a husband, too, but after the way that one ended, she was in no hurry to put her heart on the line again. Maybe single parenting was hard, but marriage wasn't everything it was cracked up to be either.

"Natalie." Her sister's insistent voice pulled her from her thoughts. "Kyle was just asking about your job."

"I'm sorry." She wiped her mouth with the stiff dinner napkin. "I'm the director at the Hope Center."

His eyes lit with interest. "That's wonderful. I have a lot of respect for the work that's done there."

Natalie acknowledged his sincerity. "Thank you." She took a bite of the duck while Paula smoothly asked about his work as an attorney.

"I mostly work with couples seeking to adopt a child. I make sure everything is done legally." He explained how the system worked. Natalie reluctantly found herself hanging on to his every word.

Kyle's arm brushed hers as he reached for his glass of iced tea, and she pulled in her elbow.

"I imagine some people must be antagonistic toward the center."

She realized Kyle was talking to her. "Most of the people I associate with support our efforts."

"Of course. But do you ever get opposition from the Women's Health Clinic or pro-abortion groups?"

"Would anyone like cracked pepper?" Paula passed the pepper mill to David.

Natalie noted her sister's smooth change of topic. But she was feeling a tad defiant tonight. "In answer to your question, Kyle, we do occasionally get nasty letters or have a few people picketing the center. The other night I was actually attacked in my car in the parking lot. I can't prove it was a pro-abortion group, but he did refer to the center. Of course, it could be the boyfriend of one of our clients, too. We can't let other people dissuade us, though. We believe in what we're doing."

"Did they catch the assailant?"

"Unfortunately, no," Nat said.

"I think it's admirable what you do. It must be stressful. There must be times when clients refuse to listen."

"Yes, and they sometimes come back to the center after the abortion. You've heard of Post Abortion Syndrome?"

"Yes, the pro-abortion groups deny its existence, don't they?" Kyle asked.

"That's because they don't get the fallout after the abortion," Nat said.

David adjusted his trendy glasses. "One of Natalie's clients committed suicide recently after having an abortion."

"How awful," Kyle said.

Natalie's stomach clenched like a tight fist. She'd tried to befriend Dana, had tried to inform her of the facts, but like so many young girls, she just wanted the pregnancy over. Thought her life would go back to normal if she just had an abortion.

"Kyle, what got you interested in private adoption? It's a rather narrow field." Paula steered the conversation in a different direction.

Kyle set his fork on his plate. "Well, my parents were unable to conceive, so I was adopted at birth. I guess I've been fascinated by the process all my life because of that. When it came time to choose a career, I chose the legal field, but eventually drifted into adoptions because of my passion for children."

Was it Natalie's imagination, or did Kyle's voice sound a bit choked? She didn't risk a look. And she didn't want to feel sorry for Kyle. He'd apparently had a perfectly fine childhood; there was nothing for her to feel sorry for.

Somewhere along the meal, she'd lost her appetite. The pecan stuffing on the plate looked about as appealing as a lump of Cat Chow. She poked her fork into it and slid it into her mouth.

The conversation turned to real estate, and David entertained them with stories of impossible-to-sell homes and loan-closing disasters. Paula filled any conversation lapses with well-timed quips, and before Natalie knew it, the meal was over.

Paula and David excused themselves to the kitchen to get coffee, leaving Natalie and Kyle alone.

Natalie placed her napkin on the empty plate, noticing for the first time how quiet the house was. For the life of her, she couldn't think of a thing to say. Why had Paula gotten all the conversation genes?

Beside her, Kyle shifted in his chair.

In the kitchen, the coffee bean grinder buzzed to life. Oh, man, it would take forever for that coffee to brew. She was just trying to decide if she could figure out a way to leave without appearing rude when Kyle spoke.

"Look, this has been a little awkward. When Paula invited me for dinner, she didn't say anything about—well, you being here."

OK, so he'd been innocent about Paula's dinner arrangements.

Natalie glanced at Kyle, but the glance turned into a stare. She hadn't looked at him all through dinner and had forgotten—or hadn't noticed before—how attractive he was. His deep-set gray-green eyes and strong jaw line would set him apart in a crowd of men.

"Your sister couldn't know this, of course," he said. "But I'm not at a place in my life where I'm ready for a relationship. I don't want you to take this personally. You seem like a really nice person."

He was rejecting her? She gritted her teeth. Why, she'd never offered him anything to begin with. Natalie's gaze snapped back to her plate. Her blood suddenly seemed to be pumping very quickly through her body. Some of it, she was sure, was rushing to her face. "I assure you, I had no knowledge of . . . of this *thing* tonight either."

"I'm sorry. I didn't mean to—"

"I didn't know you'd be here any more than you knew I'd be here, and a relationship is the last thing—the very last thing—on my mind."

The kitchen door swung open. "Coffee will be ready in a jiff," Paula said. "Why don't we get cozy in the living room?"

CHAPTER
SEVEN

"That went well, don't you think?" Paula asked her husband after shutting the door behind Kyle.

"You're kidding, right?" David was already involved in a copy of the *Jackson Hole News*. The real estate section, no doubt.

Paula sank onto the couch and flipped up the footrest. "She wasn't that upset. And Kyle's very nice, isn't he?"

"You could've cut the tension between them with a knife."

"Romantic tension is a good thing." Things had been a little tense over dinner, but whatever she'd interrupted in the dining room had followed them into the living room and hovered over them through coffee.

"That wasn't romantic tension. That was just plain old I-don't-like-you tension. I'm not sure whether Nat was aiming it at Kyle or you, but I'm pretty sure neither of you are on her list of favorite people right now."

Paula disagreed but decided to let it go. She had another issue to cover with her husband tonight, and an argument wouldn't help matters.

She kicked off her pumps. She knew without looking that David's own shoes lay under his coat by the door.

"How was your day?" she asked.

He hesitated so long, she mentally flicked the newspaper that blocked him from view.

"Fine."

All that time for a "fine." No matter. She had more important things to discuss. "I went to the doctor today. The gynecologist."

That brought the paper down. "What for?"

She hesitated, taking a moment to pull a string from the cuff of her suit. It wouldn't kill him to wait for her for a change. "She looked me over to see if she could find any reason why I'm not pregnant yet."

His glasses had slid down his nose a bit. She couldn't believe he hadn't shoved them back up yet. "Everything looked fine, as far as she could tell."

"What's that mean?"

Paula shrugged. "More testing," she said. Now for the hard part. "Apparently, we both need to be tested at this point." She used her best TV voice. Smooth. Gentle. She could use all the help she could get.

"Why me? Don't they need to rule you out first?" His eyes blinked rapidly.

Rule me out? "Even if there is some . . . abnormality . . . with me, they still run tests on the male partner because things like sperm count and motility factor into the equation."

"Sperm count? Isn't it too soon for all this? We haven't been trying that long."

"Over a year, David."

"Still, that's not long. I think we should give it some more time."

Because you don't want to put your feet in stirrups. Why were men such babies?

"And insurance is an issue, too," David said. "They probably won't cover this kind of thing." More blinking.

She couldn't believe he was thinking about money. Yes, she could. "I'll check in the morning. Would you please just make the appointment? I did my part today."

He sighed. She could see his hand itching to pick up the paper again. A barrier between them. A wall to shield him from anything unpleasant.

"Sperm count . . . how in the world do they—oh. Oh, you've got to be kidding me." He tossed his head back against the recliner.

She forced a neutral expression. It was easy; she did it every night on camera.

"Come on, Paula, I'm not going—"

"It's no big deal—"

"For you!" The blinking stopped when his frown lines cut two rigid lines between his brows. "It isn't necessary yet."

"There must be something wrong."

"It's too early to tell."

"I can't get pregnant!"

"Sure, you can!"

The words sat in the middle of the floor like the proverbial white elephant. She couldn't believe he'd brought up her pregnancy in that hateful tone. It was almost enough to make her think he knew the truth. But that wasn't possible.

She kicked in her footrest and stood calmly to her feet before leaving the room. Behind her, she heard the paper snap open.

Linn settled back onto the tissue-covered vinyl table, feeling exposed and uncomfortable in the gown. She laid a hand over her flat belly, feeling the tiny metal knob of her belly button ring through the tissue. The screen beside her was black and gray, a moving mass that didn't look like much of anything. Miss C's eyes were glued to the screen.

Over the past week she'd wondered a hundred times why she hadn't just gotten rid of it when she had the chance. What had made her panic at the clinic? She felt like a little girl who couldn't make up her mind. She needed to act like an adult and make a rational decision. What was rational about having a baby at nineteen?

"There it is," Miss C said.

Linn looked at the screen. It was mostly gray and staticlike. But there was a black area shaped like a kidney bean with something gray inside it.

Miss C pointed with her finger at the grayish area. "Right there, Linn. There's your baby. Look at the heart beating."

Linn did see it then. She saw a head. A body. With arms. Legs. And a tiny, throbbing thing. A beating heart. Her own heart skipped a beat.

"This is a really good picture. They're not always so clear. Isn't it amazing how fast their hearts beat when they're this little?" Miss C said.

Linn's eyes fastened on the little gray mass and couldn't let go. This wasn't a blob. Even she could make out the body parts. Her eyes skipped over to the heart. Her baby's heart.

"Your baby's only about two inches long, but he or she has eyes and ears and tiny little toes. It never ceases to amaze me."

Linn couldn't even find her breath. This wasn't at all what she'd expected. It was a baby! How could she get around that fact? Sure, its head was big, and its body shape wasn't real defined, but . . .

She looked away from the screen. Her stomach rolled. "I feel sick." These bouts of nausea came and went all the time now, but she wondered if it was her own conscience making her feel sick this time.

Miss C put down the wand and tugged the tissue gown over Linn's legs. "Can I get you anything? Do you want to sit up?"

Linn sat up, suddenly wanting to leave. Quick.

"Wait a minute, honey. I don't want you getting dizzy and falling."

Linn forced herself to sit on the end of the examining table. Her legs dangled over the end, and she felt like a child whose legs weren't long enough to reach the ground. She didn't want to be here talking about a baby. She wanted to be with friends talking about the latest piece of gossip about Chad Michael Murray or listening to her favorite Maroon 5 CD.

She shifted, and the tissue paper under her crackled. "I'm OK now." If you didn't count the racing heart. "Really."

Miss C squeezed her hand. "Are you sure? I can get you some water or crackers to settle your stomach."

Linn shook her head. "I want to change back into my clothes."

Miss C left her alone to change, asking her to meet in her office when she was done.

After she was dressed, she walked across the hall. Miss C was already seated next to the desk. She patted the chair beside her.

Linn sank into it. The little gray body on the screen flashed in her mind. She'd wanted to know the truth, and now she did. But that just made things harder. Suddenly, her eyes stung. She blinked them. Looked at the wallpaper to distract herself. She did not want to cry right now. She wouldn't.

"Were you surprised at what your baby looked like?"

Linn wished she would quit calling it that. But when she looked at Miss C, even she could see concern in her eyes. She looked away, blinking.

"I know this is hard for you. You don't have to do this alone, though. We'll help you through it. I'll help you through it. I promise."

"You don't understand. My dad—" Her dad would what? Kill her? Hit her? Kick her out? What was she so afraid of? He'd never hit her before, and she knew he'd never kill her. Kick her out, maybe. But was that what she was so afraid of?

He expects this of you anyway. She closed her eyes. It was true. He'd always expected the worst of her. She'd worked so hard in school. So hard to make him proud. And now look at her. She was exactly where he always said she'd end up. Knocked up and alone.

She dashed away the tears that had somehow escaped.

"There are so many ways we can help. You're not alone, Linn. You can get through this. You're a strong young woman."

"I don't feel strong. I feel stupid."

"Making a poor decision doesn't make you stupid." The gentleness in her voice drew Linn's gaze to her face. "People make poor decisions all the time. Goodness, I make them every day."

Miss C's poor decisions probably amounted to a bad hairdo or Cheetos for breakfast. "But a baby . . . I'm not ready to be a mom. And my scholarship. I'll never be able to afford college without that scholarship."

The woman squeezed her hand. "Maybe we could get them to apply it to next year. You never know until you ask. And adoption is always a wonderful option. There are so many couples looking for a baby just like yours. You can give your baby life, and they can give your baby a home and a loving family."

Linn closed her eyes. She was so confused. Miss C put her hand on Linn's shoulder.

"So many women think the problem will just go away if they have an abortion. But it only gets worse."

"How could it possibly get worse?" It seemed her whole world was a big, messy jumble.

"Oh, Linn. I've seen so many girls and women who suffered terrible guilt and distress after an abortion. There's even a name for it. Post Abortion Syndrome. Even the women who think the baby really is just a bunch of cells seem to know better after the abortion. They grieve and hurt and ache over their decision. I don't want to see you go through that. You can make a better choice."

Linn's stomach felt leaden now. Some choice she had. Abort the pregnancy and live with guilt or have the baby. But she wouldn't be able to keep it, and could she stand to give up her baby? What would it feel like to know someone else was raising her child?

"I don't know. I just don't know," Linn said.

"You don't have to make a decision today." Miss C squeezed her hand and sat back in her chair. "How've you been feeling? Nauseous?"

Linn nodded. "Off and on. And tired. I feel tired almost all the time."

"Well, the good news is that passes pretty soon. Probably in just a couple weeks. Have you been to a doctor?"

Like she could afford one. "No." How would she even be able to take care of herself if she carried the baby all those months? Her dad had no insurance, and her new job at Bubba's Bar-B-Que was only part-time. She couldn't even afford an abortion, much less a nine-month pregnancy.

She remembered so clearly, too clearly, what that little gray body on the screen looked like. It was implanted on her brain, and now it would never go away. Could she go through with an abortion now?

It's just a blob of tissue.

Look at the beating heart.

One day you'll be knocked up and alone.

You can give your baby life.

They'll just scrape away the tissue, then it's all over . . .

They'll just scrape away the tissue, then it's all over . . .

They'll just scrape away the tissue, then it's all over . . .

She put her hands against the sides of her face and shook her head, wishing all those thoughts away. "I have to go." She was through the door before Miss C could even get up.

Everything in the center rushed by her.

"Linn, please call or come back anytime, OK?"

They were the last words Linn heard before the door closed behind her.

CHAPTER
EIGHT

Eyes closed, Paula could feel the brush gliding up her cheekbones. Then gentle fingers stroked in an arched pattern. She felt his breath tickling the hairs by her ear.

"Ah, that is much better," Dante said.

She opened her eyes and watched him in the mirror. He began singing "Return to Me," his Italian accent soothing away her worries. He picked up the eyeliner brush, wet it, then swept it through the brown powder.

"Close your eyes, *mia cara.*"

Ah, she loved the way he said that. It was a good thing he wasn't doing her lips yet. She didn't think she could tug the corners down if she tried. Dante was the result of eighteen months of begging for a makeup artist. That was the problem with this small-town network. They thought small. If you thought small, you'd be small. One day she'd be at a larger network, doing more important work, but for now, she'd make do with what she had. It was a small town, but she *was* the news anchor.

Next on her list of accomplishments was pregnancy. She hoped it didn't take as long as the career goal. David had hardly said anything when she'd left the house. But then, that was normal. He'd dropped his perfunctory kiss on her cheek and—

"Open," Dante said.

She did. His handsome face was inches away.

"Perfect."

He moved away too soon. When he returned, she closed her eyes again, feeling the sweep of the tiny brush across her eyelid.

"How was your group this morning?" she asked. Dante's makeup job was only part-time. His other job as a whitewater boatman at Snake River Adventures was what kept his muscles so defined.

"Ah, they were a lot of fun. Teenagers from a church group. Good kids."

Paula bet the girls all hoped they'd fall in so Dante would have to rescue them.

"Open." He gave a satisfied grunt, and she closed her eyes again as he went to work on her eye shadow. He'd choose the right shades to bring out her green eyes. When he was finished, her face would look natural, as if God had created it that way.

God. It seemed like she hardly ever thought of Him anymore. She knew her parents were disappointed with her sporadic appearances at church, but she couldn't live her life to please them. She was a grown woman. And so often, David had open houses on Sundays. She hated going to church alone.

She wondered if David would make a doctor's appointment today. She'd already made hers with the fertility specialist her doctor had recommended. At first, the secretary said it would be a two-month wait to get in, but once Paula had ever-so-subtly dropped her name, the woman had somehow found an opening in about a week. Fame had its privileges.

"Open." His long, wavy hair hung down both sides of his face, framing his high cheekbones. How could a man with long hair look so incredibly masculine?

"Perfect." He practically purred the word. His eyes connected with hers. Her stomach clenched. Then his gaze flitted down her face and settled for just a second on her lips.

"Twenty minutes!" Ron Hall, the producer, called out the warning.

Dante turned to find the right shade of lipstick, and Paula drew a deep breath, determined to put thoughts of Dante behind her.

"See you next week," Natalie said to Angela, a volunteer. "If Linn should call—"

"I know, I know, give her your cell number." Angela softened the reply with a smile.

Natalie slung her purse over her shoulder and exited the center. Her thoughts turned to dinner. Did she have any spaghetti sauce, or had she used that jar last week?

Her heels crunched across the scattered gravel on the lot as she made her way to the Suburban. Suddenly, a blast exploded from somewhere. The ground shook under her feet. *What in the world?* It was too loud to be a backfire, and fireworks didn't shake the ground. She turned and rushed back to the center.

Angela was already outside. "What was that?"

"I don't know." Around them, people filed out of buildings. "But it sounded pretty close. And it came from that direction, I think." She pointed toward the edge of town.

"Do you think it was a bomb?" Angela asked.

"I can't imagine that happening here." But what else could it have been? Thankfully, her parents' house, where her boys were, was in the opposite direction. The station where Paula worked, however, was not. "I think I'll go check it out."

"I'll go flip on the radio," Angela said.

Natalie rushed to her Suburban, turning the key over with hands that shook. Bombs didn't happen in Jackson Hole, Wyoming. It was a ski resort town. A tourist attraction. A scenic, picturesque place where people came to experience peace and nature's beauty.

She only made it a few blocks before she had to park. People were milling everywhere. Business people, waitresses, tourists. She joined the throng.

Black smoke filled the air. The sheriff was already on the scene, pushing the crowd back and putting up barriers. When Natalie stood on her tiptoes, she saw the busted windows of the Women's Health Clinic. The side of the brick building was crumbled. Debris littered the road and sidewalk. Muted chatter surrounded her.

"Wow, I wonder if anyone was hurt?"

"I feel like I'm still in L.A. Can you imagine, something like this happening here?"

"Is that an abortion clinic?"

"I'll bet one of those pro-lifers did it."

"I've never felt anything like it. It was like someone pushed me as hard as they could."

"I hope everyone's OK."

Natalie heard a siren wailing. She pushed through the crowd to get closer. Maybe she could help.

"Excuse me, excuse me. I'm a nurse." Some parted willingly; others resisted. It didn't matter; she had to help if she could.

She was nearly to the blockade when an ambulance arrived, its siren shrieking across the block. The workers jumped out and rushed into the building.

She got an officer's attention. He must've been new, since he didn't look familiar. "Excuse me, I'm a nurse, can I help?"

He looked at the building, where the clinic's sign lay among glass shards on the sidewalk. "Fire department is assessing the situation, but I think we have enough help."

A gray-haired woman shoved through the crowd across the street and approached an EMT. From her panicked gestures, Natalie guessed she had a loved one who worked at the clinic.

She breathed a prayer for the building's occupants as she turned to make her way back to her vehicle. An attack in her own car, a bomb at a clinic . . . what was happening to their town?

Her car seemed to find its way to her parents' without any help. She tapped on the door, then opened it.

"Mom?"

"We're in the kitchen," her mother called.

Taylor stood on a chair beside her mom, stirring something in a mixing bowl. Beside him, Alex wore a white apron that dragged the ground.

They greeted her enthusiastically, and she hugged them, not caring about the flour that transferred onto her blouse.

"My turn," Alex said.

"Is not, is it, Grammy?"

"One more minute, Alex." She tossed Natalie a smile that made her look ten years younger than her actual fifty-five years. "How was your day, dear?"

"Fine, Mom." Natalie glanced at her watch. The news would be on in three minutes. "Can you come in the living room a minute?"

Her mother assessed her with a quick look. "Sure. All right, Taylor, it's Alex's turn." He reluctantly turned over the wooden spoon.

Natalie went to the living room and flipped on the small television to see a local commercial.

Beside her, her mom wiped her hands on a checked dish towel. "What's wrong?"

"There was an explosion in town. Just as I was leaving the center. It was the Women's Health Clinic."

"Oh no. Are you sure?"

She nodded and nudged up the volume button. "I went to the scene. I was worried about Paula because of the direction the blast came from. An ambulance, the fire department, and the police were there."

"Was it a bomb, do you think?"

"I don't know. I hope not, but since it's the clinic, it makes you wonder."

The news came on, showing a close-up of Paula and the other reporters. The music faded away, and the camera panned in.

"Good evening, I'm Russ Marrick."

"And I'm Paula Landin-Cohen. Thanks for joining us. At four thirty-eight this afternoon, an explosion rocked the northeast quadrant of Jackson Hole. For more on that, let's go to Mike Henkly, who's on the scene. Mike, what can you tell us about the situation?"

The picture changed to Mike, who stood in front of the clinic. Behind him was a gaping hole where the windows had been.

"Good evening. I'm standing on Pearl Street in front of the Women's Health Clinic, where a bomb apparently detonated at four thirty-eight this afternoon."

"Oh, good heavens," her mother said.

"Firefighters, police, and EMS immediately reported to the scene. Initial reports suggest there are two people injured, but no one is believed to have died in the blast. Police aren't speculating yet who may be responsible for this act. That's all the information I have for now. Back to you, Paula."

The picture switched back to the newsroom.

"Thank you, Mike. We'll get back with you later as more details are available." Paula went on to other news, but Natalie turned down the volume.

"I just hate it when this stuff happens," Natalie said. "People get hurt or killed, and what does it solve?"

"Do you think it was some misguided pro-lifer?" her mom asked.

"I hope not." Actually, that was exactly what she thought, but she didn't want to believe it herself. Why did these people think they could change anything this way? All it did was cast a shadow on the pro-life cause.

They flipped off the TV and joined the boys in the kitchen. Since her mother had already started dinner, Natalie and the boys joined her. She was thankful she didn't have to go home and figure out what to make tonight.

Later that night, after the boys were tucked in bed, she sat up waiting for the late news. When the news channel music began, she turned up the volume on the set.

"Good evening, I'm Russ Marrick."

"And I'm Paula Landin-Cohen. This afternoon at four thirty-eight, two people were injured when a bomb ripped through the Women's Health

Clinic on Pearl Street. Investigators on the scene say the bomb was planted in a dumpster behind the clinic. One nurse and one patient received minor injuries. Here's what Doctor Lewis, one of the clinic's doctors, said."

The screen filled with a man who looked to be fortyish and wore a white lab coat. Natalie had seen him before, but they'd never spoken. "I was in my office at the time of the explosion. I've never felt anything like it. There was smoke and chaos . . . it was just terrible. Thankfully, no one was killed."

A voice sounded, though the camera stayed on Doctor Lewis. "Do you have any idea who might have done this?"

The doctor shook his head sadly. "We've gotten two letters recently. Threats. I'm afraid the clinic, and the two injured women, have been targeted by some anti-abortion group."

Natalie closed her eyes. She could hardly believe she was watching the local news. This was something they sometimes saw on the national news, but not here. Not in Jackson Hole.

Paula appeared on screen again, her auburn hair glistening under the lights. "There you have it. Join us tomorrow morning for another update and tomorrow night for an interview with Barbara Franklin from the National Pro-Choice Organization."

Natalie grabbed the remote and flipped it off. Great, just great. They were going to point fingers at the pro-lifers and paint them all with the same brush as some demented idiot who may or may not have done this.

She went to bed and set the alarm to catch the early news. It was her day off from the center, but this was too important to miss. She lay awake thinking of the news and Paula. She couldn't help but be perturbed at her sister. She may not write all the news, but she surely had some say in what was done. She wondered where her sister even stood on the issue of abortion. But for the first time, she wondered if she even wanted to know.

Natalie barely had time to make coffee before the news began, so when she sat on the couch, her mind was still sleep-fogged. She flipped the TV on and sank against the cushions, hoping the coffee would brew extra fast this morning. Hopefully, the boys would sleep in, since they'd gotten to bed late.

The morning news team welcomed the viewers before pitching right into a recount of the bomb story.

"Because the Women's Health Clinic is the only abortion provider in the area, and because the clinic had been receiving threatening letters, investigators believe the bomb is the result of opponents of abortion. Recent violence by anti-abortion demonstrators has included the killing of a doctor in Seattle and bombings in Atlanta and Chicago."

The screen showed pictures of the results of those bombings, then cut to another picture.

Natalie sucked in her breath. It was the center. *Her* center.

"Centers such as this one, the Hope Center, here in Jackson, discourage women from having abortions. Here's what Dr. Addison from the Women's Health Clinic says about the Hope Center."

The picture cut to a woman Natalie didn't recognize. She leaned forward, fully awake now.

"I'm sure they're doing what they think is right. But they're spreading inaccurate information to the women who go there. The misinformation confuses girls who are already in a state of confusion and lays a heavy load of guilt on their young shoulders. And the misinformation fuels people to violent behavior."

The newscaster reappeared at her desk.

"Join us tonight for an interview with Barbara Franklin from the National Pro-Choice Organization. And now for a look at the weather."

"Oh no. No no no!" How could they allow such things to be said on TV? It wasn't true! She flung the remote control down on the couch and glared at the screen. She and her colleagues told the truth to these girls; it was the clinic that spread lies. Why hadn't they contacted her for a statement? It was all so incredibly one-sided, she wanted to shriek in anger. How many women had heard that statement, and how many would never go to the Hope Center because of it?

Had Paula known about this? She walked to the kitchen and picked the phone up. With angry jabs, she punched in Paula's number.

The phone rang four times before being picked up. "Hello?" It was David, and his voice cracked.

She realized the hour, but was too upset to care. "David, it's me, Natalie. Is Paula there?"

"Um, yeah—" He cleared his throat. "Yeah, here she is."

The phone crackled. She could hear movement. "Hello?" her sister croaked.

"Paula, it's me. I was just watching the news, and I couldn't believe what they showed—"

"Nat, it's six a.m."

"I know it's early, but this is important. Did you know your station showed a picture of the center this morning? They had a statement from a doctor saying that the center was handing out false information. Did you know about this?"

"Of course I didn't know."

She heard Paula saying something to David.

"Hold on," she said to Natalie. "OK, I'm back."

"Did you know they're doing an interview tonight with Barbara Franklin?" Natalie waited. She could almost feel her blood pressure rising more by the minute. "Did you hear me?"

"I heard you. Yes, I know about the interview. It's via satellite, but Saturday news isn't well-viewed, if it makes you feel any better."

Natalie didn't know whether to be angry or relieved. Maybe her sister could help her cause. Could help the center's cause. "What's the purpose of it? Why are they twisting this bomb thing?"

"They're not twisting anything, Nat. They're just writing news. Some pro-life nut probably put the bomb there. It's happened too many times before. The media is all about angles. Abortion is a big controversy, and the media is bound to capitalize on that."

"If they want controversy, then why are they only covering one side of it?"

Paula sighed. "I don't know. Listen, I'll check into it today, all right? I'll see what I can do."

Natalie covered her face with her hand. "I can't believe this."

"Calm down. I'll look into it and get back with you, OK?"

"All right."

She got off the phone and paced around like a mental patient. *This is ridiculous. I have to stop this. It isn't doing any good.* She stopped in her tracks, remembering the One who could do something about the situation.

OK, God, I don't understand what's going on here. We're trying to do something good at the center, and along comes some psycho and ruins everything. She took a deep breath and let it out. *Help me to give this to You and trust You to work it out.*

"Mommy, I'm hungry." Taylor stood in his superhero jammies, rubbing his sleepy eyes. Those were always the first words from his mouth in the morning.

"What are you doing up so early, Sport?"

"I'm hungry."

She got up and looked through the pantry. It was time to go to the grocery. Past time. She pulled out a box of pancake mix, relieved that it only required water. "All right, it's going to be a few minutes. How about you help me with it?"

Alex was up by the time the pancakes were stacked on their plates. After smearing pats of butter on their stacks, the boys dove in like they were starving. Maybe she should cook breakfast more often. And spend more time just doing fun stuff together. It seemed she was always working at the center or catching up on chores here at home.

She looked at the clock, wondering when Paula would call her. Was there anything her sister could do to stop the fallout from the bombing?

"Are we going to the grocery today?" Alex asked. "It's my turn to pick out the cereal."

"Is not. It's my turn!"

"You picked the Waffle Crisp last week. Didn't he, Mom?"

Someone had picked Waffle Crisp, but darned if she could remember who.

"You picked it, Alex!"

"Did not!"

"Did too!"

"Hey, hey, hey! Stop it, now. Since I can't remember, you can both pick out a box, OK?"

"Woohoo! I'm gonna get Lucky Charms, and you can't have any!" said Alex.

"Yes, I can. You have to share. Don't he, Mom?"

"Go get dressed, boys, before I change my mind and get oatmeal for breakfast all week."

She ushered them up the stairs, then went to clean up the breakfast mess, her mind back on the center. And Linn. What if Linn or one of the other girls heard the news and decided to have an abortion because of it? Would Linn call back, or would she disregard what she'd seen on the ultrasound?

The trip to the grocery passed with only one major argument over who got to help push the cart. They went home and put the groceries away. There was no message on the machine, which meant Paula hadn't called.

She began making a mental list of everything she needed to get done today: laundry, vacuum, clean the bathrooms—

"Mommy, will you push me on the swing?" Taylor asked, his feet swinging from the barstool. The untied shoelaces clicked rhythmically. "Pleeaaase?"

She sighed. "Honey, I've got so much to do today. Maybe Alex will push you."

"I don't want Alex to push me." He propped his chin on his hands, the corners of his mouth pulling down.

She put the jugs of milk in the fridge. "Maybe I'll come out and push you after I get the laundry and stuff done, OK?"

"You don't have to do laundry. I'll wear dirty clothes this week, OK? Please?"

She looked into her son's big, blue eyes and felt herself caving. Would it really be so awful if she got behind in the housework? She remembered reading some poem about the chores being there to stay, but the kids growing up and leaving all too quickly.

She closed the fridge, feeling rather good about the decision. "All right, Sport, no work today. And not only will I push you on the swings, but I'll take you to the park."

Seeing his eyes light up and his back go straight was enough to make her wonder why she didn't do this more often.

They put their shoes back on, and with one last glance back at the silent phone, Natalie ushered them out the door to the SUV. They would be back in plenty of time to grill out for lunch.

As she had since that night when she was attacked, Natalie thought of the terror she'd felt as she climbed onto the leather seat. Strange that she had gotten attacked for being pro-life, and the clinic had gotten attacked for being pro-abortion. What was this world coming to?

It was the perfect day for a romp in the park. A blue sky above, with the beautiful Tetons rising in the distance. She knew she took the beauty of Jackson for granted. It was hard not to when it was there every day.

When she parked, the boys scampered out, slamming the door behind them. She watched them run across the grass to the teeter-totter and laughed when Taylor jumped up, trying to get on it after his heavier brother.

She locked the doors, leaving her purse inside, and went to lift Taylor onto the teeter-totter. She sat in the middle of it and acted as if she lost her balance whenever the wooden board shifted. Soon, they ran off to play in the tunnels, and she made her way to the swings, where she'd sit until the boys begged for a push.

She was nearly there when she saw a girl sitting in a swing, facing the other way. The girl's feet shuffled back and forth, hardly moving the swing. Her back was hunched over, her head was down, but even so, Natalie would have known her anywhere.

CHAPTER NINE

Linn lifted her foot and propped it on her knee, the swing swaying at the movement. She removed a wood chip from under the loose flap of her shoe. Usually, coming to the park made her feel good, gave her a quiet place to think, but today, it only made her feel sad. She used to come here to play when she was a kid. And now she sat here on the same wooden slat swing, pregnant with a baby.

She gripped the chunky metal chain with her fists. She wished she could talk to Megan or Trisha about this. But they had drifted apart since they'd graduated. They'd gotten full-time jobs at the Majestic's restaurant, and Linn felt left out. She'd gone out with them a couple weeks ago, but all they talked about was waitressing, music, and all the hot guys who worked with them. Linn used to talk about that stuff, too, but now everything was different.

Guys weren't worth talking about anyway. She wouldn't be in this mess if she hadn't been so gullible. She couldn't believe she'd waited all those months for him just so he could dump her. Now her whole future was on the line. She wanted to go to college so bad. It would be like starting all over, where everyone didn't know that your dad was a drunk and that you lived in the wrong part of town.

In college, she could just be one of the girls. One of the smart girls, who happened to be pretty nice-looking, too. At least that was what *he'd* said. She put her foot back down and shuffled through the woodchips, drawing a line through it with the toe of her good shoe.

"Linn?"

Startled, she turned. It was Miss C from the Hope Center. "Hi."

The woman smiled as though she was actually glad to see her. It had been a long time since anyone had looked at her like that. Miss C took a seat on the swing beside her, facing the opposite direction.

"What are you doing here?" Linn asked, just before she heard kids squealing behind her. *Dummy, she brought her kids. You didn't think she came here just for you, did you?*

"Just wanted to get out with the boys. I'm so glad I ran into you."

Her face tilted, her eyes so kind, Linn felt like soaking up everything Miss C said and did.

"Do you come here a lot?" Miss C asked.

She shrugged. "Sometimes. Just to think."

"I know what you mean. Sometimes I just like to get on a swing and push off and go as high as I can. Feel the air going through my hair, lean back until I'm looking at the world upside down."

Linn had trouble picturing Miss C doing anything of the kind.

The woman laughed at Linn's expression. "Even us old people can let loose a little, you know."

"You're not old."

"Tell that to these crinkles at the corners of my eyes."

Linn didn't see a crinkle at all. Miss C was pretty in a natural way. Today, she had her hair pulled back in a low braid with wavy tendrils escaping on the side. She looked more like a teenager than an old person.

"Mommy, come look!" one of the boys called.

Miss C seemed to waver between staying and going. "I'll be right back. You're not going anywhere, are you?"

Linn shook her head. Where would she go? She wasn't scheduled to work today, and home was no place she wanted to be on a Saturday.

She pushed off and pumped her legs. Moments later she was soaring up, almost as high as the fir trees in front of her. Coniferous trees, meaning "cone bearing." She remembered it from Mr. Dooley's biology class, ninth grade, fourth quarter. She loved science and was looking forward to the science classes she'd have to take for her psych degree.

She pumped her legs hard and leaned way back as she went forward. She closed her eyes, feeling the warm wind smack her face. A funny, fuzzy feeling came over her. Dizziness. She opened her eyes and tilted her head upright. Things seemed dark around her peripheral vision. She dragged her feet until she stopped and blinked hard. She never used to get dizzy on swings. Was it the baby?

"You OK?" Miss C settled into the swing beside her again.

She nodded, glad the yucky feeling had gone away. The nausea she'd felt for several weeks had subsided. Sometimes she wished it would all go away. Wished she'd just miscarry so she wouldn't have to make this decision. *What kind of a person thinks like that? You're pathetic, Linn!*

"You know, I was planning to grill out hamburgers with the boys for lunch. If you don't have any place to be, we'd love to have you join us."

Linn wondered if her kids would feel so good about it. Nothing more she hated than being unwanted.

Miss C seemed to sense her reluctance. "The boys would love to have someone new to show off for. They're always doing their stunts for me, and saying 'Look, Mom!'"

Just then a squeal pealed across the park. "Look, Mom!"

Linn's and Miss C's gaze met, and they broke into laughter. Her bigger boy was hanging upside down on the monkey bars.

"Very nice, monkey boy!" Miss C said.

What would it hurt to go to her house? She had nothing better to do today. She did like kids, and she had lots of experience baby-sitting. Maybe they'd like her, too. "All right, I'll come. Thanks."

Linn was rewarded with a big smile. "Great! You're welcome to ride along with us. There's plenty of room."

"Oh. I rode my bike. Is it far?"

"No, not at all." She explained where they lived, and Linn knew the area. It was at the base of the buttes, where the rich people lived.

She'd known someone who lived in there once. *Stop thinking about that.*

"We can put your bike in the back if you want."

"That's OK. I don't mind riding."

One day she'd have a car to drive, and she wouldn't have to ride around on Megan's castoff. If she still remembered how to drive, that is.

Miss C pushed off and began going higher and higher. She laughed like a little girl, and for a moment Linn felt jealous. She'd noticed the woman didn't wear a wedding ring, so she was probably divorced. What would it be like to be so independent? Miss C seemed so sure of herself, so calm and capable. Linn felt just the opposite.

"Fifteen more minutes, boys!" Miss C called.

Linn figured she'd better get a head start if they were leaving soon. "I think I'll start off now. That way, we'll get there about the same time."

"Oh, OK." She repeated the directions to make sure Linn knew where her street was. Linn memorized the address.

As she hopped on her bike, Linn realized she was looking forward to the afternoon more than she'd looked forward to anything in a long time. It was a sad statement about her life. And how long had it been since she'd had grilled-out food? Her stomach rumbled at the thought.

For the first time in weeks, she noticed the tall buttes skirting Jackson Hole like a huge wall of safety. The summer sun heated her skin even as the warm air whispered across her face and through her hair. She felt her lips curve in a smile. Maybe everything would be all right. Her grandmother used to say that everything worked out in the end . . . or something like that. Maybe she'd been right.

The roads winded and curved. She took all the right turns and felt her legs burn as she pumped up the rise in the road. She was out of breath by the time she reached the right street. She turned onto it, vaguely aware of its familiarity. But she immediately began looking at street numbers. The first one on the street was 5665, so she knew she didn't have too far to go. The first home was a huge two-story brick thing that had the look of an estate.

The homes were big enough to be hotels, with manicured lawns and flowerbeds. Streetlights, not the tall metal kind, but the shorter black streetlamps, lined the street. What would it be like to live in a place like this? She passed 5669 and looked ahead to the next one, which should be it. Something in the sight of it brought her heart to her toes.

Toot toot! A friendly horn sounded beside her, and she saw Miss C go by in an SUV. She pulled into the drive.

It can't be . . . Linn's heart spun as fast as her wheels. She braked, her tires bumping up the curb of the drive. Her bike coasted to a stop beside the SUV.

The house. She couldn't take her eyes off it.

Beside her, Miss C opened the door of her car. "OK, guys, everybody out!" She opened the door behind her, and two boys jumped from the vehicle.

Linn looked from Miss C to the boys to the house. Maybe she was wrong. It had been dark. Megan had been driving. She really hadn't been paying much attention to how she got here. Anyway, people sold houses. It had been over a year ago.

"Linn, I'd like you to meet my two boys, Taylor and Alex. Guys this is Linn, a very special friend of mine."

Oh no. Oh no.

"And, Linn, I was thinking it's kind of silly for you to call me Miss C. Why don't you call me Natalie."

Oh no. No no no. This isn't happening.

CHAPTER
TEN

Paula ambled into the kitchen and plugged in the coffee maker. A glance at the clock told her she could make it to church, but did she want to?

She pulled her silky robe around her and eased onto a barstool to await the aroma of her favorite Starbucks Breakfast Blend coffee. One of these days, if she could get David hooked on espresso, maybe he wouldn't balk at the price of a commercial espresso machine.

A slip of paper on the counter caught her eye, and she reached for it. David's neat script slanted across the paper.

Paula, sorry for my reluctance re: the testing. Wanted you to know I did make an appointment. Love you. David.

A smile pulled her lips upward. Well, that was a nice surprise in the morning. Sundays with a real estate agent husband meant a day alone while he shuffled from one open house to another. He would at least get home in time for dinner, and at the moment, some warm place in her heart wanted to fix him something special.

The phone rang, and she picked it up off the battery base. "Hello." Still possessing her morning voice, she cleared her throat.

"Hey, it's Natalie."

"Good morning. Did you get my message yesterday?"

"I did. Thanks, that's why I was calling. I've never done an interview. Should I do something to prepare?"

"No, relax. Russ is a real pro. The interview will last about five or ten minutes, but the clip they'll show will be very short. Don't worry if you mess up or have a memory lapse or something. They'll pick something clean for the clip."

"And it will air tomorrow?"

"Yes, in the evening. Russ will put you at ease and tell you what to expect, but don't be caught off-guard if he asks you some sticky questions."

"Sticky questions? Like what?"

The coffee stopped dripping, and Paula slipped her favorite coffee cup from the cupboard and poured the dark, rich brew.

"Well, if I were doing the interview, I'd probably ask something like, 'Doesn't the anti-abortion stance taken by the Hope Center encourage violence on abortion providers like the Women's Health Clinic?'" She took a sip of the coffee, her taste buds instantly awakened. "Nat?"

"I just thought—well, I guess I thought he'd go easy on me since I'm your sis." Her chuckle sounded wry.

"In a perfect world, he would. But this is the news, and they're not going to air a boring, pat-on-the-back interview. It could be tense for you at moments, but you can handle it."

"I'd feel a lot better if it were you."

Paula gave a sharp laugh. "Oh no, you wouldn't. I'd have to be my usual barracuda self, and you'd get all angry with me for it. No thanks. I don't interview family."

"I guess you're right."

"You might be interested to know that we did get some unhappy phone calls and e-mails about our coverage of the Health Center, though. One of the first ones was Gram."

Natalie laughed. "Good for Gram."

"How's she doing these days? The Alzheimer's—does the medication seem to be slowing it properly?"

"It really has. Thank God for meds. And, Paula, really, you could just pick up the phone and call." Her voice softened the words. "Or go see her at the lodge. She and Hanna aren't so busy they couldn't stop and have lunch with you or something."

Nat was right, she knew. She was so bad about staying in touch with people. She even had trouble staying in touch with her own husband, and he lived with her. "You're right. Maybe I'll pop in at church today." If she hurried, she could be presentable in an hour. She could see her whole family in one shot; how was that for efficient?

"That would be nice. Just no matchmaking, OK?"

"You didn't like Kyle?"

"I didn't like being set up for the slaughter."

Paula laughed. "It was hardly that. Just a friendly dinner. So does that mean he hasn't called?"

"Paula . . ."

"All right, all right. If you don't recognize a catch when you see it, I can't help you."

"I don't want a catch right now, good or otherwise. Why is it so hard for you married people to understand that? And for your information, Kyle isn't looking to make a catch anytime soon either. He told me so rather explicitly."

"Ahhhh, that's what I interrupted in the dining room that night. He's got your hackles up."

"I don't have hackles—whatever they are. And in case you didn't know, you can't know if someone's a good catch in one meeting."

Paula knew Natalie was referring to Keith. Who knew when they'd gotten married that he would cheat on her and conduct his bank business so unethically? He was lucky to get off with only eight months in the pen after trying to sabotage Gram's lodge. It was only because of Hanna's mercy on Keith and Natalie's boys that he got off so easily.

Paula heard Taylor squeal through the phone line. "Listen, I'd better go if I'm going to make it in time for church."

"You? We're all still in our pjs." Natalie's voice grew muffled, as if she held a hand over the receiver. "No, Taylor, don't put the Cheerios in your hair!"

Paula smothered a laugh that somehow turned to a groan. She

looked around her pristine kitchen and longed for a little pajama-clad boy or girl slurping up a bowl of cereal. Her eyes started to sting.

She cleared her throat and turned on her TV voice. "Well, it sounds like you need off even more than I do, so I'll see you at church."

She placed the phone back in its cradle, her heart clenching as she looked back at the empty kitchen.

"So, how did the interview go?" Hanna asked.

Hanna and Micah, Gram, her mom and dad all sat around the TV set in her living room waiting for the news to begin.

"I think it went OK. Mostly he asked good questions, and I think I handled it all right. He did ask a couple sticky questions, but Paula told me to expect that." Natalie glanced at the clock on the wall. Four minutes and she would be on TV. It was enough to make her as nervous as she'd been at the interview.

"Have they found out anything more about the bomber?" Gram asked.

"I don't think so," Natalie's mom said. "And what with all the people coming and going through town, I'll be surprised if they do."

"How much time are they going to give the interview on the news, Natalie?" Micah leaned back and put his arm across the back of the sofa behind Hanna.

"Paula didn't say for sure."

"Don't be surprised if it's short." Her dad crossed his shoes, a burgundy pair of wingtips that he thought went with anything he wore. "They like to keep things brief."

"They sure didn't keep that Barbara Franklin brief," Gram said.

"Guess you have to be a big name to get that much time," Micah said.

"I'm sure they'll be fair to Natalie," her mom said. "She's a hometown girl, after all. That should count for something."

Alex plopped on her dad's lap. "I'm hungry, Mom."

"We'll eat after the news, honey. Remember, Mommy's going to be on TV tonight."

"Shh-shh-shh, it's coming on." Her dad picked up the remote and jacked up the volume.

"—and I'm Paula Landin-Cohen."

Everyone grew quiet while Paula covered three different local stories. Natalie felt her heart thumping in her chest. Her mouth grew so dry she nearly got up for a drink but didn't want to take the chance of missing it.

"In other news tonight," Russ began, "the person responsible for the bombing of the Women's Health Clinic still remains at large. Police are asking that anyone with information on the crime contact them directly. The bombing of the clinic has stirred up local controversy about abortion. Earlier today, Natalie Coombs, director for the Jackson Hole Hope Center, had this to say."

The screen switched to a picture of Natalie behind her desk at the center. "Our goal is to help the young women who come through our doors. We try to educate them about the facts of pregnancy and abortion."

Russ's voice sounded, though the screen continued to show Natalie. "Does that education include telling them that an abortion takes a life?"

"Well, yes—"

"Does the center take an anti-abortion stance?"

He skipped her whole answer! She'd given a long, detailed—

"Yes, we are against abortion."

Fire burned in Natalie's gut. "He skipped the whole—"

"Do you feel that anti-abortion groups such as the Hope Center play a part in creating the political climate that feeds violence on abortion clinics?"

"Of course we're against all violence. We view the taking of a baby's life as tragic as any person's life."

The screen changed to Russ behind his desk. "The bombing of the Women's Health Clinic has temporarily closed the clinic, but they hope to be up and running within a month."

Natalie could hardly see straight for the emotions whirling in her. "I can't believe it." She stood up and paced across the room.

"What's wrong, Nat?" Hanna asked.

"Those answers didn't sound anything like what I said. He took bits and pieces of it and—I qualified those answers. Like the one on whether we were anti-abortion or not. My answer focused on the women, our clients. I talked for a good two minutes about how the women are our main concern, and how we're trying to do what's in their best interest, and he took it all and boiled it down to 'Yes, we're against abortion.'"

Her hands shook as she smoothed her hair back from her forehead. "I wish I'd never had the interview. It's done nothing for our cause."

"Now, honey,"—her mom stood up and put her arm around her—"the start of it sounded positive."

"How could Paula have let this happen?" Nat asked.

The room grew silent. Her dad crossed his legs. Natalie didn't know how much say Paula had in the editing of these tapes, but surely she could have done something. If she cared nothing for the pro-life cause, she should have at least cared enough for her own sister to step in and do something.

Natalie was still mulling over the broadcast interview on the way to work the next morning. Her family's presence had been comforting the night before, and she thought perhaps she'd overreacted to the coverage. They had played that bit at the beginning about helping clients and giving them information. And people were smarter than they were sometimes given credit for. Some would see through the editing and know there'd been more to her answers.

She turned off the ignition and grabbed her purse, finding the center's key on her key ring. She stepped outside and breathed deeply of mountain air and the refreshing scent of spruce trees. This was still Jackson Hole, the hometown she loved with the views no other place could compete with.

She rounded the corner onto the sidewalk. Maybe she'd hear from Linn today. She'd behaved strangely on Saturday when she'd come to Natalie's house. She suspected she might have felt overwhelmed by the size of the house and the grandeur of the neighborhood. It hadn't taken long for the boys to warm up to her, though, and things had seemed OK after that.

In front of the center, a flash of red on the light brick caught her eye, and she turned. *Oh no.* She froze in place, her eyes skimming the words that seemed more gruesome because of their blood-red color.

Go away liars.

Who had done this? It was that news interview that had ticked someone off. She had to get the spray paint off the brick. She took another few steps before her shoes crunched on something. She looked down. Eggshell pieces lay scattered across the concrete as if a massive hatching had just occurred. Her gaze skimmed up the brick wall of the center, following the clear line of lacquered liquid.

Only then did she see the mess on the picture window. Tiny fragments of shell were set in the hardened splats of liquid. *What a mess.* It looked like the work of teenagers. She sighed as she unlocked the front door. It would take all day to clean it up, and that was assuming she'd be able to remove the spray paint from the brick. She turned the key with more force than necessary and jerked it from the keyhole. A whole day lost because some stupid—

"Wow, what a mess." A voice from behind made her jump.

She turned. It took a moment to place him. Kyle. He looked different than he had at Paula's that night. More professional. Cuter somehow. She turned and pulled open the door, disliking her train of thought.

Her heart still raced from the scare he'd given her. She wasn't sure what bugged her most. His sneaking up on her or his inane comment about the graffiti. "Just what I needed today."

He followed her inside as she dumped her purse on top of the filing cabinet. "I saw the interview last night."

"Some interview. Score one point for pro-abortion people every-where." She glanced pointedly to the blurry front window. "Make that two points." She turned and perched on her desk. "What are you doing here?"

He shrugged, looking boyishly charming.

She crossed her arms. He wasn't boyish. More like boorish.

"I guess I thought you might need a little encouragement."

Oh, really? What happened to that gigantic wall you had so firmly in place at Paula's? She cocked her head, in no mood to make things easy on him.

"I know how the media can creatively distort things. I'm sure your real answers were much better than the ones they aired."

So she'd come across as a dunce on TV? "Thanks a lot."

He stuffed his hands in his pockets, his suit coat flapping out and around them. "Hey, I'm on your side."

The phone rang, saving her from responding. She hesitated before picking it up. What if it was the person who'd vandalized the center? What if they started getting ugly phone calls?

So what? Some jerks weren't going to stop her from helping these girls. Defiantly, she picked up the receiver. "Hope Center, Miss C speaking."

It was a young, pregnant girl they'd been working with for several months. Since she wanted to talk to a particular volunteer, Natalie looked at the schedule and told her when she'd be working.

When she was finished, she hung up the phone. Kyle was still standing around. She noticed the briefcase in his hand. "Can I help you with something?"

The center's door opened, and Natalie leaned around to see who'd come in.

"Linn!"

"Hi, Miss C—I mean Natalie." Linn looked awkwardly at Kyle's back, then at her again.

Just then Kyle turned to face Linn, and Natalie couldn't miss the change in expressions on Linn's face. The smile fell from her face. Her eyes widened, then narrowed, her lips going taut. She darted another look at Natalie. "Did you call him?" It was an accusation as much as a question.

"Call who?" Natalie looked at Kyle, then to Linn.

"Hello, Linn," Kyle said.

Linn's eyes narrowed farther. She crossed her arms over her chest protectively. "What's he doing here? I thought you said everything was confidential."

Natalie felt Linn's trust slipping away and was desperate to save it. "It is. I didn't call him, Linn."

"She didn't call. I just stopped by," Kyle said.

"I take it you two know each other." Natalie moved closer to Linn, but she took a step back.

"I was married to her sister."

Oh, my. Married, past tense. Probably a divorce situation. Obviously there was bad blood between the two of them. Natalie had thought Linn was an only child.

"If you didn't ask him here, what's he doing?"

"I didn't even know the two of you knew each other," Natalie said.

"Natalie and I know each other, Linn. That's the only reason I'm here." Kyle rubbed a hand across his face. "I didn't mean to upset you."

His softened tone did nothing to alter Linn's demeanor. Natalie needed to get him out of here before she lost all the ground she'd made with Linn.

"How's the family?" he asked.

"None of your business."

Natalie spoke. "Kyle, why don't you—"

"Why should you care anyway? It's all your fault," Linn said.

Natalie glanced at Kyle. His gaze fell to the floor.

"I wish you'd just leave us alone. You're the worst thing that's ever happened to us!"

"Linn, you know I didn't—"

"Just go away!" Linn started for the door.

"Wait, Linn." Natalie rushed ahead of her and stopped her with a hand on the arm.

"I'm sorry." Worry lines creased Kyle's forehead, and his eyes drooped at the corners like a sad puppy. "I loved your sister."

"You killed her!" The words shot from Linn's mouth like an arrow, and judging by the look on Kyle's face, they'd made their mark.

CHAPTER
ELEVEN

You killed her. Linn's words echoed in Natalie's head.

Natalie looked between Linn and Kyle. One looked as sad as the other looked angry. What had gone on in their family? It didn't seem possible that Kyle could do anything like Linn had said. But then, she hardly knew the man. One thing was clear, looking at Linn's set jaw and flashing eyes. She believed exactly what she'd said.

"I'll be going now." Though Kyle's tone was calm, the pink flush that climbed from beneath his collar betrayed his emotions. He slipped past them and out the door, stopping for a moment on the door stoop. "You might want to call the sheriff about this vandalism." With that, he was gone.

Natalie turned her attention to Linn. The girl was as taut as a tug-of-war rope. Natalie put her arm around her. "Let's go have a soda, OK?"

Linn hesitated, her gaze bouncing off Natalie, as if trying to figure whether or not Natalie deserved her trust.

Natalie went to the back room, where the soda machine was. "What'll you have?" She dropped in two quarters and waited, hoping against hope Linn wouldn't leave. It took so much effort to gain these girls' trust and so little to lose it. She prayed she hadn't done that today.

"Root beer?" The voice came from the doorway.

Natalie couldn't keep the relieved smile from forming. "Root beer it is." She pushed the tab, and the soda can clunked down the machine. She handed it to Linn and selected a Diet Pepsi for herself.

"What happened out there?" Linn asked, pointing to the front of the center.

Natalie knew she'd have to call the sheriff, and she really needed to clean up the mess, but right now, Linn was more important. The rest would have to wait.

"I guess some teenagers had too much time on their hands," Natalie said.

"I can help you clean it up."

Natalie stopped in the middle of popping her soda open. "I couldn't ask you to do that. Besides, I have to do a little research to find out how to get the egg and paint off. I probably won't get to it until later this morning. What I really want to do right now is talk with you."

"You should call the cops right away if you want to catch these guys. Otherwise, the crime scene will get messed up."

Why hadn't she thought of that? "You're absolutely right."

Linn shrugged. "I guess I've watched too many *CSI* episodes."

"First, let's talk." Natalie sat down with Linn in her office. She hated to bring up a sore subject again, but she wanted to be sure Linn understood. "Are we clear about Kyle, then? I don't want you thinking I've betrayed your confidence."

Immediately, Linn leaned back and looked away. "How do you know him?"

"We had dinner together awhile back."

"You're *dating* him?"

"No. No, we're not dating at all. He was at my sister's for a dinner party. That's all there was to it." Did Linn believe her? She couldn't tell by her expression. "I can see there's a lot of animosity between you two, and I just wanted to make sure you knew you could trust me."

"Why do you care so much?"

The question took her aback. Why did she care so much? It was hard to put into words.

Linn began biting her nails, and Natalie could see there wasn't much left to bite.

"To explain that, I have to explain something else. It's kind of like me asking you why you really disliked a teacher. You couldn't explain that without telling me something about your background with him, right?"

Linn nodded.

"We talked a little about God on your first visit here. Do you remember?"

"Sure," she said, paying particular attention to her pinky nail.

"Well, when I was a little girl, I decided I wanted a relationship with God. I know that might sound funny, but all my little life, I'd been told how much He loved me. That was easy for me to understand, since my parents loved me, and my life was so good, you know? They told me He loved me more than anyone in the world could love me. It made me feel really special.

"It was easy to believe when everything in life was great, but sometimes in life, things get shaken up. Things go wrong, and all of a sudden your world seems to turn upside down. It's then that you begin to wonder what's real. What's important. I put my trust in a man, a man I thought loved me more than anything, and he failed me. It was then I really started realizing who God was and how much He loved me.

"You asked me why I care, and I don't know if I can explain this right, but I care because I know how much He loves you. I know how much He loves you because I feel the love He has for me, and I want you to feel it, too. Does that make sense?"

"Kind of." Linn took a sip of her root beer. "That thing you said about your world turning upside down." Linn wiped her mouth with her fingers and began twisting the soda tab back and forth. "I feel like that now."

Natalie felt such a tugging in her heart, she wanted to reach out and make the girl believe in God. But it didn't work that way. "I know you do, Linn. You're going through a very difficult time. You have to make a tough decision. When my world turned upside down, the decision was made for me, and there was nothing I could do about it. But you have a choice."

"You've never been in my situation."

"True." Sometimes, she realized not having a choice was the easy way out. And it was easy to tell someone else what the right thing to do was when she didn't have to live with the consequences.

"There are volunteers here who have been, though," Natalie said. "Some have had abortions, and now they know they made a terrible mistake. But it's too late for them, so they help other girls make good decisions. Would you like to talk with one of them?"

She shook her head. "Not yet. Maybe later."

Help me, Jesus, to give this girl what she needs to hear to make the right choice. Help her to do the right thing, no matter how hard it is.

Would you?

The voice whispered into her heart but had the impact of a thunderous boom. Would Natalie do the right thing regardless of the consequences? She feared she'd have to know the consequences before she could make a decision.

And if the consequences were too great?

She had to stop thinking about herself. This was about Linn, not her. And the girl clearly needed her help.

"What can I do for you, Linn? How can I help you?"

She shrugged. "I don't know. I guess I need to know what my options are. Besides abortion, I mean. If I decide to keep the—the pregnancy, how does all this work?"

Natalie explained how some girls kept their babies and others found good families to love and raise their child. She explained that some birth mothers wanted to be kept updated on the child with pictures and letters and so forth.

Linn's eyes lit up at that piece of information, and hope sprung in Natalie's heart. She felt such a connection with Linn, such a need to help her. If she could help it, Linn would not wind up like other girls who lived in anguish over their choice for years. Nor like Dana, who hadn't lived at all.

"Would you like to come over for dinner one night this week?" As soon as she said it, she cringed. It was the center's policy not to involve the clients in their personal lives. She'd have a fit if one of her volunteers invited a client to her home. And Natalie had already done it once. Still, she felt Linn was so close to making the right decision. And what could it hurt, really?

"Depends what night. I have to work a few nights this week, but I can't remember my schedule."

"No problem. If it's OK, I'll call you, and we'll work it out." Linn seemed open to learning about God. She'd listened intently while Natalie shared her testimony. Wouldn't God want her to open her life to Linn?

After Linn left, Natalie called Sheriff Whitco to report the vandalism. She'd thought they'd come out and at least look for evidence of some kind, but they only filed a report over the phone.

Even when Natalie reminded the man that she'd received a physical threat from someone, he said the best they could do was tie the two reports together. So much for catching the culprits.

When Sheri, one of the morning volunteers, came in, she commiserated with Natalie over the mess. She recommended a good scrubbing with dish soap for the egg, so Natalie went home to get a bucket and some abrasive sponges.

When she got back, she scrubbed the hardened mess, wishing she knew who had done this so she could put them to work. Despite the attack on her in the parking lot, she still believed this to be the work of some teens, the result of last night's interview on TV. Someone who was serious enough to attack her wouldn't resort to a petty act like tossing eggs on the window.

She was almost done, her fingers wrinkly and white, her khakis and shirt splotched with dirty water, when Paula approached.

"Oh, Nat, who did this?"

Somehow seeing her sister, whose station aired the incriminating interview, standing there all impeccable in her Anne Klein pantsuit, irritated Natalie to the bone. She turned back to the window, scrubbing extra hard at the remnants of lacquered egg white. "Well, if I knew that, they'd be cleaning it up, not me."

The silence was only broken by the squeaking of her sponge on the glass.

"Are you unhappy with the interview Russ did?"

"Which one, the one he did at the center, or the one he aired on TV?"

Paula slid her sunglasses up on her head. "You know that's the way they do things in the media. I didn't think the center came across badly."

"Well, someone obviously did." Nat tossed the sponge in the soapy water. "And coming on the heels of a physical assault, it's not very reassuring."

"Does the sheriff's office think they're connected?"

She shrugged. "They said they'd tie the two reports together. It's all they can do when they don't have any suspects."

Paula glanced at the red paint against the beige brick, and her manicured brows drew together.

Natalie looked at the words. *Go away liars.*

No. She would not go away. They could throw eggs at the building every day and spray anything they wanted on the front of their building, but they would not go away.

"If it makes you feel any better," Paula said, "they haven't found who did the bombing at the clinic either."

Did Paula think she'd be glad about that? That Natalie wanted such a hateful crime to go unpunished? "It doesn't make me feel better at all, Paula." She grabbed the bucket and tossed the water onto the grass lining the sidewalk before entering the center.

CHAPTER
TWELVE

Kyle slid the adoption petition closer and proofread the copy. He'd be finalizing an adoption later today in court and wanted everything to go smoothly. Somehow, finalization days no longer carried the excitement they used to. It was still rewarding to unite couples with a child in need of a family, but he remembered when he used to thrive on it. So much had changed since then.

To his right sat a mountain of paperwork, his task for the morning. If only he could keep his mind on his work. After running into Linn at the Hope Center, his mind had been on only one thing.

Jillian.

He set down his pen and leaned back against his padded chair. After almost two years, he'd finally managed to get on with his life. Finally managed to stuff the guilt and confusion down deep inside. But then he'd run into Linn, and now everything had bubbled back to the surface.

On his way to the office, the smell of summer and newly mown grass had drifted through his windows, reminding him of that last tragic day. He'd put up the window and put in a WOW CD. Even so, the day was burned into his mind like a brand.

They'd been returning from church, of all places. The Sunday night service had gone well, he'd thought. Jillian had gone to her small group class, and the pastor had spoken on Jeremiah. But something must have happened in Jillian's small group, or maybe she'd just reached the end of her rope. He'd never know for sure.

"We have to talk, Kyle," she'd said.

He pulled out onto Broadway, and he turned down the radio so he could hear her. "What's up?"

Her voice seemed tense, but lately, the pregnancy had her emotions teetering all over the scale. "Maybe I should wait until we get home."

He noticed the way she twisted her purse strap in her fingers. "What's wrong, hon? Did I do something?" He immediately thought of the bookshelves he'd promised to put in her office. And the closet door she'd been asking him to fix. He had been negligent, but the cases he was working on were taking up so much of his time. And he didn't want to do anything to let these couples down. Or the birth mothers.

He braked for a stoplight, and tourists began crossing in the crosswalk toward the Town Square.

"It's about the baby, Kyle."

The baby? His gaze skimmed her face. Under the glow of the street-lamps, he could see her brows were pinched together. Her hand went to the gentle swell of her abdomen. "What's wrong? Is there something wrong with the baby?" Had she had an appointment lately? He couldn't remember.

She shook her head. "No, the baby's fine. It's—" She looked out the window, turning away from him. Her thick, curly hair shielded even her profile from his view.

He wanted to pull the words from her, but forced himself to be patient. She was probably overreacting to something. It had been the way of things these past few months.

"I guess it's about more than the baby," she said.

The light turned green, and he accelerated.

She sniffled, and he looked her way again. She'd been a little weepy lately, but he was beginning to think this was more substantial than a neglected "honey do" list.

He reached over and covered her hand that still rested against her stomach. "Talk to me, hon. What is it?"

"I can't say it. I just can't say it!" She covered her face with her hands and wept.

One part of him wanted her to tell him what was wrong, and another wanted to plug his ears shut. His mouth went sticky-dry while his mind worked for an explanation.

"I don't know where to start."

"Start at the beginning."

She wiped her eyes with her fingers and sniffed, then rifled through her purse for a tissue. She pulled it from the mini packet and wiped her cheeks.

"Remember when we were arguing in the spring?" She tossed him a glance.

He remembered well. She'd passed a house on Pine Drive and had fallen in love with the five-bedroom home with a cedar shaker roof. She'd even gone through it with a realtor before telling him about it. Kyle had gone through it eventually, but it hadn't changed his mind. Regardless of what the realtor said they could afford, the house was out of their budget. And he wanted to get the mortgage paid down on their house before they even thought about buying another. They'd argued about it for weeks.

"Remember how busy you were and how you didn't go to my reunion with me?"

He let the accusation slide. She was right. He'd had a heavy load in the spring. Then on the night of her class reunion, he'd had a birth mother who nearly backed out of an adoption plan, and the prospective adoptive couple was frantic. He'd talked to them all evening, and eventually, the adoption had gone through as planned.

"I was so mad at you that night for not being there, for not being home much anymore, for not letting us get that house. I was in no frame of mind to see Jeff again."

Jeff Kline? "You never told me Jeff was there." Thoughts of his wife's high-school sweetheart sent a pang of regret through him. Regret that he hadn't been with her that night. Suspicion buzzed like a fly in his ear.

She met his gaze, shaking her head. "I didn't mean for it to happen, honest I didn't, Kyle."

Didn't mean for what to happen? He searched her eyes, dread squeezing his throat like a vice. "What happened?" His calm tone belied the riot in his head.

Tears leaked from her eyes again and trickled down her face. "It didn't mean anything. I was just angry and confused, and seeing him again brought back stuff. He was divorced, and we were just talking . . . that's all I ever meant it to be."

"What happened, Jillian?" A logjam clogged his throat, but somehow the words slipped past.

"I had a drink. I know I shouldn't have, but I just thought one little drink wouldn't hurt anything. And then there was another in my hand, and I drank it, too."

His heart raced, pounding through his shirt. He felt almost like he'd explode. Jillian didn't drink. Had sworn she wouldn't because of what it had done to her father. *This can't be happening.*

"He invited me to go back to his hotel to see the plans he was working on for some building he's designing. You know I was always interested in that." She shook her head slowly, as if still trying to figure out how it had happened.

His gut hardened to a tight knot. "You slept with him?" The words grated across his throat, across the rock that seemed stuck there. "You slept with him, Jilly?" He couldn't believe it. It couldn't be true. Not Jilly. His world spun crazily.

"I'm so sorry, Kyle. I didn't want to tell you. Didn't want to hurt you like this, but I just can't stand it anymore. I just can't keep it from you anymore." She sobbed into her hands.

His eyes glazed over. "How could you do this? Why, Jilly? Why?" The last word tore loudly from his mouth. He looked into the seat next to him where his wife—his wife—sat crying like a baby.

The baby. The thought hit him like a tidal wave. Didn't she say this had something to do with the baby? He stared at her in horror. She looked out the window and suddenly jerked back, her hands flying up.

"Kyle!"

It was the last thing she said, though it had taken a few days for him to remember. He hadn't remembered the red light either, or the delivery truck that had barreled into his wife's side of the car, but plenty of eye-witnesses attested to it.

He'd walked away with a concussion, but his wife hadn't walked away at all. And the baby . . .

He'd lost his wife and baby that night. And though he'd never know for sure if the baby had been his or not, he knew one thing was true. The thing Linn and her family would never let him forget. He'd been re-sponsible for their deaths.

"Close your eyes," Dante said.

Paula let her eyelids fall shut and turned her face up for the eye shadow. Dante's brush glided across her lid with smooth strokes.

It had been a week and a half since Natalie's interview aired, and thankfully, her sister was speaking to her cordially now. All marks of vandalism were gone, and no one else had tried to deface the Hope Center. Unfortunately, the authorities were still clueless about who set the bomb at the Women's Health Clinic.

"What did you do on the weekend?" Dante paused to dab the brush in an olive green shadow.

"Oh, nothing much. Shopped on Saturday, lazed around on Sunday."

"No big date with your husband?" His inflection begged a flirtatious response.

"He's not home much on the weekend." Pleased with her restraint, she closed her eyes again. She really must be more careful with Dante. Sure, he made butterflies dance in her stomach, but she loved David. Maybe their relationship had fizzled fast after they'd married, but she supposed that was to be expected.

Dante was a temptation she could control. Heaven knew she'd con-trolled herself many times before. She knew she was attractive. A woman didn't get an anchor job without beauty, and her auburn hair and green eyes had always snatched the attention of men. She couldn't help that men were attracted to her. It was a shame David seemed less so after their years of marriage. Even when they were dating, he'd been a real challenge. That had been part of his charm. Little did she know that the challenge would wear old after a while.

"You are going to get unsightly lines on your face if you do not stop frowning," Dante said. He began applying eyeliner along her upper lid.

A smile curved her lips. "Is that better?"

"You just make me draw a crooked line, *mia cara*. You are going to look like a clown instead of a beautiful woman."

She smiled fully. "Dante, I'm quite certain you could make even a clown look beautiful."

"Ah, not so. You just make my job too easy. It is like a piece of pie."

She laughed and opened her eyes, meeting his gaze head on. "Piece of cake."

His eyes laughed, and she wondered if he'd messed up the cliché on purpose. He lifted a finger to smudge the line at the corner of her eye. "There now, it is all fixed, and you are as beautiful as ever."

It was then she saw someone in the mirror, standing behind her at the door. "David."

Dante pulled back and leaned against the makeup counter.

"Have you met Dante?" Paula asked. "He's the new makeup artist. Dante, this is my husband, David."

Dante spoke first. "It is a pleasure, Mr. Landin."

"Cohen. Landin is Paula's maiden name."

Paula cringed. David had hated her keeping her maiden name, the way she hyphenated it with his surname. It was a career decision for her and a sore spot between them.

He stood on the threshold for a moment before entering the room. "You forgot to leave the checkbook."

He'd asked her to leave it this morning so he could do the bills when he got home. But she'd had so much on her mind . . .

"Oh, sorry about that. Excuse me a minute, Dante." She got up and retrieved her purse from the closet.

David came near as she fished through her purse. She felt the tension in him and wondered if he felt threatened by Dante. It wouldn't hurt him to know someone else was interested. Maybe it would wake him up a little.

"There you go." The checkbook was a mess, and she wished she'd had a chance to straighten it out before he got hold of it. She smiled past the thought.

"Thanks." He kissed her on the cheek. "See you later tonight."

"Bye, sweetheart." She watched him throw a stiff nod toward Dante and couldn't help feeling a bit justified.

CHAPTER THIRTEEN

Natalie glanced at her watch and saw she was running a bit late to pick up Linn. She pressed the accelerator, looking at the homes as she passed them. Most of the homes begged for a coat of paint. She couldn't help the twinge of pity she felt for Linn. It couldn't be easy growing up in a poverty-stricken area with a father who apparently didn't care much.

She'd gathered that much over the last two weeks. Linn had been a regular over at her house, so much so that the boys had really bonded with her. She was very good with them, and Natalie wondered if maybe Linn wouldn't decide to raise her baby.

She thought of something Linn had said the week before.

"You're a real good mom to your boys." Linn had just rinsed out a glass and put it in the dishwasher.

The words were a balm to Natalie's heart. "Thanks, Linn. Sometimes I get too busy doing stuff, you know? And worry I'm not such a good mom."

Linn closed the dishwasher and dried her hands on the towel Natalie handed her. "It's the good moms who worry. Bad moms don't care enough to worry."

Natalie looked at Linn, so young, yet sometimes she said the most profound things. "You know, Linn, you are one smart cookie."

Natalie read the street sign and saw she was almost to Linn's street. Linn hadn't said anything about keeping the baby or adoption. She hadn't talked about abortion much either, though, so Natalie knew she couldn't rule it out. The clinic was up and running again after the bombing, and it would only take one visit to the clinic for Linn to change everything.

Natalie had really enjoyed Linn's company, and when she'd called this afternoon, Natalie jumped at the chance to have her over. The boys were with Keith, and she was beginning to feel a little lonely with nothing to do on Saturday nights. They agreed to rent a movie and order pizza.

Natalie pulled onto Linn's street and found the right house. It was a tiny, white clapboard house with curling roof shingles. Linn came running down the crumbling porch steps before Natalie had come to a full stop.

On the way to Natalie's, they stopped and rented *You've Got Mail* with Meg Ryan and Tom Hanks. Natalie had already seen it, but she loved it enough to watch it again. The pizza came partway through the movie, but they only paused it long enough to put slices on plates and grab cans of soda from the fridge. Natalie had started stocking the fridge with root beer for Linn, but the boys were always pestering her for a can. She might have to rethink that idea.

By the time the movie ended, Linn was sprawled out on one end of the sofa, and Natalie was at the other end, her footrest kicked out. Natalie clicked the DVD player off.

"Like it?" Natalie asked.

"Um-hmm. Romantic comedies are the best." A cloud passed over her face, and she sighed. "Too bad men aren't really like that in real life, huh?"

Natalie hated seeing disillusionment on such a young girl. But in all honesty, she wasn't feeling great about the opposite sex these days either. Since Keith had left her for another woman, she'd had zero interest in a romantic relationship. Still, with Linn's father being the way he was, she knew Linn needed a dose of encouragement, not pessimism.

"We all have our faults, men and women. All men aren't like your dad, you know. There are men out there worth finding."

"Well, the last one I found left me in kind of a bind." She looked pointedly down at her abdomen.

"Did you ever tell him about it?" Only because of their friendship did Natalie feel she could ask.

Linn snorted. "No, he's, like, made it real clear it's over. And I know he doesn't want this baby." She glanced down at the sapphire ring on her finger. "I don't know why I still wear this."

"Do you still care for him?"

Linn laid her head against the back of the sofa, her dark hair spilling over her shoulders. "I don't know. I haven't seen him in a couple months. I have other things on my mind right now."

Natalie knew she was referring to the baby. "Do you know what you're going to do yet?" She teetered between wanting to know and dreading to hear.

"I've been thinking lots about it." She darted a glance off toward Natalie. "A part of me wants to have it, and a part of me just wants to have this over with."

Natalie reached out and put a hand on Linn's ankle. "It's not over with when you have an abortion, Linn. Truly, it's just not that easy."

"I know . . . I hear what you're saying." She shifted over until she was lying on her back, her head propped on the arm of the sofa, her knees poking up in the air. "I'm not taking all this lightly. I kind of did at first, but not anymore. I see you with your boys and can't help thinking about my baby and what he or she would grow up to be."

Natalie smiled. She was talking about the baby in terms of gender. That was good.

"But then I think about college just a few months away. I want to go so bad, and they haven't answered my phone call about my scholarship. What if they won't apply it to next year? I'll never be able to afford college on my own."

Natalie's heart plunged. She'd really been thinking Linn was coming around, but it seemed as if she was still up in the air. She thought of Dana and how she'd gone to the hospital to see the girl after she'd swallowed a bottle of painkillers. All pale and fragile-looking. She hadn't lived through the day.

"Maybe the scholarship can be worked out," Natalie said. "You still don't know for sure. Abortion is a decision that can never be changed. You have your whole life ahead of you for college and your career. Right now you have the opportunity to give your baby life."

Linn nodded slowly and fiddled with the ties on her shirt.

"Have you thought much about adoption?"

Linn's glance skittered off Natalie, and she wondered what she'd seen in the girl's eyes.

"You know what bothers me most about that?" Linn said. "The thought that my child would be out there somewhere with strangers. I couldn't live knowing that. I don't think I could stand it, you know?"

Natalie's heart squeezed. *Oh, Lord, help Linn to make the right decision, no matter how hard it is. This isn't easy for her, but help her to see what she needs to do.*

"The thing is, I've been thinking, and I think I have an answer that I could live with."

Hope surged in Natalie. Even looking at Linn now, she reminded her so much of Dana with the long, dark hair and eyes that looked older than her years. *Please, God, show me what to do to help Linn.* "Oh, I'm so glad. What is it, Linn?"

"Well, you know I was saying how I didn't like the idea of strangers raising the baby . . ."

Of course. A relative. Linn wanted to have a relative adopt the baby. Natalie hoped she had someone dependable in her family. Surely, she didn't think her father was up to the task.

"The thing is, I was thinking of you."

Lost in thought, Natalie only half-heard what Linn had said. "What?" Surely, Linn hadn't said what she thought she had.

"It's the perfect solution. You're a great mom, and you have a big enough house. And I know I could, like, trust you to do what's right for the baby."

Natalie was sure she'd stopped breathing. How was it then that her heart was still pressing against her ribs with enough force to bring pain? She wanted—she wanted—*oh, God, she can't ask that of me!*

"I know it's asking a lot." Linn's almond-shaped eyes narrowed. "But I know how much you care about saving the baby. So, see, you'd be saving the baby, and I'd feel good about who the parent is."

Deep breaths. Deep breaths. Adopt a child? She was a single mother, struggling just to make time for her boys. How could she possibly—how could Linn possibly ask it of her?

"You're not saying anything," Linn said.

Oh, God, what do I tell her? I can't adopt her baby! If I adopted every client's baby, why, I'd be running an orphanage here in my house. But how do I explain it to Linn?

"You don't want to do it, do you?" Linn sat up, swinging her feet to the floor. "It was a stupid idea. It's not your problem. It's mine." She slid on her clunky shoes, blinking hard.

"I'm sorry, Linn, I'm not handling this very well. I just—I guess you surprised me a little."

"It's OK." She picked up her pizza plate and carried it to the sink. "In a way, you've helped me solve the problem."

Natalie followed her into the kitchen on shaky legs. "What do you mean?"

The room suddenly seemed so quiet. She could hear the humming of the refrigerator.

Linn sat her plate in the sink and turned. "I know you think it's the wrong choice, but I'm going to have an abortion. Maybe I'll regret it, but at least it'll be over."

Natalie's thoughts swirled in her head. *Oh no. No, Linn couldn't do that.* She'd thought she'd really reached her. Her prayer from moments ago echoed in her head. *Help Linn make the right decision, no matter how hard it is.*

What about your decision?

She shook away the thought. "Please, Linn, it's just not that easy. Abortion isn't like that."

"You've been telling me how strong I am. I can get through it." Despite Linn's resolve, her eyes looked so sad.

Natalie wanted to weep with frustration. "What about keeping the baby? Or what about a relative? Don't you have some relative you'd trust the baby with?" She regretted the pleading note to her voice.

"I got that you don't want the baby, Natalie. But there is no one else. And I'm not ready to be a mom." She walked out of the kitchen. "Can you take me home now?"

CHAPTER FOURTEEN

Natalie slept restlessly that night, thinking of Linn and the bad situation Natalie had put herself in. She'd broken the center's policy where clients were concerned, and she was quickly beginning to see why those policies were in place.

During church she'd tried to keep her mind on Pastor Richards's sermon, but instead she kept reliving her conversation with Linn. As she'd taken the girl home, she'd tried her best to smooth things over, but she didn't think she'd been very successful. It seemed a wide chasm had opened between the two of them, and Natalie feared what the girl would do if she felt she had nobody on her side. Natalie had told her she'd call Monday morning, but she had no idea how to fix this.

After the service, she approached Hanna, who was standing alone after Micah went to greet a visitor. "Do you guys have any plans for lunch?" She realized her invitation sounded as if it were meant for both Hanna and Micah. "I don't want to interrupt anything you might have planned, but I really need to talk to you about something personal."

"No, we were just going to go back to the lodge to eat with Gram. What is it?" She brushed her straight hair behind her ears.

Natalie shook her head. "Too long a story to get into right now. Can we have lunch together?"

"Sure. Just let me tell Micah."

"Meet me at the Shady Nook in about fifteen minutes?"

"Sounds good."

Natalie made the short drive and secured a table in a quiet corner. She'd already ordered them both Diet Pepsis by the time Hanna arrived. They ordered the lunch special and sat back to wait on their food.

"What's up? You sounded pretty serious at church. Is it a man?"

Natalie huffed. "Not you, too. Between you and Paula, you'd think a man was as necessary as oxygen."

Hanna tucked in the corner of her lip and wiggled her eyebrows. "Mine is."

"Yeah, yeah, we know you've got it bad. Spare me the details."

Hanna took a sip of her soda. "Seriously, what's up? Something at the center? You haven't had any more vandalism, have you?"

"No, nothing like that. It's about a client."

Hanna's eyes softened. "Have I told you lately how much I admire your dedication? You're really making a difference in the world, you know."

Natalie squirmed in her chair, then shrugged away the ugly feeling stirring inside her. She had no reason to feel guilty. "Thanks. Sometimes it's stressful, that's all. And this one client . . . well, I guess I've gotten a little more involved than I should have."

"That's not like you. You're usually such a stickler for rules."

Natalie playfully narrowed her eyes. "Thanks. I think." It was true, but she'd really gone far off the rule book on this one. She explained to Hanna how she'd befriended Linn, and how Linn had seemed to be coming around.

Her mouth went dry as she thought about the previous night, and she took a sip of her soda. "Then last night happened. We were just watching a movie, having pizza, then she springs this on me."

"What'd she spring on you?"

"She wants me to adopt her baby. Me. Can you believe that?" She gave a wry laugh. Surely, Hanna would see the absurdity of it. "And she really seems to think abortion is the only other option. I don't get it. It's like she only sees two options: I adopt her baby, or she has an abortion."

"Maybe that's the way she does see it. Maybe those are the only options she's willing to consider at this point."

She couldn't believe her sister wasn't laughing at the absurdity of the idea. "Hanna. I can't adopt a baby. I'm a single mother. I have two boys already. What in the world would I do with another child?"

Hanna held up her hands, palms out. "Hey, I'm not saying you should do it. I'm just saying this girl may think those are the only options she can live with. Have you talked to her about keeping the baby?"

Natalie shook her head. "That's not going to happen. She has plans for the future, and she's hanging on to them pretty tightly. Plus, she's really in no position to keep the baby financially, and her dad will be zero help."

"What about an arranged adoption? Those can work out nicely for everyone involved."

"I suggested that. She just can't picture her child with anyone else, she says. What am I going to do, Hanna? I'm afraid she's going to up and have an abortion because I won't adopt the baby."

"Did you tell her you won't do it?" Her inflection revealed surprise.

"Well, no, not in so many words. But she could tell by my reaction—I was just so shocked."

"I can understand why you were caught off-guard, but maybe you shouldn't rule it out so quickly."

The breath left Natalie's body. "You think I should consider it?" A weight the size of a boulder sat on her shoulders. How could she do it? What would her boys think? She couldn't believe she was even giving thought to the idea. It was insane!

"Well, maybe you shouldn't rule it out just yet. I mean, this is a baby's life we're talking about here. You have the chance to save this baby, Nat. And save this girl from the biggest mistake of her life."

"Sure, bring on the guilt." The words were said lightly, but inside, her heart raged. It wasn't fair to be put in this situation.

"I don't mean to make you feel guilty. I just know how much this issue means to you. You've dedicated your life to helping these girls." She shrugged and ran the tip of her finger around the rim of her soda glass.

Natalie hated the emotions welling up in her. She'd thought Hanna would confirm her own thoughts, not make her consider this ridiculous idea. "Helping them is one thing. Adopting a child . . . well, that's huge, Hanna. I can't take that lightly."

"Of course not. I'm just saying maybe you shouldn't write it off so quickly."

Sure, it was easy for Hanna to say. She wasn't the one being asked to alter her life because of a mistake.

Isn't that what you ask girls to do all the time?

That was different. It wasn't her mistake. Why should she be the one to pay for it?

This is a child we're talking about, Natalie, not a mistake.

She buried her face in her hands. Why was she having these horrible thoughts? Of course, it was a child. A precious baby, not a mistake. She told girls this nearly every day. How could she be thinking like this?

She felt Hanna's hand on her arm. "I'm sorry. I can see you're really struggling here. I didn't mean to add to your problem."

Natalie shook her head and crossed her arms on top of the table. "It's not your fault. I'm just so confused. I never dreamed I'd be put in this position. I don't know if I should even be considering it. I don't know if I'm capable of what she's asked of me."

"I understand your confusion, but there's no doubt in my mind that you're capable, Nat. You're one of the most nurturing people I know. If anyone could love a child born from another woman, it's you."

How could Hanna be so sure? Natalie felt so incapable at the moment. Of course, she loved her boys dearly, but how would she feel about Linn's baby? Could she love that baby the same way she loved her boys? She didn't even know anyone who'd adopted a child. She'd had clients who'd successfully made an adoption plan, but she didn't know the adoptive parents.

The food was served, and after they said grace, they dug into their meatloaf. As they ate, they talked. Hanna told her Micah had started looking for his little sister Jenna.

"Sister? I didn't realize he had one."

"They were separated in foster care when Micah was young. She's been on his mind for a while, and he's determined to find her."

Natalie wished him luck, what with all the red tape he'd probably have to go through.

On the way home from lunch, Natalie's mind returned to her own situation, and she had an idea. Kyle was an adoption attorney. He'd seen lots of couples matched with children in need of a family. He definitely wasn't the one to talk to Linn, since she clearly despised her brother-in-law. But maybe he was someone who could offer her advice.

When she got home, she phoned Paula for Kyle's number. She needed to speak with him today if she was going to call Linn in the morning. When Paula answered, she wasted no time getting to the point.

"Hey, I was wondering if you might have Kyle Keaton's number. His home number, I mean."

"Well, well, well. Finally coming around, are you?" Paula's voice dripped with amusement.

"It's business, Paula. I can get his work number from the directory and call him tomorrow, but I really need to reach him today if at all possible."

"Business. On a Sunday. Sure, Sis, whatever you say."

"Paula . . ."

"I think I have it here somewhere. Let me check."

Moments later, Paula rattled off the phone number, and Natalie said good-bye before Paula made any more suggestive comments.

Before she could change her mind, she dialed Kyle's number. It rang three times before he answered, out of breath.

"Hello?"

"Uh, is this Kyle Keaton?"

"Yes, it is."

She was starting to feel really stupid for calling him at home. And what if he thought she was interested in him? "This is Natalie Coombs. From the Hope Center? Paula Landin-Cohen's sister?"

A pause. "Sure. What can I do for you?"

Was it her imagination, or did he sound guarded? Was it their uncomfortable meeting at the center with Linn or the awkward dinner they'd shared at Paula's? He probably thought she was going to ask him on a date or something. She quickly stepped in to break him of that notion.

"I have a . . . a situation with a client. A really unusual situation involving adoption. I know you're busy, but I was wondering if you might have time to meet me today. I need some advice."

The moment stretched on. She was feeling more stupid by the moment. Why had she called him? Maybe he thought this was a ploy to get to know him.

"I have to call this client tomorrow," Natalie said. "Or if you don't have time, maybe we could just discuss it on the phone."

"No, we can meet if you like. I'm busy this afternoon and have plans for dinner, but maybe after that?"

Natalie breathed a sigh of relief. Maybe she could invite him over for coffee. Then she remembered Linn's vehement accusation about Kyle killing his wife. She wondered what that meant. Surely, there wasn't anything substantial to it. Wouldn't he be in jail if that were the case? Nonetheless, maybe someplace public would be smarter. "That sounds great. I really appreciate it. How about the Hard Drive Café?"

They agreed on a time and hung up. Next, she called Keith and asked if he would bring the boys home a little later than usual. He agreed, and it was all set.

With the details out of the way, Natalie was restless all afternoon. There was nothing on TV, she hadn't bought a new book in ages, and she'd cleaned out the last of the Rocky Road two days ago. Seeing her Bible on the end table, where she'd dropped it after church, she decided to have some alone time with God. She ended it with a heartfelt prayer for guidance.

That evening, after she ate a sandwich and bowl of soup, she tidied herself up and went to meet Kyle. She wondered what questions to ask him. She hardly knew where to start.

When she arrived at the Hard Drive Café, Kyle was already there, sipping a coffee at a table against the far wall. She almost didn't recognize him in a black T-shirt. After waving, she ordered a decaf vanilla latte and went to join him.

"Thank you for meeting me." She hung her purse over the chair back and sank onto the chair. She was struck by his good looks as a distant smile formed on his lips. She wondered if he felt awkward because of Linn's accusation three weeks ago.

"No problem. I come here a lot anyway." He took a sip of his coffee from the big mug and licked the foam from his lips.

"I didn't know who else to talk to about this. It concerns adoption, so I thought maybe you . . ."

"Sure, have at it."

Natalie sat back in her chair and put her hands on the table. Her fingernails still sported a coat of clear polish, but the tips had flaked off. She breathed a sigh and explained the situation with Linn, making sure to leave out her name. Not only did she need to protect client information, but with Kyle being her brother-in-law—and family enemy—it was important he not know who she was talking about.

The girl at the counter called for her to come and get her latte. After getting it and adding a little cinnamon to the foamy top, she sat back down across from Kyle and took a sip of the hot, sweet brew.

"So, let me get this straight. Your client threatened to have an abortion if you don't adopt the baby?"

"Well, no, I wouldn't say 'threatened.'"

"What would you say?" he asked.

Natalie thought back to the night before. She hadn't gotten the feeling at all that Linn was trying to force anything on her. "It was more like she felt those were the only two options she would consider."

"So, she's leaving her decision, her mistake, up to you to solve. Putting it in your lap." Though the words were harsh, his tone wasn't. His eyes flickered in the dim light.

"It feels that way, but I don't think she means it that way. She's young, frightened. She feels safe with me, I guess."

"It's an awful lot to ask." He leaned back in the chair and tilted his head. "Look, adoptions are complicated. Even in the best of situations, where there's a birth mom wanting an adoption plan and an adoptive couple wanting a child, it's hard. There are a lot of emotions going on, and adoptions take a long time. There's the wait through the pregnancy, then the placement period after the baby comes. Have you ever thought about adopting a child?"

"No. No, of course not. I'm a single mother with two boys. My hands are pretty full as it is."

"Well, if you ask me, there's your answer."

"But what about the baby? What if she has an abortion?"

He looked down at his hands, which were wrapped around his mug, then met her gaze. "You can't hold yourself responsible for someone else's decisions."

"But I can do something about it." Her insides flopped over. She *could* do something about it. The weight of the thought was both exciting and nerve-wracking.

"Look, I'm as pro-life as they come, but think about it. Couldn't all of us do more about any issue we believed in? I could get involved in politics and try to change the laws about abortion. I could picket the Women's Health Clinic every Saturday. I could write an article every day for the rest of my life in hopes of persuading somebody of the value of life. But I don't. I just place children with adoptive families. That's my part. You work at the Hope Center. That's your part. You have to draw the line somewhere."

"I don't remember anything in the Bible about drawing that kind of line. The disciples were willing to die for what they believed. That's asking so much more than raising a child."

It was his turn to sigh. "Think about the baby, then. Doesn't every child deserve to be wanted?"

"Doesn't every child deserve to be born?" Her eyes stung at the thought. She took a sip of her latte, more to distract herself than anything else. "And the mother is a concern, too. She doesn't really have anyone else in her life supporting her."

"It sounds like you've allowed the relationship to get pretty close."

It wasn't an accusation, yet Natalie felt the lump of guilt anyway. From one professional to another, he was letting her know she'd over-stepped the boundaries. "I know. I know." She shook her head, still feel-ing the heat that rushed up the back of her neck. "I let things go too far. I did befriend her, and I broke the rules. Now look where it's gotten me. This is really my own fault."

"Maybe you did break some rules, but you aren't responsible for her pregnancy." He leaned against the table, bringing him closer. His gray-green eyes had flecks of gold.

"She's so alone, though, and I fear I'm her only real friend right now. If I disappoint her like this, I'm afraid she'll think everything I've said and done was phony. I mean, shouldn't I be able to practice what I preach? I *say* abortion is wrong. I *say* an unborn child is a life. But how far am I willing to go to protect that life?"

"You shouldn't have to change the entire course of your life."

"I ask girls to do that nearly every day. They want an end to their pregnancy, and I try to convince them to have their babies. Whether they raise the child or make an adoption plan, isn't that changing the en-tire course of their lives? Have I been asking something of them that I'm unwilling to do?"

"You're being too hard on yourself, Natalie. You can't save the world."

"But I can save this baby."

"Look, even when adoptive parents desperately want a child, they sometimes have trouble bonding. How do you think you're going to bond with a baby you never wanted?"

"That sounds so callous."

"You have to consider what's best for the child. It takes eighteen years to raise one."

"I just want this child to *have* eighteen years. But it's not just the baby. If the mother decides to abort . . . This client isn't a Christian, but she really seemed open to talking about God. If I let her down, where does that leave her?"

He quietly observed her. Natalie felt self-conscious under his appraisal, as if he were looking into her instead of at her.

"It sounds as if you've already made your decision," he said.

Natalie's thoughts seemed to freeze at a stand-still. Her body locked up like brakes on icy pavement. Could it be true? She thought back over the things she'd said since she arrived at the coffee shop. It seemed Kyle had been arguing against the idea, and she had been arguing for it the whole time. What did it mean?

CHAPTER
FIFTEEN

Linn turned off the blow-dryer and began gathering her hair up on top of her head. She was due at Bubba's Bar-B-Que at ten o'clock, but the thought of waiting on a bunch of tourists today held no appeal. *Oh, well, it'll get you out of the house awhile. And add more money to your savings.*

And if the way things went Saturday night were any clue, she'd need that savings for an abortion. Her stomach clenched at the word. She didn't want to do it. Not after she'd seen those pictures, seen her own baby on that ultrasound screen. She put the image from her mind.

If only Natalie would agree to take the baby, everything would be perfect. But that didn't seem likely. A dull ache had settled over her Saturday night and hadn't left her since. She'd thought Natalie cared about her and the baby. Obviously that wasn't the case, and now everything was ruined. No one wanted her, and no one wanted her baby.

The phone rang, and her fingers tightened on the hairclip. It was probably Natalie. Just thinking about talking to her made her nauseous. Everyone in her life had betrayed her, and now Natalie had done it as well. But what if she'd changed her mind? Telling herself she was a fool for hoping, she dropped the hairclip and sprinted for the phone.

"Hello?"

"Hi, Linn, it's Natalie. Did I catch you at a good time?"

"I guess." She clamped her mouth shut. Why should she make it easy on her? If Natalie cared all that much, wouldn't she help? Now all that God stuff she'd been talking about sounded so lame.

"I wanted to see how you're doing this morning. I really enjoyed watching the movie with you the other night."

"I'm fine."

A long pause. A sigh. "I also wanted to talk to you about what you asked me. I'm sorry I reacted the way I did. You just really took me by—"

"Whatever. It's fine." Her words were clipped, but she didn't care.

"It's not fine, Linn. I feel really bad about how I handled it. And I need to tell you something else, too."

Linn waited, her heart in her toes, where it had been since Saturday night.

"I want you to know I'm considering your offer," Natalie said.

Linn waited for her to say more. Could she be understanding this right? Was Natalie really thinking about adopting her baby? She sank onto the old plaid couch.

"I know I didn't seem very open to the idea at first, but I realize I shouldn't have been so quick to make a decision. I'll seriously consider it, OK?"

Linn nodded, then realized Natalie couldn't hear that. "OK."

"This is a big decision, and I'm going to need time to think and pray about it. Is that OK?"

"Sure." Linn barely managed to get the word out. She felt near tears, which was stupid, when this would be the perfect solution.

They set up a time to get together later in the week, then said good-bye. Linn let the phone drop into the cradle. *Please, oh, please let Natalie agree to adopt my baby.* She wasn't sure if it was a prayer or a wishful thought.

Ever since that day three weeks ago when she'd first gone to Natalie's house, the idea had been forming in her mind. Sure, she'd been surprised when she'd ridden her bike into the driveway and realized who Natalie was. Shocked, really. Who wouldn't have been? It wasn't every day you discovered something like that.

Keith. Just thinking about him made her stomach feel all hollow and achy. He used to make her feel so beautiful and alive. They'd had so much fun together, and she'd thought he was her "happily ever after." Ha. What a joke.

She'd thought if she could just get Keith to divorce his wife, everything would be perfect. She'd spent all those months feeling nothing but envy toward his wife. Well, maybe she'd felt a little hatred, too. After all, Natalie had been the obstacle that stood between her and Keith. Or so she'd thought. Linn had wanted him, and she'd eventually gotten him. And Natalie had lost him. Now Linn had lost him, too. She only had one thing left of Keith, and that was the baby she carried.

It was a bizarre situation, but she decided it must have been meant to be. The thought of leaving her baby for strangers to raise had never held any appeal. But this was so much better. Now she had an opportunity to place her baby with real relatives. And she couldn't think of a better place for her baby than with his or her real brothers.

CHAPTER
SIXTEEN

Natalie closed the door of her office and sank into her chair. She didn't know what was wrong with her today. She'd been scattered all morning, hardly able to complete any task she'd started. Truth be known, she'd been this way for two weeks, ever since she'd told Linn she would consider adopting her baby.

Even at home, she'd been so consumed with her thoughts that she didn't hear what the boys said until several seconds after they said it.

All she could think about was the possible adoption.

And Dana. She'd thought about Dana a lot. About how similar she and Linn were, about how tragically Dana's life had ended. About how she couldn't let that happen to Linn.

Her gaze skidded over to the file cabinet where the old files were kept. Ever since Dana had committed suicide, she'd done her best to forget. But Dana had been her first client, her responsibility, and how could she help but feel accountable?

She leaned over and pulled the metal tab, slowly opening the drawer. Her fingers shuffled through the manila folders until she came to the right one. She hesitated for a moment, then she pulled it and set it in front of her. Her heart raced, and she drew a deep breath. It wasn't as if opening this file would change anything. Dana was gone. But she was tired of trying to forget. It was time to remember.

She opened the folder and let her gaze skim Dana's loopy cursive handwriting. A sad smile tugged her lips at the way she dotted each "i." She had been a junior in high school, a member of student council, and an honor student. She read the entire file, then sat back in her chair.

Natalie closed her eyes and remembered the way Dana had lit up when she'd talked about science. She'd wanted to discover cures for diseases and give people hope for a future.

Now there was no hope, no future for Dana.

She closed the file and rubbed her face. *I did try, God. You know I did. But she was so set on not having that baby. And now Linn . . .*

What should I do? I don't want her to have an abortion. I don't want her to have to live with that regret, or worse. And there's an innocent child involved here, too.

She heard the center's door open but knew Cheryl was covering the desk.

Lord, I really need Your guidance here. Please show me what to do. This is too big a decision to mess up, and it affects so many people: Linn, the baby, me, the boys . . . and I'm really to the point where I just want to do what's right in Your sight.

A rap sounded on her door.

She rubbed her face and leaned back. "Come in."

The door opened and a face peeked in. "Morgan." She hadn't seen this client since she'd had her baby two months ago. She stood up and walked around the desk, eyeing the bundle in her arms.

"Hey, Miss C. Brought you a surprise."

Little Mattie wore a floral sundress with a matching bonnet. Two big blue eyes peeped out from beneath it. "Oh, Morgan, she's just an angel." Natalie put her arm around Morgan and gave her a sideways hug.

"Wanna hold her?"

"Absolutely." Natalie took the baby from Morgan's arms and cradled her in her arms. The baby had been born a few weeks premature and was still on the small side. But so perfect. Her little nose so round, her blond eyebrows so delicate.

"Have a seat, Morgan."

She sat down, and Natalie took the chair beside her, hardly taking her eyes off the baby.

"How are you getting along?" Natalie asked.

Morgan was only eighteen, but now she had the support of both her parents. She'd been so afraid of telling her parents in the beginning, she'd wanted to have an abortion. But her parents had handled it very well once they'd had time to get used to the idea. And now look at them.

Mattie let out a little squeak.

"It was really hard at first. Especially the delivery. Ugh! I was not prepared for that!"

Natalie laughed at Morgan's dramatic expression.

"And then the night feedings and diaper changing, and did you know babies go through, like, four outfits a day? Well, I guess you did know that, seeing as you have kids."

Natalie shifted Mattie in her arms, and the baby locked eyes with her. She had bits of silver in her eyes.

"But, know what, Miss C? I wouldn't trade it for the world. Sometimes I look at her, even in the middle of one of those night feedings and think, 'I almost didn't have you.'" Her words choked off.

Natalie laid a hand on Morgan's. "But you did. You made the right decision for your baby, and I'm so proud of you."

Natalie's own eyes stung. She looked down at the precious bundle in her arms. It never failed to amaze her. This little life could have been snuffed out so easily, yet by the grace of God, here she was, a perfect little angel. How many jobs had the opportunity for such rewards as this? She was so blessed that she could make a difference in lives.

You can make a difference in Linn's life, too. Her baby is just as precious as this one.

The thought hit Natalie like a concrete slab, then sat upon her heart like a crushing weight. Linn's baby was precious. All of them were; she'd always believed it.

But did she believe it enough to change her life? Did she believe it enough to add another child to her single-parent home?

Isn't that what faith was all about? Stepping up to the challenge and doing what you believe, no matter what? She thought of the student who'd professed belief in God in the face of a gunman. She'd stepped up to the plate when her life was on the line.

Was Natalie capable of the same thing? Her heart thumped in her chest. She looked at the baby in her arms and pictured Linn's there, cuddled in the curve of her elbow. A sweet little girl or boy who deserved life and love.

Mattie squeaked and pursed her little rosy lips. "She's so adorable."

"Miss C?"

Natalie looked up at the serious note in Morgan's voice.

"I came by to show Mattie to you, but I also wanted to say . . . thank you." Her voice sounded as though her throat was stuffed with tears. "I would have had an abortion if it wasn't for you."

"Oh, Morgan." A sweet feeling welled up in her.

"Really, Miss C. You were the one who convinced me to tell my parents. It was hard at first, but you were right. They did support me."

"They're good parents. You're very blessed." She thought of Linn's dad and wished she had been so blessed. Her dad was in no condition to support Linn or her baby.

But you can.

Natalie looked down again at little Mattie and touched her hand with a finger. The baby grasped on to her pinky, holding it like a lifeline.

She could be a lifeline to Linn's baby. A lifeline to Linn in her time of need. Her breath caught in her chest. Maybe she could do it. Maybe she could love that baby as her own. Maybe God could use this situation to win Linn. She had an openness toward godly things.

"Well, I just stopped by real quick on my way to her doctor's appointment."

Natalie handed the baby back to Morgan. "Thanks so much for bringing her by. Don't be a stranger around here, OK?"

"I won't." Morgan stood, the jumbo diaper bag swinging from her shoulder.

Natalie walked her to the front door, where they said good-bye. As the door swung closed, Natalie watched mother and child go down the sidewalk, her heart full of the things God had done through the center.

"Amazing, isn't it?"

She didn't know Cheryl had walked up beside her until she'd spoken. Natalie drew in a deep breath and let it out. She didn't have to ask what Cheryl was talking about. They were all here for the same reason. "It sure is."

CHAPTER
SEVENTEEN

Natalie snagged the pillows off the floor and tossed them onto the couch. "Pick up your Legos, Alex."

"When will Daddy come?" Taylor asked, his three-year-old eyes turning up to her. He'd sat on the couch wearing his Bob the Builder backpack for the past half hour.

"Any minute, sweetie."

She took a dirty glass to the kitchen and came back, surveying the carpet with a sigh. She thought there was more mulch in the house than in the landscaping outside. Oh, well. Too late to do anything about it now.

Why are you cleaning up for Keith anyway?

She shrugged away the thought. She would tidy up for anyone who was stopping by, she told herself.

"Good job, Alex." He carried the tattered Lego box to his bedroom.

A car door slammed, and Natalie made her way to the front door. Taylor raced around her and threw open the door. He ran down the concrete path and grabbed his dad's legs in a tight embrace. "Daddy!"

An ache started in her stomach and winged its way outward. Would she ever get used to seeing her kids leave with Keith? Though she no longer loved him, it pained her that the boys didn't have a dad who lived with them.

"Hey, buddy." Keith embraced Taylor. "Got your stuff?"

"Uh-huh. Are we going fishing?"

"You bet. Where's your brother?"

"Here I am!" Just in time, Alex slid through the door and went to hug his dad.

"Hi, squirt." His gaze met Natalie's over his head for just a moment. "Hey, you two, go get in the car. I need to talk to your mom a minute."

"Awww . . . I wanna go now." Alex slumped toward the car.

"There's a bag of Fritos in there you guys can split."

"All right," Alex said and headed for the car.

"Share," Natalie said, as if that one motherly comment would do any good. She eyed Keith, who approached.

He stepped up on the porch, sliding his hands into the pockets of his khakis. She could see him with objective eyes now. He looked older than he had when they were married, and his hairline had receded a bit more. She wondered what he wanted to talk about.

"How's your work at the center going?" he asked.

"Fine." The last thing she wanted right now was small talk. "How's the Wort?" If his brother hadn't given him a management position in the historic hotel, he would have had trouble finding anything to support himself. After serving jail time for his part in the bank scheme that almost closed Hanna's lodge, who else would have hired him? She was thankful, since she needed the child support to help with Alex and Taylor.

"Good." He looked back at the car. "Listen, I wanted to let you know the boys'll be meeting a friend of mine this weekend. My girlfriend."

Her heart sunk like stone in her chest. Hearing him talk about another woman brought back all the pain. From the moment of finding the condom in his pants to the moment of realization that he was having an affair with some other woman. Natalie didn't want the boys to meet her. She was the one who'd caused this whole mess in the first place.

"It's been two years, Natalie."

"As if time can really fix things." Why was her heart pounding as if she'd just run a marathon? Two years was a long time, and she no longer had any feelings for Keith. She'd been surprised he hadn't brought Lindsey around the boys before now. She'd wondered why, and now that he was going to do it, she questioned that, too.

He sighed. "Look, I just wanted to let you know."

"I wish you'd told me earlier so I could've prepared the boys. They don't really know about—about Lindsey." She tried really hard to say the name without coating it in bitterness.

His eyes widened marginally. "Actually, it's not her. Things have been over with her for a while. This is someone else."

She felt a momentary pang of satisfaction. So, it hadn't worked out with him and Lindsey. Served them right. Maybe Lindsey was feeling the same pain she'd caused Natalie. She closed her eyes, batting away the ugly thoughts. Why was it so hard to be Christlike when it came to Keith?

"Her name is Alisha, and she's really good with kids, so it'll be fine. I just wanted to prepare you."

Somehow, knowing it wasn't Lindsey made it better. "All right." She gritted her teeth and forced out the next words. "Thanks for telling me."

"Taylor isn't sharing!" Alex's voice called through the open window of Keith's car.

"I guess I'd better go," Keith said, backing away.

She nodded. "Bye, boys. Be good," she called, waving toward the car.

They barely gave a distracted wave in their fight over the Frito bag. Oh, well, it was Keith's problem now. She closed the door and went back inside.

The house was so quiet she could hear the mantel clock ticking. The house was clean, except for the carpet, and she had two days and two nights to herself. She spied the book she'd picked up at the library. It was a book on adoption, and it was rated high on Amazon.com.

She picked it up and flipped through the pages. Was she really considering going through with this? What would it be like with a baby in the house again? She'd be doing it all by herself this time.

A wry grin formed. Of course, she'd practically done it by herself with Alex and Taylor, too. The difference this time would be that she had to work outside the home. Would her mother be willing to care for the baby while she worked? It was one of the many things she had to think about if she was going to consider adopting Linn's baby.

She began reading the book, and before she knew it, she was on chapter five, and darkness had fallen behind the curtained windows. She was learning a lot. The adoption process was long and complicated, but reading about it had done something inside her. A tender fire was blazing in her heart toward this baby, and she wondered if it was God's way of preparing her for this job.

A glance at her watch told her she'd missed dinner. She wasn't hungry, though. She had too much nervous energy to eat. What she really wanted was to talk to someone.

She picked up the cordless and punched in the number for Higher Grounds. Gram answered the phone.

"Hi, Gram, it's Natalie."

"Well, hi, honey, how are you?"

"I'm just fine." She asked about the business and about Gram's friend Gerdy, and when their conversation began to wind down, she asked if Hanna was there.

"No, honey, she and Micah took a group up Mt. Moran this morning. It's just me and Mrs. Eddlestein."

Natalie was glad they'd had the foresight to leave their housekeeper with Gram. Ever since the onset of Alzheimer's, they'd realized it wasn't safe to leave her alone. But since Hanna would be gone overnight, Natalie had no one to talk to. Her spirits sank.

She talked to Gram about the boys for a few minutes, then hung up and walked to the fridge. She opened the freezer and saw the Rocky Road container on the top shelf, where it stayed the perfect temperature. She sighed and turned away. What was she thinking? She hadn't even had dinner yet.

She wandered back to the couch and sat down. She thought of Linn and wondered if she should call and invite her over. She'd talked to her quite a few times over the past couple weeks. Linn had gone to Burger King with Natalie and the boys, they'd gone to the park, and Linn had come over for dinner twice.

But what Natalie felt a need for right now was advice. And her Dear Abby was gone. She considered calling her mom but tossed the idea aside. Although she was a great listener, she rarely gave advice. Sometimes Natalie wondered why such a wise woman kept all that wisdom to herself, but she knew her mom was just trying to be careful not to guide her in the wrong direction.

Paula was undoubtedly home alone on a Friday night, but her sister's advice wasn't the kind she wanted. Maybe she was being too picky.

She thought of Kyle for a moment, then let the thought slide by. She'd already bothered him once before. He wasn't family, and he certainly wasn't interested in her, so it would be selfish of her to call and pick his brain again.

Wouldn't it?

She let the idea linger a moment. What could really be the harm in calling? If he was busy, he was busy. And she could make it clear he was under no obligation. She was pretty good at reading people, and he hadn't seemed at all bothered when they met for coffee before.

She eyed the phone on the end table. Had she kept his number somewhere? She got up and rooted through the junk drawer. Under the phone book and two coloring books was the scrap of paper with his number.

She grabbed the phone and dialed it, waiting for it to ring. A thought occurred to her. It was Friday night, and he was a handsome, single man. He was probably out with a woman or . . . what if he had a woman at his place? What if she was interrupting something? She should hang up. She pulled the phone from her ear.

"Hello?" Kyle's voice sounded faintly.

She pulled the phone back to her ear, wondering what she'd been thinking. She cleared her throat. "Um, hi, is this Kyle?"

"Yes."

"This is Natalie. Natalie Coombs . . . we met for coffee a couple weeks ago." She closed her eyes, suddenly feeling very stupid. Why was she insinuating herself upon this man she barely knew? He was going to think she was completely self-absorbed.

"Sure. Hi, Natalie."

Well, that didn't sound so bad. Now if she could only figure out what to say. "I really appreciate the help you gave me before. I . . . I guess I'm still struggling with this decision and wondered if—look, maybe I shouldn't have called. You hardly know me from Adam, and this certainly isn't your responsibility, and you're probably busy right now anyway."

"No, it's all right. Really. What do you need?"

Her eyes stung at his offer, and she chided herself for being so ridiculous. She felt the sigh that seemed to well up from her stomach. "I guess I need some answers about the adoption process." It occurred to her he did this daily in his job. For money. "I'd be glad to pay you for your time," she added.

"No, you're all right. Go ahead, ask away."

She sank onto the couch and opened the book she'd been reading. For the next forty-five minutes, she barraged him with one question after another about the adoption process. He was patient and thorough in his answers. The book was a great overview, but Kyle provided the nitty-gritty details as well as the relationship problems that sometimes surfaced in what he called the adoption triad—the adoptive couple, the birth parents, and the child.

"What about the baby's father?" Kyle asked. "If your client has the baby, is he willing to sign away his rights?"

"I don't know. The client says he wants nothing to do with her or the baby. But I don't know if she's asked him that question point-blank."

"Hmm."

Silence hummed across the lines a moment, and Natalie shifted to lie down on the couch. "I guess I should ask that, shouldn't I?"

"It sounds as if you're really serious about going ahead with it."

She drew a breath and let it out. "I am. And that's really amazing, because I was so dead-set against it at first. Do you think I'm crazy?"

She heard him breathe a laugh. "No, I don't think that at all."

There was a silence, but after all their time on the phone, it wasn't the awkward kind. More like the kind of quiet that passed comfortably between friends.

"Do you have anything else you've been wondering about?" Kyle asked.

"Shoot, I have so many questions, I could keep you up all night with them." She wondered if he wanted to get off the phone. "But you've been really kind to answer my questions, and I've taken enough of your time."

"I don't mind."

A silence, this time awkward.

"Listen, I was wondering . . . ," he said. "I know it's late, but have you had dinner yet?"

Was he asking her to dinner? Warmth kindled inside her. How long had it been since she'd been to dinner with a man? Of course, this wasn't a date or anything. Her stomach gave a hefty growl as if in encouragement.

"Oh, your kids are probably in bed," he said.

"No, their father has them for the weekend. And I missed dinner." Why was her heart wobbling all over the place?

"Would you like to, then? Meet me someplace?"

He was only being nice, trying to answer her questions. "Sure, name the place."

"How about the Shady Nook?"

They set a time and got off the phone. Natalie looked down at the knit short set she'd put on and ran up the stairs to find something more appropriate. It was a casual restaurant, but she didn't want to walk in looking this ratty.

Why hadn't she done her laundry this week? She was down to almost nothing. And why did she care so much anyway? She pulled a black blouse from the closet and looked for something to go with it. Nothing. She put the blouse back and picked up a lavender short-sleeved sweater. Jeans. All she had in the pants department were jeans. She slid the sweater back on the shelf.

This was ridiculous. She had twenty minutes to get there, and she hadn't even assessed her hair and makeup.

She slid into a nice pair of trendy jeans, added a black belt and a black T-shirt, then went to look at her reflection in the mirror. Fortunately, she'd touched up her makeup before Keith had come. But her hair was matted and messy from lying on the couch, so she twisted it up and secured it with a clip. She arranged the pieces as best she could in the few minutes she had, then grabbed her purse and keys and was out the door with five minutes to spare.

Kyle stopped in front of the Shady Nook to pet Daisy, the owner's dog. The collie wagged her tail, then watched him as he entered the restaurant. The place wasn't very crowded, since it was late for dinner, but it was still a little on the noisy side. He snagged a booth in the corner and opened his menu, keeping an eye on the front door. He'd been chastising himself ever since the invitation had slipped out of his mouth. What had he been thinking? Meeting her for coffee had been one thing. She'd been desperate for answers that night. He'd only been trying to be kind. But tonight he could've answered all her questions on the phone. There was no need to meet face-to-face.

You were hungry.

He recognized it for the excuse it was. He could've fixed himself a turkey sandwich and ate while they'd talked. But he'd wanted to meet with her, and that was why he'd been calling himself every kind of fool for inviting her here.

He hadn't been out with a woman since Jilly. Just the thought of his wife was like a punch in the gut. He didn't want to think about her tonight. Not the accident or the baby or the affair.

The waitress came, and he ordered himself a Coke. As she walked away, he saw Natalie approaching the table. He took in her cute figure in the jeans and top and felt his mouth go dry. When was the last time he'd looked at a woman that way? Feeling disloyal to Jilly, he glanced down at his water glass.

"Hi." She slid into the booth.

"I didn't know what you'd want to drink." He gestured to the water the waitress had set there.

"No, that's fine. Water's all I want anyway."

He handed her the menu, and she smiled her thanks. She wore her dark, wavy hair up in a way that looked messy and mesmerizing all at the same time. A few pieces looked as if they'd escaped and grazed the sides of her face.

After they'd placed their orders, he leaned back against the booth and told his heart to settle down.

"I haven't been here in a while," she said.

"I imagine with kids, you don't eat out much."

"Sure I do. Ronald McDonald and I are on a first name basis." Her lips curved up, and her dark eyes sparkled in the dim light.

"So what do you do for fun when your kids are gone for the weekend?"

Her eyes simmered with the lazy seductive look of Catherine Zeta-Jones. "Laundry . . . weeding . . . mopping . . . I could go on and on."

He leaned forward. "You lead a very exciting life," he deadpanned.

She smiled then in a way that reminded him of a little girl. It touched a place in him that he'd thought was dead.

The waitress came to refill their drinks, and he found himself eager to resume their conversation. When the waitress left, he took a sip of his Coke.

"You know, I've been thinking about what we can do to help with your decision about this adoption. A good friend of mine adopted about a year and a half ago. I'm sure I could set something up if you want to talk to him."

Her eyes lit. "Oh, that'd be great. Do you really think he'll talk to me?"

"Sure, he's a good friend, and he loves talking about their little girl." In fact, Joe and his wife had often gone out with him and Jilly. And though he and Joe still kept in close contact, it seemed they had less in common than ever before.

"It would be really helpful. That's been part of my problem. I don't know anyone who's been in my shoes. I don't suppose he's a single parent, too." Her eyes sparkled playfully. "Divorced, with two boys, maybe."

"And a young, pregnant girl offered him her baby? No, I'm afraid you're not that lucky."

Her lips tipped up at the corners before she sipped water through her straw.

"He's married, and he and Kristin couldn't have kids of their own."

"I was only kidding. It would mean the world to get to talk to them."

"I'll set it up, then."

They talked about Kyle's friends for a minute, then conversation turned to work.

"Has the controversy surrounding the center died down?" he asked.

"Yes, it has, thank goodness." He saw a flicker of concern before her gaze swung down toward the table.

"That must've been pretty stressful."

She took a sip of her water. "The vandalism was a drag, and the news coverage bothered me, too. But what's really messed with me was the assault. I've never been attacked before."

The assault? His confusion must have shown.

"I think I mentioned it the night we had dinner at Paula's."

"Oh, right. I can't believe I'd forgotten."

"I wish I could." She toyed with a napkin on the table.

"Police never caught him?"

"No. I guess I didn't really expect that they would. Jackson Hole is full of tourists who come and go. I couldn't even see his face." She shuddered at the memory of that night.

She looked small and vulnerable in the big booth. He resisted the urge to put his hand on hers. "Tell me about your boys." Her brows rose at the change in subject, but he could see her warming to the idea.

"Hmm. Well, Alex is six, and he's the big brother. He's charming, playful, and will manipulate anyone, anytime. He's also a huge showoff, especially where hockey is concerned. He's actually pretty good."

He found himself smiling at her description and the proud look on her face. "Maybe he'll be recruited by the Jackson Moose." Their local hockey team was very popular with the town's residents. "Well, probably not for a few years at least."

"Taylor is three and a half. His favorite activity is pestering Alex, and I might add, he's quite good at it."

"Sibling rivalry."

"At its finest," she added.

"Do you enjoy your time alone on the weekends, or does it seem lonely?" His own loneliness seemed to seep into that last phrase. He hoped she hadn't picked up on it. He didn't want sympathy.

"A little of both, I guess. On Saturdays and Sundays I get a lot done, errands and cleaning. You know, all that exciting stuff I mentioned before." Her lips curved into a nice smile. "But in the evenings when it's quiet, I guess I get kind of bored."

"Not lonely?" Why had he asked that? She would think he was interested.

Aren't you?

"There's a difference?"

"I think so. Bored means you're looking for something to do. Lonely means you're looking for someone to do it with."

She blinked, her dark eyes studying him. "I've never thought of it like that. I guess I'm both. Nothing to do and no one to do it with." She twisted the napkin on the table, and he sensed her vulnerability. "How about you?"

It was his turn to feel awkward. Why hadn't he realized the question would come back around to him? Maybe he could skirt the question.

"Actually, I don't mind being alone. Suits me well. So, how long ago was your divorce, if you don't mind my asking?"

She hiked a brow, and he realized he hadn't pulled a thing over on her. She'd seen his non-answer for what it was. He felt a moment's guilt for evading the question when she'd answered so honestly.

"About two years. Though it doesn't seem like it."

He wondered if she had a boyfriend but didn't want to ask. She hadn't mentioned anyone.

She glanced at him, then back down at the table, and bit her lip. He wondered if she'd been about to ask him about his marriage. After what Linn had said to her about murdering Jilly, she was probably afraid to mention it. Just as well.

The waitress arrived and set the plates down on their table, and he was grateful for the interruption. While they ate, Natalie asked more questions about adoption, and he did his best to answer. When they parted, he promised to get in touch with her about a meeting with Joe and his wife. He walked her to the car and saw her safely away before turning toward his own. As he walked in the quiet night, he wondered why he suddenly felt lonelier than he had in a long time.

CHAPTER EIGHTEEN

Natalie was helping Taylor into his pajamas one night a week later when Alex asked the question.

"When are we going to have another baby, Mom?"

She almost put Taylor's arm through the head opening of his pjs. Kids asked these questions sometimes, she knew, but Alex never had. Had he overheard her on the phone with Linn or Kyle? She didn't think so. She'd been very careful.

"Why do you ask, honey?"

He sat beside her on the living room floor, gathering his knees up close to his chest. "Brandon's mom just had a baby girl, and I want a sister, too."

Natalie chuckled. "You already have a brother."

Alex gave Taylor a glare. "He annoys me." The adult word sounded funny coming off her six-year-old's lips.

"Do not!" Taylor slugged Alex.

"You don't even know what it means," Alex said.

"Stop it, both of you," Natalie said.

"We have an extra bedroom. She could sleep in there."

"Honey, there's a lot more to having a baby than where you're going to put her. Besides, you don't get to pick whether it's a boy and girl. God decides that."

"Can't we just ask God for a girl?" Alex asked.

She smiled. "Sure, you can ask, but He can say no if He wants to."

She could hardly believe Alex's timing with this question. Only yesterday she'd met with Kyle's friends and discussed their adoption process. Their little girl was adorable and seemed as happy and secure as any one-year-old she'd ever seen. Joe and Kristin had been very convincing. Not that they'd *tried* to convince her, but their attitude toward their little girl and toward adoption in general was hard to overlook.

"Go brush your teeth, Alex." She took Taylor up to his room and tucked him in, listening to his little boy prayers.

"Pray for Mom and Alex and Dad and Granny and Papaw and Aunt Hanna and Unca Micah and Aunt Paula and Unca David and . . . help tomorrow and the new baby. Amen."

Natalie opened her eyes.

Taylor was snuggling into his pillow and comforter, a content smile on his face.

"Taylor, what new baby?"

He looked up at her with his big, innocent eyes. "Our new baby."

Her breath stuck in her lungs, where it seemed to accumulate until she felt she'd explode. *Is this You, God? Is this Your way of telling me what I should do?*

No, not telling, but confirming. Maybe she was crazy, but she'd been leaning very strongly toward the idea of adopting Linn's baby. She'd been concerned, though, about how the boys would accept a new brother or sister. She guessed she needn't worry about that anymore.

She tucked the comforter up to Taylor's chin and said good-night.

Over the next two days, the idea of adopting the baby grew in Natalie's heart until she knew it was the right thing to do. She'd even begun to get excited about the thought of a baby in the house again. It had always been her favorite stage with the boys.

She had Linn over for dinner and a game of Monopoly, but still, she sheltered the idea in her heart. Linn had been feeling her out by the things she said, and Natalie knew she was anxious for an answer. What was she waiting for?

On Thursday of that week, the last day in June, Natalie looked at her refrigerator calendar and decided. Tomorrow, on the day that marked Linn's nineteenth week of pregnancy, she would tell Linn she would raise the baby as her own.

Paula flung her purse on the table and went to pour herself a glass of wine. She felt like celebrating. Tonight's broadcast had gone flawlessly. It was one of those nights when she was just on. Every word came out with just the right inflection, every segue smooth as satin, every ad-lib perfect. And her boss Donald had noticed. He'd asked to speak with her after the show.

"Did you know there's a temporary position in our affiliate station in Chicago, Paula?"

She'd known, but she generated just the right amount of surprise.

"You're too good to be tucked away here in the mountains. I'm sending them your tape."

Her heart had nearly stopped beating. It was her dream to be a news anchor for a large station in a city like Chicago, and this temporary job as an investigative reporter was just the break she needed.

She filled her goblet and took a sip, allowing herself one giddy moment. She could see herself on Chicago's evening news in front of thousands of viewers. She had a sense of destiny about the possibility.

Her mother would say something about God's will, but she'd worked too hard for it to lay the credit at God's feet.

The front door opened and clicked shut. David. She could hardly wait to tell him. She met him in the foyer, feeling exceptionally frisky.

"Hello, handsome." She curved her lips in a smile she reserved just for him.

"Hi." He brushed past her.

She watched him remove his wallet from his pocket and set it on the shelf. Next, he removed the coins from his pocket and placed them in the sterling canister.

She took a sip from her glass and followed him into the room. "Can I get you a drink?"

"No, thanks."

She watched him take off his shoes and set them in the closet. Hers were still by the front door, where she'd kicked them off. Is that why he was acting so short? She went and picked them up and tucked them under the end table.

"How was your day?" she asked. He shot her a glance, and for a moment she thought something was very wrong. But just as quickly the look was gone.

"Interesting." He flicked on the TV with the remote control. A sitcom came to life on the screen. He didn't turn it.

She sat on the couch and studied him. He never watched sitcoms. He hated the canned laughter. "Did you eat dinner?"

"Yeah." He leaned back in his recliner and kicked out the footrest.

So much for her news. She wanted to tell someone who would be as excited for her as she was. In his present mood, he might not even offer her an offhand congratulations.

She sighed. "Is something wrong?"

His jaw clenched, and the shadows moved there in the crevices of his face. He was really quite handsome. When they were dating, everyone had said they looked perfect together. Though she was tall, he still cleared her head by three inches, even in heels. The perfect dancing partner.

She realized he'd never answered her. "Hon, are you all right?"

He looked at her, his eyes blazing with something she couldn't define. He looked away.

Something in her shuddered. She'd never seen that look. David was always so controlled. So charming with impeccable manners. She couldn't imagine what would provoke the emotion she'd seen in his eyes, but it was clearly aimed at her. What had she done? She automatically thought of the pregnancy three years ago and her deceit. Her stomach clenched in dread.

But no, he couldn't know about that.

She sensed it was time for a change of topic. So much for waiting for an eager listener. "You didn't get to see the news tonight, did you?"

He seemed absorbed in the program. "No."

"I think it was my best ever. Apparently Donald thought so, too."

The canned laughter sounded, and he picked up the remote and changed the channel. As much as she wanted to share her news, she decided to wait. He was obviously in a snit about something. She picked up her glass from the end table and started for the kitchen. Must've had another picky client. Maybe if she just gave him some time to cool off.

"I got my test results today."

She barely heard the words, spoken so calmly and quietly. Test results? Her brain jogged. The sperm test.

She walked back into the room and sank onto the couch close to his chair. Something was wrong with his test. That's why he was in this mood. She put her hand over his. "What is it, hon?" Inside, her nerves pulled taut.

He jerked his hand from under hers and crossed them over his chest.

She blinked at the abrupt movement. He was starting to scare her. This wasn't David at all. "Is it bad?" She searched his face for answers. Why didn't he just spill it? Her own appointment with the specialist was later in the week, but if there was a problem with David . . . well, she didn't know what it would mean exactly.

His gaze was glued to the TV, where a commercial for Paxil CR was running. His nostrils flared. Whatever it was, this was serious. She braced herself.

"It turns out I have a low sperm count. And low motility." He drilled her with a look. "It's very unlikely I can get you pregnant, Paula." The corner of his nose turned up in a snarl.

The way he said it, with hatred almost, made her flinch. Why was he acting this way toward her? She allowed herself a moment to catch her breath. She'd read about problems with male infertility. The problems he mentioned weren't rare, by any means, but when you combined both the low count and the low motility, it severely limited the chances for pregnancy.

"How bad is it?" Why wouldn't he look at her? Why was he acting so cold? Maybe he was feeling responsible for their problem conceiving. "Hon, this isn't all bad. In fact, if there's no health problem with me, I'll bet in-vitro is a strong possibility."

He fixed her with a glare, then pushed up his trendy glasses.

She'd never seen him this way. Didn't know how to handle him. And she always knew how to handle people. Right now, though, her emotions teetered between rank fear and justified anger. What had she done to deserve his silent treatment? It wasn't her fault he had an infertility problem.

He flicked off the TV and tossed the remote on the table. It clattered, then spun and plunked on the carpet.

She looked at her husband, suddenly feeling that she didn't know him at all. "What is wrong? This is more than just a test result."

He turned toward her then, and she saw the full weight of his anger. "I can't get you pregnant, Paula." His spat the words as if spewing some nasty food from his mouth.

Her heart pressed against her ribs, her blood gushed through her veins, but still, she couldn't figure out why—

And then a terrible thought occurred to her.

"Do you get it now? Yes, I see that you do." He blinked rapidly.

"You can't be serious."

Silence. So heavy and oppressing, it felt as if she smothered in it.

"You are." She couldn't believe he thought she'd—

"What am I supposed to think? The doctor told me it was highly unlikely I could get you pregnant. 'Practically impossible,' she said."

"But you did. We did."

"Did we?"

The words hung in the air between them. Suspended like a poisonous cloud of gasses. It sucked the air from her lungs. Her eyes stung. "Of course, we did. Think what you're saying, David."

"I've had all afternoon to think. And you know what I thought about? I thought about the time I found a bunch of e-mails from Evan in your inbox—"

"He was just seeing how—"

"I thought about the time we had those mysterious hotel charges on our credit card—"

"That was—"

"And I thought about how you act around other men, how you flirt and act so coy, and how you and that . . . that Dante were acting two weeks ago when I walked in on you at the TV station." His voice escalated. "That's what I thought about, Paula."

He shoved in the footrest, stood, and left the room.

She felt as if some heavy boulder sat on her chest. Sure, she'd been attracted to Dante. And maybe she did act a little coy with men, but that was just her personality. Couldn't he see that?

Maybe he senses your guilt.

She shoved away the thought. That was a whole separate matter. He was accusing her of cheating on him.

She followed him into the kitchen on legs that felt uncharacteristically wobbly. When she reached the kitchen, he was making a pot of coffee. She leaned against the counter.

"I know I sometimes act a little flirtatious with other men, but I have *never* cheated on you."

He emptied the water into the reservoir and shoved the pot on the burner.

"That baby was yours, David," she said emphatically. Her heart turned flip-flops in her chest when he didn't respond. She'd told him the truth. Why wouldn't he believe her? She trembled now, but not from fear. "How could you even think it?"

He took a mug from the cabinet and turned to get the half-and-half from the fridge.

She grabbed his arm. "Why are you doing this? Talk to me!"

He flung the creamer across the counter, where it slid and toppled.

"The doctor said 'practically impossible,' Paula. Do you understand what that means?" He jerked his arm away, and her hand fell. "I grieved that baby. For weeks, I grieved that baby. And it wasn't even mine."

"Yes, it was." How could he think this? It was so unfair. She flicked away the tear that escaped.

"Whose was it, Paula? Have there been others?"

"There hasn't been anybody! Would you listen to yourself?" Her eye started twitching. "Maybe you've only recently become infertile. Have you considered that? Did you ever think about that before you started accusing me of adultery?"

He nailed her with a glare and left the room.

Her insides clamped in knots until they ached. Beside her, a heavy puddle of creamer pooled around the lip of the container.

CHAPTER
NINETEEN

Linn swung her bike into Natalie's driveway and hopped off. Shoving down the kickstand, she walked up to the door and rang the bell. She felt grimy and sweaty from the hours she'd put in at Bubba's. She'd been stiffed a tip twice and run around by the spoiled tourists like she was a slave or something. Thinking of a nice quiet night at Natalie's house was the only thing that had kept her going today.

Natalie opened the door and embraced her. "Hi, Linn. Come on in." Natalie was the only one who hugged her. Though she kind of liked it, Linn never knew what to do with her hands. She followed Natalie into the living room and dropped her purse on the end table.

"Want a root beer?" Natalie asked.

"Sure. The boys gone?" Linn had been careful to time their meeting after Keith had picked up the boys. But in the back of her mind, she still worried about running into him.

"Yeah, they're with their dad. Just you and me tonight."

Maybe Natalie would finally make a decision about the baby. Her tummy had a little pooch to it now, and Linn could hardly stand the thought of having an abortion. Why was it taking so long for Natalie to make up her mind? Didn't she want to help? She smothered the spark of irritation. No sense getting all worked up now. She would do whatever she had to do to survive. She always had.

She'd finally gotten through to the scholarship people, and they'd said she would be able to use her scholarship money beginning in

January. It was all settled on her end. Now, if only Natalie would co-operate.

Natalie handed her a root beer and took a seat on the other end of the sofa. Funny how they already had regular spots to sit in. It was always exactly this way, even when the boys were here.

"How was work tonight?" Natalie asked.

Linn sighed. "I'm so sick of working around tourists. You'd think they might be generous on their vacations, but I keep getting stiffed. And I don't deserve it either. I'm a good server."

"I used to be a server when I was in high school. Back then we called them waitresses, though. And we got stiffed sometimes, too."

"I can't wait to get out of this town." She wanted to go off to college and get a job in some big city. She'd wear suits to work every day and do something real important.

"Well," Natalie said. "I'm thinking it might be awhile."

Linn looked at Nat and tried to read her face. What was she talking about?

Natalie reached out and grabbed her hand. "I've been doing a lot of thinking about your offer, as you know. It's an important decision, one I didn't want to take lightly."

Linn's thoughts froze, and her breath swelled in her lungs. This was it. She didn't think she could stand not knowing another second. Would she have to abort her baby, or would it get raised with Natalie? With its own brothers. Her tongue felt like sandpaper against the roof of her mouth.

"I've talked to several people about the adoption process and gotten a lot of advice and guidance. Mostly, though, I've been praying very hard. I believe God has in mind what's best for all of us. And if we ask Him what that is, He'll show us. He showed me."

Linn just wished she'd get on with it. Her insides ached with wanting to know, but somehow she couldn't seem to make her lips move.

"Linn, if your offer is still open, I want to accept it. I want to adopt the baby."

Linn's thoughts spun through her mind like a Tilt-a-Whirl. *She wants to adopt the baby. She wants to adopt the baby.*

Suddenly, the emotions she hadn't even known she was holding back gushed out. She put her hands over her face and felt it crumple like a wad of newspaper. She cried into her hands. Her baby was going to have life. Her baby was going to grow up and play with his or her real brothers. She wouldn't have to have an abortion and live with the guilt of what she'd done.

"Hey, it's OK."

She felt Natalie's arm slide around her shoulder. She wished she could stop the flow of emotions, but somehow she couldn't seem to control it. She was just so relieved. So happy and grateful. Natalie held her until she pulled herself together.

They pulled apart as Linn sniveled, feeling like an idiot. "I don't know why I'm crying like a big baby."

"You have every right to each emotion you're feeling right now. You've been through so much." Natalie nudged her shoulder. "And the pregnancy hormones don't help either."

Lynn smiled but felt it wobbling on her face as more tears filled her eyes. "Good grief, here I go again."

Natalie got up and returned with a box of tissues.

"I hope I'm not gonna need that whole box." Linn grabbed a tissue and wiped her face, then blew her nose.

"So, can I assume your offer still stands?" Natalie asked.

If Linn wasn't mistaken, Natalie looked almost afraid that her answer would be no. "Yeah, it's what I've been dreaming about, hoping for." Natalie and her boys were the closest thing this baby had to a real family. Nothing could make her happier than to know her baby was going to be raised in this house, with these people. She felt a smidge of guilt. What would Natalie think if she knew the truth?

"You know, once I started considering the idea, I started finding myself eager at the thought of raising this baby."

"I know you'll be a good mom. You're a good mom to Taylor and Alex."

"You should see me with a baby." Natalie's lips lifted in a dreamy smile. "I could hardly stand to put the boys down when they were babies. I just adored every minute."

"Even the nighttime stuff?" Linn didn't see how anyone could adore that. The thought of getting up every few hours every night sounded like a cruel form of torture to her.

"Well, at first it was hard, but you get used to it." She squeezed Linn's shoulder. "We have so much to talk about."

"Where do you want to start?" Linn's own mind was a mass of knots, like a ball of yarn all in tangles. How would she get through the pregnancy? She hadn't even seen a doctor. Who was going to pay for the doctor and the birth? And how would she tell her dad? Just the thought sent ripples of apprehension up her spine.

"What's wrong?" Natalie asked.

Part of her was afraid to say anything negative about the adoption. She sure didn't want Natalie to change her mind.

"It's OK," Natalie said. "We have to be honest with each other if we're going to do this together. Let's make a deal that we can say whatever's on our minds. That we'll be honest about our feelings when we speak and understanding as we listen. OK?"

Guilt bubbled up in Linn's gut. She couldn't be completely honest with Natalie. Not about the baby. That would ruin everything, and she'd come too far to ruin this. "I just realized I'd have to tell my dad."

Natalie offered a sad smile. "Oh. That's going to be hard for you, isn't it?"

"It's just—he's always said this would happen to me. And now it has, and he's going to be so like 'I told you so.'" Linn lowered her voice to sound like her dad. But her dad would sound worse than that. He'd yell and rant and call her names. And that was if he wasn't drunk.

"I'd be willing to go with you, if you think that would help."

Linn sighed. She didn't know which was worse. Facing her father all alone, or having someone else overhear the things he would say about her. "I don't know yet."

"That's OK. You have time to decide."

"I'm nineteen weeks now." Linn was carefully marking it off on her purse calendar. She was almost five months along, and it wouldn't be long before she couldn't hide it anymore. Already she wore her jeans unbuttoned.

"How do you think the boys will feel about having a new brother or sister?" Linn asked. She listened as Natalie told her about what Alex and Taylor had said. She couldn't believe how this was working out. Everything had felt so over. Her life had seemed like a waste, and her future had seemed as dark as a cave. Now there was hope. She could give her baby life, and Natalie could give her baby love.

"Thank you, Natalie." She whispered the words but put everything she was feeling into her expression. Her eyes began to sting again.

Natalie embraced her. "Thank you, Linn. For giving me the opportunity to love this baby."

By the time they parted, they both had tears streaking their faces. They looked at each other, and a smile connected the two of them in a way Linn had never experienced before.

"Pass the tissues," Natalie said. Linn handed her the box as laughter replaced the tears.

The Fourth of July dawned sunny and clear, and Natalie spent the day with the boys. She made them pancakes for breakfast and sat them down to talk about adopting Linn's baby. Over the past three days, she'd been nervous about telling them and had decided to wait until the holiday, when she had the whole day to spend with them.

Ironically, though, her nervousness was wasted, and the speech she'd rehearsed turned out to be a non-event. After she'd told the boys in a simple way all that was transpiring, Alex had only one question. "When do we get our new sister?"

She couldn't help but laugh at all the preparation she'd done going into this conversation. She'd been prepared to explain everything from where babies come from to who's going to be the daddy, but the boys hadn't cared about any of that. It was as if they'd known this was going to happen all of their little lives.

Since Keith was taking them to the fireworks in the evening, she made the most of the afternoon by taking them to Music in the Hole, an outdoor concert that was part of the Grand Teton Music Festival. She enjoyed the patriotic music and festive atmosphere, but as soon as they'd scarfed down all the junk food they could handle, Alex and Taylor were bored.

The whole family had decided to have a picnic at her parents' house before the fireworks, so Natalie took the boys there next. Keith was picking them up there, and Natalie was planning to tell her family about the adoption while she had them all together.

Hanna, Micah, and Gram picked them up from their house, and they drove to their parents' house. When Natalie walked out on the back patio, her mom was unpacking the hotdogs. Natalie set down the bowl of potato salad she'd made and embraced her. Alex and Taylor ran off to where their grandpa had set up a croquet set.

"Happy Fourth," her mom said.

"You, too, Mom. The boys have been looking forward to this all afternoon." Natalie grabbed a package of Oscar Mayer hot dogs and ripped it open.

"Me, too," Hanna said. "As much as I love the lodge, it does feel like I have to baby-sit it sometimes."

Micah joined her father in the yard, and Gram walked over to Paula, who was sitting on a camping chair a short distance away. When they looked her way, she waved, then addressed Hanna. "Who's watching the lodge?"

"The two summer students we hired. The rooms are all set, so all they'll have to do is check people in. Besides, just about all our guests are out enjoying the festivities. Did you go to Music in the Hole?"

"I took the boys, but let's just say I don't think they appreciate fine music yet."

"Did you go, Mom?" Hanna asked.

"Ha. Your dad wouldn't be caught dead at a concert, free or not."

"You could've tempted him with the junk food," Natalie said.

"He knew he'd get plenty of that tonight," her mom said. "Look at him out there. Like a kid."

Natalie followed her mom's eye out to the field, where her father, Micah, David, and her boys were reacting to a shot Micah had made. Her dad was shaking his head while the others laughed.

"I hope it doesn't get too competitive out there," Natalie said. "I'm not up for a family brawl." She smiled the thought away. Their family had hardly even argued in all the years since the girls had left home. They were tight that way. They could really confide in one another and trust one another.

As she watched her mom and Hanna preparing all the food, Natalie felt the urge to tell them right then about the baby. She had planned to tell everyone together, but somehow it seemed right to do it now.

She peeked a glance as she ripped off a length of tin foil.

"Mom, Hanna, there's something I've been wanting to tell you."

Both women looked up at the same time, their eyes brimming with concern. She realized her voice carried levity, and it wasn't often she had news to spring on anyone. The last time she'd said those words to her mom, it had been to tell her that Keith was leaving her for another woman.

"Mom, don't look like that. It's nothing bad. In fact, I'm pretty excited about this, but I need you to hear it with an open mind."

She glanced at Hanna and saw realization dawning in her eyes. She hadn't talked to Hanna about it since that Sunday at the Shady Nook.

She explained the situation with Linn starting from the moment Linn had first walked into the center. She talked about how Linn reminded her of Dana and how she feared Linn would never be able to live with the horror of abortion.

Paula and Gram wandered over, but sensing their private conversation, started to walk away. Natalie took Gram's hand. "No, you two stay here. I'm glad you came over, because this is something I want you to know, too." She looked out at the yard, where her father and two brothers-in-law were playing. She would tell them later. It just seemed right for all the women of the family to hear the news together.

She caught Gram and Paula up on the details she'd shared so far, then continued the story, admitting her failure to keep her relationship with Linn on a professional level. Telling them about how Linn bit her nails when she's nervous, and had a thin layer of false bravado that covered a sensitive heart. She told them about her sad home life, and finally she told them about Linn's offer.

"After a lot of prayer, I've decided to take her up on it. I'm going to adopt the baby."

Only Hanna didn't gasp or visibly react to the words.

Everyone seemed to freeze in time, and she could almost hear an imaginary clock ticking away the shock.

"Somebody say something." Natalie tucked her hair behind her ear. The looks on her mom's and Paula's faces would have inspired laughter if she wasn't so nervous.

"I'm really proud of you." Hanna walked around the picnic table and embraced her.

Natalie released a sigh that she felt from her toes up. "That day we met at the Café was the beginning of my decision. I would never have considered it until you encouraged me to."

They drew apart, and Natalie looked reluctantly at her mom. What would she think? What mother wanted her single-mother daughter to take on someone else's child?

But the look on her mother's face wasn't what she expected. A smile tugged her mom's lips, and her eyes filled with tears.

"You are an amazing woman, sweetheart."

Gram pulled her into a enthusiastic embrace. "Such compassion. I'm so proud of you."

This wasn't what she'd expected. She'd braced herself all day for opposition. She'd been afraid her family would think she was crazy for what she was about to do. But then she realized Paula hadn't said anything yet. Her sister's flawless face revealed something less than excitement. She crossed her arms over her green blouse, and her green eyes held some flicker of emotion she couldn't identify, but then Paula looked away.

Before Natalie could say anything, her mom and Hanna asked her questions about the adoption process. Some Natalie could answer, but some she would just have to learn as she went. She still hadn't figured out how she'd afford to adopt this baby. She didn't even know if Linn had medical coverage. It wouldn't be an inexpensive proposition either way. There was still the attorney fee.

"Do the boys know?" her mom asked.

Natalie thought back over the past few days, about how the boys had seemed to know before she had about the new addition to the family. She told the other women about it.

"Well," Paula said, "it'll certainly be interesting to see how they adjust once the baby's here."

Natalie wondered if she imagined the starchiness in her sister's voice. Why couldn't Paula just be happy for her?

"Oh, they're going to love it," her mom said. "You should see Alex at the park when there's a baby there. He'd just as soon play with the baby as climb on the monkey bars."

"And Taylor is always wanting to be the big brother," Hanna said. "He'll enjoy having a younger sibling to teach."

"And boss around." Paula's voice was terse. "I think I'll take these hot dogs over to Dad." She picked up the platter and carried it toward the grill, where their father was talking with Micah.

Natalie watched her go, noting her stiff posture.

"What's Paula's deal?" Hanna asked.

"She seems distracted today," their mother said.

Distracted wasn't the description that came to Natalie's mind. She hadn't said anything about Natalie's big news. She seemed almost critical, though Natalie couldn't see any reason why Paula would feel that way.

"Paula's just a little stressed, I think," Gram said. She squeezed Natalie's arm. "We are just so excited about your news, dear. It's been a few years since we've had a baby in the family."

Natalie grabbed the hot dog buns and set them beside the condiments. "Has Micah made any headway toward finding his sister?"

"He found the family who adopted her," Hanna said. "Unfortunately, Jenna ran away from home awhile back, and they don't know where she is."

"That's too bad."

The conversation switched to babies while they readied the table. A while later, Alex accidentally hit Taylor with the croquet mallet, sending Taylor into a fit of tears.

Finally, the food was ready, and a line formed for everyone to fill their plates. It was then that Hanna pulled Natalie over by the pine trees.

"Well, Sis, I have a little news of my own today." Her eyes sparkled, and Natalie's breath caught.

"Are you pregnant?"

The smile said it all. "I am."

Natalie squealed and hugged her sister. "Shhhh!" Hanna said, laughing. "We haven't told anyone yet."

"When's the baby due? Do you know yet?"

"I haven't been to the doctor yet, but I think around the end of February."

Natalie couldn't seem to stop smiling. Hanna and Micah were so in love, and they would be great parents.

"When are you going to tell the family?"

Hanna wrinkled up her nose. "Well, that's the thing. We were kinda going to tell them today, but with your big news, I was thinking maybe we should wait. I don't want to—"

"No, Hanna, no. Tell them today. Really, I want you to." It was sweet of Hanna not wanting to steal her thunder, but Natalie thought this just capped the day off.

"Hey," Natalie said. "Won't it be cool to have babies at the same time?"

"I've already been thinking about that. Our baby and your baby will only be a few months apart."

Natalie's heart stopped at the words. *My baby.* She hadn't started thinking of this amazing child as hers yet. Not really. It was hard when this child was in someone else's body. But in a few short months, someone would place this infant in her arms, and she would be a new mommy. Again.

Hanna and Natalie joined the rest of the family. After filling their plates, they seated themselves at the two picnic tables that had been pulled together and covered with blue-checked plastic tablecloths. Next year, this time, there would be twelve at the table instead of ten.

Word of the adoption had spread to her dad and Micah, but David seemed surprised when the topic came up. Natalie wondered why Paula hadn't told him.

Her dad asked about Linn and her situation, and Natalie filled them in on the details, still being careful to leave Linn's name out of the conversation. She wondered at what point she could dispense with that rule. She at least wanted to get Linn's permission.

Alex wolfed down his hot dog and chips before dashing out toward the croquet game. Taylor picked at his food, and she finally got him to eat a hot dog sans the bun and a spoonful of baked beans. Realizing that was the best she'd get, she set him free, and he joined his brother in the yard.

Across from her, Paula sat stiffly, moving food around on her plate. Next to her, David ate quietly. Although he talked to Gram and her father, she hadn't noticed him speak once to Paula. Natalie wondered what was going on between them.

Before the adults left the table, Hanna gathered everyone's attention. Micah took her hand, and they shared an intimate look before Hanna spoke.

"Micah and I have some news we wanted to share today, and it goes hand-in-hand with Nat's good news." She exchanged a smile with Natalie.

"Micah and I are expecting." She looked from face to face expectantly.

"Oh, Hanna!" Her mom reached over and gave her a sideways hug. "I'm so happy for both of you." She leaned across Hanna and hugged Micah.

"My, my," Gram said. "What a day this has been. Congratulations, you two. I didn't have any idea. You've been buzzing around the lodge like superwoman."

"I've been feeling pretty good so far," Hanna said.

Natalie noticed Paula had yet to say anything. Her face looked strained.

"Congratulations," David said.

"Yes, it's been quite a day." Paula's tight smile spoke volumes, though no one else seemed to notice.

There was an air of celebration the rest of the evening. Natalie was thrilled for Hanna and Micah, and equally excited that their babies would be so close in age. But for the first time, Natalie wondered if it would bother her to see Hanna growing big with her pregnancy while someone else carried her baby.

Oh, well, at least I won't get the fatigue and swelling and backaches.

Shortly after they cleaned up, Keith came by to pick up the boys. She'd arranged to meet him in the front yard, since it was still awkward for her family. Her parents may have forgiven Keith for his desertion and what he had done to Gram, but she doubted they'd ever forget. Sometimes she didn't think she would either.

When darkness began to fall, they loaded up her parents' SUV with lawn chairs and set off toward the heart of Jackson for the annual fireworks display. In the back of the SUV, Natalie gazed out the window. The huge buttes were shadowed against the darkening sky, and the majestic houses snuggled up against the base looked like Monopoly homes in comparison.

The town would be teeming with tourists tonight, and Natalie hoped they'd be able to find a spot to watch the display. Each year the town put on a grand show at the base of Snow King, and people came from all around to see the fireworks.

Tonight Natalie couldn't help feeling a bit lonely without the boys. But Keith had asked weeks ago if he could take them, and she knew the boys were starved for time with their dad. At least she had her family. Though, with the exception of Gram, they were all couples. She wondered if she'd ever get over feeling incomplete without a husband. The thought of being married again brought only fear, though. She was in no hurry to put her heart on the line again. How could she ever trust another man after what Keith had done to her?

"I think we should have left earlier," her dad said.

The traffic was bad along Broadway. They'd be fortunate to find a place to park.

When they neared the town square, a huge crowd had already gathered. Tourists snapped pictures in front of the arch of elk antlers, the town's most popular landmark. Pedestrians flooded the sidewalks, meandering in and out of the rustic shops like busy ants.

"It may take me awhile to find a spot," her dad said. "Why don't I let everyone out, and you can go try to find us a place."

They agreed that her mom would call her dad on her cell phone and let him know where they'd settled.

They each grabbed a lawn chair from the trunk at the stoplight and made their way down Cache Street on the boarded sidewalks.

Hanna took Gram's arm and led the way with Micah and her mom behind. Paula and David strode behind them, and Natalie brought up the tail. People were everywhere. If they weren't walking, they were lined up on the edge of the sidewalks, their chairs pointing toward Snow King's steep slope. They'd arrived much too late, and she was beginning to wish she'd brought a tall ladder to climb to the roof of the center. They would have had a perfect view from up there. Already it was dark, and only the streetlamps and storefronts illuminated the street.

A pedestrian bumped her arm, and she dropped the folding chair.

"Excuse me," the woman said as she passed.

Natalie stooped over to grab the chair, and as she did, her purse slid from her shoulder, spilling out its contents.

"Wait up, guys," she called to her family as she scooped her checkbook, keys, and various coins back into her purse. She glanced in the direction she'd been walking but saw no sign of her family among all the people. *Shoot.*

"Is this yours, ma'am?" An older man she didn't recognize handed her a tube of lipstick.

"Thanks." She stuffed it in her purse and slid it on her shoulder before grabbing the chair off the boarded sidewalk. All the while, people stepped around her. Finally, she stood and rushed as quickly as she could toward her family. She looked above heads as best she could, given her short stature. Where did they go? She couldn't see a thing. Surely they'd realize they'd lost her and stop.

She kept going, past Simson and Hansen Avenues, but they were nowhere. She realized they could have turned off on either of those streets and made their way up toward King Street. At the corner, she stopped in her tracks in front of Fighting Bear Antiques. People on chairs and lawn blankets covered the yard and large rustic porch.

She'd never find her family now, not among all these tourists. Someone jostled her, and she moved toward the edge of the sidewalk and propped the closed chair against her leg.

Her cell phone. She pulled it from her purse and turned it on, waiting for it to light up. Nothing. She sighed. The battery was dead. She put the phone back in her purse. Great. Now she was out here all by herself with no car to get back to her parents' house. Just what she needed. Her parents would worry about her.

A glance at her watch told her that the display was about to begin. She looked around at the families and couples sitting in groups. At the people passing her, all talking and laughing. The warm summer air seemed almost stuffy as she stood, suddenly feeling very alone in the midst of a crowd.

She just wanted to go home. Maybe that's what she would do. It wasn't that far, and she could call her mom and let her know she'd made it home fine. She wasn't interested in the display anymore. It was no fun watching it alone. She looked at the darkness around her. It would be very dark in her neighborhood without all the store lights. Her heart beat quickly at the thought. Did she really want to be walking alone at night? Memories of the attack surfaced.

Don't be silly, she told herself. *Nothing's going to happen.* She picked up her chair and hiked her purse higher on her shoulder.

"Natalie?"

She turned toward the Fighting Bear's lawn and scanned the crowd. In the darkness, she couldn't make out anyone she recognized. She tried to place the voice she'd heard and couldn't. Maybe he'd been calling a different Natalie.

"Over here." Someone stood up on the edge of the property and waved. From his silhouette, she recognized him. Kyle.

She waved.

He maneuvered around the people and blankets until he was by her side. "Are you meeting your family?"

"Not exactly. We were together, but I kind of lost them."

She warmed at the smile on his face.

"You're welcome to join me if you'd like. I think there's room to squeeze in another chair."

It was tempting, but she was still feeling a little sorry for herself. Her boys should be with her, and they weren't. She was supposed to be enjoying the evening with her family, and she wasn't.

"I was thinking I'd just walk home. I'm not really in the mood for fireworks tonight."

A boom sounded that she felt deep in her stomach. A bright starburst exploded in the sky.

"Too late," Kyle said. "Come on. You might as well stay."

Three more colorful displays burst in the sky. She looked at Kyle. He turned from the brightened sky, his skin glowing pink from the fireworks.

"All right." She followed him back to his spot and set up the chair. It was a squeeze between his chair and the blanket beside her, where a Hispanic family of six crowded together. Finally, Natalie settled into the chair and relaxed. As the fireworks exploded above her and the deep booms rumbled in her throat, she thought of the freedom she enjoyed and wondered what her life would be like next Fourth of July.

CHAPTER TWENTY

When Kyle had looked over and seen Natalie on the sidewalk, his first thought was to hide. He was alone, but that suited him just fine. He'd come to the fireworks for something to do, and he wasn't one to need a bunch of friends around to make him feel secure.

But then Natalie had stopped on the sidewalk. Her arms hugged her torso as the chair leaned against her leg, and he thought she looked like a lost little girl. Then, suddenly she looked as if she were about to bolt. All thoughts of hiding fled as her name formed on his tongue.

He called himself all kinds of fool even while he extended his invitation. Why was he asking her to watch the fireworks with him? Was it pity? She'd looked so alone and had become separated from her family. Or did he secretly want to spend time with her?

As they walked to his spot on the lawn, he shoved the thought away. It was compassion that made him do it and nothing else.

They sat down, their chairs arm-to-arm in the tight space. Above them, the colorful display erupted rhythmically.

"Do you have a cell phone on you?" Natalie asked.

"Sure." He dug his from his pocket and handed it to her.

"Mine's dead, wouldn't you know it? I don't want my family to worry." She punched in a number.

Kyle turned toward the dark sky and watched the display. He heard her talking to someone with the reassurance that she was fine. She had to talk loud to be heard over the booms and the oooing and aaahing all around them. Not to mention the toddler who squealed on the blanket beside her. When Kyle heard Natalie telling her family she'd walk home, he spoke up.

"I can give you a lift if you want." Now, where had that come from? The last thing he needed was to spend more time with Natalie. Already, he'd admitted to himself he was drawn to her. And the last thing he wanted was a woman in his life. But it wasn't safe, even in Jackson, for a woman to be out walking alone after dark. He was surprised she was even willing, after being assaulted.

"Are you sure?" Natalie covered the mouthpiece. "It's not far."

"No problem." Except to his peace of mind.

Natalie said good-bye and handed him the phone. "Thanks."

They watched the rest of the fireworks in silence. The grand finale came, and the crowd applauded all the way through it. As the last of the fireworks sounded, the departure scramble began all around them.

"If you don't mind," he said, "I'd just as soon wait until the traffic clears."

"Don't like sitting in traffic, do you?"

"It's the one bad thing about summers here."

Natalie leaned back and rested her head against the chair back. "It's not so bad, really. It just seems bad, compared to the off-season."

"It's a unique place to live," he said. "Soon as warm weather hits, the tourists come and flood the town with their camping and climbing gear. Then it gets cold, and everyone seems to disappear almost overnight."

"And my favorite restaurants close for a few weeks."

"Then after Christmas, the skiers come flooding in and enjoy the slopes until spring."

"And then it starts all over again," she said.

He nodded. "I guess it's not surprising that there are so many transients. Not many locals left."

"Nope," she said. "I guess I'm a rare breed."

They watched the family beside her packing up their things and let the quiet fall between them. The night sky was perfectly clear, and even with the lamplights along the sidewalk, he could see hundreds of stars dotting the sky. He thought of Jillian on nights like this and wondered what heaven was like. Could she see him here on earth, or was she tucked away at the foot of God's throne?

He shook the thought away. Thinking of Jillian only left him depressed. Their relationship hadn't been very good, and his last moments with her were ones he wished he could forget. If only she'd never told him about the affair. It would have been better not to have known.

"I'm glad I ran into you tonight," Natalie said, jerking his thoughts back to the present. "I wanted to thank you for all the information you've given me on adoption."

"Have you decided what to do?"

"Actually, I have. I told my family today. I am going to adopt the baby."

He tried to keep the surprise from his face. "Well. Congratulations." He nodded thoughtfully. Inside, he was astounded at Natalie's resolve to do what she felt was right. Astounded by her bravery. How many single mothers with two young children would adopt a newborn?

"I'm not sure how I'll be able to work it all out. The finances and everything. It's not like I have money to burn or anything."

The least he could do was offer her a discount. If she was willing to put her future on the line for this baby, the least he could do was lower his fee. "I'd be glad to cut my fees to make it a little easier."

She blinked, and he saw something like fear in her eyes before she looked away.

It struck him as odd, and he wondered what caused it.

"Oh. I'm not sure how we'll be doing this," Natalie said.

How they'd be doing it? She must mean through an agency or attorney. Maybe she didn't know he was the only one in town who handled adoptions. "Sure. Well, if you choose to go the attorney route—and that's what's usually done in cases like this—I can save you a lot of money."

He stopped himself. It sounded almost as if he were begging for her business. What was wrong with him? She clearly didn't like the idea of using his services. He could almost feel her close up on him when he'd suggested it.

"Thanks for the offer. Everything is really up in the air right now. I don't even know if my client has health insurance."

She shifted in her chair, and he sensed her discomfort. "The boys with their dad tonight?"

She nodded. "He's keeping them overnight."

"How long were you married?"

"Eight years." She cradled her purse in her lap and played with the leather straps. "You were married before."

The comment caught him off-guard. She was remembering what Linn had said at the center, of course. He should have known it would come around to this eventually. It was the last thing he wanted to talk about.

"I'm sorry. Maybe I shouldn't have said anything."

She'd given him a way out, but suddenly he didn't want to take it. Was it the way she looked at him, with eyes as soft as a rose petal?

"It's true, what Linn said." It pained him to say it. Real pain that radiated out from his heart.

"I find that hard to believe." She hardly knew him, yet she believed him innocent of Linn's accusation.

If her eyes were soft, her voice was velvet. Her head was turned toward him, leaning against the canvas back of the camping chair. A vulnerable spot in him didn't want to disabuse her of that notion. But he was already feeling too warm toward Natalie. Although she'd given him no indication she was interested in him, knowing the truth about him might keep a nice, safe distance between them.

He looked away from her toward the pedestrians who strolled past on the sidewalk. "We were going home from church. I was driving, and we were having an—a disagreement. I wasn't paying attention at all, and I didn't see the red light. A truck hit on her side of the car. She was gone that quick."

"I'm so sorry. I think I remember when it happened. Seeing it on the news."

He propped his ankle on his knee, more for something to do than for comfort.

"But it was an accident, Kyle. Nothing more."

"It was my fault. I was responsible for keeping her safe. I was driving."

"That's not murder, though."

He looked at her then, his gut in a knot. "What differentiates an accident from murder? Intent? No, I didn't intend to be negligent. But a careless motorist who crashes into another car is charged with reckless homicide when someone in the other vehicle dies. So, what's the difference in this case? My wife is dead because I was reckless."

"If you were guilty of such a thing, you'd be in jail."

He'd wished he were many times. Maybe it would soothe his guilt.

"Your wife's family has held this against you all this time?"

"Do you blame them? I'm responsible for Ed's daughter's death. And Linn's only sister."

"You shouldn't accept that. You should defend yourself. It was an accident."

He felt a longing to believe her words. A longing to exonerate himself. But it didn't wash. "It's only an accident when there's no one at fault."

Her brows knotted thoughtfully. He looked away before he lost himself in her eyes. He felt vulnerable, and he didn't like it. She made him feel things he didn't want to feel. He felt her hand on his arm and turned toward her again.

"I'll be praying that you forgive yourself."

Her words took him aback. Is that what he needed to do? He'd never thought of it that way. He'd always figured this was the bitter pill he'd live with. Some things could never be undone. Maybe he should forgive himself, but it was hard when others still held him responsible for Jilly's death. He'd never forget the scene at the hospital where they'd taken Jilly after the accident. Her heart had stopped beating in the ambulance, but they'd tried to revive her at St. John's.

Ed and Linn had come after it was too late. They'd overheard the details as he was telling the officer, but they'd gotten one important fact wrong. He hadn't had the heart to correct them, and even to this day, they believed a lie.

"Think it's cleared out enough to head out?" Natalie's voice pulled him back to the present.

He looked around, noticing for the first time that the lawn and porch had cleared. "Sure. I'm parked on Milward. Not too far." They stood up and grabbed their things. He reached out and took her chair for her, and they began walking.

"Tell me how the center is going," he said.

She pulled her purse up on her shoulder. "Better. No more vandalism."

"That has to be a relief. It must be difficult to work so hard for a cause you believe in just to have people harass you for it. I guess it's true we can't change the world."

"Maybe not the world, but we can change lives one person at a time."

He used to believe that. He remembered when his work was fulfilling. When he'd place a child with a family and think God had used him to change their lives for the better. Now it just seemed like a job. A job that he'd allowed to pull him from his wife, the one person who should have been first on his priority list. He'd failed her and failed the baby she carried, and what was more important in his world than that?

When they reached his car, he helped her in and asked for directions to her home. It was only moments later that they were turning from the flat of the valley up the steep hill of Rodeo Drive. She instructed him to turn into the drive of a large home that was dark except for one porch light.

"Well," she said, gathering her things, "thanks for the ride. And for sharing the fireworks with me."

The last she said with a smile that wrapped its way around his heart.

"Anytime." He started to add a little quip about getting lost in a crowd but decided against it. "If you need any advice about the adoption, feel free to call me." *Shut up already, Keaton.*

"Thanks, I might just do that." With a little wave, she shut the door.

He watched her until she made it inside the house and wondered if she hadn't made her way inside his heart just a little.

CHAPTER
TWENTY-ONE

Paula walked around Betty's dog and slipped into the Shady Nook Café, snagging a table in the corner.

"Hi, Paula, haven't seen you in a while," Betty said as she passed the table with a tray balanced on one hand. The owner was likely to be seen doing any of the jobs necessary at the Shady Nook.

"Hi, Betty." Paula settled into the wooden chair and picked up the menu. Though she'd come here enough to have the menu memorized, the café was not a place she hung out often. Paula's tastes ran more to eclectic than country bumpkin. Still, she browsed the selection and settled on potato soup and a side salad.

When the door opened, she glanced up, but it was only a couple of tourists. She sighed and sipped from the water glass Betty had set on the table. She wasn't here to eat anyway, she realized. She'd been hoping Natalie would come in while she was here. Which was silly, when she could just call her sister and invite her over.

Why hadn't she just done that? She needed to talk to someone. Heaven knew there had been no conversation in her own home over the past week, what with David skulking around like an injured bear. What a joke that was. She should be the raging lunatic in the house. What he was accusing her of was inexcusable.

"Decide what you want?" Betty flipped open her order pad, pen poised expectantly over the paper.

Paula had just finished ordering her food when Natalie slipped into the chair opposite her. "Saving this for someone?"

Paula wondered if the relief showed on her face. "It's all yours."

Natalie slung her big, floppy purse over the chair back. "Man, what a day."

"Busy?" Paula wondered how the little Hope Center could possible be as busy as that. If Natalie ever spent a day at the station, she'd see what busy was.

"Just the usual flow of clients, but I've been training volunteers and trying to do more research on adoption in my spare time."

The adoption. How could Paula have forgotten? First a baby just falls into Natalie's lap, and then Hanna turns up pregnant. Meanwhile, Paula can't conceive, and her husband accuses her of having affairs. Film at eleven.

"How are things at the station?" Natalie poured herself a glass of water from the pitcher on the table.

"Fine." Should she tell Natalie about the job opportunity? Why not? "Actually, it's going very well. Donald has sent my tape in to our affiliate in Chicago. He thinks I might have a shot at the job."

The smile on Natalie's face was all genuine. "Paula, that's so awesome! When will you hear?"

"Well, he only sent it in this week, so it'll be awhile yet. And it's only a temporary position, but there's potential for something permanent."

"You must be so excited. David, too. I know how hard you've worked for this."

Betty brought Paula her soup and set it down in front of her. Paula was glad for the diversion and sipped the soup from a spoon while Natalie ordered.

Hadn't she wanted to talk to Natalie? Why did she suddenly want to clam up the minute David's name was mentioned? Maybe because Natalie always seemed to have it together. She had a calmness about her that Paula envied. Natalie was so solid, even through the divorce and Keith's incarceration and money worries. Paula had the marriage and money, but all the money in the world couldn't give her the peace she wanted. Besides, things weren't always as wonderful as they appeared to be.

"So, how does David feel about the possibility of leaving Jackson?"

If Paula thought she was going to avoid the subject of David, she guessed wrong. She set down her spoon and shrugged. Truthfully, she hadn't a clue how David felt about leaving, since he hadn't said a word about her job opportunity. Was too caught up in his imaginary world of accusation.

"I think we're going to wait and see if I get an offer before we make any decisions," Paula said.

"He's built a name here as a realtor. I imagine he'd have mixed feelings about leaving that."

"Sure, but what a market Chicago would be. David always was more of a city person."

Natalie smiled. "And you. You always said you couldn't wait to get out of this hole."

Paula couldn't remember a time when she wasn't longing to escape the small-town atmosphere of Jackson. What others saw as quaint just seemed stifling to her. The buttes around the town had always felt like big prison walls holding her in. It was a wonder she'd stayed this long.

"Wouldn't you miss it, though?" Natalie said. "The mountains, the skiing, the way you can't go to the grocery without running into people you know?"

"I could live without it quite nicely, thank you very much. Especially when I'd have theater, shopping, and fine dining minutes away."

Natalie laughed and shook her head.

Sometimes Paula wondered how the same parents had sired both of them. Hanna and Natalie were cut from the same cloth in many ways and very like their mother. Paula had always been the odd one out.

She finished her soup and pushed the bowl back. "So, Mom said you watched the fireworks with a male friend. Anything a nosy sister should know?" A quick study of Natalie's face showed a tinge of pink rising to her cheeks.

She tried for a nonchalant shrug but didn't quite pull it off. "I ran into Kyle Keaton by chance. We watched the fireworks, and he offered me a ride home. No big deal."

"I can see it was no big deal by the blush on your cheeks."

"I'm not blushing."

"OK." Paula sipped her water.

"Would you stop it? He's just a friend. I probably won't even see him anymore."

"In Jackson? You can hardly avoid it."

"You know what I mean."

"So, who's going to do your adoption? I assumed you'd use him as your attorney." Paula saw shutters go up over Natalie's eyes and wondered at it.

"I'll probably use another one."

"Good luck finding someone else. He's the only one in Jackson trained for adoptions."

"How do you know that?"

"From the research for that piece I did for the news a couple months ago."

"Are you sure? I guess I should have looked into this already."

Betty came and set her salad down in front of her. Natalie pulled her chicken salad plate close and bowed her head for a silent prayer.

"So, what's the big deal?" Paula asked when Natalie had finished. "Why not just use Kyle?" Something was on her sister's mind. She could tell by the knot between her brow. If she didn't stop making that face, she'd be a Botox candidate in two years.

"There's kind of a conflict of interest."

Paula stabbed her lettuce with her fork and dipped it in the Thousand Island. "What do you mean?"

Natalie wiped her mouth with the paper napkin. "Kyle knows this client. It just wouldn't be a good idea."

"That shouldn't matter. It's a small town. It's not like the adoption can be kept secret."

"I'm not trying to keep it a secret exactly. There's just bad blood between my client and Kyle. There's no way she'll agree to using him."

"Well, you don't want to drive all the way to Casper, do you?"

"Casper? Surely there's one closer."

"Not that I could find."

The change in her sister's countenance could only be described as a deflating balloon. "I can't drive over four hours for these appointments. What will I do with the boys?"

Paula wiped her mouth. "You should use Kyle." She could only guess what the problem was between Kyle and Natalie's client, but she figured it must be a doozy to make Natalie's spirits droop so much.

They ate a few minutes in silence before Natalie spoke again. "So, how's David doing these days? I didn't get to talk with him much at Mom and Dad's over the Fourth."

How was David doing? She should know, shouldn't she? But it was hard keeping tabs on him when he was hardly home. And she was lucky if he even spoke to her when he was home. "Business is good. He's got another wealthy business owner from out of state wanting to buy a bunch of land to put a mansion on. Good old Wyoming. A tax shelter for the wealthy."

She'd sidestepped Natalie's question a bit, but if her sister noticed, she didn't persist. Why was it so hard to admit there was a problem between her and David? And if she wouldn't admit it to Natalie, who would she ever be able to talk to about it? She supposed she could talk to a professional, but who had time for that?

She was growing weary of the silent stones being thrown her way. It was so unfair. How could David think it of her? She wasn't the one who needed help; he was. Maybe she should make an appointment for him with a psychologist. She smothered a laugh. That would stir up some conversation between them.

David, I've arranged for you to get some professional help for your demented delusions. Perhaps you can come to grips with your need for hurling insulting accusations my way.

Yeah, that would go over. Why was everything in her life turning to dust? Suddenly her fixation with conceiving had totally taken a backseat in light of David's cruelty. She'd had her appointment with a fertility specialist, and everything looked fine with her health so far. The news had given her relief, but had been overshadowed by David's accusation. How would David ever come to believe her when she couldn't prove the truth? And how would she ever get over his lack of faith in her?

CHAPTER
TWENTY-TWO

Linn flipped the TV channel to a sitcom and leaned back against the tattered plaid couch. In front of her, her stomach pooched under her unbuttoned jeans. She pulled her shirt down over her belly. She had yet to visit the doctor, though she knew she needed to. But she needed her dad's insurance card for that.

She had to tell her dad. She'd already wasted two weeks waiting for the right moment. When was she going to realize there would never be a right moment? Her dad would yell and scream and tell her she was just what he'd always thought she was. She was living up to everything he'd ever told her. Proved that Jillian was the good daughter and Linn was the bad. And somehow the fact that she was still here while Jillian was gone was all her fault.

Why did her dad blame her for that? It was Kyle's fault, not hers. Sometimes she wished it had been her in that crash instead of her sister. Maybe then her dad would be happy.

Her eyes burned, and she pressed her fingers against them. Stupid hormones. She used to hardly ever cry, and now she couldn't seem to stop. She felt like a big baby. Just yesterday she'd nearly cried when a customer had a fit over his cold barbecue chicken. Like that had been her fault.

She heard her dad's junky Oldsmobile pulling into the gravel drive and tensed. The headlights shone against the white wall above the TV, then went off. She had to tell him tonight. She knew he would be sober because he'd gotten off work only ten minutes ago. He hadn't had time to stop at Sidewinders and get drunk. No, he was saving that for home. But she would tell him before he got plastered.

Maybe he would surprise her. Natalie had said most parents react better than her clients think they will. She'd said nearly every girl thinks her parents would have a conniption, but they rarely do. She'd said to expect shock and maybe hurt before her dad came around and became rational. She'd offered to come with her, but Linn had thought that was a bad idea. It would be humiliating enough to tell her dad without an audience.

The front door creaked open and clicked shut. Her dad walked past her to the kitchen. Linn's breath froze in her body even while her heart set an all-time record for its speed. Her dad came back into the living room and grabbed the remote control off the table before sinking into the recliner. She could see him out of her peripheral vision take a swig from the beer bottle.

He turned the channel, surfing through twice before settling on *PrimeTime*. Linn scarcely noticed the segment about shady jewelry businesses. She was too caught up trying to think of the right way to say what she had to say.

Maybe she shouldn't tell him tonight at all. Had he had a bad day at work? She turned her head just enough to look at him over the end table and around the lamp. It was hard to tell. His weathered face looked blank. He hadn't said anything yet, but maybe that was good. From the moment he walked in the door, he usually griped about the messy house or the dishes in the sink. But she'd been careful to take care of all that today, since she'd had the day off work.

Should she tell him now or should she wait?

Wait for what? What was going to get better? She needed a doctor's appointment, and he was going to notice her belly soon anyway. She pulled the couch pillow over and hugged it to her stomach. She was just procrastinating, that's all she was doing. She had to grow up and be responsible about what had happened. Maybe he would even like the idea of having a grandchild. Even if she wasn't keeping the baby. She clung to the thought as she opened her mouth.

"Have a good day?" She cringed as the words tumbled out. What a stupid thing to say. She'd never asked him that in her life. She felt more than saw him toss her a glance.

He grunted.

So much for conversation starters. She chewed her pinky nail. Maybe she should just get right down to it. "I was wondering if we could talk about something."

"I ain't got no extra money this month, so you can save your breath."

His words hit somewhere deep inside her. "I don't need money, Daddy . . ."

Daddy. She hadn't called him that in years. Her thoughts raced with words she was afraid to say. *Help me,* she pleaded, then wondered who she was pleading with. Would Natalie's God help her? Why should He? She was deceiving Natalie. She was probably rotten to the core just like her dad said.

"What is it, then?" her dad asked.

Was there a softening in his voice? Was it because she'd called him "Daddy" or because of her prayer? "I have a problem you need to know about. Remember that guy I was seeing awhile back?"

"How would I remember him? You never brought him home."

How could she bring a married man home to her dad? Besides, she would have died before bringing Keith into this dump to meet her drunk father. Why had she brought up Keith anyway? Was she trying to prove that at least this baby was the result of a relationship and not a trashy one-night stand? What did it matter anyway? Pregnant was pregnant. He would see it all the same.

"That thing I needed to tell you," she said, bracing herself and making the words form on her tongue, "is that I'm pregnant, Daddy." She squeezed her eyes tightly shut, glad for the dimness of the room and the lamp that stood between them. Her heart pressed against her ribs. The silence was louder than the blaring TV.

Then he slammed his beer bottle on the table and spit out a few choice words. "Well, I guess I shouldn't be so surprised now, should I?" The sarcasm in his tone twisted the words like someone wringing a dirty dishrag. He cursed again. "What am I supposed to do about this? No, that's not the question, is it? The question is what are *you* supposed to do about this, and I think we both know the answer!"

He leaned forward and glared at her across the table, but she couldn't look. He was talking about abortion. She blinked rapidly. He couldn't make her do it, could he? She wasn't a minor anymore.

"You're gonna get rid of it, and that's all there is to it. And you're gonna pay for it yourself because this is your mess, not mine!"

Her heart felt like it was cracking. This was his grandchild they were talking about. Didn't he know this baby had a heartbeat and tiny fingers and a little pug nose?

Of course he didn't know. She hadn't known herself until she'd seen the ultrasound. And she hadn't even told him how far along she was. She cleared her throat and hugged the pillow tighter. "The thing is, I'm further along than you might be thinking. I'm twenty-one weeks. Five months pregnant."

He shot to his feet like a Jack-in-the-Box. "Five months!" His eyebrows knotted up, his mouth practically snarled.

She looked down at her arms, curled around the pillow.

"You've been hiding this for five months?"

"Not hiding, Daddy. Just deciding."

"Ain't no decision to make, girl! We can't afford no baby, and I'm not having some squalling kid living here." He turned and rubbed his stubbled jaw, mumbling something Linn was glad she couldn't hear.

He hadn't mentioned adoption. Maybe it wouldn't seem so bad to him. He wouldn't be put out. He wouldn't have to pay for anything. Maybe she'd use his insurance, but Natalie would take care of the rest, wouldn't she?

"I know I'm not ready to be a mom yet. I wasn't thinking of keeping the baby."

"Well, that's good, but you still have to get rid of it yourself." He crossed his arms and stared at her from across the room. The light from the TV flickered on his face as the program went to a commercial break. He took a swig from the bottle.

"How could you let this happen?" he asked. "How many times did I warn you? But did you listen? No, just as stubborn and rebellious as you ever were. Not at all like Jilly. It was always you giving me the trouble."

If her heart cracked before, it shattered now. It was always about Jillian. Perfect Jillian. She blinked back the tears. "Stop it. That's not fair. Jillian wasn't perfect, you know."

"She wouldn't have gone and got herself knocked up, that's for sure! She wouldn't have hooked up with some man near old enough to be her dad neither."

No, Jillian only married a man who killed her. Linn's insides clenched tightly. "Maybe I wouldn't have either if I had a real dad," she muttered.

"What? What did you say, girl?"

She looked at him then, fear in her gut. His hair stuck up like he'd just ran his fingers through it. He looked like a madman. She should just shut her mouth before she regretted it.

"You got something to say, I can see. Go ahead. Tell me. I'm dying to know." Sarcasm again.

Fine. She would. "Ever since Jillian died, you've done nothing but drink and yell and shout. And even before, you weren't much of a dad. Maybe I'm not the perfect daughter like you've always wanted, but I'm the only one that's left. Why can't you see that?" She swiped the tears off her cheeks.

"Why, you ungrateful brat."

His tone, deceptively calm, drew her eyes to him. It scared the snot out of her.

He swatted at the nearest thing on the shelf beside him, a clay ashtray she'd made him in third grade. It fell to the wood floor and cracked into two pieces.

"I've let you live here. I've put food on the table and clothes on your back . . ." He cursed, then punched the wall beside him.

She pulled the pillow tightly to her stomach as if she could shield her baby from him.

"I'm not talking about *things,* Dad."

"What, the little girl didn't get what she wanted? You always was spoiled. Too good to live in this house. Clothes I bought was never good enough for you. Always complaining about something."

"Not like Jillian, right?" She could do sarcasm, too. She'd learned from the best.

"Leave her out of this! You have no right to talk about her with that tone."

"She was my sister. I lost her, too."

"You don't know nothing about loss! I lost your mother and my Jilly. You don't have a clue." He turned from her and brought a hand to his face. If she didn't know better, she'd think he was crying. But he never cried. Except when Jillian had died. He'd lost his child, and he was asking her to willingly kill her own.

"And now you want me to lose my baby."

"It's not a baby. It's a . . . a bunch of tissue or something!"

"No, it's not, Dad. I've seen pictures. My baby has fingers and toes and a heartbeat."

He turned, and she thought his eyes looked glassy in the dim light. "Stop it! You're getting rid of it, or you're getting out of this house. I'm not raising another kid."

"I never asked you to. You never even let me tell you what I want to do."

"You think you're so smart. Just because you got that scholarship—"

He stopped so abruptly, she knew what was coming next.

"You have to use that scholarship this year. You're going to college in two months. You can't do that with a baby."

"I know I can't." She drew a deep breath. "I was thinking of giving the baby up for adoption. I've already found a woman who wants—"

"That's crazy! How can you go off to school pregnant? You're being stupid, Linn!"

"No, I'm not. If you'll just listen. There's this really neat lady who wants to adopt the baby. You should meet her, Dad, and see—"

"The only thing I see is a girl who made a stupid mistake and found a stupid answer. You're going to college in August, and that's all there is to it."

"It's not your decision."

"You live in this house and eat my food. Don't tell me it's not my decision."

She might live in his house, but she bought more groceries than he did. He was in no mood for her to throw that in his face, though. She closed her eyes. This was going as badly as she'd feared. What could she say to change his mind?

"I can go to college in January. Would it really make that big a difference?"

"You're not putting off school." He glared until she looked away.

Was he that eager to be rid of her? She bit the inside of her lip. "I'll earn my keep. I'll cook and clean and do laundry."

"You're getting rid of it, Linn, and that's all I have to say about it."

Who did he think he was? It was her body, her baby. He couldn't tell her what to do. She clamped her jaw down before the thoughts came out. She had to handle this carefully, or she'd find herself living on the streets. Maybe she should just be quiet and let it drop for the night. If he had a night to sleep on it, he might be in a better frame of mind once the shock wore off.

Maybe she could even have Natalie over for supper or something. If he met her, maybe he'd change his mind. And Natalie could explain how it was a real baby, not a—

"When are you going to do it?"

"What?"

"That abortion clinic is back open now. The sooner you get it done, the better."

She winced. How could he treat it like this? Like it was some thing you check off a to-do list. It was her baby. Didn't he care about it?

But why should he care about her baby when he'd never cared about her? Why had she hoped for anything from him?

"I can't do it, Dad." The words just fell from her lips, and she regretted it the moment they were out. It would have been better to dodge his question and pick up the conversation later.

He put his work-roughened hands on his hips. "Don't you argue with me, girl."

"I'm not a girl anymore. I'm a woman, and it's my decision, not yours." Her words quivered like a big bowl of Jell-O.

One side of his nose curled up. "You live in my house, you abide by my rules."

"Let's just think about it for a while. It's too important a decision to make on a whim."

"Answer's no!"

He was so stubborn. She knew he'd never go back on his answer once he'd given it. He'd rather die than change his mind. Jillian was the only one who'd ever been able to change his mind. His precious Jillian.

"I'm not doing it. I've already made up my mind. I'm going to have this baby—and it is a baby, Dad. Natalie's going to adopt it, and I'll go to college next semester."

"Ain't gonna happen. You get rid of it, or you find yourself someplace else to stay."

Her stomach dropped to the floor. She was sunk now. He'd said the words; he'd never go back on them. Old man had too much pride to change his mind. She closed her eyes. Where would she go? She'd saved enough to spend a few nights at a hotel if she drove to Alpine and stayed someplace cheap.

What had she gotten herself into? She should have brought Natalie along. Maybe it would have made a difference. It was too late now. She'd never been out on her own before. She didn't make enough at Bubba's to live anywhere in Jackson. Property was a mint around here, thanks to all the rich people moving in from all over.

Maybe she could find a couple roommates and stay over in Alpine, where things were a little cheaper. She'd need time to get that together, though.

She looked at her dad and hated the way he looked at her. As if she were road kill he had to clean up off the pavement. Why did it still hurt after all these years?

"Can I at least have a few weeks to find someplace to stay?" She tried to inject the right amount of humility and gratitude in her voice.

"No way."

Her heart sunk. She gritted her teeth. What? Was he just going to toss her out on her duff? "I need some time—"

"Listen here, missy, if you want to stay here, you get rid of the problem. If not, you can get your things and leave right now."

"Now?" It was irrational, even for her dad. Who kicked their pregnant daughter out of the house at eight-thirty at night?

He turned and walked back to the kitchen. She heard the fridge door suck open and heard him open another beer. She had to think. She had to get him to give her until morning at least. Did the bus run to Alpine at night? One night at a Jackson hotel would eat up all her savings. Especially with the peak season rates.

She got up and followed him to the kitchen. He sat at the kitchen table, his face lit by the florescent light in the center of the ceiling. He didn't look at her when she stopped in the doorway. What could she say? What would Natalie say? She was so good at explaining things. Linn had been stupid to do this alone. She'd messed it up good.

"All right, Daddy, I'll leave if that's the way you want it. But can I have 'til morning? I don't know if I can get a ride to—"

"Stop your sniveling, Linn. I told you to leave tonight, and I ain't changing my mind unless you agree to my terms."

"Be reasonable—"

"Reasonable is not getting knocked up when you're nineteen about to go off to college. Reasonable is making a better choice about it when you do. Don't tell me to be reasonable. I'm done talking." He got up from the table, his chair scraping on the floor. He snatched up his bottle and left the kitchen. As he did, he tossed some words over his shoulder. "If you're not out by ten, I'll be tossing your things on the front lawn."

CHAPTER
TWENTY-THREE

Natalie finished filling out one form from the stack of papers and set it facedown beside her. This was her least favorite aspect of the job. The paper trail. No clients had come in yet this morning, but the incessant ringing of the phone had her nerves jangling. She was glad Amanda was at the front desk taking all the calls; otherwise, she wouldn't have gotten a thing done. Even worse was that she had trouble concentrating; she was already getting excited about the baby. She was starting to wonder if it was a boy or a girl and what he or she would be like.

The phone rang again, and she heard Amanda answer.

"Miss C, call on line one," Amanda called from the front room.

"Thanks." She picked up the phone and punched the lit button. "This is Miss C."

"It's me, Natalie."

It was only three words, but the tone spoke volumes. "Linn, what's wrong?"

"Dad kicked me out last night."

"What? Because you told him about the baby?"

She gave a wry laugh. "Yeah, I told him, but he, like, didn't take it so good."

"Where are you? Are you OK?"

"I'm at Kayley's house, one of the other waitresses at Bubba's, but I gotta get out of here because her mom's coming home from work in an hour, and she'd pitch a fit because Kayley's grounded."

Natalie ran her fingers through her hair. Linn had said her dad would go ballistic, but Natalie had hoped she was wrong.

"I'm scared, Natalie. I don't have anywhere to stay, and I only have enough money to spend one night in a hotel. They're so expensive here, and the bus line doesn't go to Alpine, and I can't ride my bike all the way there, since my job's here—"

"Calm down, Linn. It's going to be all right." She tried to inject the same calm assurance that had settled many of her nervous clients down. Could she offer Linn a place to stay? Did she have any choice?

"Here's what we're going to do. I'm going to come and pick you up and take you to my house. You can stay there until we figure something else out, OK?"

She heard Linn sniffle, then a round of silence.

"Linn, did you hear me?"

Another sniffle. "Why are you being so nice to me? First you agree to raise my baby for me, now you're giving me a place to stay. I don't get it. I don't have anything to offer you."

Bless her heart. Natalie's insides went as soft as freshly baked bread. "Honey, I care about you because God cares about you. I don't want anything from you. I just want to help you."

"But why?"

She looked at her watch. "I'd love to explain it to you, but let's do it later, OK? We need to get you out of there so we don't get Kayley in trouble. What's the address?"

Linn told her she was just north of Miller Park, but that she could ride her bike over. "But don't you have your things, your clothes and everything?"

She said she did, and Natalie insisted on picking her up. She left the center and made the short trip to Kayley's house. It was a beaten-up shack of a house, with missing shutters and grass growing through the cracks in the sidewalk. Linn came through the door with a giant shopping bag and a book bag slung on one shoulder. Natalie got out of the car and grabbed the bike off the porch. She patted Linn's shoulder as they piled the things inside the SUV.

Once they hopped in, Natalie took a good look at Linn. Her face was devoid of makeup, and her hair needed a good washing. Natalie had the urge to take her home and pamper her all day. But that couldn't happen today. "I'll take you to the house, but I have to get back to work because I have a client coming in to see me at ten-thirty."

"I appreciate this. I'm hoping I can find a couple roommates to share someplace cheap with. I'll start asking around tomorrow at work."

"We'll just take one day at a time. I have an extra bedroom, and you won't be in the way."

Linn turned her face to the side window, but Natalie could see her lashes blinking rapidly. She pretended not to notice.

They pulled up Rodeo Drive and curved around and up the butte. She depressed the gas to give it enough juice to make it up the incline. After they pulled into the drive, she helped Linn into the house with her meager belongings.

"Help yourself to the fridge and TV, whatever. You can reach me at the center if you need anything. I'll be home around six-thirty with the boys. You don't work tonight?"

"No."

"Good, it'll give us a chance to talk." She hugged Linn, noticing the girl hugged back for the first time. Her lips tilted as her heart warmed. "Everything's going to be OK."

"Thanks, Natalie. I don't know how I can ever pay you back."

Natalie pulled back. "You can take good care of yourself and that baby. Deal?"

Linn nodded.

Throughout the day, Linn was constantly on her mind. When she picked up the boys from her mom's, she explained that Linn was temporarily staying at her house. The boys were excited, but she saw the concern in her mother's eyes. Perhaps it wasn't the ideal situation, but it was necessary, at least for the time being. She could hardly let Linn live on the streets.

When she arrived home and opened the door, a slight aroma of garlic assailed her. She walked through to the kitchen, following Taylor and Alex, who were calling Linn's name.

"I'm in here," Linn called.

They entered the dining room, where Linn had covered the table with a tablecloth and set the table.

"It's ready, if you're hungry," Linn said.

"Linn. You didn't have to do all this."

"I didn't have anything else to do, and I want to be helpful. I cooked at home all the time. I'm, like, not such a great cook, though."

Natalie slid her purse off her shoulder and walked into the kitchen. A pot of spaghetti sauce bubbled on the stovetop.

"Yummy, spaghetti!" Alex said.

"Go wash your hands, boys." Natalie lifted the pot from the stove and poured it over the top of the cooked pasta while Linn removed a pan of garlic toast from the oven. "It smells wonderful."

As they ate, the conversation was lively, and Linn seemed to bask in the praise from Natalie and the boys. She didn't know how long Linn would be staying, but it was good to see Linn intended to be helpful while she was here.

After dinner, Linn insisted on loading the dishwasher while Natalie helped Alex with his Lego house. By the time she was finished, she was a whole hour ahead of her usual evening routine. She was glad, since she had a lot to talk about with Linn. There was the housing issue, the health insurance dilemma, and the problem of Kyle. Natalie knew she needed him to be her attorney, but Linn wouldn't be one bit happy about it.

After she shooed the boys out to the backyard to play hide-and-seek, she poured Linn a glass of root beer and joined her in the living room. Linn's eyes were glued to the *Jeopardy* game on TV.

"Thanks," Linn said when Natalie handed her the soda.

Natalie settled on the opposite end of the couch. "I sent the boys outside so we'd have a few minutes to talk. I'm sorry your dad reacted the way he did."

Linn shrugged. "I knew he'd get all mad. I just didn't think he'd toss me out right that minute, though, you know? I thought he'd at least let me work something out."

Linn went quiet then, and Natalie thought the pain of her father's act must be hitting home. She tried to put herself in Linn's place and imagine what it would feel like to have her father wash her hands of her so easily.

"He wanted me to get an abortion." The words were barely above a whisper. "He would've let me stay if I had an abortion." Linn looked at her then, tears shining in her dark eyes.

Natalie's stomach clenched. "How did that make you feel?"

Linn's eyes fixed on *Jeopardy* again. "I've never felt he cared for me. Especially after Jilly's death. But when he insisted I kill my baby . . . what's worse than that? And then to throw me out of the house, pregnant and all." Linn caught her lip in her teeth as she blinked back tears.

"It's a bitter pill to swallow, Linn. You can't change your dad, but you can focus on taking care of yourself and the baby. You're doing the right thing."

She nodded. "I know. And I don't need him anyway. I think it's better to be away from him."

It was a sad thing for a girl to feel about her father, but Natalie suspected she might be right. Under the right conditions, she felt Linn could blossom into something special. Her father only filled her with self-doubt and insecurities.

They talked about doctors and health insurance for a while, and Natalie insisted Linn make an appointment with a doctor the next day. They decided to use the obstetrician Natalie had used for Taylor and Alex.

When the medical details were covered, Natalie knew she had to address the other issue. And this one was not going to be easy.

"I wanted to talk to you about the adoption process." Natalie took a sip from her soda, more to stall than anything else. "I have a book you can read if you want. It cleared up a lot of details for me."

When Linn expressed an interest, Natalie pulled it from the bookshelf and handed it to Linn. "The first thing I need to do is select an adoption attorney. Unfortunately, I've found there's only one in Jackson Hole."

Linn flipped through the pages.

"The nearest adoption attorney other than that one is hours away."

"So use the one here."

Natalie cleared her throat. "Well, that's what I was thinking. I really couldn't drive four hours away every time I had an appointment. I'd miss an entire workday."

Linn didn't seem to see the problem. Surely she knew her brother-in-law was an adoption attorney. She was too busy reading snippets from the book to put it together.

"Hey, listen to this," Linn said. She read a fact about birth mothers that Natalie remembered reading weeks ago.

"There's all kinds of interesting details in there," Natalie said. She had to tell Linn about Kyle, and she wished she hadn't handed Linn that book yet.

"Linn, here's the thing. That adoption attorney, the only one in Jackson is, well, he's Kyle Keaton. Your brother-in-law."

Linn's head shot up then. "What? You're not, like, going to use him, are you?"

Natalie didn't know what to say. Had Linn heard anything she'd just said? Surely she wouldn't expect Natalie to drive four hours for every appointment just so Kyle wouldn't be involved. "Linn, I know this must come as a surprise to you. But please take a minute and think about what I'm saying. Kyle is the only attorney in town suited to handle adoptions. The nearest one is—"

"I heard what you said! I don't want him involved in this!" Linn crossed her arms over her chest, and Natalie thought she looked every bit of the teenager she was.

Her mind spun for ideas, angles that might make a nineteen-year-old pregnant girl with a grudge understand. "I know you have bitter feelings toward Kyle, but—"

"He killed my sister!" Linn's eyes narrowed stubbornly.

Natalie sighed. This was going even worse than she'd thought. She injected her tone with a measure of patience. "If we're going to work out all the details of this adoption, we're going to have to communicate better than this, Linn. Will you please let me finish my thought, and then you can respond, OK?"

Linn only looked back at the TV.

Natalie took her silence as acquiescence. "First of all, I want you to consider—and this is going to be hard—but please, just consider for a moment that maybe Kyle isn't the monster you believe he is."

Linn stiffened but still stared at the TV.

"I know you think he killed your sister, but isn't it possible it was just an accident? A terrible, unthinkable accident? He was driving, and he ran a light. Careless, yes. But murder?"

Linn's jaw worked, and Natalie knew she was only making her angrier by the moment. But the girl needed to face reality. She'd needed someone to blame for Jilly's death, and Kyle was the convenient one.

"Kyle was only distracted by the . . . conversation he was having with your sister. He never meant to—"

"You've already met with him." The accusation was in her voice and her eyes.

"It wasn't like that. I haven't formally met with him, but we've been talking, and I really think—"

"What are you, like, dating him or something?" She had enough sass in her voice to fill a canyon. "You said you weren't."

She gritted her own teeth. *Patience, Nat.* "No, Linn. I'm not dating him."

"'Cause he cheated on my sister, you know. He was a two-timing jerk, and I don't care what you say. He wanted her dead so he could run off with his girlfriend!"

Natalie's breath caught in her lungs. It wasn't true, was it? Kyle cheating on his wife? She couldn't reconcile that with the Kyle she was beginning to know.

"Yeah, he didn't tell you that part, did he?"

Natalie shifted in her seat and tried to gather her thoughts. This last piece of news had shaken her more than it should. Why did she care so much if Kyle had cheated on his wife? What was it to her? Maybe an overdeveloped sense of righteous anger from a woman who'd been duped by her own husband?

But it wasn't anger she felt. That yucky feeling curdling in her stomach felt more like supreme disappointment. And there would be only one reason for that. She shrugged off the thought. Regardless of what Kyle had done, she still had no other option for an attorney. Linn was just going to have to adjust to the idea.

"Look, I know you feel Kyle has hurt you and your family. I'm sorry about that. Truly. But I still have no other option. You won't hardly have to see him, anyway, and he's offered a huge discount because of the situation—"

"He knows it's me?" Linn drilled her with a glare.

"No, I haven't mentioned you by name. He only knows it's a client of mine."

Linn snapped her head back toward the TV. "Then why's he giving you a discount?"

"I guess he supports what we're trying to do at the center. It's a substantial discount, and it would really help."

"Like you need help." She gestured around the great room. "You're obviously loaded. You can afford any attorney you want."

Natalie gave a wry laugh. Linn had no clue. Nothing could be further from the truth. But then she remembered the tiny shack that Linn had lived in with her father. It was only natural that she'd take one look at this place and assume Natalie had it made.

"Don't let the house fool you. I only have it because my ex-husband owned a bank, and I got it free and clear in the divorce."

Linn shifted, and Natalie thought she saw something flicker on the girl's face. Maybe she was starting to make sense.

"I don't earn much at the center. If this house weren't paid off, there's no way I'd be able to afford it. I don't have a bunch of money sitting around, and I was really starting to wonder how I would be able to afford the adoption until Kyle offered to do it for less."

"So, you're saying if I don't want you to use Kyle, you're not going to adopt the baby?"

"Calm down, Linn, that's not what—"

"That's how it sounded to me. It sounds like you're threatening to back out if I don't go along with what you want!"

"I'm not backing out. I'm only saying we don't have another option."

"Well, you're not the one who holds all the cards. Maybe I don't want you to have this baby anymore!"

The patio door few open. "Mom, Taylor's being a big baby!"

Taylor rushed through behind his brother, crying. "Alex is cheating!"

Natalie got up and went to mediate the sibling bickering. If only there were someone to mediate the conversation between her and Linn.

CHAPTER
TWENTY-FOUR

Linn tugged on her Bubba's T-shirt and slid into her favorite pair of jeans. She couldn't believe she'd hung around in pajamas all morning. It had been so quiet when she'd awakened, she'd known Natalie and the boys must have been gone. She'd been relieved at first.

But then as the morning crawled by and her mind replayed the argument she'd had with Natalie, she wished Natalie were home. Anything to stop the anxiety buzzing through her.

What had she done last night? She'd practically told Natalie she didn't want her to adopt the baby. Linn rubbed her rounded belly with her hand. *Stupid, stupid.* As if she had women waiting in line to adopt her baby. As if she had anyplace else to live right now.

Why had she run off to her room last night like a spoiled brat? She went to the bathroom she was sharing with the boys and pulled her hairbrush through her hair. Maybe Natalie wouldn't want the baby now. Maybe Linn had ruined everything with her big mouth and bad attitude. She had a chance to place her baby with his or her real brothers and a loving mom, and she'd probably blown it.

Would it really be so awful if Natalie used Kyle? What she'd said about Jilly's death being an accident had struck a chord with her. Was it possible Linn's family had overreacted or been too quick to blame him?

Regardless, she'd determined one thing this morning. If she wanted Natalie to adopt her baby—and she did, more than anything in the whole world—she was going to have to compromise about Kyle. He already ruined their lives once. There was no way she was going to let him stand in the way of her baby's future.

Natalie hadn't focused on anything all day. All she could think about was the argument she'd had with Linn last night. She should've waited to have the conversation about Kyle. What had she been thinking? The girl had just been kicked out of her home by her father. Her whole future was up in the air, and Natalie had gone and heaped another problem on top of her.

She shook her head. *Not the brightest move, Nat.* She looked at her watch, pleased to see that it was almost time to go. She wanted to resolve things between her and Linn tonight, even if they couldn't come to an agreement about Kyle.

When closing time rolled around, Natalie left to get the boys. Her mom wanted to talk, but the boys were eager to get home to Linn. "I'll call you later, OK?" she said. She knew her mom was probably concerned about her taking in Linn, but what was the harm? Once her family got to know Linn, they'd see she wasn't some leech coming to suck up all their time and money.

When they walked in the door, the boys ran to the kitchen. "Linn, we drew a picture for you!" Taylor called.

"Hush, dummy, it's a surprise!" Alex said.

"Alex. Apologize."

He mumbled, "Sorry," with less sincerity than Natalie would have liked.

They entered the kitchen, but Linn wasn't there. A stone formed in Natalie's stomach. What if she'd left? What if she really didn't want Natalie to have the baby anymore?

Her gaze darted around the kitchen, around the living room for some sign of Linn. Nothing.

"Where's she at, Mom?" Alex asked.

"I don't know." Maybe she had to work tonight. But Natalie thought she only worked until five today.

Upstairs. She'd check her room. Her feet flew as rapidly as her mind. What if Linn had taken off with no thought of where she'd go? What if she ended up staying with people she hardly knew? She could unknowingly put herself in danger. And all because Natalie had bombarded her with too much.

And what about the baby? If Natalie had decided anything today, it was this: she loved and wanted Linn's baby. She'd begun to think of the baby as hers and was looking forward to raising another child more than anything.

Her feet took the stairs two at a time, then she entered the spare room. Her breath left her body. There on the dresser were Linn's pajamas and her purse.

"She's outside, Mom!" Alex's voice called from downstairs.

Natalie took a minute to gather herself. Everything was fine. Linn was fine; the baby was fine. Linn must not be too angry if she hadn't left.

Natalie trotted down the stairs and slid out the patio door. The boys and Linn stood around the grill, where Linn was tending half a dozen hamburger patties. She turned as the door slid open.

"Hi, there." Natalie tested the waters and was relieved when Linn smiled.

"Hi. Hope you all like hamburgers."

"I like mine plain," Alex said.

Linn laughed. "That's so boring." She tousled his hair.

The picnic table had already been set with paper plates and cups. "You don't have to cook dinner every night, Linn. You're going to spoil us."

"I don't mind."

When Natalie retrieved the condiments from the refrigerator, she saw a freshly made salad and pulled it out, too.

They ate together on the patio, exchanging quips about their days. Linn made the boys laugh with her exaggerations about the tourists who ate at Bubba's. Cleanup after dinner was a snap because of all the paper ware, so by the time Natalie fixed one of Alex's broken trucks, it was still too early for baths.

They settled on the couch and watched *Finding Nemo*. Afterward, Natalie helped Taylor with his bath while Alex took a shower, then she tucked them in bed.

When she went downstairs, Linn had poured her a glass of Diet Pepsi and turned the TV to a sitcom. Natalie sank onto the couch with a weary sigh and felt an awkward silence settle around the room. She felt the need to address last night's conversation, but wasn't sure how to bring it up without causing another argument. Linn had been her old self since she'd been home, but how did she feel now about the adoption? She was afraid to ask.

"I'm sorry about what I said last night," Linn said.

The words took Natalie aback and warmed a place deep inside her. "No, Linn, I'm the one who's sorry. I shouldn't have asked you about Kyle last night, not after the day you'd had."

"I didn't mean it." She shook her head as if for emphasis, and her eyes seemed to be a bit glassy. "I want you to adopt my baby more than anything. If you need to use Kyle to get it done, then I can live with that."

Natalie could hardly believe what she was hearing. She'd hoped to reconcile with Linn, but she hadn't imagined the girl would change her mind about Kyle. "Thanks. That's very mature of you."

"So you still want my baby?" Fear flickered in her chocolate-brown eyes.

It hadn't occurred to Natalie that Linn might be worrying about that. Judging by the look on her face, she'd been stewing about it all day. She reached out for Linn's hand and gave it a squeeze. "Oh, honey, more than anything. Don't ever doubt that."

Linn fell into her arms, and Natalie held her. "I was so worried," Linn said. "I was stupid to say that last night."

"It's OK. I wasn't thinking straight myself." She held Linn for a moment more before the girl pulled away and wiped her eyes on her shirt-tail. "Stupid hormones."

Natalie asked if Linn had set a doctor's appointment, but Linn shook her head no.

"Tell you what. Tomorrow, you set that appointment, and I'll make an appointment for this week to get the adoption process started."

Linn nodded, her lips tipping in a smile. "It's really going to happen. My baby's going to have a cool family, and I'm still going to get to go to college next semester and finally get out of this rinky-dink town. I feel like celebrating!"

Maybe a celebration was in order. "That's a terrific idea. Let's plan a little party with just us and the boys. Do you work Saturday?"

"I get off at four."

"Perfect. Keith is bringing the boys home at two, so we can have a special dinner together."

Some emotion Natalie couldn't define crossed Linn's face.

"What is it? Do you have other plans?"

"No, I was just . . . This is Keith's weekend with the boys?"

Natalie was baffled by Linn's dampened enthusiasm. "Yeah, but he's only going to have them for part of Saturday, so it won't interfere with our celebration dinner. Sound like a plan?"

Her face cleared, and her sunny smile came out. "Sounds like a plan."

They talked the rest of the night about their celebration dinner and Linn's plans for the future. Whatever had come over Linn disappeared as quickly as it had come. By the time Natalie went to bed, she was so excited about the future that she lay awake for over an hour.

It turned out their plans for the celebration dinner had to be put off, since Natalie couldn't get an appointment with Kyle until the end of the following Friday. Linn's appointment with Dr. Hart was scheduled for the same day, and they had squeezed her in because of how much time had passed in her pregnancy already. At nearly twenty-four weeks, Linn definitely looked pregnant, with her belly pooching out and resting snugly against her T-shirts.

Nat had desperately wanted to go to the appointment with her, but she wanted to get the adoption plans underway. She gave Linn her insurance card and made her promise to call if they decided to do an ultrasound. For that, she would leave her appointment early if she had to.

They'd planned the celebration dinner for that night, and Natalie thought that was perfect, since both of them had their appointments that day. She was eagerly awaiting a chance to talk with Linn about the doctor's appointment when she got home. She breathed a prayer for a healthy baby.

On her way home from Kyle's office, she'd stop and pick up the steaks and potatoes and some balloons for good measure. They had so much to be excited about and thankful for. The boys had insisted on making signs to hang up around the house. Taylor drew a little figure with a big head and hair that stuck out on the ends. "That's our baby, mommy," he'd said. Alex's artwork was more complex and was labeled with big block letters spelling out "Congratulations!"

When it came time to go to Kyle's office, Natalie eagerly left the center and made the short drive. His office building was on the second floor of the Ellis Building above Pica's Mexican Restaurant. She pulled into a slot directly below his office and took the stairs up to the wooden balcony that rimmed the upper floor.

When she entered the office, an older woman with hair as black as soot greeted her from behind a desk. "Good afternoon."

Nat had seen the woman around town a few times but didn't know her by name. "Hi, I have a four o'clock appointment with Kyle."

"Natalie." Kyle peeked out from what she assumed was his office doorway. "Come on in."

Natalie slipped into his office, noting that it was very tidy and very small. His desk took up half the room, and he seemed to take up the other half. She slid into a chair across from the desk and told herself that she was nervous about the adoption. Not about the man behind the desk.

"Big day for you," Kyle said. "You ready to get the ball rolling?"

She nodded, unable to stop a smile from curling her lips. "This is all so new to me."

"Don't worry. I'll guide you every step of the way."

Kyle explained what they would need to do, starting with lots of paperwork. He asked about her client, and Natalie realized she would have to tell him who it was if he was going to do the adoption plan. She bit her lip. How would he react to that? Would it change his mind about helping her? Linn's family had been nothing but cruel to him since Jillian's death.

"What's wrong?" he asked.

She looked down at her purse resting on her lap. She twisted the straps in her fingers. "I've never given you the name of my client—the birth mother. I suppose you're going to need that information sooner or later."

"This is a small town, and believe me, we've arranged adoptions with birth mothers we know. We'll handle everything carefully and confidentially."

"That's not what I'm worried about." Her mouth felt as dry as sawdust. "I'm more concerned about how you're going to react." Before he could speak, she continued, "The birth mother is Linn."

Kyle's mouth parted slightly, lines of concern furrowing between his brows. If his silence was any indication, she'd taken him completely off-guard. The crinkles at the corner of his eyes disappeared completely.

"Linn?" His eyes softened until she thought they seemed to glaze over. He looked down at the paperwork he'd begun.

"I know this must come as a shock. I would've told you before, but there's client confidentiality, and I didn't want to—"

He held up a hand, palm out. "I understand." He leaned back in his padded chair and steepled his hands. "Poor kid. She must be scared."

She'd expected anger or bitterness, not this. His compassion stirred something in her that made her squirm in her chair. "She's doing OK now."

"Ed must be having a fit."

It took Natalie a minute to realize he was talking about Linn's father. She explained how Linn's dad had given her an ultimatum and kicked her out of the house, and how Linn was now living with Nat temporarily.

He slowly shook his head.

Immediately, her walls of defense went up. "She had no place else to go. I know it's probably not wise for a birth mother and adoptive mother to live under the same roof, but . . . really. Well, what else was I supposed to do?"

"You are something else, Natalie."

She didn't know what to say. Didn't quite know what he meant.

"First you agree to adopt her baby, and now you take her in because she has no place to go. If every Christian put her feet to her faith the way you do, the world would be a different place."

She felt heat coil in her neck and wondered if it was now flowing into her cheeks. She could see from the expression on his face that he meant every word.

"I've embarrassed you. I'm sorry, but I wanted you to know that." He paused, folding his hands on the desktop. "Thank you for taking care of Linn. Jillian loved her little sister very much. She would have wanted someone like you to take her under your wings."

Natalie felt her own eyes glazing over and looked down at her purse again. She swallowed past the lump in her throat.

"Does she need anything? Is there anything I can do to help?"

She breathed a laugh. "You are helping. You've agreed to give me a much-needed discount."

He absently straightened the stack of papers on his desk. "In light of what I know now, I can't charge you for the adoption plan, Natalie."

"No, Kyle, that's not why I told you."

"I want to do this. For Linn. For Jillian."

The lump in her throat felt like a whole can of Play-Doh. She never dreamed, never expected . . . "Thank you."

The awkward moment stretched, and she felt a connection with Kyle. She was adopting what would have been his niece if Jillian were still alive. She wondered if the connection she felt could ever evolve into anything significant.

Linn's words from the week before thundered in her ears. *He cheated on my sister, you know. He was a two-timing jerk, and I don't care what you say. He wanted her dead so he could run off with his girlfriend!*

Natalie could easily discount the last part. She already knew enough about Kyle to know that couldn't be true. But maybe he'd had an affair. Maybe that's why he felt so much guilt over Jillian's death. Maybe that's what they'd been arguing about in the car when he'd had the accident.

As they got the paperwork underway, Natalie decided it made sense that Kyle had had an affair. It would account for his self-blame over his wife's death and explain the antagonism Linn's family felt toward him. She didn't want to think it of him, but she'd learned the hard way that it can happen to just about anybody, given the right set of circumstances. No one would have suspected her ex-husband of being unfaithful either, and he had managed to keep it a secret for months. An ugly mass of hurt surfaced, and she shoved it away. It was all in the past now. No sense dredging up ancient history.

After the appointment with Kyle, she picked up the boys and headed toward the grocery. While she drove, she determined to keep her head when it came to Kyle. It would be hard enough to trust any man again, but she would never put herself into a relationship with a man who'd already proven himself untrustworthy. Her heart couldn't take that kind of betrayal again.

CHAPTER
TWENTY-FIVE

Natalie flipped the steaks on the grill and checked her watch for the dozenth time. Why was Linn's appointment taking so long? If she'd known it would go so long, she would have joined her at the doctor's office after her appointment with Kyle. She'd expected Linn to be here after she'd returned from the grocery, and now she was getting worried. Natalie had had sufficient time to start cooking, and the boys had put up all the decorations. What if something was wrong with Linn or the baby?

Oh, she should've just postponed her appointment with Kyle and gone with Linn. Maybe something *was* wrong, and Linn was there all by herself.

Don't be such a worrywart, Natalie. Doctors run late all the time, especially obstetricians. She was just getting ready to call Dr. Hart's office when she heard the front door open and shut.

"I'm out here, Linn," she called through the screened patio door. She slid the screen open, glad the boys were playing next-door with Brandon so she and Linn would have a chance to talk. Linn was wearing a smile, and everything in Natalie went limp with relief.

"Everything went OK, then?" Natalie asked.

Linn nodded. "It took forever, though." She crinkled up her nose. "And the exam was, like, so embarrassing."

"I know. Believe it or not, you'll get used to it. At least Dr. Hart is a woman."

"No kidding. I can't imagine letting a strange man do that to me. Oh, and I got to hear the heartbeat! That was so cool." Linn's excitement was contagious.

"I wish I could've been there," Natalie said. "Did you set your next appointment? Will they do an ultrasound?"

"Dr. Hart thought they should 'cause I'm so far along and 'cause of my age, I guess. They set it for next Tuesday. Can you come?"

Natalie smiled as a rush of anticipation went through her. "I wouldn't miss it. They can tell the sex now, you know." It occurred to her that maybe Linn wouldn't want to know. "Unless you don't want to know."

She shrugged. "I think it would be OK." Linn went to the grill and checked on the steaks. "Actually, it would be great." She glanced back at Natalie before turning to the steaks again. "I've kind of started a journal for the baby. You know, just thoughts and stuff I'm having while I'm pregnant. I was thinking you could, like, give it to him or her later."

Natalie's heart squeezed. "Oh, Linn. I think that's wonderful. What a beautiful gift. Someday this child will be able to read your thoughts and know how much love you had for your baby." Natalie's eyes burned.

Linn nodded but didn't turn to look at her, and Natalie wondered if she was having trouble getting her emotions in check.

Finally, Linn turned and gave a watery smile. "Would you look at me? This is supposed to be a celebration, and here I am getting all weepy."

"Linn!" Alex called as he ran to the patio. "Did you see our decorations?" Taylor followed him, his chubby little legs working hard to keep up with his brother.

"I sure did! You guys did great."

"Let's celebwate!" Taylor said.

Natalie and Linn laughed.

"I think the steaks are done," Linn said.

Natalie retrieved the baked potatoes from the oven and took the phone off the hook while Linn stacked the steaks on a plate. They'd decided to eat in the dining room, where the boys had put streamers of crepe paper around the walls.

Since the dining room opened up to the living room with the vaulted ceiling, they'd tied the balloons to the back of the chairs to keep them from getting away. Natalie had set the table with her ivory tablecloth and gotten out the delicate china she and Keith had received as wedding presents. They'd only been used a handful of times and didn't have a chip or scratch on them. Watching Taylor settle into his chair beside her, she hoped she could say the same thing by the end of the evening.

Linn took a seat next to Alex, against the wall, while Natalie distributed the steaks, cutting one in half for Alex and Taylor.

Alex picked up his fluted glass and sipped the milk from it. "This is fancy, just like TV."

She dished out the French-cut green beans, giving the boys a tiny serving, and watching Alex's nose crinkle up.

"This smells heavenly. I'm so hungry," Linn said.

"Me, too. I skipped lunch." Natalie put a hand on Taylor's as he was about to shove a bite of potato in his mouth. "Wait for prayer."

Finally, they were all settled around the table, and it grew quiet. Natalie held out her hand for Taylor, and Linn joined in until they were all connected.

"We have so much to be thankful for." She looked around the table at her boys and the young woman God had brought into their lives. "Not only has God blessed me with two wonderful boys, but He's brought you into our lives, Linn."

Though Linn looked down at her plate, Natalie could see she was pleased. "You've enriched our lives just by being you, and we're grateful we've had the chance to get to know you."

"And she plays a wicked game of Uno, too." Alex's serious expression only made the comment more comical.

Natalie chuckled, then paused a moment until the room grew serious again. "I'd like to offer a prayer of thanks now."

Everyone bowed their heads. Natalie closed her eyes and took a moment to formulate her thoughts.

"Our dearest heavenly Father. We are so grateful for the love You have for us. For keeping us safe and giving us peace and joy. Right now, we're so thankful that You've brought us together at this very special time in our lives. Thank You for making Linn the special person she is, and for helping her see the dear value of the life she carries. Thank You for this wonderful opportunity You've given me to raise another child. What an awesome responsibility. I pray that You will help the boys and me to be everything this child needs.

"Bless us now and keep us safe. Help us to bear with one another and love one another. Help us to be fully committed to doing whatever task You have for us, always keeping You first in our lives. For it's in Jesus's name we pray, Amen."

"Amen," Linn said, her glassy eyes focusing on Natalie.

Natalie picked up her goblet and held it in the air, waiting for Linn and the boys to do the same. Alex quickly caught on, but Taylor only watched with furrowed brows.

"Put your glass up, dummy," Alex said. Before Natalie could correct him, he apologized.

Taylor put his glass up as high as he could reach. "Are we gonna get the baby now?"

Linn chuckled. "No, sweetie, it's not ready to be born yet."

"And 'sides," Alex said, "we don't have no baby bed to put it in yet."

"My arm's getting tired," Taylor said.

"To Linn," Natalie said. "For her willingness to share the most precious gift in the world." Natalie started to clink her glass with Linn's, but Linn pulled back.

"And to you and the boys," Linn said. "For being willing to love and raise this baby."

Natalie and Linn shared a smile, and for a sweet moment, it felt as if their hearts were connected by a string. "Here, here." They all clinked glasses, and nobody said a word when Taylor's milk sloshed out a bit.

The boys mimicked the way Natalie and Linn took a sip from their goblets and set them down.

Before they could pick up their utensils, Linn started to get up. "Wait a minute. I have something I want to read to you. I wrote it this week in my journal." She scooted her chair out and dashed around the table and up the stairs.

"I'm hungry. Can we eat?" Alex said.

"Wait a minute. Linn has something special she wants to share."

"Where's the baby?" Taylor asked.

"It's still in Linn's tummy," Natalie said. "But in a few months the baby'll be born. Would you like to help feed the baby?"

"I will. I ain't changing no diapers, though," Alex said.

Natalie thought she heard a car pull into the drive and sighed. She didn't want their celebration interrupted. It was probably Paula or Hanna dropping by to chat. She got up and peeked out the picture window.

Keith. A ball of disappointment formed in her belly. *Shoot.* Of all the people she didn't want showing up right now, his name topped the list. He was picking up the kids tomorrow morning, so why was he here now? He got out of his car, so she walked to the front door at the base of the stairs to head him off. She swung it open as he was getting ready to ring the bell.

"Oh," Keith said. "Hi."

"Hello, Keith."

"I tried to call, but it was busy."

"We're kind of in the middle of something . . ."

Keith glanced toward the dining room, where the boys were starting to eat despite her request to wait for Linn to return.

"I didn't miss a birthday, did I?" Keith asked, referring to the balloons and crepe paper.

"No, it's something else." The boys would no doubt spill the beans about the adoption tomorrow. That was OK. She wondered briefly how he'd react. "What are you doing here? We didn't get our arrangements mixed up, did we?"

"I was wondering if I could pick the boys up a couple hours early tomorrow. I was thinking of taking them up to Jenny Lake."

"Sure, that's fine." She just wanted him gone. "We'll see you then."

"Found it!" Linn called from the top of the stairs. Natalie could hear her bounding down the steps behind her. She was about to turn and tell Linn to slow down, but she saw Keith's eyes widen, his jaw go slack. Natalie turned in the direction of his gaze.

Linn. She'd stopped three steps up from the foyer, a look of pure shock on her face. Her body frozen as if it were in a cryonic deep-freeze. All the blood had drained from her pink cheeks, leaving them pasty white. Her eyes looked as if they'd just spied a semi-truck getting ready to barrel her over. The journal slipped from her hand, clanking against the sofa table before hitting the floor.

"Lindsey . . . ," Keith rasped.

Natalie heard the word from over her shoulder.

Then the name registered. Lindsey?

Lindsey. Lindsey. She looked from Keith, then back to Linn. Inside her, fingers of dread curled in a tight fist. Why was he calling her that awful name? The name that had ripped their marriage in two? Why were they staring at each other as if they'd seen ghosts?

The horrible heaviness in her gut spread to every part of her body. It was Linn, not Lindsey. Right?

They didn't hear the question. It only bounced around her mind like a super ball gone wild. This was Linn. Her Linn. She looked back to Keith. His eyes had narrowed as he looked at Linn.

"What are you doing here?"

She looked at Linn. The girl's eyes swung crazily from Keith to Natalie. What was it on her face? Shock? Terror? Yes.

And guilt.

Oh, God. Oh, God, no.

CHAPTER
TWENTY-SIX

Paula was floating on a cloud. She'd hardly been able to make it through the evening broadcast without spilling the news to all her viewers: she was almost finished with this pokey little town. Donald had told her this afternoon that their Chicago affiliate had called while she was at lunch. They wanted to set up a time for her to come to Chicago for an interview.

She'd called immediately and set it up. Miles, the station manager, was eager to have her there; she could tell it in his voice. Next week they were flying her to the big windy city, and she could hardly wait. She looked at the little two-story wooden stores as she drove down Broadway on her way home. Next week she would be driving through downtown Chicago with its majestic skyline along the lake.

She needed to make plane reservations. She needed to get her hair trimmed and the highlights retouched. She needed a new outfit! Something classy and hip. Would they put her up in a fancy, towering hotel?

She wondered briefly what David would say. He'd been nothing but cold since their argument about her supposed affair. They had polite conversations and nothing more. He hugged his side of the bed as if her side were infested with the Black Plague.

She shrugged. His loss, not hers. Despite his righteous attitude, he was the one who owed her an apology. She'd done nothing wrong.

She pulled into the drive, her heart still flying high, as though it were filled with helium. She was so close to her dream. All her efforts were paying off. Chicago. She could hardly believe it. The temporary job would lead to a permanent one, she just knew it.

She walked in the door and followed the sounds coming from the kitchen. She didn't know how David would react to her news. She hoped he could put their differences aside long enough to be excited for her. It would be pure selfishness to do anything else.

When she walked into the kitchen, David was putting a plate into the dishwasher.

"Hi," she said, testing the waters.

He smiled at her for what seemed like the first time in weeks. "Hi, there."

She set her purse on the countertop and studied his face. "Have a good day?"

"You could say that. Want something to eat? I made a meatloaf. There's a plate for you in the fridge."

She blinked. It was usually self-service around here. Especially lately. She pulled the plate from the fridge and heated it in the microwave. "Thanks. I have some great news, too. But tell me about your day first." If it had made him this happy, she'd be glad to let him go first. She was just glad to see him back to his old self. And this good mood definitely boded well for his reaction to her news.

When her food was hot, she placed it on the bar and sat down on a stool while David leaned against the counter.

"So spill it, what happened?" Paula asked. It had to be something great to get David this excited. She hadn't seen him like this since her pregnancy. She pushed the thought away and forced a smile on her face.

"You know how Stewart has been talking about retiring the past few years," David said.

"Sure." The owner of Jackson Hole Realty was way past retirement age and had a dozen realtors working for him, but Stewart had always been a workaholic.

"You're not going to believe this. He took me to lunch today and told me he's decided to sell. He wants to move out to Colorado to be close to his kids."

He paused long enough to draw her complete attention. "Paula, he offered me ownership. Full ownership. He said he thought I could take the company to the next level."

Paula let her fork down slowly. Ownership in JH Realty? It was a wonderful opportunity. But that meant—David would have permanent roots in Jackson if he owned it.

David was watching her expectantly. Her mind worked for something to say. She had to handle this just right. "David, that's so wonderful. He must trust you enormously to leave his baby to you."

"No kidding. Stan's going to be so jealous. He thinks he's the best thing to hit JH since the low interest rate."

"Did you discuss any details?" How was she going to turn this around? She couldn't stay here. She'd suffocate if she had to live here another year, much less the rest of her life.

"He's not in a huge hurry, but he'd like to have everything done by the beginning of winter."

"That's three months away."

He pushed his glasses up. "You sound upset."

She collected herself. "It's just sooner than I expected. You have so much to get in order, so much to think about."

"What's to think about? This is my dream."

His dream? What about her dream? She'd sacrificed so much for it. She'd sacrificed her baby . . . Her breath felt as if it had caught in her lungs. She pushed the stool back and walked to the window facing the backyard.

"What about my dream?" she asked, trying to rein in her temper. "I'm happy for you, David, really, but I don't want to be stuck here forever."

The dishwasher whirred into a different cycle. "You're happy for me, but you want me to pass it up." His voice was flat. "Isn't that thoughtful."

She clenched her jaw and turned around. "You're not the only one who got an offer today, David."

That gave him pause for thought. She could almost see the wheels turning before his eyes narrowed. "Who was it? That Dante creep you've been fawning all over?"

Dante . . . ? What did the job offer have to do with him? She replayed her words in her mind. *Got an offer.* He thought she'd gotten an offer from a man? Her blood raged. *"What?"*

"Or was it someone else?"

"A man? You think I'm talking about an offer from a man?"

He began to look a little uncomfortable. But not enough. "Is that all you ever think about anymore? That stupid affair I supposedly had? I told you it wasn't true!"

His face went hard.

So did her heart. "You're never going to believe me. I'm wasting my breath."

"I knew there was something going on after you had the miscarriage. You acted so strange. I just couldn't figure it out. You were relieved, weren't you?" His voice rose. "Relieved because you wouldn't have to pretend it was my child anymore."

Her insides coiled like a snake getting ready to strike. She had acted strange. She had been hiding something. But not an affair. She couldn't tell him then, and she couldn't tell him now.

"I can see the guilt all over your face."

What could she say? She'd dug herself an awful hole, and there was no easy way out. It was better for him to believe the affair than to know the truth. He'd never forgive her for aborting her pregnancy. He wouldn't understand that it had been her choice, not his.

She walked out of the kitchen. Behind her she heard him have the last word.

"That's what I thought."

CHAPTER
TWENTY-SEVEN

Natalie looked from Keith to Linn in shock. Denial. Linn couldn't be Lindsey. She just couldn't. Lindsey was an awful woman. A hateful witch who'd stolen her husband, her life, her marriage. Lindsey was not a nineteen-year-old girl who'd become a dear friend.

"What is she doing here?" Keith asked, looking at Natalie.

"I don't understand." The words choked Natalie's throat. She was all too afraid she understood perfectly. *Please, tell me it's not true.* She silently begged it of Keith, of God, of anyone who would say it.

"I can explain," said Linn, whose face looked like terror etched in stone.

"Daddy!" Taylor called. As he got up from his chair, the balloon came loose and floated up to the chandelier.

"Dad, I thought you were coming tomorrow," Alex said, coming toward them.

The boys hugged their father.

It was too much. Natalie couldn't assimilate it all. She felt as if she were in someone else's body, as if this whole thing were happening to someone else. She wished it were.

Keith was explaining that he would be back for them in the morning.

"Boys, you can go eat," Natalie said. Alex complained briefly before obeying. The sudden silence shook the room.

Linn's hand gripped the stair railing, the bones of her knuckles standing out like white bony beads. Keith stood in the doorway, still gripping the door handle.

And Natalie stood in the middle, her heart still searching for another reason Keith may have called Linn by that awful name.

"What are you doing here?" Keith asked Linn. His jaw had gone hard, and Natalie knew he was angry.

"It . . . it's not what you think," Linn said, looking at Natalie instead of Keith.

Natalie read the fear in Linn's eyes but felt detached from it. "What is it then, Linn?" Natalie asked.

"You're pregnant," Keith said.

The words seemed out of place. Her heart froze. The baby. Keith and Linn. How long ago had Keith and Linn broken up? Her thoughts flashed back to all the conversations she'd had with Linn about the baby's father. Facts. She needed to remember facts. Linn had dated the father for almost two years. He didn't care about the baby. But did he know about the baby? She looked at Keith, whose eyes had gone wider. Her thoughts spun dizzily as a chill worked its way up her spine. *Oh, please.*

Keith swore. "You're pregnant." This time the word held revulsion. "Will someone tell me what the—what she's doing here? Is this some kind of a sick joke?"

If it was a joke, it was on Natalie, but it wasn't funny.

"I didn't mean for any of this to happen." Linn's eyes clouded with tears.

Natalie couldn't bring herself to care about Linn's pain. It was obvious by the guilt on the girl's face. She was Lindsey. She wasn't the sweet young girl Natalie had thought her to be. She wasn't the naïve girl or the self-conscious teenager. She was Lindsey. The Other Woman.

The flashbacks started. She remembered the condom falling from the pocket of Keith's pants, she remembered how she sank to the floor when he admitted to the affair, she remembered him telling her the marriage was over.

It was starting to soak in now, to feel more real, but with the reality came an ugly feeling. Just the tip of it, like the first drop of rain from gathering storm clouds. She felt the enormity of what was coming and was helpless to stop it.

"Is it mine?" Keith asked.

Natalie looked at Linn in time to see her slight nod.

Oh, God, no. How could this happen?

"How could you let this happen?" Keith said. He cursed again, slamming his hand on the door. It bounced against the wall. "I don't want it."

"I know," Linn whispered. "I was going to put it up for—"

She looked at Natalie. Adoption. Yes, well. That was all going to change, wasn't it? It was Keith's baby. Linn and Keith's baby. She wanted that baby now like she wanted a tumor.

A thought occurred to Natalie that sent suspicion careening into the wall of her stomach. Had Linn known all along who she was? Hadn't Natalie talked about Keith? She had to know. And Linn had kept it from her.

"How long have you known?" Natalie asked Linn, anger bubbling in her gut.

Linn looked at Keith as if he were going to save her the trouble of answering. Ha! He looked mad enough to tar and feather her.

"I didn't know for a long time, I swear!"

"Will somebody please tell me what's going on?" Keith grated.

Natalie held Linn's gaze for what seemed like minutes. "I'll tell you what's going on. Your little tramp has connived her way into my life. She was going to pawn your baby off on me without even telling me whose it was." Her voice had risen, shaking and out of control.

She must've gotten the boys' attention because Keith went to the table and said something to them. A moment later, they carried their fine china plates out the patio door.

Natalie turned and glared at Linn.

Lindsey.

Whoever she was.

The girl's lips quivered, but not even the tears that chased each other down her face softened Natalie. This was way beyond tears and sympathy and compassion. This was too much.

"I was afraid to tell you," Linn whispered. "I didn't mean for this to happen."

"You mean you didn't mean for me to find out. Were you just going to let me raise your and Keith's child and never tell me? That's sick, Linn."

Keith returned. "You're going to adopt Linn's baby?"

Absurdly, a gurgle of laughter bubbled up in her throat, but she strangled it. "Of course, I'm not."

"Natalie, please . . ." Linn reached out her hand.

Natalie batted it away. "Don't touch me."

"I didn't know in the beginning, I swear!" Linn said.

"When did you find out, Linn?" Natalie asked. It didn't matter now, not really. But she had to know how long she'd been played the fool.

Linn's wiped her face.

"How long?" Natalie's tone demanded an answer.

"Since that day we met at the park."

"Which one?" How many times had she taken Linn to the park with the boys? How many times had she included her in her little family? For heaven's sake, she'd taken the girl into her own home.

"That first time," Linn said. "The first time I came here and saw the house."

Natalie thought back to that day. It seemed forever ago, but when was it? It was the day after the bomb had gone off at the clinic. Natalie had been stewing about the news coverage that day. It had been May. She felt her jaw harden, her teeth squeeze together.

"That was three months ago," Natalie said.

"Please don't be mad, Natalie. I swear I didn't mean to—"

She laughed then. At the absurdity of Linn's request. At the absurdity of this whole situation. *Don't be mad. I've only slept with your husband,*

*broken up your marriage, and tried to pawn off our love child on you. Please
don't be mad.*

She looked at Keith. He had a look on his face she'd never seen before. Did he think she'd gone mad? Maybe she had. Had anyone else on
this planet ever been subjected to such a mess? She was entitled to a little
madness. What had she done to deserve this? *What have I done, God?*

"Why didn't you tell me about the baby?" Keith drilled Linn with
a look.

Linn sniffed. "You didn't want it."

"That's right, I didn't. So why'd you get pregnant to begin with?"

"I wasn't trying to!"

"You should've had an abortion then. Look how far along you are!
I don't want another child." He ran his hand through his hair. "It's not
too late, is it? You can still have an abortion."

This wasn't happening. Her ex-husband and his mistress, standing
in front of her, fighting about the child they'd conceived. Natalie put her
hands over her ears and closed her eyes. She just wanted them gone.
Both of them.

"Get out," Natalie said. "Get out." She pulled her hands away from
her ears. The two ex-lovers were still exchanging words, Keith's heated,
Linn's regretful. They didn't seem to hear Natalie.

"Get out! Both of you, just get out!"

Keith looked at her as if just realizing she still stood there.

She looked at Lindsey. "Get your things. You're leaving." She looked
at Keith and pulled the door from his deadened fingers. "Go." Her tone
brooked no argument.

He looked back at Lindsey. "You figure it out. I don't want anything
to do with this baby."

When he left, Natalie closed the door behind him with stunning
calm. As she turned, her eyes caught sight of the balloon that had
crawled across the dining room ceiling and was now flying out of reach
to the highest peak of the vaulted ceiling.

Natalie looked at Lindsey, whose face was now mottled red.

"Please, Natalie, I don't have anywhere to go. Can we just talk about it?"

"You've had three months to talk about it." Bitterness made camp inside her. "I'm going out back with the boys. In five minutes I'm coming back in. You'd better be gone."

Kyle had been disquieted all evening, and he knew it had nothing to do with the paper he'd forgotten to have Natalie fill out. He couldn't get Linn off his mind. And Natalie. And Jillian. It all just spun around in his mind until he was dizzy.

He could hardly believe Jilly's little sister was old enough to be pregnant, but, of course, she was nearly twenty. Still, he'd always think of her as the little fresh-faced kid who followed Jilly around on spindly legs.

He sank into a booth at the Shady Nook Café and looked over the menu he knew by heart. Betty waved at him as she passed with a tray of food. "Be right with ya, Kyle."

"Take your time."

He had nowhere to go. Home was a dark, empty building that held no appeal. That's why he ate out for dinner too much. He looked at his watch and wondered what Natalie was doing. She was probably still celebrating with Linn and her boys.

A grin tugged his lips. What a woman. Who else would adopt a stranger's child just because that child needed a mother? And her a single mother. Just when he'd lost all hope in the world, a woman like Natalie presented herself and made him think the world wasn't such a bad place.

Natalie would have her hands full once the baby came, but that didn't stop her from doing what she felt was right. For the first time he'd really noticed her wide brown eyes tonight. She had a natural beauty that was very different from Jillian's put-together appearance. Yes, Natalie had caught his attention today in a way that disturbed him. He wasn't ready for a relationship. Didn't know that he ever would be after what Jillian had done. How could he ever trust someone again after his best friend and lover betrayed him? He'd never gotten to talk it out with her, to figure out why she'd done it. He'd never gotten to tell her how angry he was for what she'd done. She'd deserved to hear how much pain she'd caused him.

But she hadn't deserved to die. No, he wasn't ready for a relationship. Wasn't even sure he deserved a happy ending.

A new waitress took his order before returning to the kitchen. A few minutes later she brought out his Coke and tried to make small talk, a flirtatious sparkle in her eyes. He responded politely, offering no encouragement, and finally she went away.

The Friday night crowd was streaming in the door in groups of two and threes. He opened his briefcase and pulled out the paperwork he'd brought with him.

When his food arrived, he put the work away and ate, then paid his bill. As he drove home, he wondered why he felt so restless. This evening was like so many others since Jillian's death. It had never bothered him to be alone before.

He pulled into his drive and went through the garage, flipping on the kitchen light as he passed through. He set his briefcase on the floor next to the end table with every intention of working on the stack of papers. When he sat in his favorite recliner chair, though, he didn't feel like working. Not even thoughts of the Graber's adoption finalization spurred his desire to complete the paperwork.

He flipped on the TV and surfed. He found a legal thriller but changed the channel when it failed to hold his attention. The same held true for a drama involving a crime scene investigation and for a sitcom. What was wrong with him tonight? He flipped off the TV and glanced at the wall clock.

He wondered if Natalie and Linn were finished with dinner. He supposed he could call and tell Natalie she needed to stop by the office and fill out that paper. He jumped at the excuse and went to retrieve the cordless from the kitchen cradle. For a moment, he thought he didn't have her number, then he remembered the paperwork in his briefcase. After rifling through it, he pulled out one that had her number on it.

He had a strange stirring in his gut as he dialed the number, and he told himself to get real. He was only calling to tell her about the paperwork, not to ask her out.

A busy signal bleeped in his ear, and he told himself it wasn't disappointment fanning through him. He clicked the off button and resigned himself to a quiet night at home. Somehow, it didn't hold the same promise it used to.

CHAPTER
TWENTY-EIGHT

The next morning, Natalie checked the clock, realizing that Keith would be arriving any minute. She'd sent the boys to their rooms to clean up their toys and make their beds and made herself a second pot of coffee. She needed caffeine like she needed air.

Last night had been the second worse night of her life. Only her discovery of Keith's affair had been worse, and it didn't escape her that last night's event was a direct result of that. The sin her husband had committed had created an avalanche of suffering. Would it ever stop?

Upstairs she heard Alex complaining that Taylor had made the mess of blocks and demanding that his brother pick them up. She sipped from her Jackson Hole mug and ignored the argument. They'd argued last night, too, but it had been with her.

Why did Linn leave? Where'd she go? But we're having a party . . .

She only told them that Linn had to leave for a while. Still, they'd kept after her until she wanted to scream, and finally she'd pulled out the much-coveted tub of Play-Doh. That had distracted them for a while. She'd locked herself in her room while the food congealed on the table.

She lay on her bed, seething and shaking, but strangely, there were no tears. Not then, and not in all the hours she'd lain awake in the night.

The doorbell rang, and Natalie's heart kicked into gear. The boys came clambering down the stairs and flung the door open, hugging their father.

She got up and approached warily. Keith's eyes had a half-moon circle beneath them, and she knew he'd had a rough night, too.

Tough luck. Wasn't this his doing? His and his precious Lindsey's?

"Boys, grab your stuff and take it to the truck," Keith said. "I'll be out in a minute."

They obeyed, eager to spend the day at Jenny Lake with their dad. Natalie called out a good-bye as they slid out the door.

She crossed her arms, unable to summon a smile or even a greeting for Keith.

He stood awkwardly in the same spot he'd stood the night before. He glanced outside, probably making sure the boys had made it into the truck.

"Is she gone?" he asked.

What business was it of his? He'd caused more pain and damage in her life than any person had a right.

"Don't look at me like that. It's not my fault what she did. I didn't even know she was pregnant."

"It's your fault she's pregnant, Keith. That's the problem."

"Like I wanted a baby?"

She narrowed her eyes, hoping some of the venom poisoning her insides would infect Keith. "There are ways to prevent it, you know. Abstinence, for instance."

He ran his hand through his hair. "Look. We don't even need to have this conversation. This has nothing to do with you now."

Could he really be so clueless? "Nothing to do with me? I was going to adopt this baby for heaven's sake. I was expecting—the boys were expecting—to have that baby in this house in a matter of weeks! This changes everything. I feel like I've been—"

Betrayed all over again. That was how she felt. But he didn't need to know it.

"You just need to leave, Keith." Her voice shook.

After a moment, he pulled the door closed. She sagged against it and closed her eyes. Her heart was pumping madly, her insides twisting like a wild roller coaster. She'd wanted to be alone, wanted the boys to be gone so she could sort out her thoughts. But now she was afraid. She didn't want to think about Linn or the baby.

The baby. A heavy weight sunk in her belly. She felt almost as if she'd had a miscarriage. She'd wanted that baby. Loved that baby. And now the child had been ripped from her.

She considered whose child it was and felt a stab of revulsion toward it. She shook her head. How could she feel that way about a baby? Mothers and babies were her life's work.

She went up the stairs, seeking the solitude of her bedroom. She didn't bother turning the light on, just slipped under the covers and burrowed into her pillow.

Just yesterday she'd been starting the adoption process. She'd been looking forward to adopting a baby into their family. She'd been feeling so good about helping Linn by giving her a place to stay. Today all that was gone. How had so much changed in one day?

The phone rang beside her bed, and she groaned. She didn't want to talk to her mom or Paula or Hanna. She just wanted to stay under these covers and pretend last night never happened.

But it could be something about the boys. They'd only just left, but maybe they'd forgotten something. She forced herself to reach over and pick up the extension.

"Hello." Her efforts to disguise her feelings fell flat.

"Natalie?"

The sound of Kyle's voice brought relief. "Hi, Kyle."

"I just called to let you know there was a form I forgot to have you fill out." His voice was guarded and questioning, as if he could tell something was amiss. "I discovered it after you left. It can wait until Monday, of course."

It hit her what he was saying. Forms. Paperwork. The adoption. Should she just tell him OK and wait until later to explain?

"Or maybe I can drop them by and save you the trip."

He probably took her silence as irritation that she'd be inconvenienced.

"No, no need." If only he knew. Maybe she should tell him now instead of waiting.

"Are you OK? I thought you'd be pretty excited after yesterday."

She let the silence hang as she tried to figure out what to say. This was Linn's brother-in-law, after all. Even Kyle was related to this whole mess between her ex-husband and his mistress. Was there any part of her life that had gone untouched?

"The adoption is off," she said.

"What?"

She could hear the surprise in his voice.

"What happened?" he asked.

Suddenly, the weight of the situation bore down on her until she felt she had to unload it on someone. Why not Kyle?

"It happened last night. I found out who Linn is." Did Kyle know Keith was the baby's father and her ex-husband. Was it possible he had kept it from her, too? The thought brought another stab of fear.

"What do you mean?"

"I have to ask if you knew. Did you know about Linn and my ex-husband, Kyle?" Her voice held a hint of accusation. But it would make sense if he knew. Maybe he'd even seen Linn and Keith together at some point. It was a small town, after all. While everyone didn't know everyone's names, you certainly knew all the locals' faces.

She rolled over on her back, holding the phone tight to her ear. She didn't think she could bear one more deception.

"Natalie, I have no idea what you're talking about. I promise."

She sighed. She didn't know why, but she believed him. Maybe it was desperation.

"Look, do you want to meet somewhere and talk tonight? I know this isn't any of my business, but I'm a good listener."

The thought of going out held no appeal, but maybe a listening ear would offer some relief. "Could you come over here?"

"Sure. I have to help a friend move into his house this afternoon, but I'm free tonight. I'll bring something for dinner if you like."

Natalie gave him directions to her house, then they settled on take-out from the Mangy Moose, set a time, and said good-bye.

All day Natalie's thoughts tossed about like a rowboat on open seas. She didn't understand why this had to happen. Why, when she'd been doing the right thing, did she get a knife stuck in her back?

Why, God? I was only trying to help a girl in trouble. I was only trying to do what You'd asked of me. I was really taking a step of faith, a step of obedience in adopting this baby. Of all the women in Jackson Hole, of all the unborn babies, why did it have to be Linn?

Later that evening, Natalie walked into the great room but felt too restless to sit down. Dusk was settling outside, and it was nearly time for Kyle to arrive. She was still in her denim shorts and T-shirt. She hadn't looked in the mirror since she'd run a comb through her hair this morning, but she couldn't bring herself to care.

All she could think about was Linn. Why had Linn done this to her? Hadn't she hurt her enough with the affair? Did she have any idea of the pain she had caused Natalie's family?

It occurred to her that Linn was only nineteen, hardly even an adult, but that sickened her more. How old had she been when her husband had been having the affair? Seventeen?

She'd lost her husband to a seventeen-year-old girl?

The thought set a lump in her gut the size of Grand Teton. What kind of man turns to a mere child for love?

What kind of woman loses her husband to a girl that age?

A knock came at the door, rescuing her from the uncomfortable thought. When she opened the door, Kyle stood in a pair of jeans and red shirt. A delicious aroma escaped from the Mangy Moose bag in his arm, and she realized she hadn't eaten yet today.

"Hi, come on in."

He eyed her warily as he stepped inside.

They made small talk as they set the food and plates on the table.

It surprised her that Kyle found the silverware drawer and poured drinks. A man that helped without being asked was a rare find in her experience.

They made it through the meal without bringing up the subject of the adoption. Natalie didn't want to think about it until she finished eating, and Kyle seemed to sense that. Instead, they talked about the tourists and the Jackson Hole Moose, their local hockey team. She was pleasantly surprised how natural it seemed to have Kyle in the house. She hadn't had a man at her dinner table since Keith had left.

When the food was gone, they cleared the table together, and Natalie led them to the great room, where she sat on the sofa. Kyle sat at the opposite end and turned toward her, propping one knee on the seat.

"Do you want to talk about what happened?"

She noticed how gentle his voice was. It warmed her from the inside out. She shook her head. "I still can't believe it." She relived the moment when Keith and Linn saw each other, and shivered. "While we were having our celebration last night, Keith stopped by. He and Linn saw each other, and I found out that"—she looked at Kyle—"Linn is the one who broke up my marriage. She's the one my husband had an affair with. The one my husband left me for."

Natalie saw the emotions work on Kyle's face. Confusion, shock, all the things she'd felt yesterday. Finally, his gaze turned downward. "I'm so sorry. That must've been a terrible discovery."

She breathed a laugh. "That's not all, I'm afraid. I also found out the baby Linn's carrying is Keith's."

His eyes darted up to hers. "What?"

"So you can see why I'm wanting to back out of the adoption."

His jaw worked. "This is insane."

No one needed to tell her that. She was still reeling, and she had to admit, there was something satisfying in seeing Kyle's reaction. Almost protective toward her. How long had it been since someone had protected her, even cared for her?

"No one would expect you to follow through on an adoption like that. It's unthinkable—" He stopped abruptly and looked at her. "Linn—she didn't know about this, did she? About who you are?"

Natalie felt the hard lump inside her swell. "Yes, she did." She didn't want to say too much. Kyle might sympathize with Linn. She was his sister-in-law, after all. Natalie didn't think she could stand that.

"She knew?" Unbelief was etched on his face.

"She's known for three months."

Kyle reared back as if smacked. It seemed to take a moment to formulate his thoughts. "What in heaven's name was she thinking? How could she—I'm so sorry, Natalie."

"Stop apologizing. It's not your fault."

"You must be a wreck."

She gave a wry laugh. "That's a pretty accurate description." Silence hung as the weight of what had happened sank in further. Her future had changed so drastically in just one moment. The thought of losing the baby was unbearable. The thought of raising Linn and Keith's child was even more so.

"Where's Linn now?"

She looked at Kyle and felt a moment of dread at having to tell him the truth. Would he hate her for kicking Linn out? She wet her lips. "I told her to go."

Mixed emotions swam on his face. He was torn, and Natalie hated that. She wanted him to take her side. She was the one who'd been wronged. Linn had fixed her own mess. Why should she feel bad about that?

"You think I should've let her stay in my home, eat my food, and pretend she isn't the person who wrecked my life?" Her voice shook, she couldn't help it.

Kyle rubbed his fingers over his mouth. "No. Of course not."

"But you're wondering how I could just kick her out on the street, aren't you?"

"Natalie, I don't want to argue."

"I know she was your sister-in-law, Kyle, but I don't give a fig where she is. What she did was inexcusable. She's young, but she's old enough to know better. She deserves whatever she gets, and if my saying that makes you hate me, then that's too bad." Her eyes stung, burning deep in the sockets, then her vision blurred. Cursed tears. She didn't want to cry. She wanted to hit someone.

He reached out and put his hand on hers. "I don't hate you." He squeezed her hand. "I could never hate you."

She felt her face crumpling and covered it with her hands. Then he was there, close to her, holding her. She buried her face in his shirt, inhaling his musky cologne, drawing comfort. Her hands balled into fists, clutching the material of his shirt.

"You're going to get through this," he said. "You're a strong woman."

She didn't want to be strong anymore. She was tired of being strong. Tired of taking care of everyone. She wanted to lean on someone else for a change. It felt so good just to be held.

She let the emotions from the past day pour out of her. She wept for her broken marriage, and for the way Linn had betrayed her, and for the loss of the baby.

The baby.

Her heart constricted at the thought. *Oh, Jesus, I wanted that baby! And I thought You were leading me to adopt the child. But I must've been wrong. How could I have been so wrong?*

She cried for all the loss, grateful for Kyle's strong arms and gentle touch. He was quiet all through it, as if sensing she just needed to let go of the pain.

When she was done, she was spent from the emotional release, from the lack of sleep the night before. She felt strangely content to just be in Kyle's arms. He, too, must've felt comfortable enough, for he didn't move, didn't shift, just continued to hold her. Her thoughts turned toward him, and she thought how odd it was to feel so at home in his embrace. No man had held her since Keith.

She heaved a deep sigh and turned her face so that her cheek rested against the soft, damp material of his shirt. Beneath the material, his heart beat strong and steady. She should pull away, she'd leaned on him long enough. But she couldn't bring herself to do so just yet. Just a few more minutes, and she would leave the comfort of his arms. But a few minutes later, she was lost in the depths of sleep.

CHAPTER
TWENTY-NINE

Paula took the elevator from the garage, and when the door whooshed open, she walked out into the lobby. Chicago was a wonderful place to be. She'd enjoyed every minute of her two days here. Seeing the station had been an eye-opener. It was nothing like the podunk station in Jackson. And the people were quick and professional and hip. She'd gone out earlier just to walk the streets. The city was so alive. You could almost feel the energy. She belonged here. She only hoped Miles, the station manager, felt the same way.

She thought of David and how he'd not even said good-bye before she left. Her stomach took a dive at the thought. Over the past few days, he'd started the process of buying out JH Realty without so much as checking with her, so why should she care what he thought about her career direction?

She glanced around the lobby for Miles. He was taking her to dinner on her last night in Chicago. She saw him across the lobby seated beside an enormous marble stand sporting a large vase of fresh flowers. She approached, confident that the suit she'd selected made her look every inch a big-city reporter.

"Paula, right on time." Miles shook her hand. His salt-and-pepper hair was wind-blown, but it only added to his good looks.

She put on her prettiest smile. "You're not a man to be kept waiting, Miles."

He laughed, and she knew he felt appropriately flattered. Men like him wanted to matter, wanted people to sense their importance. Paula would make sure he felt respected on this, their last evening together. Her dream job might depend on how well this meal went.

He ushered her into a taxi that was waiting at the curb, and within moments they were at Narcisse, seated across from each other. Instead of the quiet atmosphere she'd expected, the restaurant bustled with activity, and the tables were crammed together. It was so different from Jackson, where most of the locals knew each other, at least by face. Here, no one spoke to anyone at the other tables. And that meant there was none of that small-town gossip she despised. No one knowing all your business.

Paula knew Miles had spent time this afternoon reviewing her test tape. She was more than eager to hear what he had to say, but she wouldn't appear eager. She had to play it cool, as if there were other networks beating down her door.

He ordered a bottle of wine and turned off his cell phone. A good sign; he didn't want to be interrupted. After the waiter had poured their drinks, Paula took a sip, noting the Merlot was one of the best she'd ever had.

"I reviewed your new tape this afternoon, Paula," Miles said once he set his glass down.

She cocked her head, eager to hear more. She was glad he couldn't see the rapid fluttering of her heart.

"You're good." He nodded slowly. "Very good."

"Thank you." She took another sip, glad her hand wasn't trembling. Would he offer her the job tonight? What would she say when she hadn't come to an agreement with David?

"Even though the tape your station sent us was terrific, we honestly didn't expect to find such talent in a small town like Jackson Hole. Your delivery today was exceptional, your ad-libbing brilliant, and you're not too hard on the eyes either."

She laughed, enjoying the compliments. She knew she was good at what she did, but she could hardly believe this big-city pro was impressed. She was beginning to think she had the job all sewn up.

"Now, you know the job is a temporary assignment, but whomever we hire has an opportunity for something more permanent. And it's no secret that our key anchor is thinking of retiring. I can see you in that role easily."

She wondered if her head were swelling visibly. "Thank you. I'm passionate about working my way up, and I think you'll find me dedicated to whatever job I'm entrusted with."

He nodded. "Your station manager told me as much, but it's nice to hear it from the horse's mouth, so to speak."

When the waiter came and took their orders, Paula stifled a pang of irritation. Miles was on the cusp of offering her the job, and she just wanted to hear the words. She allowed him to order for her, since she hadn't even opened her menu. When the waiter left, Miles's attention returned to her.

"What time is your flight tomorrow?"

The question caught her off-guard. She was hoping they'd pick up right where they'd left off. "Seven-thirty. So you can't keep me out too late." She smiled coyly.

He returned her smile. "You do know how to burst a man's bubble." He winked.

The conversation turned to the business of TV news in general, but the whole time Paula wondered why he hadn't offered her the job. The food arrived, and the conversation trickled off a bit, since they were busy eating. Only after Miles had paid the bill did he finally bring up the job.

"I'm sure Cindy told you about the other reporters we're interviewing," he said.

Her heart stopped cold. His assistant had failed to mention that little detail.

"We won't be needing the job filled until December, so it may be a month or two before you hear back from me." He stood up and helped her from her chair.

She smiled confidently. "I'll look forward to hearing from you, then." Inside, she was deflating like a punctured raft.

Natalie dropped off the boys at her mom's house and rushed back to the car. She was running behind again, this time because she hadn't been able to get the garage door to close. And when she'd gotten into her car, she'd realized she needed gas *now*.

Everything seemed different since that awful day a week and a half ago. She'd finally broken the news to the boys about the adoption. Alex had gotten mad, demanding to know why. It seemed impossible for him to accept her generic "it just didn't work out" answer. But she wouldn't tell him more. She had never told him about his father's affair and wasn't planning to start now.

Her family had been a different story. Paula had nodded and murmured her sympathies, while her eyes betrayed no surprise at all. Hanna and her mom had offered the support she'd expected. They'd had just the right amount of righteous indignation to leave Natalie feeling justified. Only somehow, the justification was wearing off. She shrugged away the thought as she signaled a left turn.

Kyle had also been a great support. The night she'd told him about Linn, she'd fallen sound asleep in his arms and hadn't woken up until the next morning. At first, she'd been confused, waking up on the couch. When she saw the throw cover over her, she remembered crying in Kyle's arms and realized he must've covered her and left. Even now, the thought brought a warm, cozy feeling to her insides.

As she drove by Bubba's Bar-B-Que, she glanced at the building, wondering if Linn was working.

She tore her eyes away. What did she care if Linn was working? Not

Linn. Lindsey. She should start calling her by her real name. Linn was a friend. Lindsey was a betrayer. The name brought up every ugly feeling a person could have. She'd honestly wondered if she was capable of hurting the girl. She'd had thoughts she hadn't had since discovering the affair. *I thought I'd forgiven this, God. I thought I was over it, yet if I was, why is this weighing on me so heavily? Why am I so angry?*

She turned down Pearl Avenue and turned her thoughts to her day ahead. She had a new volunteer starting today and would need to show her the ropes. Beth had gone through training like all the others, and Natalie had high hopes she would be good at counseling the clients.

She pulled into the parking lot behind the center, slid into a slot, and exited her car. She had about an hour to get some things done before Beth arrived. Not as much as she'd hoped for, but enough to get most of it done if the phone stayed quiet.

She rounded the corner of the building and walked along the sidewalk. The August heat had started early on this day. She figured it must be in the eighties already. She thought of Linn again and wondered how she was coping with a pregnancy during this heat. She shoved the thought firmly away. She didn't want to think about Linn today. She was sick to death of thinking about Linn.

It was the crackle of glass under her feet that caught her attention first. She looked down at the pebble-sized pieces, her mind wondering quickly where they had come from. Before she could finish the thought, her eyes swung to the center's plate glass windows. The tempered glass was shattered, and hundreds of glass shards lay at the base of the building.

She approached the door with her key in hand but quickly saw she didn't need the key. The glass on the door was broken, and the door was ajar. Instinctively, she took a step back.

"Oh, heavens! What's happened?" The voice came from behind Natalie.

She jumped before turning and seeing Betty, the owner of the Shady Nook. "I don't know. I just got here," Natalie said.

"I was just getting ready to flip the 'Open' sign in the window when I looked out and saw. Oh, honey, what a mess."

"I need to call the sheriff," Natalie said. *But not from in there*, she thought. What if someone was still in there? She backed away, almost stumbling down the curb.

Betty took her arm. "Come on. You can call from the diner."

After Natalie had made the call, she sipped the coffee Betty had perked and stared at the center across the road. She was shaken, and she hated that. Memories of the night she'd been held in her car came flooding back with such reality she could almost feel the sting of her scalp as her assailant grasped her hair.

She shuddered. Was this vandalism related to that? And what about the graffiti incident? Was it all related or just a set of coincidences? Had someone vandalized the center because of their work there, or was it just some drunk tourists with too much time on their hands?

"Here they come," Betty said, peeking out the window where the sheriff's car was pulling to the curb.

She poured two cups of coffee for Sheriff Whitco and his deputy as they entered the diner. They took off their hats and greeted the women.

"You're having a bad year, Natalie," Sheriff Whitco said.

He didn't know the half of it. Between the violence and harassment at the center and the strife in her personal life, she was beginning to think there was a sick joke being played on her.

The officers went to investigate the center while Natalie kept Betty company. The woman started the food prep while they talked, but Natalie found herself wanting Kyle's company. She felt insecure. Her world was being shaken from all directions, and he was a great stabilizer in her life. She toyed with the idea of calling him, biting her lip until she tasted blood.

She forgot about Kyle when she saw Beth rounding the corner of the center. She'd forgotten all about the volunteer. She rushed out the door and crossed the street.

"Oh, my goodness, what happened?" Beth asked.

"Just a little vandalism. Nothing a good security system won't cure." The sarcasm in her voice made her cringe. "Sorry. It's been a rough morning."

"You weren't here when it happened . . ."

"Oh, no. It was like this when I got here. Hey, why don't you take the morning off? We're not going to get any training done today."

"No way. I'll stay and help you clean up this mess." Beth gave a sharp nod, and Natalie felt like hugging her.

Sheriff Whitco and his officer came out the door, and Natalie studied him, waiting for answers.

He shrugged. "It's a royal mess in there, but I guess you'd already figured on that."

Thank God for insurance, but it would be a nuisance to clean the building and replace everything that had been damaged. And some things would never be replaceable. She thought of the collage with pictures of clients and their babies and hoped it hadn't been ruined.

"Is this related to the other incidents?"

"Hard to say for sure, but it's likely at least two of the three are related."

She stifled her frustration. Why couldn't they get to the bottom of this? Her attacker had never been identified, the graffiti incident had hardly even been looked into, and now this. What would happen next?

"You need to get yourself an alarm and a better lock on that door."

"And you need to figure out who's doing this stuff," she said sharply. She never spoke that way to an elder, much less an authority, and one she'd known for years.

He raised his brows. "Yes, ma'am."

She apologized for her tone, then Sheriff Whitco recommended some safety measures, promising to do his best on the case.

After they left, she and Beth entered the center. Natalie stopped dead in her tracks. Nothing was as it had been before. Every table, chair, and shelf was overturned. Papers were strewn everywhere;

equipment was demolished. She closed her eyes against the sting in them. *Oh, God, why is this happening? How are we ever going to get this back the way it was?*

"Well"—Beth laid an arm across her shoulder—"the sooner we get started, the sooner we can set it back to rights. If you give me some names of other volunteers, I'll see if anyone's available to come help."

Natalie offered a feeble smile. "Let's get to work."

CHAPTER THIRTY

Linn shut the break room door and pulled a chair to the corner, where the phone sat on a table. She wasn't sure she could do this. But what choice did she have? Her shift was over, it was dark out, and she had no place to stay tonight. She looked at her bare finger. She'd already sold the sapphire ring Keith had given her. Good riddance. But she hadn't gotten much for it, and that money was long gone.

She eyed the phone again and wondered if she had it in her to make the call. Natalie had been the kindest, most compassionate woman Linn had ever met. She'd wondered a dozen times why Keith had left a woman like that for her. He must've been crazy. But Linn had totally blown it with Natalie. She could surely never forgive Linn for what she'd done.

It had been almost two weeks. Maybe Natalie had calmed down some. Like a lot, if she had any chance at all. She picked up the extension and dialed before she could change her mind. She pictured Natalie's face the last time she'd seen her. She'd hardly seen the woman upset, much less seething with rage. And Linn deserved her anger, didn't she? She didn't deserve Natalie's forgiveness. Her eyes began to burn again.

"Hello?"

It was Natalie, and her voice sounded calm and cool. She couldn't do it. She didn't have the gall. She hung up the phone, her heart skittering in her chest.

The break room door burst open, and her friend Kayley entered. "Still here?"

Linn shrugged. Like she had any place to go.

Kayley took off her apron and stuffed it in her locker. "Can't find a place to stay? Did you try your dad again?"

"Not yet." Her friends from high school had left for college the previous week, and she had no family other than her dad. She was out of luck.

"Kayley, can I maybe just come over one last time? I'll work something else out tomorrow—" She stopped when she saw her friend shaking her head slowly.

"Sorry, Linn, but Mom's on days now, so she's home at night. And she 'bout had a fit when she found out you stayed last week. I'm practically grounded till I graduate."

Linn nodded. "Sorry you got grounded." What was she going to do? She glanced at her watch and saw it was almost ten o'clock. What would happen to her if she slept outside somewhere? It was warm enough, but was it safe? She felt the baby move and put a hand on her belly.

Kayley gave her a sympathetic hug and slipped out the door. What would she do now? The only other option was to call her dad. He would ask her if she'd had an abortion. She was beginning to think that was her only option. What was she thinking trying to have a baby when she didn't even have a place to sack out at night? Her baby had no loving parents, no future. It would have been great if things had worked out with Natalie, but she didn't have the luxury of thinking that way now. She didn't even know what the laws were. It might be too late to have an abortion here. But Kayley had told her of someplace in Kansas that did late-term abortions. She cringed at the thought and shook the thought away.

She picked up the phone before she could change her mind and punched in the numbers. The phone rang and rang, and she feared he wasn't even home. She looked at her watch. He should be home from work by now unless he'd stopped at Sidewinders for a few beers. She hadn't talked to him in the three weeks since he'd kicked her out. Maybe he had softened a little.

"Hello?" Her dad sounded out of breath.

"Dad?" The silence was deafening and awkward. She searched for something to say. "How've you been?"

She could picture him rubbing the black whiskers on his chin. "Linn. What are you calling for?"

She heard laughter in the background, a woman's laughter.

"Daddy, I . . . I need a place to stay, just for a little while." She closed her eyes, twisting the old-fashioned corkscrew cord around her index finger.

"Did you take care of that issue we talked about?"

Her eyes came open as her stomach bottomed out. "I don't know what I'm going to do yet. I need some time to think about it." It broke her heart to even consider it, but—

"You know what my offer was. I haven't changed my mind." The woman in the background squealed, then laughed as if he'd pinched her or done something equally revolting.

"Please, Daddy. I promise I won't be there long. I just need a place to sleep. I won't be in the way."

"Now's not a good time. You'll work something out."

She heard another cackle. Her heart raced and her eyes tingled the way they did when she was about to cry. "All right," she said before he could hang up. "All right, I'll get the—I'll have it done. I'll call tomorrow and make the appointment."

"No, you have it done first. Then you can come home." Click.

"Dad?" Nothing. She sighed and dropped the phone back in the cradle. She remembered all the pictures she'd seen of fetuses. She knew what hers looked like now.

Don't think about that. The choice is out of your hands now. You're not a bad person, just a kid with no other options.

She buried her face in her hands. Why had she gotten herself into this mess? She was so stupid! She'd had it made with a college scholarship. Now she was pregnant, homeless, and had no way of paying for medical care. There was no future for her or her baby.

It doesn't have to be that way. If you just have the procedure, everything will be the way it was before.

She sniffed and wiped her cheeks. Tonight, she didn't know what she'd do. But tomorrow she would call the Women's Health Clinic. It wasn't like she had a choice, right? Her eyes burned. Her feet hurt, her back ached, and she just wanted to go to sleep for a long time.

"Who was it?" Kyle asked Natalie as she hung up the phone. He didn't like the fear he saw on her face.

"I don't know. They hung up."

Upstairs he could hear the boys bouncing on the beds and giggling hysterically. "Has that been happening a lot?"

She shook her head as she placed the phone back in its cradle. "That's the first time."

"I don't like this. Not after what they did to the center." When he'd found out about the center the day before, he'd called Natalie. He'd felt so many things. Worry for her safety, a desire to protect of her, and hurt that she hadn't called him right away. Her invitation to dinner tonight had helped.

He walked over and picked up the phone, then punched *69. A mechanical voice repeated the number, but when he punched it in, a busy signal beeped out through the lines. "It's busy. Probably a wrong number, and they hung up and dialed the right one. But if it happens again, dial star sixty-nine and call back and see if they answer. Maybe you should get caller ID so you can screen your calls."

"If it keeps up, I will." She folded her arms and looked into his eyes. "What if they know where I live?"

The tremor in her voice beckoned him. "Come here."

She walked toward him, and he pulled her into his arms. Ah, sweet heaven. Did she know how good he felt when he held her? The way she burrowed into his chest sent warm shivers through him. The night he'd held her until she'd fallen asleep was a memory that had replayed itself in his mind a dozen times. Just thinking about the comfort and trust required to make herself so vulnerable nearly crushed him. He'd wanted to hold her all night, but that was hardly appropriate. He'd only let go of her when his back ached unbearably from sitting still so long.

Natalie squirmed in his arms, pulling him from the memory, then she stepped away. She didn't look him in the face but walked to the sofa as if to put some distance between them. Was he rushing things? Did he even want this to go further than friendship?

Who was he kidding? He'd never enjoyed holding anyone so much. Maybe distance was what he needed. Not wanted, mind you.

He took a seat across from her on the chair and turned his mind back to their problem. Their problem. Funny how he'd begun including himself in her world.

"I don't like this," he said. "If they're calling you at home, I have to wonder about your safety here."

"They vandalized the center, so I don't think it's personal. It's probably some angry boyfriend of a client."

"How can you say it's not personal? You were attacked in your car a few months ago." He watched her swallow and look at her hands on her lap. "I'm not trying to scare you, but I want you to be careful."

Her lips tipped up as she met his gaze. "I appreciate that."

He wasn't spouting platitudes. He was genuinely worried for her. "I don't want your appreciation," he said gently. "I want you to promise to be careful."

She cocked her head, and he wondered if he'd overstepped his boundaries. He had no rights to her. All they'd shared was some conversation and a couple embraces, but darn it, he was worried about her.

"I'll be careful," she whispered.

Their eyes met and clung. She looked like a woman who liked what she saw. He wished she wasn't across the room with a coffee table between them. Was he reading too much into the look?

She looked away. "I should get the boys bathed and in bed." She stood.

He stood with her. Well. Not exactly a little hint. "I should be going, then." He hoped he'd misread her. He hoped she'd tell him not to move, that she'd be back down shortly, and they could pick up right where they'd left off. She didn't.

"Thanks for coming over," she said.

She walked him to the door, and he pulled it open and turned. "Thanks for having me. Dinner was great. I don't get homemade meals very often."

She laughed, and he thought he could drown in the sound. "I don't know if I'd call spaghetti with Prego homemade."

"If you were a bachelor you would."

"You make a good point."

He wanted to kiss her. Or hug her, at least. But she crossed her arms over her chest, and he could feel her pulling away.

"Well. Good night," he said.

"'Night."

He walked out the door but turned before she could shut it. "Be careful."

"I will."

The door closed softly. But he feared her heart had, too.

CHAPTER
THIRTY-ONE

"I don't know how in the world I let you guys talk me into this," Natalie said, huffing the words as she attempted to draw air.

Ahead of her, Hanna stepped easily up a rocky incline, then turned to help her. "You wanted to come and you know it."

The small entourage of guests from Higher Grounds Mountain Lodge trudged ahead of them, following Micah.

"That was before I remembered how out of shape I am." Natalie focused on putting one foot in front of the other.

"Isn't the air great out here, though?"

"It's going in and out of my lungs so fast, I hadn't noticed."

Hanna laughed.

"You seem to be feeling pretty good," Natalie said. Hanna hadn't had the fatigue Natalie had in the beginning of her pregnancies. Lucky girl.

"I feel great. I'm at that perfect stage where my energy is high and I'm not huge yet."

"You're not even showing."

"Don't let the baggy T-shirt fool ya. There's a little belly under here."

All this talk about Hanna's pregnancy was making Natalie think about Linn. She stuffed the thoughts in a dark corner of her mind and focused on the trail.

They climbed in silence for a while until they came to a flat space, where they rested and sipped from their water bottles. Micah talked to the family of four and two male friends, who seemed intent on showing off for the teenage girl with the family.

"So how's everything at the center?" Hanna asked.

It had been five weeks since the center had been vandalized, and everything was back in order. So why did her life feel so unsettled?

"It's fine. We finally got reimbursed for the equipment and got everything replaced."

"And you got a security system, too, right?"

"Yes, Mom."

"Someone has to watch out for you. I was hoping something would develop between you and that attorney."

Kyle. Just his name evoked all kinds of feelings. He'd called and even stopped by the center, but she wouldn't let herself fall for him. According to Linn, he'd had an affair on his wife, and she would never give her heart to him knowing that.

"Nope. That was a dead end." If she kept telling herself that, maybe she'd start believing it. If only Kyle would stop coming by the center, it would make resisting him a lot easier.

"Mom told me Keith took the boys camping this weekend."

"They were so excited. I think Alex was awake half the night anticipating it."

"Are things still awkward when he picks them up?"

She shrugged. They'd gotten over the awkwardness. Even the anger toward him had faded. "I forgave him a long time ago. This new development with Linn just brought it all back up. And I'm over the shock of it now, so I guess there's no sense in holding it over his head."

Hanna took a gulp from her water. "What about the adoption? I know you were excited about the baby."

Her stomach clenched. She didn't want to think about the baby. She'd tortured herself with thoughts of Linn having an abortion. What if she'd gone through with it? What if she'd been that desperate for a place to stay that she'd done as her father had demanded? What if

Natalie's kicking her out had resulted in the baby's death? She shook off the terrible thought.

"You're really struggling, aren't you?"

Only Hanna could be so honest with her. "I guess I am. I'm still mourning the loss of the baby."

"Have you heard from Linn?"

"No." Her tone left no doubt that she didn't want to either. And yet . . .

"So you don't know where she is?"

"Time to move on!" Micah called from his spot near a rocky incline. He walked toward them and slipped an arm around Hanna, rubbing her back. "You doing all right?"

"Now I am." Hanna reached up and pecked Micah on the cheek.

Natalie felt relieved that she didn't have to talk about Linn anymore. One of the reasons she'd wanted to go on this trek was so she could get away from her thoughts. She was tired of thinking about Linn and the baby. Her ex-husband's baby, she reminded herself. She was tired of fighting her attraction to Kyle. She probably just needed to tell him the truth. Well, not the whole truth, but at least tell him she just wanted to be friends. She cringed. No one wanted to hear those words.

Later that night, they settled around the campfire. Dinner had been simple but filling, and with her belly full, Natalie found herself feeling relaxed for the first time in weeks.

The young men turned in first, followed by the Mitchner family. The teenage girl practically had to be peeled off Micah.

"She's at that age," Hanna said as Mr. Mitchner zipped the tent flap behind him. Micah poked at the logs in the fire in front of them, and Hanna leaned over toward Natalie. "And it doesn't hurt that he's such a hottie," she said in a stage whisper.

Micah turned and smiled at his wife. The look they shared made Natalie wonder if they remembered she was there at all.

"Did I tell you Micah thinks he knows where his sister Jenna is?"

Micah took a seat on the other side of Hanna, the log tipping a bit when his weight sank on it.

"No, where is she?" Natalie asked.

"Well, I don't know exactly," he said. "But I tracked down some friends of hers who said she went to L.A. with a boyfriend."

"L.A. That'll be like finding a needle in a haystack." Natalie wished she'd kept her mouth shut. She should be encouraging him, not dissuading him. Misery loves company.

"Normally, you'd be right," Hanna said. "Tell her what you found out." She nudged Micah.

"Some relative of her boyfriend owns a bar out there. I'm still working on finding out the name of it. Once I have that, I'll have someplace to start."

"That's terrific, Micah."

"I'm going to find her." He gazed into the fire, his jaw set, his eyes determined. Natalie didn't doubt it for a minute.

He sighed. "I think I'll turn in."

"I'll put out the fire," Hanna said. When Micah kissed her goodnight, Natalie looked the other way.

After Micah disappeared into the tent, she and Hanna listened to the fire crackle and pop for a moment.

"It sounds like Micah's close to finding Jenna. It seems to mean a lot to him."

"It does. Especially after—well, he found out a few weeks ago that his mom died several years back."

"Oh. I didn't know."

"He's still working through that one. Even though she abused him, she was still his mom."

"How old was he when he was put in foster care?"

"Six, I think. He remembers quite a bit, though. More than he wished he did."

"Was Jenna abused, too?"

Hanna shook her head. "She was just a baby when they were taken from their mom. Micah remembers feeding her bottles and taking care of her. He felt protective of her, even as young as he was."

"Why weren't they put in the same foster home? Don't they try to keep siblings together?"

"They were in the same home initially. But at some point, the foster parents didn't want Micah anymore—I guess he was a difficult child—and they couldn't find a home that would take them both. So they ended up separated."

"That's so unfair. They'd already lost their mom, and then they were taken from each other, too."

"I know. It seems to have worked out pretty well for Jenna, though. The family adopted her."

"Don't they know where she is?"

Hanna shook her head. "They tried to find her after she ran away, but they came to a dead end. And they have five foster children, so they have their hands full. Micah let them know we think she's in L.A."

They let silence fall around them for a while.

Natalie's thoughts went back to Linn and the baby. She'd been by Bubba's many times in the past weeks, and she hadn't seen Linn's bike in the bike rack once. What if something awful had happened to her? Who would even know if she disappeared? She clenched her teeth. Why should she care what happened? Didn't Linn deserve everything she got? Hadn't she dug her own hole?

Natalie closed her eyes and breathed deep of the fresh, pine-scented air.

She'd thought if she got away from home, she could forget her troubles. But no matter how far away she got, the troubles seemed to follow.

Natalie watched the young woman walk out of the center and felt like her stomach was anchored to her feet. According to the test, the girl was pregnant, and there was no doubt in Natalie's mind that she would be getting an abortion. She was from Alpine and had come here for the free test. Natalie had never seen anyone so close-minded. She hadn't wanted to hear about the baby forming inside her or Post Abortion Syndrome. She wanted a quick fix, and she was convinced an abortion was it.

Natalie put her face in her hand and closed her eyes against the sting. Would it ever get any easier? She couldn't save every baby from death, couldn't save every mother from the agony of regret.

But you can save one.

She sat up straight, jarred by the thought. No. She wouldn't think about Linn and her baby. Keith's baby. She couldn't do anything about it, and no one could ask that of her.

Besides, it may be too late for Linn's baby.

Linn could have aborted the baby by now. The weight attached to her stomach dragged downward. *That's Alex and Taylor's half-sibling.* She closed her eyes. This was all so twisted. So awful. What a terrible mess.

No matter how much she detested what Keith and Linn had done together, she knew the baby was innocent of that.

Still.

There was nothing she could do. And she was so angry with Linn. Time had eased the shock, but she couldn't forget what Linn had done.

She'd thought she'd gotten over the affair after the divorce. She'd forgiven Keith. It had taken a long time and a lot of praying, but she'd forgiven him.

But what about Lindsey?

She hadn't even known who the other woman was. Just that it was someone who'd worked for Keith at the bank. Someone named Lindsey. How could you forgive a ghost-woman, a woman you didn't know and had never seen?

She hadn't even realized, but now she knew. She'd never forgiven the other woman. Maybe it should be easier to forgive now that she had a face, a person to attach to the crime. But it seemed harder than ever because now Linn had betrayed her twice: once with Keith, then again by hiding her identity.

Help me, Lord. If I could forgive Keith, maybe I can forgive Linn, too, but I need Your help.

Her afternoon volunteer, Amanda, walked through the door. "Good afternoon!" She shrugged her purse off her shoulder and set it on the filing cabinet. "What's wrong?"

Natalie forced a smile to her face, but it felt plastic. "Rough day." She explained about the client who'd just left, and Amanda consoled her, then they prayed together that God would direct the woman's footsteps.

Later that night, as she was putting the boys in bed, Kyle called. "I was hoping we could talk," he said. "But I hear the boys, so I guess I've caught you at a bad time."

"I'm just putting them to bed. Why don't I call you right back?"

"Actually, I was hoping we could talk in person. There's something I wanted to talk about."

Natalie cringed. She needed to back off from the relationship, and that was much harder when he was with her. She needed to tell him she only wanted to be friends, and that would be much easier over the phone.

"There's something I want to talk to you about, too." No time like the present. At least she could get it out of the way. Having him around all the time was getting harder all the time. He was too easy to lean on.

"How about a half hour or so?" she asked.

"Sure."

He sounded cautious, and Natalie realized he was probably wondering what she was going to say. What if she couldn't work up the courage to say it at all?

They hung up, and Natalie finished tucking in the boys and saying prayers. Only then did she allow herself to consider what she'd say to

Kyle. It was too tempting to have him in her life. He fit so well. He was easy to talk to, a good listener, and he wasn't hard on the eyes either.

Her thoughts drifted back to the time he'd held her while she cried. He had a strength about him that was magnetic. She felt so safe and cared for in his arms. Just thinking about it sent warmth spreading through her.

She had to stop thinking like this. She didn't want a man who'd already betrayed one wife. *Remember what that was like, Natalie? Remember the pain you went through with Keith? You do not want to go through that again. And you have the boys to consider. Another failed marriage is not an option.*

Before she was ready, a soft knock came at the door. Her heart pushed against her chest, and when she opened the door, her knees went weak all over. Did he have to be so handsome?

"Come in." She tried for a smile but was sure she'd failed.

"Thanks for letting me come over so late," he said quietly.

She asked him to have a seat while she poured him a Pepsi. He was so thoughtful. Wouldn't most men ring the doorbell and waltz in talking loudly, mindless of the boys sleeping upstairs? Maybe she was making a mistake in letting him go.

No. She had to stop thinking like that. Remember the affair. Remember the pain. Nothing was worth experiencing that again.

She went into the great room and handed him the drink.

"Thanks."

He wore the moss-colored shirt that brought out the green in his eyes. For the first time, she wondered what he was going to say. What if he was going to tell her the same thing she was planning on telling him? What if he was going to dump her before they even began dating? *Isn't that what you wanted, you goof?* Why did she suddenly feel like a junior-high girl?

"Boys asleep?" he asked.

"Probably. Taylor was nearly asleep by the time prayers were over."

He smiled so warmly, she looked away. He looked too comfortable on the other end of the sofa. She envisioned herself cuddling up to him, her head on his chest. Why hadn't she sat across the room in the recliner?

"Are you doing OK?" he asked. "You haven't talked about Linn and the baby lately."

Was this what he'd wanted to talk about? The thought brought relief, and she immediately wondered why. She shrugged. "God's working on me with that. I know I need to forgive her."

"It can't be easy."

He wasn't one to give advice, and she loved that about him. He listened, he encouraged, but he didn't try to fix everything. "I've been praying for you."

Her heart squeezed. Had a man ever told her that? How often had she prayed for Kyle? She felt a prick of guilt. Even knowing the load of guilt he carried about his former wife, had she really prayed for him?

"Why the frown?"

She tipped her lips. "You're a special man, Kyle." *But we need to keep our relationship on a friendship level.* Now was the perfect time to say it. Why wouldn't it come out?

"I think I hear a 'but' after that," he said.

How had he known? Now she had to say it. She looked him in the eye. His hair looked as if he'd just run his hand through it. Or as if he'd just woken up and hadn't combed it yet. He looked sweet and vulnerable. She looked at his arm curled around the back of the sofa. His hands were strong-looking, tapering down to squared-off fingers that were capable of amazing tenderness.

She looked away. "You know I have a lot going on in my life right now. A lot of unresolved issues." She hoped he'd jump in and agree. Or something. He didn't.

"While I've appreciated your friendship, I want to be honest and tell you I'm not ready to go any further with it at this time."

She darted a glance at him. His little smile looked frozen on his face.

What if he didn't want any more than friendship? Had she just made a complete fool of herself? "I mean, maybe you never intended— I didn't mean to imply—"

He held his hand up as if to ward off her words. "No. You were right." The stiff smile was gone. She could read disappointment in his eyes. That is, if he'd look at her again. But he looked everywhere else.

"Well." He took his arm from the couch and leaned his elbows on his knees. "This is awkward."

If only he knew. She wanted to put her arms around him and tell him how much she cared for him. She wanted to tell him she didn't mean it, that he was just the kind of man she could love. And he was. That's why she had to end it.

He gave a wry laugh and shook his head.

"What?" she asked.

His profile gave nothing away. "It's just the irony of it." He stared at his hands before turning and offering her a gentle smile. "I thought we had that special something, you know?"

Yes, she knew. Boy, did she know. Even now, she wanted to be in his arms instead of across the sofa.

"It's hard for me," she said. "This is the first time I've allowed myself to open up at all to a man since Keith."

"I'm in the same boat."

It wasn't the same, though. How could he know what it was like to be betrayed by the one you trusted more than anyone in the world? She couldn't make herself that vulnerable again—not to someone who'd already been unfaithful.

"When Keith had the affair, it really rocked my world. I guess that's why I haven't gotten back into the dating game yet." Right now it didn't feel like a game at all. In fact, it felt pretty rotten.

"I have to admit, I'm disappointed. But I do appreciate your honesty." He turned toward her again, his naked gaze baring all. "And I understand about unfaithfulness more than you know."

She fought the urge to cover her ears. She didn't want him to tell her about the affair he'd had. Didn't want to sully the way she thought of him. Didn't want to put him in the same category as Keith.

"I've never told another soul this, but Jillian had an affair," he said.

It took a moment for his words to sink in. Jillian had an affair? What about his?

"It's what we were arguing about when I wrecked the car." He rubbed his face. "Well, I guess I did tell one other person. The officer who took my statement after the accident. I don't even remember what I said exactly. I was a mess."

"But . . . I thought . . ."

He looked at her, seeming to hear the confusion in her voice. "What?"

"I thought . . . Linn said . . ."

Understanding dawned on his face. "Linn told you I'd betrayed Jillian."

Confusion warred with disbelief in her mind. She wanted to believe it, but maybe she'd misunderstood.

He shook his head. "Her dad overheard some things I said to the officer that night. He thought I was the one who'd had the affair. I didn't have the heart to tell him the truth."

Her heart swelled with hope, but she had to be sure. "You didn't have an affair?" She kept her voice level, disguising any trace of expectation.

"No. I was completely faithful to her. I guess that's why it hurt so much when she told me that night."

Her mouth had gone dry. She should have poured herself a drink, too. But she didn't think this little chat would take long. How was she to know her preconceptions were wrong? But this changed everything, didn't it?

"So, I do understand about having to be ready," he said. "It's taken me a long time, too. And I appreciate your honesty."

He didn't know. He didn't know why she'd backed away from him. And how could she tell him now that she'd already said the words?

He stood as if to leave.

But she didn't want him to. She wanted to take back everything she'd said.

"What's wrong?" he asked.

Everything. Everything was wrong. She stood and met his gaze. "I'm afraid I owe you a big apology."

His forehead creased, his eyes looking more gray than green at the moment.

"Sit down," she said.

He sank right where he stood, and she sat beside him, their legs touching. He studied her, and she knew he was confused.

She felt so stupid! Why had she believed Linn when everything she knew about Kyle pointed against it?

She wet her lips. "When Linn told me weeks ago that you'd been unfaithful to Jillian, I believed her. I'm sorry—I shouldn't have judged you without knowing the facts."

He lifted and lowered one of his shoulders. "Water under the bridge. You don't owe me an apology."

But she did, couldn't he see? She'd based her whole decision to back away from him on that one flimsy piece of evidence. How could she take back what she'd said? *Oh, Lord, I've made a mistake. And what if he's not interested now, after I've judged him and deemed him unsuitable?*

She might as well tell him the whole truth. What did she have to lose now? "You don't understand," she said. She could feel heat pooling in her cheeks and regretted the bright overhead light she'd left on. "That was the reason I . . ." She forced herself to meet his gaze. "When Linn told me you'd been unfaithful, I purposely held you at arm's length because . . . well, because I didn't want to find myself involved with—"

She couldn't finish the sentence. It was bad enough she knew how unfair she'd been, but admitting it to him was humbling.

His head reared back slowly. Ah. It was all starting to connect.

She looked away. What must he think of her? How prideful of her to play judge and jury on his life. Hadn't she made her share of mistakes in her own marriage? What if he hadn't wanted to be involved with her because she hadn't been enough to hold on to Keith? Her breath felt trapped in her lungs.

She felt his hand on her chin, turning her face. She dreaded looking into his eyes, sure of the disappointment she'd see. But the gray-green of his eyes looked as inviting as a warm sea.

"I understand," he whispered.

Her breath caught in her throat. Time froze in place. Just two words, but they meant everything. He leaned toward her so slowly she thought she'd die from anticipation. But when his lips touched hers, she knew she was wrong. She'd die from pleasure. Surely she would.

His lips teased hers softly, like a butterfly's wings. The gentle movement started a riot inside her. His hand caressed the side of her face. She felt the back of her eyes sting.

He drew back too soon.

Those eyes. Did he know she was thoroughly captured? She wanted to reach out, take him by the collar, and pull him back toward her. She clenched her fists, afraid for a moment her body would act on the thought.

A little smile played at the corner of his lips. A smile was good, wasn't it? His eyes crinkled at the corners in the way she loved.

"What a night," he said. "It took me all day to work up the courage to call you and ask to come over."

And to think she'd almost told him no. She let her eyes roam his face, wishing her fingers could follow.

"Keep looking at me like that," he said, "and I'm going to think it's an invitation."

Her heart leaped. Her lips curved. "Maybe it is." Was that her talking this way? She didn't care who it was. All she knew was that Kyle was leaning toward her again, and in that moment, nothing else mattered.

CHAPTER
THIRTY-TWO

Kyle could hardly keep the smile off his face. He hadn't felt this happy for—well, he didn't remember ever feeling this happy. He gathered his papers off the desk and walked out of the courtroom. Finalizing the Graber's adoption today had been icing on the cake.

Last night had been a turning point for his relationship with Natalie. A turning point for him personally. He was finally putting his heart on the line again, and it felt good. Scary but good. Natalie was helping him see he wasn't responsible for Jillian's death. The guilt was slowly evaporating, leaving him feeling more free than ever before.

There was only one little black cloud hanging over his head. Linn. His former sister-in-law was out there somewhere, alone and helpless.

No, not helpless. She was nineteen now, hardly a child. And yet, she was fresh out of high school with no family to help.

She doesn't want your help.

He couldn't deny that. But she might need it, whether she wanted it or not. Weeks ago, he'd made some calls, but he'd been unable to track her down. He'd called all the cheaper hotels. But in Jackson, even the cheaper ones would be a fortune to live in. He'd even tried the hotels in the smaller surrounding towns. It was as if she'd disappeared. She wasn't working at Bubba's anymore. One of the waitresses had said the manager had fired her when she'd failed to show up twice in one week.

He walked out the courthouse doors and made his way to his car. Did she have another job? Who was hiring this time of year when all the summer tourists were gone and the winter ones had yet to arrive?

He opened his car door and slid inside, setting his briefcase on the seat beside him. Moments later, he found himself going in the opposite direction from his home. It didn't take long to near the other end of Jackson.

He drove north on Cache Street, passing Snake River Kayak and Canoe. The town was all but deserted now, compared to a couple months ago. He looked at each establishment as he drove by, wondering where Linn could be. It was entirely possible she'd left Jackson. And, as Natalie had said, entirely possible she'd had an abortion. How long had it been since she'd left Natalie's house? Eight, nine weeks? A lot could happen in that time.

He was almost to the north point of Jackson. Once he reached the end of town, the road would lead past the elk refuge, then past the airport and toward Grand Teton National Park. Nothing out there for a young girl all alone with little money.

He would turn around just ahead in the Dairy Queen parking lot. He put his foot on the brake, and just then his eyes brushed by a familiar sign. Wagon Wheel Campground. Something in him seized. He pressed the brake and turned in, all the while chiding himself. She wouldn't be at a campground. It was downright cold at night in late September, and the campground would close up in early October.

But he'd tried everywhere else. And he knew the owner, George Hutchins, would be able to tell him if Linn was there. It wouldn't take long to inquire.

He stopped in at the office and found George leaning back in his chair watching *Oprah*.

George flicked off the old portable TV. "Kyle. How's it going, pal?"

Any other time, he would tease George about his TV viewing habits, but not today. They shook hands. Last time Kyle had seen George, he'd been hanging business fliers at Kmart.

They made small talk before Kyle got to the point. "I'm looking for a girl who's missing. She's Jillian's little sister, and I think she's pregnant."

"Haven't heard nothing about a missing girl." George's bushy brows drew downward, the gray hairs sprouting wildly in all directions.

"Well, she's of age, not a runaway or anything. But I am concerned for her."

"She by herself?"

"Yes, so far as I know."

George rubbed the top of his head, where a shiny spot gleamed in the florescent light. "I do have a young missy camping in a tent. Been here awhile and keeps to herself. She's a local, but can't recall her name. He flipped open an old-fashioned reservation book.

"Linn something," George said. "Can't read her last name."

Relief filled Kyle. "That's her. It has to be. Is she pregnant?" He prayed she hadn't had an abortion.

"Yep. Awful young-looking to be having a baby."

Kyle felt a heavy weight roll off his back. "Where's she staying?"

George jerked his head toward the buttes. "Over thataways. Last tent site."

What was he thinking? He couldn't just go over there and get her, take her home. She wanted nothing to do with him. He could give her money, but would she take that?

He remembered the last time he'd seen her at the Hope Center. No, he couldn't imagine her taking a thing from him. *What should I do, God? I want to help her.*

"Good thing you came 'round if she's got no place to go. We're closing in a few days. Getting too cold to camp."

Kyle thought of Linn out sleeping in a tent while the temperatures had gotten down nearly to freezing some nights. He hoped she'd had warm blankets. What would she do when the campground closed? Did she have any money?

He turned toward the window and ran his hand through his hair. "She won't come with me. I need to figure something else out." But what? He ran through his list of friends. Would one of them take in a single pregnant girl? Could he ask it of them?

"I got a cot in the back of the restaurant. Ain't much, but it's a warm place to bed down."

He turned and looked at George. A perfect solution. Linn would be out of the weather, and George would look after her. His throat closed up. "I'd appreciate it, George. I can pay you something for it."

"Naw, never mind that. The old cot's just sitting there unused."

They discussed how George would offer it to Linn, then Kyle insisted he take some money to be sure Linn had food and anything else she needed.

"Shame I can't hire her," George said. "But with the season over . . ." He shrugged.

Kyle would figure something out. Linn was still pregnant, and she needed more than food and water. She'd need medical care.

"I'll check back in a few days, all right?" Kyle said. In the meantime, he'd pray Linn would take George up on the offer.

CHAPTER
THIRTY-THREE

Natalie went into her office and closed the door. The center was quiet today, and that was just as well, since she had boxes of baby clothes to sort through.

In the two weeks that had passed since she and Kyle had kissed, their relationship had taken off. While the feelings of growing love made her spin at times, she couldn't shake the terrible feeling in her gut.

Sometimes she felt as though someone were watching her. The week before, as she'd walked from the center to her SUV, a bolt of shivers had gone up her spine. She'd looked around at the empty gravel lot to the surrounding evergreen cedar bushes, feeling as if someone were going to jump out any moment.

Later, she'd berated herself for being so paranoid. But just the night before, when she'd taken the boys to the park, she'd gotten the same feeling all over again. It was dusk, and with night falling quickly, she'd hurried the boys into the car, ignoring their protests at the abrupt departure. After the boys were in bed, she'd called Kyle and finally told him about her uneasiness. She'd expected him to shrug it off—it was just a feeling, after all.

But this morning he'd shown up on her doorstep and insisted on driving the boys to her mom's house and Natalie to work.

She felt a smile tug at her lips. Maybe she was just being paranoid, but it felt incredibly good to have someone care so much about her and the boys.

She walked to the corner of her office, where the boxes of baby clothes sat. A woman she attended church with had dropped them off the day before.

A stack of mail on the corner of her desk caught her eye. Underneath the pile was a bulky box, and she stopped to pick it up. She'd been expecting an order of brochures on pregnancy for days now, as the center had run out two weeks ago.

She looked for the return address label to see if it was the company that printed the brochures. Seeing no label, she turned it over.

Strange. No return address. The box was the right size, but it was heavily taped. A niggle of suspicion crept under her skin. Hadn't she read a warning somewhere about opening mail that was heavily taped? And lacking a return address?

Maybe she was being overly cautious. It might be a thank-you gift from a client. She looked closely at the package. There was tape on every corner of the box. Otherwise the box looked normal. The center's address was typed on a regular address label. What should she do? She set the box down gently on her desk and stared at it. She remembered the bomb that had gone off at the Women's Health Clinic months ago. They'd never found the bomber. Would he target the center, too?

She opened her office door. "Amanda, can you come here a minute?"

"Sure."

Amanda entered her office. "What's up?"

She explained the situation with the package, feeling a little silly. "It's probably just a gift from a client or something, I know, but . . ." She shrugged.

"I think you should call the sheriff," Amanda said.

"Really?" Maybe she wasn't crazy after all.

"After everything that's gone on here, sure. I think it's wise to be cautious. Worst thing that can happen is they'll say it's nothing, and there's no harm done."

Natalie went to the main desk and placed the call. When she hung up, she looked at Amanda. "They said to leave the package where it is and exit the building."

Suddenly, it all seemed very real, and Natalie couldn't leave quickly enough. They grabbed their purses and walked out, continuing across the street toward the Shady Nook. When they reached the other side, they turned and looked back at the center.

Natalie felt awkward standing in the middle of the sidewalk in front of the café. In a few minutes the sheriff's car would pull up, and people would walk out onto the street to see what was going on. And what would she say? *I got a package with no return address. And it was all taped up.* Whoopdedoo.

"OK, I admit, I'm feeling a little silly," Amanda said.

Natalie gave a wry laugh. "I was just thinking the same thing."

Moments later Sheriff Whitco arrived with another officer. He came over and asked her a few questions while they waited for help to arrive. By this time, Betty and a few customers had come out on the sidewalk. It would be the talk of the town by closing time, even if the package turned out to be a cuddly teddy bear.

Soon the specialists arrived and went through the center's doors, leaving Natalie to bite her nails for a while longer. She had a strong desire to call Kyle, but what if it turned out to be nothing?

"Do you think we did the right thing?" Amanda asked.

Natalie thought she was going to be embarrassed royally in front of the whole town, but she didn't need to tell Amanda that. "We did the safe thing." She hoped it didn't make the news. She made a note to herself to call Paula and put in a special request.

It took an eternity for the men to come out, and by this time, Betty had talked her into having a cup of coffee in the café. When the men exited the building, Natalie jumped up from her chair and went out to the sidewalk.

Sheriff Whitco met her there, but she couldn't read anything on his face. "Good thing you called," he said. "It was an explosive."

A bomb. In her center. Her knees went wobbly.

"It's been defused, and it's safe to go back inside."

"But—who—?"

He shrugged. "We'll be looking into that. We've got some samples of the materials used. We might come up with something on this one."

They talked a few more minutes before the sheriff left.

At some point, Amanda had joined her on the curb. "Wow," she said. "That was a close call. What if you'd opened it?"

Natalie didn't even want to think about that.

CHAPTER
THIRTY-FOUR

Natalie put the bowl of macaroni and cheese on the table as Kyle placed a hot dog on each of their plates.

"Alex, your turn," Natalie said after they were seated.

They bowed their heads, and Alex blessed the food.

The boys dug in with vigor. Natalie choked down a bite of hot dog. A week had passed since they'd found the mail bomb. Sheriff Whitco had assured her they were looking into a few leads, but she couldn't help wonder what terrible thing was going to happen next.

Kyle had started taking her to work and picking her up. He helped her make dinner every night and stayed until after the boys went to bed. When he left her house, he always waited to hear the click of the lock. His protective attitude was endearing and his good-bye kisses breathtaking. Natalie knew Kyle wasn't just a man she could live with. He was a man she couldn't live without.

Kyle winked at her over a forkful of macaroni, and Natalie couldn't help the smile that curled her lips. The boys were telling Kyle about the snake they'd seen in Grandma's backyard today.

Natalie couldn't believe how well Kyle fit into their little family. The boys seemed to accept him as easily as they'd accepted Linn.

Not a day passed that Natalie didn't think about the girl. She saw her in every pregnant client that walked through the center's doors. And she couldn't deny that God was tugging on her heart. Sitting through Sunday services had been torture lately. It seemed Pastor Richards knew exactly what she was dealing with, although she knew that couldn't be true.

What do you want from me, God? I don't even know where Linn is or if she's still pregnant. And even if I did, what could I do? Surely, You wouldn't ask me to adopt that child.

Would He?

She stuffed the thought back into a corner of her mind. She didn't think it was even possible. How could she raise a baby, love a baby, who'd been conceived through her husband's betrayal?

She shook her head. It was impossible.

What is impossible with men is possible with God.

The scripture verse came unbidden. She supposed she could thank her mother for that; all those years of Bible verse drills.

She took a bite of macaroni, wondering why the boys never got tired of it.

The phone rang, and she hopped up to get it. "Hello?"

Silence sounded on the other end.

"Hello?"

She plugged her other ear against the boy's raised voices.

Kyle put his fork down and turned to look at her with a question in his eyes.

The phone clicked as the other person hung up. A sliver of fear cut into her. Goose bumps tightened her skin. She hung up quickly, drawing her hand from the receiver as if it were poison. Her heart echoed in her chest. Why were they doing this? Should she call the sheriff? And say what? *Someone just called and didn't say anything.* Yeah, that would go over well. If they could just figure out who was doing all this.

"Who was it?" Kyle asked.

Aware of the boys' eyes on her, she shrugged, and tried for nonchalance. "They hung up. Probably just a wrong number."

Kyle's eyes fixed on her in a knowing look. "Give me the phone."

Before she could grab the phone, it rang again, and she jumped. She didn't want to answer it.

"I'll get it." Kyle took the phone.

"Hello?"

He looked at Natalie. "Just a minute." He handed her the phone. "I think it's Paula."

Natalie answered the phone.

"I only have a second," Paula said. "But turn on the TV and watch the news, OK?"

Watch the news? "Sure, OK."

Paula hung up, and when Natalie glanced at her watch, she saw why Paula had been in such a rush. They'd be airing in less than a minute.

"What's up?" Kyle asked.

"She said to watch the news."

Together they went to the great room. Kyle turned on the TV, then sat beside her on the edge of the sofa. "What do you think this is about?"

"I don't know."

The news jingle came on, showing Paula's and Russ's pictures and their logo before finally zooming in to Russ at the news desk.

"Good evening, I'm Russ Marrick."

"And I'm Paula Landin-Cohen. Thanks for joining us. At five-twenty this afternoon, police arrested Frank Schlater at his home after finding evidence that he may have been behind the recent bomb mailed to the Jackson Hole Hope Center." They flashed a picture of a young man on the screen.

Natalie gasped. She turned up the volume on the remote.

"Sheriff Whitco stated they were able to lift a fingerprint from the package and match it with fingerprints they had on file. It's not yet known why Schlater may have sent the bomb, but police will investigate whether he was behind recent problems at the Hope Center, including an attack and vandalism."

The camera switched to Russ. "Also in local news, an old home-town favorite restaurant is closing after eighteen years in business . . ."

Natalie turned down the volume. "I can't believe it."

"Who is this Frank guy?" Kyle asked.

"I don't know. His name isn't familiar, and I don't recognize him either." Could it really be over? The danger, the fear, the waiting?

"The police should know more soon. I'm just so glad you're going to be safe now." He drew her into his arms.

"You're not going to have an excuse to come over every night now. Or to pick me up every morning and take me to work."

His eyes sparkled. "Do I need an excuse?"

She answered the best way she knew how. She leaned toward him and caressed his lips with hers. He reciprocated in a way that stirred her blood and sent her belly turning flip-flops.

In the two days following Frank Schlater's arrest, the police had sorted through all the information. Frank confessed to attacking her in her car, the vandalism, and sending the package bomb to the center. At first, Natalie figured he must be one of her client's boyfriends, but then Sheriff Whitco had called yesterday with some startling information.

"He was hired to do it," the sheriff had said. "He says Doctor Lewis was behind it."

Doctor Lewis? "From the Women's Health Clinic? But why?" He was the one Paula had interviewed on the news months ago after a bomb had ripped through his clinic. None of it made sense.

"According to Schlater, Doctor Lewis wanted to shut you down. Apparently you've put the hurts on his business."

It was her job to save lives. She supposed it was the doctor's job to take those lives. She was struck by the irony of that. "Still, though, his own clinic was bombed. It doesn't make sense."

"It does when you take into account that Schlater was paid to do that, too."

"What?" She was starting to think Schlater just wanted a scapegoat.

"The good doctor wanted a little sympathy. And some new equipment, apparently."

"I can't believe this," she said. She dragged a hand through her hair.

"Believe it. Case is just about wrapped up."

She had thanked him and immediately called Kyle at his office. He'd been as baffled as her about the doctor.

The phone rang, snatching Natalie from her thoughts, and she picked it up. "Jackson Hole Hope Center."

A slight pause. "I need to talk to someone," a girl's voice said.

"I'd be glad to talk with you. I'm Miss C."

"Do I have to tell you my name?"

"No, of course not. Would you like to come here and talk?"

"No."

"We can talk over the phone, then."

Natalie tried to place her voice. It sounded familiar. She heard a sniff.

"I had an abortion." The last words were choked off by tears.

Natalie's spirit slumped. Her heart went out to the girl. "Do you want to talk about how you're feeling?"

Natalie could hear her crying and wished she could put her arms around the girl.

"It was, like, so awful!" More crying.

But Natalie's heart froze. Something in her voice reminded her of Linn. *Oh no, God, please.*

But it wasn't. It couldn't be. Linn wouldn't call here for help, would she? *And where else would she go? Who else did she have to help her after you practically threw her away.*

She shuddered at the thought. How had she been so selfish as to put her own anger and bitterness before one of God's children? In front of an innocent baby? Her thoughts condemned her.

"We talked before," the girl said. "I came in a few weeks ago and took a test."

The client who insisted she was having an abortion. Not Linn. Relief whooshed through her.

"Are you there?" the voice asked.

"I'm here." It was all she could manage. Her throat had closed up; her mouth had gone dry. It wasn't Linn. Her heart cheered at the thought. She had a second chance now, didn't she? How would she use it?

But first, the girl on the phone. She talked to her, telling her about hope and forgiveness. She could hear the girl quietly crying. By the end of the conversation, she'd talked the girl into coming to the center again. It would take more than one phone call to get through a crisis like this. She hung up the phone, saddened, but confident she'd be able to help this girl.

But what about Linn? She put the thought on hold. It was something she needed to address, but later, when she had time to give it her full attention.

Later that night, after the boys were in bed, she flipped through the channels on the TV. She was restless, and she knew why. She couldn't get Linn out of her mind. She knew she had to forgive Linn. Just as she'd known she'd had to forgive Keith when she discovered the affair. It had taken awhile, but with God's help, she'd done it. Never once had she thrown it up in his face or told the boys what he'd done.

But can I forgive Linn too? She stole my husband, connived her way into my life, and convinced me to adopt her baby.

As she ticked off Linn's sins, her own came racing to the forefront. She closed her eyes. She wasn't perfect either; she realized that. But still. What Linn had done was—

Unforgivable? No, she knew she was supposed to forgive everything. How many times? Seventy times seven, Jesus had said.

She clicked off the TV and stood. She was tired of thinking. She wanted to do something else. She looked around the room at the Legos scattered in one corner and the DVDs strewn across the coffee table. Under that was two weeks of dust. Ugh. Had she really let the house go that long?

She collected the toys and stray items and put them back in their places. The Legos had spilled behind the table along the stairwell, and she pulled it out from the wall. She really should have Alex clean up his own mess.

As she dragged the table out, something caught her eye. A book. She picked it up and almost dropped it. It wasn't a book. It was Linn's journal, the one she'd been keeping for the baby. She stood motionless, her emotions clamoring. She remembered Linn standing on the staircase that day almost three months ago. Remembered vaguely the sound of her journal clanking on the table when Linn had dropped it. The feelings of shock and betrayal came racing back, but she shoved them away. *Oh, God, help me to do what's right.*

She turned from the pile of Legos, journal in hand, and sat on the sofa. She stared at the small booklet in her lap. It was pink and purple and white with hearts splattered over the cover.

Her fingers slid over the cold, smooth cover. Should she open it? She remembered how Linn had gone upstairs to get the journal that night. She'd been about to read them something she'd written.

Natalie opened the cover. The first page was solid pink and blank except for the words Linn had written there.

To my baby, with all my love,
Mom

Her heart catching, Natalie turned the page. The first entry was dated July 28.

Dear Baby,

I've decided to write you letters so you will have something of mine when you grow up. I want you to know how much I love you. Hopefully, when you finish reading this you will know that I am doing what is best for you.

Love, Mom

Natalie felt a lump clog her throat at Linn's words. She truly did love the baby. She wouldn't have had an abortion, would she? She turned to the next page, dated August 3. Before reading it, she fanned through the rest of the journal and saw there were no more entries. Her heart sunk a little, and she wondered why.

Because the entries ended when you kicked her out.

She flipped back to the second entry and began reading.

Dear Baby,

We are so lucky. There has already been so much that has happened that I want to tell you about. I have found a wonderful mommy for you. She has two boys, and she is going to love you so much. I know you already know her now. But maybe you're a teenager like me, and you're fighting with her all the time about your friends and grades and stuff.

I want to tell you what I know about your mommy. She has been beside me since the beginning of my pregnancy. When there was no one else who cared, she took care of me, talked to me, listened to me. And when I had no place to go, she asked me to live with her for a while. (That's where I am right now.)

I still don't know why she's done all this for me. She says she cares about people because we are all God's children. She cares about us so much that she's going to adopt you. I don't understand it, but I want you to grow up with a mommy like her.

Natalie blinked away the tears that stung her eyes. Linn had so much respect for her. And she didn't deserve it.

Natalie had felt as if Linn had played her for a fool, tricking her into adopting her ex-husband's baby. But this entry didn't sound that way at all. Was it possible Linn was just desperate, that she'd kept quiet about her and Keith because she was scared of losing a mommy for her baby?

Linn's words from that awful night of discovery replayed in her mind.

"I was afraid to tell you. I didn't mean for this to happen this way."

Natalie's eyes went back to the page. She found her place and began reading again.

So, even though it is breaking my heart to think of losing you, I know I am doing what's best for you. I want you to have the loving family I never had, and I know your mommy will give that to you.

Love, Mom

Natalie closed the book, her eyes starting to overflow now. She couldn't begin to describe the emotions she was feeling. But she couldn't deny the one that was surfacing fastest. Guilt.

Sure, Linn had done an awful thing. Two awful things. She'd stolen her husband, and she'd kept a terrible secret from Natalie. She was guilty of both of those, no getting around that.

But did she deserve to suffer forever? Did the baby deserve to suffer? For all she knew, there may be no baby now. Her stomach clenched at the thought. She knew the baby was innocent. Worthy of love. Worthy of life. But would he or she get a chance at either?

Please, God, help me do the right thing.

But what was the right thing? She remembered worrying all her life about her lack of faith. About failing God when the moment of testing came. Was this her moment of testing? Was she failing miserably?

Oh, God, give me strength! I don't want to fail You. What should I do?

Forgive. Yes, she knew she had to do that. Her heart toward Linn had changed at the reading of the girl's words. She could forgive a desperate girl who, out of love, wanted the best for her baby. *I do. I forgive her.*

She remembered hearing somewhere that the Greeks' word picture for unforgiveness was a load tied onto another person's back. She'd never felt the truth of that as she did now. It was as if she'd cut the rope and let loose of the terrible weight.

She closed her eyes and leaned back against the couch. Relief, such tremendous relief. She realized her unforgiveness had been about making

Linn pay for what she'd done. Making Linn suffer for her mistakes. But Natalie's unforgiveness had made her suffer, too.

And we know that in all things God works for the good of those who love Him, who have been called according to His purpose.

Natalie knew it was true. Hadn't He worked even Keith's affair for the good? She would never have started working at the center had Keith not left her. And how many lives had she helped touch? How many babies were alive because of Him working through her there?

And now she had a precious man in her life again, and she could see the blessing of that. Yes, God worked all things for the good of those who love Him. *But I have to let Him do that.* She could walk around with a grudge tied to her back for the rest of her life, but to what end? When she didn't forgive, He couldn't complete that good work. He couldn't take the painful experience and make something good of it.

And then, all the pain she suffered would have been for nothing.

Thank you, Jesus, for helping me forgive again. Show me what to do.

If He'd taken her husband's betrayal and brought good from it, what good would He do through this?

She thought of Linn and the baby she hoped Linn still carried. Could she love Linn despite what she had done?

Haven't I loved you, despite what you have done?

It was true. *Oh, Father, it's true. Who am I to judge Linn? Help me to be merciful to her as You are merciful to me.*

She knew what she had to do. She got up and paced across the room. She had to find Linn. She glanced at the clock. Impossible. It was nine thirty-two. Dark outside. She didn't have a clue where to start.

She glanced at the calendar that hung on her wall. If Linn was still pregnant, how far along was she? She counted up the weeks. Thirty-five weeks tomorrow. Five weeks from full term.

What if Linn hadn't been able to take care of herself? What if she hadn't had food and water, and all the things she needed? And medical care. There was no way she'd had medical care.

Oh, Lord, don't let her have had an abortion. She could hardly bear the thought. She could hardly bear the burden of responsibility. She shook the thought. She had to find Linn. But where to start? She looked at the phone and considered calling every hotel in the area. But there was something she wanted to do first. She wanted to tell Kyle what had happened. He'd be happy for her, that she'd found peace in her soul. And maybe he would help her find Linn.

CHAPTER
THIRTY-FIVE

Paula hung up the phone, then stood motionless, her hand still cradling the receiver. Her heart skittered as if she'd just upped the treadmill ten notches. She looked out the glass front of her home to the western buttes of Jackson Hole. The home had gotten a lot of attention when they'd built it, a contemporary mansion next to a bunch of rambling cedar homes.

She paced around the great room, a pulse of energy zinging through her. *I got the job. I got the job.* The words kept replaying in her mind like a scratched CD.

Miles had been enthusiastic about her coming on board. The salary he'd named was more than satisfying, and she'd wanted to scream at the top of her lungs, "YES!"

She'd played it cool, though, and told him she'd talk it over with her husband and get back to him.

David. He hardly seemed like her husband anymore. They didn't talk. They didn't cuddle. And they sure didn't make love anymore. Not since his ridiculous assertion that she'd cheated on him.

Is it ridiculous? Wasn't the abortion a form of betrayal? She pushed the thought away. It wasn't the same at all. She would never cheat on him with another man. And the fact that he'd thought it of her ticked her off.

The way he was buying out JH Realty put another brick in the wall between them. How high was that wall now? She wasn't sure she could even see him over it anymore.

Surely he would be happy for her, though. She remembered how supportive he'd been for her when she'd gotten the job at WKEF. Even though they both knew it was just a little local station, it was the best Jackson had for someone in her field. He'd taken her to the Rendezvous Bistro to celebrate. She remembered the night well. Especially the love-making they'd shared later.

She ran her hand through her short auburn hair. It was a different story now, but she hoped he could pull himself out of his own success long enough to congratulate her for hers. She looked at her watch. If he ever got home, that was.

She went to pour herself a glass of Cabernet Sauvignon. She savored the smell of the liquid before she raised her glass in a silent toast. She took a sip, and the smooth liquid glided down her throat. As fulfilled as she felt about the job offer, she wanted to tell someone. Celebrating in solitude felt empty.

She heard the garage door open and the door's security beep sound. She put the glass down and walked to the hall, where David was standing with his briefcase.

"Hi," she said.

"Hi." He set the briefcase on a shelf in the closet, then walked around her toward the kitchen.

"Want me to fix you something?" she asked.

He glanced at her, and she knew what he was thinking. So it had been awhile since she'd done something nice for him.

"I'll just grab a sandwich." He opened the stainless steel refrigerator door and pulled out the deli meat she'd picked up the day before.

"Good day?" she asked. Might as well start small and build from there. It felt awkward springing such exciting news on someone who'd shown zero interest in her for months.

"It was OK."

One thing she appreciated about David. He never failed to be polite. Another man might ignore her after all the tension they'd had between them. Not David.

She watched him fix his sandwich, and when he took a seat on a barstool, she leaned back against the counter. She was about to burst. The only thing that stopped her was wondering what David's reaction would be.

"What's got you so nervous?"

She realized she'd been drumming her fingers against the Corian countertop. She stopped and took a deep breath.

David took another bite of his roast beef, eyeing her strangely.

"I heard from the station in Chicago a few minutes ago," she said.

He put the sandwich down and wiped his mouth on the napkin. "And?"

Did she detect caution in his tone? "I got it, David. They offered me the job." There was a day the words would have had her jumping up and down. David would have embraced her, and they might have done a joy jig together. She envisioned it happening, knowing a giddy smile was crowding her face.

"You told them you couldn't take it, didn't you?"

Pop. She could almost hear the sound of her bubble bursting. "What?" He expected her to dismiss it, just like that? Her dream job in one of the country's biggest cities, and he thought she'd turn it down?

"It's obvious the job may become permanent. Well, we can hardly move, Paula."

Distaste. Anger. Frustration. They all beaded up on the surface like water on a waxed car. "You can't be serious."

He blinked, finally setting his sandwich on the plate. "I can't move to Chicago. I'm buying JH Realty, in case you'd forgotten."

"And who told you to do that? Did you even once ask my opinion?"

"It was a once-in-a-lifetime opportunity!"

"So is this." She struggled to keep her voice down. Her heart raced. This was not going as she'd hoped.

He pushed his glasses up higher on the bridge of his nose. It was as if he hadn't even considered asking her about the buy-out. Now he was.

"I guess I should've asked you. But there's no way I can leave now. It's already a done deal."

"What about my career opportunity? You knew I didn't want to stay here. You knew it before we ever married."

"I thought you were happy here now."

"Who are you to decide where I'm happy? How would you know, anyway? We haven't talked in months."

His eyes narrowed. "That's not my fault."

She gave a wry laugh. "Of course not. It's my fault for not owning up to the affair that I never had in the first place!"

She felt heat rushing through her, making her skin hot. She knew her face was turning red and hated that she couldn't stop it.

She could see him trying to gather himself. He took a sip of Evian. "Arguing isn't going to get us anywhere."

No kidding, Sherlock.

"Let's look at the facts. I'm going to own JH Realty. Obviously, I can't leave."

"Can't or won't?"

He blinked rapidly. "You know what absentee ownership does to a business. I might as well throw away all the money I've invested."

"And you just expect me to give up my career opportunity?"

"Well, I'm not giving up mine."

So many thoughts. So many emotions. Too many to decipher. She knew one thing, though. She wasn't giving up her big chance.

"I'm not either. You didn't consult with me on your opportunity, and I'm not consulting with you on mine. I'm taking the job." She turned and walked away.

Linn shoved a pair of jeans in the Kmart bag and looked around the tiny room she'd been staying in. It was the size of some walk-in closets, but it had been a safe haven for almost a month.

She grabbed her tablet of paper off the makeshift nightstand and tucked it carefully inside. Her letters to her baby were her most precious belonging. Well, that was everything.

She picked up the letter she was leaving for George and read it one more time.

George,

Thanks again for letting me stay here. You'll never know how much I appreciate it. Maybe one day, I'll be able to pay you back.

I wanted to let you know that I am taking a bus to Chicago. One of my friends from high school has an apartment there and has agreed to let me stay with her for a while. Her aunt is even giving me a job in her bookstore. Don't worry. We will be just fine. Well, I guess that's all. Take care, and don't let the bedbugs bite.

Linn

She smiled as she read the last part. George had said that to her every evening when he'd checked on her. He was a funny old man, and she'd miss him.

She bundled up her things and left through the back door. A glance at her watch told her she had twenty minutes to get to the bus stop. She could make it easy in ten.

Once her bike was loaded down, she carefully straddled the seat and rearranged the duffle bag that was throwing her off balance. Wasn't easy riding a bike at eight months pregnant, especially when it was loaded down with everything she owned. She gave a wry laugh. Not that she had much.

Haltingly, she took off, shivering in the late October wind. They'd had lots of snow already, but the streets were clear now. It would be a long day for her. She hoped the bus had a bathroom. Otherwise, she didn't know how she'd make it without an hourly bathroom break. She glanced down at her swollen belly. Sometimes she could hardly believe there was a baby in there.

She felt the baby twist inside her, then thump her with what must have been a foot. "Settle down, stinker, it's going to be a long day."

Her legs pumped rhythmically, and her breath came heavily. There didn't seem to be enough room in her chest for her lungs to inflate anymore. She kept telling herself it would all be over in a matter of weeks, but with her baby's future up in the air, it didn't make her feel any better. She'd have to figure out where she was going to have the baby. Would the hospital take her in if they knew she didn't have insurance? Surely they wouldn't turn her away.

Her friend's aunt knew a social worker who was going to help her find parents for her baby. Much as she loved the little one, she knew she was in no shape to raise this child. She dreaded the thought of giving the baby up, though. It would have been so much better if things had worked out with Natalie. It would have been perfect, then. Her baby would have been raised with his or her brothers. But now some strangers would raise her baby, and they probably wouldn't let her keep in contact or send her pictures of her little one.

When her eyes teared up, she blamed it on the cold wind. She sniffed, her legs beginning to ache in earnest now. She passed the town square with its arch of elk antlers. The place was deserted this time of year. "Bye, Town Square," she whispered. She wondered if she'd ever be back. Her father was still not speaking to her. Maybe, someday, when her pregnancy was a distant memory.

When she reached the Greyhound depot, she slid off her bike, pulled it up onto the curb by the bus stop, and put down the kickstand. She felt in her jeans pocket for the ticket, then went into the shelter of the bus stop to wait.

CHAPTER
THIRTY-SIX

Natalie stuffed Taylor's blankie into his backpack and zipped it shut. Keith would be here any minute, and shortly after that, she would take a step that may change her life forever.

Last night was almost a blur. Finding Linn's letters to her baby, her phone call to Kyle. But she would never forget his words when she'd told him she forgave Linn and wanted to find her.

"I know where she is."

Even now, the words sent goose bumps up her back. He'd told her how he'd found her three weeks ago at the Wagon Wheel Campground. How he'd made sure she'd had a place to stay and food to eat. He'd spoken with caution in his voice.

"I'm sorry I didn't tell you before. I've been feeling guilty about that," he'd said. *"I felt like I was keeping something from you."*

She'd tried to imagine him telling her three weeks ago, and knew he'd done the right thing. She hadn't been ready to hear he was sympathetic toward Linn. Now it made her heart swell to see how he'd taken care of his former sister-in-law. And it made sense. Of course Kyle wouldn't have been able to stand by and let Linn suffer.

But the other thing she'd never forget was Kyle's assurances that Linn was still pregnant. She closed her eyes. *Thank you, Jesus.* Linn hadn't had an abortion, and in five weeks, she'd have a baby. Natalie wondered so many things. Had she had medical care? Had she arranged for another adoption? Had she decided to raise the child herself? Natalie didn't see how, since Linn had hardly been able to look after herself, but she'd known many girls who had unrealistic expectations when it came to raising their own children. Kyle told her Linn had lost her job at Bubba's and hadn't yet found another job. It would be hard for a very pregnant woman to get a job anywhere, much less a girl who had no car.

She'd wanted to go see Linn last night, but it was late, and Taylor and Alex were already in bed. Kyle convinced her to wait until morning, after Keith picked up the boys.

A knock on the door shook her from her thoughts.

"Alex, do you have your things packed?" She trotted down the stairs and opened the door.

"Hi, Keith."

He seemed surprised at her upbeat tone. "Hi." He eyed her sideways.

"Boys, are you ready?"

Alex and Taylor abandoned their spots in front of the Saturday morning cartoons.

"Grab your bag, Alex."

She handed Taylor's backpack to him and kissed the boys good-bye.

After they left, she paced, glancing at her watch every two minutes. Why had she told Kyle nine-thirty? She wanted to go now. What would she say to Linn? Would the girl even forgive her after what she'd done? She'd kicked a pregnant girl out on the street.

Oh, Lord, show me what to say.

Maybe Linn wouldn't want to speak to her, much less forgive her. Linn had trusted Natalie—the only person in her life she could trust. What kind of a Christian witness had Natalie been? She was supposed to show Christ's love, and instead, she'd only been selfish. Only thought of her own hurts.

At the same time, she wondered about the baby. Would Linn still let her adopt the child? It was a question she wouldn't find the answer to until Kyle took her to Linn.

She looked at her watch again. If he ever got here. She was being unfair, and she knew it. He wasn't even due for four more minutes. She walked to the window and pulled back the sheer drapes. Kyle was just pulling into the drive.

She grabbed her purse and left the house, turning to lock the door before getting into his car.

"Ready?" he asked.

She looked into his gray-green eyes, noting the peace that radiated from them. "I'm ready," she said.

The ride over to the campground was excruciating. Would Linn forgive her? Would she let Natalie back into her life again? When they finally arrived, they knocked on the restaurant door. After knocking several times, Natalie began to worry.

"Where could she be?"

"Let's check with George," Kyle said.

They found George raking leaves in front of his house. After explaining the situation to him, Natalie and Kyle followed George to the tiny room at the back of the restaurant.

As they entered the little room, George scratched his head. "Well, she was here last night, but I don't see hide nor hair of her things in here."

"What's this?" Kyle picked up a sheet of paper that had been propped on a thin, lumpy pillow.

"Oh no," Kyle said.

"What?" Natalie asked. "What is it?" Something in his voice scared her.

She couldn't read the letter, since George was standing over Kyle's shoulder reading along.

"Shoot," he said.

"What?" Why didn't someone tell her? She squiggled between the wall and cot to get to Kyle's other side. She'd read it herself.

"She left," Kyle said.

"How long ago, you reckon?" George asked.

Natalie read the note. No. Why did this have to happen now? "We have to go after her. Maybe we can catch her."

"Let's go." Kyle dropped the note, and they ran to his car.

"Good luck, you two," George called.

"We're not far from the bus stop. Maybe we'll make it in time." Kyle squeezed Natalie's hand.

They had to catch her in time. How would Natalie live with herself if they didn't, knowing the way she'd treated Linn? How could she live without knowing that child was safe in a loving family? *How will you live without having that child to raise as your own?*

The note had left no clue about where she was going, only that she would live in an apartment in Chicago with a friend. Finding her there would take a miracle.

Lord, please let us get there in time. Why had she wasted so many weeks soaking in self-pity and righteous anger? Where had it gotten her? *Forgive me, Lord, for taking so long to see the truth.*

"Almost there," Kyle said, laying a hand on her knee. "Do I see someone in the bus shelter?"

Natalie straightened and squinted through the dirty, scratched Plexiglas. There was someone in there. They neared the spot. A woman.

"There's her bike." Propped right beside the shelter and loaded down with bags was Linn's old bike.

Kyle pulled into the adjacent Wendy's parking lot and stopped the car. "I'll wait here."

Natalie started to argue, then realized he was right. Linn wouldn't want to see Kyle. It would only make this more difficult than it would already be.

She ran toward the shelter, slowing as she neared it. Suddenly, fear seized her. What if Linn rejected her apology? What if she'd already made other arrangements for the baby? Natalie didn't think she'd be able to stand either of those possibilities.

Lord, You've given me the strength to do what's right. Now help me explain it all to Linn in a way she can understand.

She rounded the Plexiglas sides and came face-to-face with Linn. The girl's eyes widened, and her head, which had been resting against the bench's back, came upright.

Natalie stopped. Linn looked so sweet sitting there. So young and vulnerable. Just like the first time she'd seen her walk into the center all those months ago. Natalie's eyes darted down to the volleyball-sized belly peeking out from under Linn's coat. She remembered praying with conviction about that baby when it was only the size of a seed.

"Linn." So many emotions darted through her. Longing for the relationship they'd had before this mess. Love for the girl who'd trusted Natalie with her baby's future. Regret for the way Natalie had responded that day so many weeks ago. Her eyes burned in their sockets until Linn blurred in front of her.

"I'm so sorry. I was wrong." Her body was frozen in space.

Linn also seemed too stunned to move.

When would the bus arrive? Natalie needed to explain before it did. The words gushed out, and she was acutely aware they weren't in any semblance of order. Was Linn making any sense of it?

"And I found your letters to your baby, and that's when I knew—Oh, Linn, I've been so wrong."

Linn's brown eyes began overflowing with tears. Her face scrunched up, and she covered it with her hands.

Natalie sat on the bench beside her and put her arm around the girl's shoulders. "Shhh, it's OK. Everything's OK now." But was it? Where would they go from here? Had Linn already promised the baby to someone else? Would Linn still go to Chicago? Natalie didn't want her to leave. She'd never told Linn how God wanted a relationship with her.

Beside her, Linn sobbed quietly. "It was all my fault. You didn't do anything wrong."

"Oh, honey, I did." Natalie stroked her hair. "I should have forgiven you long ago. I never should have put you out on the street with no place to go. That's not what God wanted me to do."

Linn lifted her head off Natalie's shoulder and wiped her face on the sleeve of her nylon coat. "How can you forgive me after what I did?"

Her face crumpled again, and Natalie knew she was thinking of the affair she'd had with Keith. Something in her went as soft as fleece. Linn hadn't had a man in her life to show her love. It was no surprise she longed for an older man to fill that void. It was all over now. She felt a strength inside her that grew until she was almost overwhelmed with it. What she was doing felt so right. So good.

She went back to Linn's question. How could she forgive Linn for what she'd done? It was simple, really. Why had she made it so hard?

"How could I not forgive you? Do you think I'm perfect? My God forgives me every time I mess up. Who am I to judge your mistakes? That's not my job. My job is to forgive, and that's what I'm doing, Linn. I'm choosing to forgive."

Linn sniffed and pushed her straight, brown hair behind her ear. Tears trailed down her face, her lashes still spiked with them.

Now that the forgiveness issue was settled, Natalie knew she needed to say the next part, and quickly before the bus arrived. "I don't know what plans you've made for the baby." Linn's face gave nothing away, and Natalie felt her mouth go dry. "If you still want me to, and if you haven't made other arrangements, I'd love nothing more than to raise your baby."

A loud noise cut off the last words, and Natalie looked up to see the bus pulling to the curb. *Oh, please, no. Not yet!*

She looked at Linn and saw another batch of tears starting.

"Please say you'll stay, Linn. You can stay at my house again, and it'll be just like before. I'll help you find a job and get back on your feet after the baby."

Linn looked at the bus, then back to Natalie.

The bus door squeaked open, and a big, burly driver climbed down the steps. "These your things?" he asked.

"What do you say, Linn?" Natalie asked.

A quivery smile broke out on Linn's face. "You still want my baby?"

Was that regret on Linn's face? Natalie's worst fear gripped her. "Have you promised the baby to someone else?"

Linn shook her head.

"Hey." The driver hiked his pants up on his mounded belly. "Do you want me to load your stuff or not?"

Linn's gaze seared Natalie's. The connection was a deep, soul-reaching one. Slowly, they both smiled.

"No," Linn said. "I'm staying."

Tingles of relief shot through Natalie. She embraced Linn, rocking back and forth. Yes! Yes! Her eyes began to burn again. When they pulled apart, she saw the bus door sliding shut, the driver shaking his head.

Then she saw Kyle rounding the corner of the shelter. She wanted to hug him, too. But just then Linn saw her former brother-in-law, and the smile slid from her face.

"What's he doing here?"

Natalie let her gaze linger on her man for just a moment. How could Linn not know what a wonderful man he was? Of course, she didn't yet know how Kyle had secretly taken care of her these last weeks.

Natalie turned Linn's face toward her. "Do you trust me, Linn?"

Her brown eyes questioned. Natalie wanted to smooth the frown puckering between her brows. "Yes," Linn said.

"I have so much to tell you. Things that have happened since we've seen each other. Things I've discovered. There've been misunderstandings between Kyle and your family."

Linn shivered and pulled her coat tight over her belly.

"I promise I'll tell you everything, but I want to get you out of this cold." She put out her hand, palm up. "Come with us?"

Linn's eyes went to Kyle then, and Natalie followed her gaze. The look on Kyle's face melted her heart. His eyes shone with his love for Linn, and Natalie had never been so proud to call a man hers.

Without taking her eyes from Kyle, Linn put her hand in Natalie's. "I'll go with you." The very words Natalie longed to hear.

CHAPTER
THIRTY-SEVEN

Natalie spread the tablecloth over the extended table and smoothed the lines from the fall-foliage material. Kyle was in the great room, and Natalie could hear him explaining to Alex the rudiments of the football game they were watching together.

"Need any help in there?" Kyle called.

"You're helping plenty by keeping the boys occupied." She winked at him as she walked back into the kitchen, wondering at the love growing in her heart toward him. He was an amazing man, and she wasn't about to let him go.

When she entered the kitchen, she saw Linn studying the stuffing recipe, a frown between her brows. Her belly was huge—there was no other word for it. But then, she was due the next day, so she was supposed to be huge.

"Linn, honey, go sit down. Your feet are going to swell to the size of Texas."

"Too late." She held up her sock-encased foot and gave a wry grin.

"Go. Sit." Natalie ushered her out of the kitchen, before returning to the stove, and watched her fall into the overstuffed sofa.

The past four weeks had passed quickly. They'd gotten the adoption process started with Kyle. Once Linn had heard how Kyle had taken care of her while she was at the Wagon Wheel, her heart had begun softening toward him. Kyle hadn't wanted Natalie to tell her about Jillian's affair, but Natalie had insisted it was the only way Linn would understand. At first, Linn hadn't wanted to believe it, but the details she'd coaxed out of Kyle were convincing. Linn remembered Jillian's high-school boyfriend, remembered the reunion Jillian had gone to alone. It all started making sense to her. And the fact that Kyle had taken blame for the affair rather than hurting her family with the truth had gone a long way toward mending things between Linn and Kyle.

Natalie could hear them in the other room even now, talking about Loyola University, where Linn would go in January. Natalie and Kyle talked to her about it often to remind her she had a great future ahead of her.

Natalie had gotten Linn's medical care covered under her insurance. She'd offered to let Linn stay after the baby's birth, but Linn decided it would be too hard to see her baby every day. After she left the hospital, she would go live with her friend in Chicago and recover there. Her friend's aunt agreed to keep the job at her bookstore open until Linn arrived and was able to work. And it made Natalie feel a little better to know that Paula would be in Chicago, too. Maybe if Linn had any problems, she could ask her sister to help out. Natalie thanked God that everything had worked out so smoothly.

The hardest part of the adoption process had been convincing Keith to go along with the plan. When she'd told him she wanted to adopt his and Linn's baby, he'd gotten as angry as she'd ever seen him. He'd even called her crazy. But after a few weeks of cooling down and the realization that adoption meant no child support for this baby, he'd agreed to sign away his rights. It would be awkward when he came to pick up Alex and Taylor, knowing he was leaving another child of his with Natalie. But he'd made it clear he didn't want to be a part of this child's life. It was as if he'd written this baby off. Perhaps he didn't believe the child was really his. No matter. It had worked out. They'd take one step at a time, one day at a time.

Natalie peeked through the oven door and read the thermometer on the turkey. Almost. The doorbell rang, but before Natalie could straighten, she heard the door opening.

"Happy Thanksgiving!" her dad called.

"Grandpa!" She heard the boys go running toward the door.

Natalie went to greet them. Kyle took their coats as Hanna, Micah, and Gram filed in behind her parents.

Natalie took the Crock-Pot from Gram's hands. "Yum! These sweet potatoes smell great."

"Wish I could take credit, dear," Gram said. "But Hanna made them this year. It was all I could do to keep my fingers out."

Hanna shrugged out of her coat and handed it to Kyle. Natalie noted her rounded belly. "Look at you! You're finally showing."

Standing behind her, Micah wrapped his arms around her, his hands on her belly, and kissed her on the cheek. "Isn't she cute?"

"Oh, stop it you two," Hanna said. "I feel like a whale. Where's Linn? I need to see someone bigger than me."

"Like, thanks a lot!" Linn called from her spot on the sofa. Everyone laughed, including Linn, who looked as if she was enjoying the attention.

Kyle carried the coats upstairs to her bedroom. The fact that he was acting as host was not lost on her mother, who wiggled her brows Natalie's direction.

The hubbub continued as the men settled in front of the TV and the women went to the kitchen. Later, Hanna paused from stirring the gravy to speak. "Isn't it funny how after all these years of women's lib, we're still doing all the cooking, and the men are still watching TV?"

"Some things never change," her mom said as she wiped her hands on a dishtowel.

"We should make the men do cleanup," Hanna said as Kyle walked in.

"I think I picked the wrong time to get a soda." Kyle smiled cautiously.

"Now's your chance to impress them," Natalie said in a stage whisper. "By showing them how helpful you are by offering to do the dishes."

The doorbell rang, then the front door opened, and Natalie heard Paula and David telling everyone hello.

"Saved by the bell," Kyle said.

Natalie snapped a dishtowel at him as he left the kitchen.

A half hour later, they gathered around the table, which was extended to support their growing family. As was their tradition, they paused to go around the table and share their blessings over the past year. Her dad, at the head of the table, nudged his wife. "Mom, why don't you go first?"

Her mom sighed, a content smile on her face. "I'm thankful for all this wonderful family around the table. God has been so good to us." She looked at Natalie and Hanna and Linn. "I'm excited that we'll be having two additions to the family very soon." She looked at Linn. "I'm thankful to God for bringing Linn into my daughter's life. Into our lives. I have to admit, when I heard what Natalie was doing, well"—she blinked back tears—"I had my doubts, I'm sorry to say. But we serve a God who's capable of that kind of love, that kind of compassion." Her words choked off, and she squeezed Paula's hand to let her know she was through.

Paula looked everywhere but at David, who was seated across from her. Natalie wondered if everyone else noticed.

"I'm so thankful for my new job in Chicago . . ." Her voice crescendoed with enthusiasm.

The words fell awkwardly on Natalie's ears. It was hard to be excited about something that was separating Paula from her husband. Her family had tried to be happy for Paula, but she was well aware they didn't approve of her being away from David.

"It'll be hard, traveling back and forth so much," Paula said, "but I'm so excited about this opportunity."

Silence spread awkwardly as she ended.

"What are you thankful for, Alex?" Natalie cued her son, who was next in line.

"I'm thankful that there's no school today, and that I get to stay up late tonight, and that I'm getting a new brother or sister soon." Next to him, Kyle ruffled his hair, and her son smiled shyly.

"You finished, pal?" Kyle asked.

When Alex nodded, Kyle spoke. "Wow, what a year." Under the table, he squeezed Natalie's hand. "I'm thankful God brought me through some personal issues, baggage I've been carrying around since my wife's death. I'm grateful He's restored my relationship with Linn." He looked at Linn, but she was staring at her empty plate. "And I'm grateful that Frank Schlater and Doctor Lewis were caught and appropriately charged."

"Amen!" her dad said.

Chuckles sounded around the table.

"And the reason I'm thankful for that," Kyle said, "is because those men compromised the safety of a woman who's become very important to me."

When he met Natalie's eyes, she wanted to drown in the stormy depths. Her stomach fluttered the way it did every time he looked at her that way. She wanted to touch those crinkles at the corners of his eyes and trail her fingers down his face and across his lips.

Her dad cleared his throat loudly, and everyone laughed again.

Natalie could swear she saw a flush creep up Kyle's neck as he continued. "I'm thankful for this family, and for two little rascals who've livened up my life." He ruffled Alex's hair again and winked at Taylor across from him.

"What's a rascal?" Taylor asked.

"He's talkin' about us. Right, Kyle?" Alex said.

"You bet I am. You guys are stupendific."

Natalie laughed at the word Kyle and the boys had made up together, a combination of "stupendous" and "terrific."

"You want to explain that one?" Micah asked.

"Later," Natalie said. "It's my turn, and the food's getting cold." She grabbed Linn's hand on the table. "I'm thankful for my family, my precious boys. I'm thankful to God for bringing two very special people into my life this year." She looked at Kyle on one side of her, then Linn on the other side. "Well, three, actually," she said, smiling. "When Linn walked into the center all those months ago, it was my prayer that she'd discover that God wanted a relationship with her and that she would value the life inside her enough to continue the pregnancy."

Her eyes burned. How could she have known the way God would answer those prayers? That He would use her so powerfully? Linn had accepted Christ the week after she'd come back home with Natalie, kneeling by the couch in the other room. She was growing in her faith and was so curious, she asked almost as many questions as Alex.

Natalie blinked back the tears, determined to get all the way through her blessings. "God answered both of those prayers, and now we'll be blessed with a baby in our family. I'm so thankful for Linn's courage to carry this baby and that she's trusted us with the most precious gift in the world." She swallowed against the lump in her throat.

She was so thankful that God had given her the courage to put her feet where her faith was. That in the midst of hurt and fear, He'd given her the power to do the right thing. She'd always been so afraid she didn't have it in her to make the hard choice when her back was up against the wall. But she'd found she didn't need to have it in her. It was God who did these things through her. She wanted to share that thought with her family but couldn't speak past the lump in her throat.

She squeezed Linn's hand.

"Um, I know I'm supposed to say something I'm thankful for, but"—Linn's eyes met Natalie's—"I, like, think my water broke a few minutes ago."

The words dropped and silence followed. Then everything was confusion.

"Why didn't you say something?" Natalie said.

"I didn't want to interrupt," Linn said. "Sorry about your chair."

"We need to get you to the hospital," Natalie said. "Isn't that what they said in Lamaze? If your water breaks, you're supposed to go straight to the hospital."

Everyone was talking at once, and the food was forgotten as Natalie helped Linn up. After she changed into dry clothes, Kyle stowed Linn's hospital bag in the car while Natalie called the doctor. The three of them piled into Kyle's car, leaving the boys in her family's care until Keith arrived to pick them up.

"Ready?" Natalie asked Linn.

Linn nodded, and Kyle pointed the car toward St. John's. In a matter of hours, Natalie would hold a miracle in her arms. Was she ready? Were any of them?

"That's it, Linn!" Natalie said. "One . . . two . . . three . . . four . . . five . . . Let your breath out. Take a cleansing breath." The redness faded from Linn's face once again as she began breathing. Her hair hung in limp, damp strands around her face. Whether it was from the tears or sweat, Natalie wasn't sure.

"You're doing terrific!" Natalie said, hoping to perk up Linn, who was exhausted. "Almost there. Just a few more pushes and that baby will be here."

"Maybe not even that," Doctor Hart said, patting Linn's leg.

Linn had succumbed to an epidural at five centimeters, and everything had progressed slowly but smoothly until she'd reached full dilation at four in the morning. She'd been pushing since then, and a glance at the clock told Natalie she'd been at it almost two hours. She brushed the hair back from Linn's face.

"Hang in there, Linn," Natalie said.

"I'm so tired." Her eyes closed, as though she wanted nothing more than a full night's sleep, but Natalie could see from the monitor that another contraction was starting.

"OK, here we go again, deep breath."

"I don't want to." A tear slid from Linn's eye and trickled down into her hairline.

"Come on, honey, it's almost over! Deep breath." Natalie took a breath, hoping Linn would follow.

Linn raised her head and took a breath, holding it while Natalie counted to five in three sets, guiding Linn to take a breath between each set.

"There's the head," Dr. Hart said as Linn collapsed on the pillow. "One more good set of pushes, and I think we'll hear some screaming in here."

"Yeah, like mine," Linn said, "if this baby doesn't hurry up and come out."

Doctor Hart laughed. "I've heard many women scream long before this, Linn. You're doing fantastic!"

The nurses were scurrying around the room, prepping for the baby's arrival.

Natalie wiped Linn's forehead with a damp cloth. "You're doing great, honey. You're bringing life into this world, and I'm so proud of you."

Linn's eyes were closed, and she was still catching her breath. She'd attended Lamaze and seen a video of a birth, but nothing could really prepare anyone for childbirth.

And no amount of preparation could prepare Linn for the feelings she would have when she left this hospital without her baby. *God, be with her. Give her the strength she needs.* Whenever Natalie had brought up the fact that some birth mothers change their minds after the baby is born, Linn had been firm that she wouldn't. She continued writing letters to her baby and said her words and a loving family were the best gifts she could give her baby.

But Natalie knew feelings could be unpredictable sometimes. In the past weeks, she'd sometimes wondered if she would think of Keith's painful betrayal every time she looked at this baby. But she and God had put those feelings to rest. No, she was more afraid that Linn could change her mind. She didn't know if she could bear losing this baby. That alone assured her that her feelings for the child were strong and pure.

"Here we go," the nurse said, shaking Natalie from her thoughts.

"Ready to bring that baby into the world?" Natalie asked Linn.

Linn lifted her head from the pillow and grabbed the backs of her knees.

"One . . . two . . . three . . . four . . . five . . . breathe!"

Linn gulped another breath and began pushing again.

"One . . . two . . . three . . . four—"

"Here we are," Dr. Hart said. "It's a girl!"

A girl! Natalie's eyes felt prickly before tears slipped out. She watched the baby slide into the doctor's arms. A feeble, furious cry filled the air. One of the nurses raised the top of the bed, sitting Linn up a bit. As they had discussed before, the nurse wrapped the baby in a blanket and laid her in Linn's arms.

"Shhhh," Linn said. "It's all right, little one."

Linn's face was a sight to behold. A mixture of awe, love, and sorrow. Tears leaked from her eyes as she gazed into the baby's eyes. The baby's eyes were fixed on Linn's in a mother-child bond. Natalie turned to give her a moment alone. She walked from the room and leaned against the wall outside the door. She wasn't prepared for the ache she felt at seeing Linn and the baby together.

So many feelings came in around her. Joy at the beautiful gift of life. Gratitude that God had intervened in saving this baby. Sadness at Linn's sacrifice. And a bit of fear that Linn would change her mind.

She wiped the tears from her eyes and tried to swallow the lump that had swollen her throat. *Help me to bear it, Lord, if she changes her mind. Help me to stand by her and do what's right.* He would, Natalie knew. He had never failed her when she needed Him or given her more than she could bear.

She should go tell Kyle that the baby had arrived, but she couldn't seem to separate herself from this wall. She didn't want to leave Linn. She didn't want to leave the baby, even for a few moments.

She didn't know how much later it was when one of the nurses peeked through the door. "Linn is asking for you."

Her heart stopped. That must be why she felt so dizzy all of a sudden. She stood up straight and wiped her face dry. She could do this. She could. With God's strength.

She walked into the room and neared the bed. A nurse was handing the baby back to Linn. The sight was precious and painful all at the same time. Linn stroked her daughter's red little cheeks, her own face streaked with tears.

She looked up at Natalie's approach. "Isn't she beautiful?"

Natalie leaned over to look into the tiny face. Her eyes were the color of Jenny Lake on a clear, summer day. Her nose was flat except for the little pug on the tip. "The most beautiful little girl, ever." Natalie realized she meant those words.

"Have you decided on a name?" Linn asked.

Natalie's heart skittered. Linn was looking at her expectantly. They'd talked about names several times. Natalie had asked Linn's opinion, but Linn had always deferred to Natalie. Now Linn was clearly leaving the choice to Natalie, and that could only mean one thing.

She hadn't changed her mind. Natalie could almost feel the joy unfolding inside her. She looked at the baby and ached to hold her in her arms. To feed her and dress her in little terry-soft sleepers. To put her finger in the palm of the tiny hand and feel those fingers curl around it. And yet . . .

She looked at Linn. She thought about the selfless way she'd made the best choice for her baby, regardless of the pain she would suffer. And Natalie knew what she could do.

"I want you to name her," Natalie said.

Linn looked at Natalie, a question on her face.

"Give her a name."

Linn looked back at the baby. She bit her lip and blinked several times. She stared into her baby's eyes for a few minutes, and the silence that wrapped around the room felt like peace itself had come and enveloped them like a mountain mist.

Then Linn spoke, her voice soft and strong at the same time. "You once told me that's God's grace was a gift, something we didn't deserve." She looked at Natalie. "This sweet little bundle in my arms is just that—a gift I didn't deserve. So I want to name her Grace."

A smile blossomed on Natalie's face as chills chased up her arms. Grace. It was perfect. "Oh, honey, I love it." She brushed Linn's hair back from her face. Grace. God's grace.

"There's a man out there 'bout to pace the carpet clean away," the nurse said.

Natalie chuckled. "I'd better go put him out of his misery." She turned to go.

"Wait," Linn said. "Take Grace." She handed the little bundle over to Natalie.

Her arms felt full, though the weight of Grace was next to nothing. She paused long enough to smile at Linn. Then she walked slowly, not wanting to take her eyes off Grace for even a moment. Time was too precious. Life was too precious to be wasted.

She found Kyle around the corner, sitting in the waiting room, his hands steepled under his chin. He turned and saw her. She could almost hear his breath sucking in at the sight of the baby in her arms. He stood slowly, the look on his face priceless.

She neared and stopped when she was a breath away from him. "Kyle Keaton, meet baby Grace."

A smile played on his lips. He reached out and touched Grace's cheek with a hand that looked super-sized next to the baby's face. "A girl. Hello, little Grace." He looked at Natalie. "How's Linn doing?"

"She's great. She did great."

"How's the new mom doing?"

He studied her so carefully, Natalie felt as if her whole heart was exposed, and she didn't mind. "I'm so happy. This just feels so right. I know it won't be easy for me or for Linn. She's losing her baby, and I've committed to something that most people would think is just plain crazy, but today we're starting a future together, and I just have so much peace—"

Kyle put his finger on her lips. "Shhhhhh. You don't have to explain. I feel it, too."

Their eyes met, and not for the first time, Natalie wanted to drown in their grayish green, stormy depths. His hand cupped her jaw, and she couldn't look away. Didn't even want to. His lips came down over hers, lingering slowly, as if to savor every second. Her skin tingled with awareness, her pulse raced.

When Grace stirred, they parted, and their eyes fixed on the little miracle between them.

"I just want you to know," Kyle whispered. "I plan to be there for you and Grace and the boys. I hope you have room for me in this future of yours."

Natalie liked the sound of that. She met his gaze. "Are you up for diaper changings and feedings and sibling rivalry?"

"I'm up for anything you need."

Outside the picture window, tinges of pink and periwinkle swept across the sky. A new day dawned, bringing with it an uncertain future, but Natalie knew it was the future God had planned. And that was all that mattered.

THE END

Discussion Questions

1. Natalie's passion in life is helping women avoid abortions. What are you passionate about, and how are you living out that passion?

2. Jeremiah 1:4–5 says, "The word of the LORD came to me, saying, 'Before I formed you in the womb I knew you, before you were born I set you apart; I appointed you as a prophet to the nations.'" Based on this biblical truth, when do you think life begins?

3. Sometimes pro-lifers focus on the unborn child, while those who support abortion focus on the woman. When you were reading about Linn's predicament, did you tend to worry more about Linn or her baby? What are some of the hazards we face if we aren't concerned about both the woman and the unborn child?

4. When Natalie discovered who Linn was, she experienced shock and anger, while Linn experienced fear and confusion. Whom did you sympathize with more, Natalie or Linn?

5. Even though Natalie believed in her cause, she still balked when it came time to put feet to her faith. Has there ever been a time when you knew what you should do and you still faltered? Did you eventually make the right decision? Why or why not?

6. If you had been in Natalie's place, would you have adopted Linn's baby? Why or why not?

7. Kyle carried a great deal of guilt over his wife's death, even though it was an accident. Have you ever felt guilty about something that was not your fault? Why do you think we sometimes feel guilty about things that are out of our control? How can we get rid of the guilt?

8. As the story progresses, Paula and David's marriage begins to unravel. What do you think causes this to happen?

9. In the story, Paula harbors a secret from her husband. Is it ever OK to keep a secret from a spouse?

10. Who in the story did you most identify with? Why?

READ MORE ABOUT THE LANDIN FAMILY!
READ A BONUS EXCERPT FROM

SECRET PLACES

THE THIRD BOOK IN
THE NEW HEIGHTS SERIES
BY DENISE HUNTER

CHAPTER ONE

Paula Landin-Cohen pushed the latches of her suitcase, and they closed with a snap of finality. She checked her bag for her boarding pass and driver's license and slung it over her shoulder.

"I'm ready to leave," she called to her husband, David. The house rang with a familiar silence.

She hefted the suitcase down the curved staircase, looking out the bank of windows on the front of the house. December had blown in to Jackson Hole with bitter cold winds and at least a foot of snow. Chicago's weather would be no better, she knew, but just the thought of the big city left her feeling as though she could soar there without benefit of Delta.

She set her suitcase by the door and checked her Movado. "David, we have to go." Her voice echoed up the vaulted ceiling and through the cavernous kitchen, but this time it drew a reply.

"Fine," he called, from the office, she thought.

OK, not the tone she'd hoped for, but at least he was talking to her today.

She grabbed her Burberry coat from the closet and wondered if she should take her warmest one, too. Fashion overruled practicality, and she pushed the closet door closed just in time to catch David's hand.

"Do you mind?" he said.

She backed away, ignoring his snippy tone. She wasn't going to let him ruin this for her. She checked her bag again for the boarding pass and license. She was being compulsive, but she couldn't let anything go wrong with this flight. She went through the list of things she'd need over the coming week. Did she pack her tape recorders? Before she could panic, she remembered sliding them into her briefcase.

David stepped around her in his charcoal woolen coat, picked up her suitcase, and walked out the door. Paula turned on the threshold and looked at her home. Sweeper marks striped the beige carpet, parallel lines running across the expanse of the great room like yard lines on a football field. Her socks from yesterday lay in two distinct balls by the sofa.

She turned the lock on the doorknob and pulled the door shut behind her. David placed the suitcase in the back of the Cadillac Escalade and pushed his trendy glasses up on the bridge of his nose in a movement that was as familiar to her as the smell of her own home. So familiar that she rarely noticed it unless she was away for several days. She wouldn't see David push his glasses up, smell his spicy cologne, or watch him squint over the *Wall Street Journal* for six days.

He opened the door for her, and she slipped inside before he clicked it shut. In spite of their problems, in spite of his relentless blaming and silent treatment, she didn't want to part this way. Not now, when she was about to do the most exciting thing of her life. She wanted someone to share it with. Someone to be happy for her. Someone to cheer her on back home. Heaven knew her family wasn't doing that.

David slid in behind the wheel and started the vehicle. His movements were sure and precise. Another man's motions would betray his anger, but not David.

"Well," she said, "at least you'll be able to keep the house clean this week." She delivered the line with just a hint of humor, planted there in hopes of coaxing him from his bitter mood. She turned her head just the tiniest bit so she could watch him from her peripheral vision. His face gave nothing away, and she wondered if she'd spoken the words aloud at all.

Paula turned forward and looked out her window. It was fine with her if David wanted to leave things this way. She could do this alone; she was a grown woman.

They headed up Snow King Avenue toward the Snow King Ski Resort. Already a few dedicated skiers were swooping down the slope on this lazy Sunday morning.

She looked at her watch again. Her parents would be getting up for church about now, her mom boiling a cup of water for that wretched cup of instant coffee. Hanna and Gram would be making breakfast for the guests of Higher Grounds Mountain Lodge while Micah shoveled the two inches of snow that had fallen overnight. Natalie would be scurrying to get breakfast ready for Taylor and Alex after an undoubtedly sleepless night with her adopted newborn baby, Grace. Paula's stomach tightened at that thought.

She looked out the front windshield, up Cache Street, the road that would take her out of here. They were making good time. Most of the tourists probably stayed out too late to do anything more than loll about in bed.

As they crossed the line that demarked the edge of Jackson Hole, Paula almost expected the raucous blowing of party horns. She'd waited all her life to exit this miserable little hole in the middle of nowhere, and today was the beginning of that dream. But instead of party horns, there was only silence. She wished the radio were on so she didn't feel as if she were about to choke on it. She struggled to think of something to say. She, whose words came easily and flawlessly.

"Your clothes should be ready at the cleaners by five tomorrow," she said. It was lame, unnecessary even, since David knew very well when his clothes would be ready. At least she was trying.

But he sat beside her as cold as a mountain glacier. Couldn't he at least grunt?

This is Paula Landin-Cohen reporting from inside an SUV, where a man is attempting to freeze his wife with the cold vapors emanating from his body. Join us at eleven, and we'll give you all the details on this story.

They passed the elk refuge, but all Paula saw was acres of snow behind the fenced, rolling pastures. She looked at her watch again.

"You've got plenty of time," David said.

She didn't know whether to be thankful for his first voluntary words or peeved at his tone. She decided on the latter. He'd done nothing but snub her for months, and for what? She was innocent of cheating on him, and he was too stubborn to believe it.

"You know, we're married, David. A little kindness wouldn't hurt."

His jaw twitched. "Married people don't live across the country from each other."

Like he cared. "It's only temporary."

The last word rang out in the car like an echo across Granite Canyon. At least they were talking. OK, arguing, but it was better than the silence.

"Not if you get your dream job."

If words could wear a sneer, those two did. And it rankled her. Heat prickled her skin under the coat, and she felt like her temperature shot up ten degrees. "Why do you care anyway? You've walked around me for months, giving me your self-righteous silent treatment. Now I won't be in the way. Not me or my soggy bath towel or my dirty dishes. You can live in your sterile house and keep it just the way you like it."

He had no right to deny her this opportunity, nor to guilt her about leaving. He'd made decisions without her approval; why should she have to get the cold shoulder?

He turned the car into the airport, and she realized this was it. They were parting as enemies on the biggest week of her life. Why had she imagined calling him on Monday night from Chicago and sharing everything that had happened? She had no reason to call home. She would go back to her apartment after work tomorrow with nothing to greet her except silence.

David pulled the vehicle up to the building and popped the back open before exiting. Paula got out and stood on the curb, waiting as he lifted the suitcase out and set it at her feet. He straightened and looked her in the eye for the first time in weeks. Face-to-face, they stood closer than they had in weeks. Was he regretting his harsh tone?

Their breaths expelled in cold puffs of air and mingled together in a dance more intimate than anything they'd done together in a very long time. She had a sudden memory of their first kiss.

It had been their third date. She'd been teaching him to ski at Snow King, teaching him how to plow to control his speed, when the tips of his skis crossed and he went down. She plowed to a stop, laughing. They'd spent the whole day laughing. But when she saw he wasn't moving, her laughter stopped.

"David?" She sidestepped up to him, kicked off her skis, and went down on her knees. That was when he reached for her and pulled her down on top of him. Bundled in so much clothing, he felt like a big cuddly teddy bear under her. His eyes sparkled with laughter.

"That was not nice," she said.

"It worked, though." His glasses were slightly cockeyed, and Paula felt a stirring in her stomach that felt right and wonderful. His grin melted away, and the look in his eyes should have melted the snow around them.

She went warm all over in spite of her bibs and coat. Their winter breath met and blended together. He cupped her face and pulled her toward him until their lips met.

"I'm sure you can get a porter to help you from here."

The cold words yanked her from the memory.

"Or maybe you can charm some guy into carrying them for you."

The words cut deeply. He was so wrong about her. So wrong about all of it. When would he believe her? What did she have to do to prove it wasn't true? Somehow, he made her feel guilty, like a little girl sitting in a principal's office.

Yes, the words hurt, but she didn't allow a trace of it to show on her face. Wouldn't have mattered if she had, since David was walking away, walking toward his side of the car. Getting in. Driving away.

Paula picked up her suitcase and walked toward the airport's door. *And that's a wrap.*

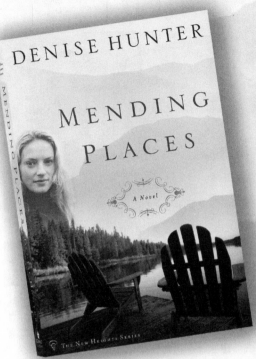

Read more about the

Landin Family in

Mending Places,

the first book in

The New Heights Series

by Denise Hunter.

Available where good books are sold.

Hanna Landin's past holds her captive, but Micah Gallagher, the rugged mountain guide she hires to help the family's foundering mountain lodge, makes her wish she could move beyond it. Together Hanna and Micah face the past. But it's more horrifying than either of them feared, and Hanna faces the ultimate challenge. ISBN:1-58229-358-9

THE NEW HEIGHTS SERIES
Mending Places • Saving Grace

OTHER BOOKS BY DENISE HUNTER
Kansas Brides • Stranger's Bride
Never a Bride • Bittersweet Bride • His Brother's Bride

NOVELLAS
Reunions "Truth or Dare" • *Aloha* "Game of Love"
Blind Dates "The Perfect Match"

www.denisehunterbooks.com

ABOUT THE AUTHOR

DENISE HUNTER is the award-winning author of eight novels and three novellas. A voracious reader, she began writing her first Christian romance novel in 1996, and it was published two years later. Her husband, Kevin, claims he provides all her romantic material, but Denise insists a good imagination helps, too. She and Kevin live in Indiana with their three sons, where they are very active in a new church start.

You can visit Denise's Web site at www.denisehunterbooks.com.

Enjoyment Guarantee

If you are not totally satisfied with this book, simply return it to us along with your receipt, a statement of what you didn't like about the book, and your name and address within 60 days of purchase to Howard Publishing, 3117 North 7th Street, West Monroe, LA 71291-2227, and we will gladly reimburse you for the cost of the book.